T0367502

THE
LAST
COUNTY
FAIR

Stan Matthews

THE LAST COUNTY FAIR

iUniverse books may be ordered through booksellers or by contacting:

iUniverse
1663 Liberty Drive
Bloomington, IN 47403
www.iuniverse.com
1-800-Authors (1-800-288-4677)

ISBN: 978-1-4917-8560-7 (sc)
ISBN: 978-1-4917-8559-1 (e)

Library of Congress Control Number: 2016901102

Print information available on the last page.

iUniverse rev. date: 03/10/2016

CONTENTS

THE FIRST DAY

A HANDFUL OF DIRT

CHAPTER ONE

A strange quietness hung over the Star's newsroom when I came in. It wasn't that it was nearly empty--only old Hilaire was there, reading the competition, the morning Monitor, as usual. And it wasn't that it was Monday morning either, because almost any morning at seven o'clock the room had the same lonely look--row on row of desks, each with its typewriter, where we reporters sat, piles of handouts and carbon copies on them. Beyond was the copy desk, a horseshoe with shaded fluorescent lamps hung over it, and then the glass-enclosed offices of the editorial writers, vacant now.

No, the office was the same--and yet I couldn't help feeling that the silence was somehow deeper, profound, even forbidding. I suppose I was more tired than usual because I had been on duty as emergency reporter the night before, staying up until one, calling the police and hospitals every hour. There hadn't been anything worth going out to report on, just a couple of traffic fatalities. Still, I had tossed all night, it was so hot, dreaming that I got a Page One byline and all the fellows slapped me on the shoulder as they went by my desk, and the glory of it kept waking me and got me thinking up trick story leads. I was fully awake before my clock's alarm went off, so I pushed in the stopper, noted that my little calendar was telling me it was Monday, August 23, 1967. I got up and showered. I'm a six-footer, so I kept banging my head on the shower spout. My mirror showed no blood but it did tell me that I needed a haircut because my uncombed black hair fell all the way to my rather prominent nose.

So I was feeling a bit wobbly as I passed Hilaire and he said "Hi, Art," and grunted without looking up. I sat down, relieved, at my desk a couple of rows over from him and slid out the leaf board on which the telephone numbers of the hospitals and suburban police stations were listed. I began phoning them, asking "Anything new?", and most often getting the usual negative reply from sleepy outpatient nurses and apathetic desk cops. The clicking of the circular phone dial echoed in the vast room, and I kept looking at Hilaire, who had got to the Monitor's obituaries and was looking down the column to see if there was anybody important. He picked up his scissors and clipped a couple, pasted them on a piece of copy paper and spiked it. Later, Johnny, our city editor, would go over these and assign someone to dig out biography files in the morgue. I hoped I wouldn't get any to write up, because if there's anything I hate writing it's obits.

When I finished the phoning I decided I might as well write up the four weekend traffic accidents I had been told about and get them out of the way, so I called to Hilaire and he brought me the Monitor stuff. There wasn't too much and I had the column finished in fifteen minutes. I took the copy to the city desk and put them in Johnny's box. I asked Hilaire to cover the phone for me and I took the self-service elevator to the lobby, went out to the street and hastened to the coffee shop on the corner.

A fellow Star reporter, Frank Lawton, was drinking his coffee in a dark booth as usual. He pushed over and beckoned to me to sit down beside him. He's a tall lean man of about fifty with a flimsy mustache and iron-gray hair. I waved to the shop manager, Charley. I ordered toast with my coffee. I was starving.

"You on emergency, Art," he asked.

"Yeah, I've been on it since Saturday," I replied. "Couldn't go anywhere, didn't go anywhere. Nothing much happened, nothing worth reporting anyway."

"That's too bad," Frank said. "Johnny assigned me to take emergency next weekend. I hope he changes his mind and decides somebody else deserves the punishment more than me. Johnny's the best city editor I ever had but I have to admit he makes me awful sore sometimes. He can be as capricious as hell when it comes to handing out night and weekend assignments."

"How many features you working on now?"

"About twenty."

"How do you do it?" I asked, and I was sincere, because I could never for the life of me figure out where he got so many tips for his feature stories, all of which got his byline.

"Just luck," Frank said. "Not having a regular beat like you, Art, I lick the cream off the top. When you've been around this town as long as I have, people like to help you," he said. "They call me up. I do them a favor, giving them publicity."

"Sure wish I had your gift," I said. I couldn't help it, that noticeable touch of envy in my voice. I knew it was against the rules of good manners among reporters.

"My what?" Frank asked.

"Your touch."

"Just another word for luck and intuition. You look for an angle in every story, some item that will lift the story from a routine report into a feature."

"You don't do straight stuff anymore, do you?" I could have bitten my tongue with that one, because for years Frank had been a straight reporter. He had covered all the beats. He still does a good job when Johnny assigns him to weekend emergency and rewrites.

Frank laughed. "We could chat about that all morning," he said, "but I heard a rumor that Johnny would like to get out a paper today."

Just the same, we took our time getting back to the Star. I hardly noticed that the day was turning out cool and bright. I was eaten up by jealousy and I knew it. I had tramped my legs off scouring Richland for feature stuff ever since I quit the Monitor and started work at the Star two years before. I had written batches, but only a small fraction of them got a byline. I suppose that was because my stories didn't have the twist that turned a straight story into a human interest one with a two-column headline.

We reached the building and went up in the elevator together. Toddling old Manny was there to greet us. He was a combination receptionist and copy boy who used to be a reporter until he hit the skids on drink and wasn't good enough for anything except being a doorkeeper. He stopped musing over the Monitor comics and waved to us in greeting. Frank said "Poor beggar. Why don't they give him a pension instead of keeping him around here like a lamp post?"

"He's what makes newspaper offices so colorful, haven't you heard?" I said.

"That's crap," said Frank.

The newsroom was full, it being eight o'clock, and Johnny was there on one side of the city desk. I went over to him and stood there until he looked up. He was a tall thin fellow with sandy hair. There was a long scratch on his forehead. He'd been in the war, serving in Italy until he got shot up at Anzio. It was said they had to patch the pieces together. I had learned long ago how to approach the city desk. You didn't barge right up and ask for instructions. You stood there until Johnny noticed you.

"That's all the accidents there were?" he asked. That's another thing: Don't expect any formal greetings, even on a Monday morning.

"All I thought were important," I said.

"The Safety Council predicted a real smasheroo."

"Guess the public is heeding the warnings," I said. "There's an angle. How about I call the Council and report this and they give me a statement commending the public?"

I expected Johnny would chew me out for being so stupid, but he said "Give it a try." Then: "Have you looked at the assignment book?" He gave me a fishy stare and I said to myself: *Oh, oh, what have I done now?* The book was on the edge of his wide desk. Johnny said: "If you don't mind, Art, if it wouldn't be askin' too much, you might glance at it once in a while?"

I never could stand that sort of sarcasm, and I felt the blood rushing to my face and a retort on my tongue, but I held it back and looked down at the Monday assignments page. On the P.M. side it had: *Chesterton County Fair--Art James.*

"You're kidding?" I said. I tried to think it was a joke.

"Since when did I ever kid you?" Johnny asked, and he was serious. It was true he never kidded me. He was my boss. He left issues of discipline to T.D., the managing editor, his boss. Johnny did the important stuff, like layouts for the City Page, checking length of stories and assigning size and width of headlines. He recommended hires and made beat assignments. He looked sternly at me. "I put the dope in your mail box," he said. "Look at it and talk to me about it."

I went to the rack of mail boxes and grabbed my handouts. My regular beat was minor courts and state police. It was strictly junior league, but not cub stuff. Those days were long behind me. What I really yearned for was the city police beat, because the few times I had filled in for the regular man, Steve Marks, I'd had a ball. Still, I was luckier than some, because I got a few general assignments and out-of-town trips, mainly because I had a car of my own. There were two staff cars, but one always had to be on the private parking zone for emergencies. Our photographers usually used them, taking along any experienced reporter available.

At my desk I piled the stack of mail on the square foot of space that wasn't occupied by piles of paper and began looking through the new stuff. There were the usual handouts from the welfare agencies and the hospitals, stuff I needed to keep my interest in the field.

In the middle of the stack was a sheaf of mimeographed stuff with the face-sheet labeled *News* in big red letters. Usually that's the kind that doesn't have any news in it at all. It announced the opening of the annual Chesterton County Fair, the centennial. It was starting the next day, Tuesday, and would run for four days, closing Friday night with *a final gala,* which, I supposed, was an odd-job, written by some cub reporter with the Chesterton Daily Times. I had been down there once covering a convention, and had been in the Times newsroom. It was a small daily with only five editorial employees, including the editor, whose name was Blanchard. However, it was a daily, that much could be said for it, with about six thousand circulation and real loyalty among Main Street advertisers.

After I had looked over the releases on the fair, of which there were several, each covering a different pavilion, I went back to the city desk and stood there with the stuff in my hands. Johnny kept on talking across his double-person desk, to Max Armstrong, his assistant, about which city page story should be the lead that day, Mondays being a bad day to find anything really lively to print.

At last Johnny turned to me. "Art, I want you to go down there this afternoon and dig up some features."

At first I could hardly believe that's what he said, but he didn't seem to notice and went on: "There's a big fight going on among the farm groups, Farm Service on one side, Grange on the other, something like that, about the future of the fair. Maybe this will be the last fair ever in Chesterton County. Check on that with the officials of both groups and anyone else you can dig up. You can wire the story. That's all."

Johnny was like that. He told me when he recommended me to T.D. for hiring that nobody got on the Star staff who wasn't experienced, and they wouldn't hire me unless they were convinced I knew how to write. I had passed a couple of journalism courses at Richland University, had graduated with a major in English literature, and had a few months at the Monitor. I had brought along a batch of my stuff, financial department mostly. Johnny said it wasn't much but they needed someone on emergency and they would give me a three-month trial. He made it clear that the Star wasn't a journalism school and not to think I was a trainee. He had been true to his word, because I never got an ounce of instruction from him, and if it hadn't been for the other reporters, not one of whom was ever unwilling to coach me, I'd have been sunk long before my three months were up. As it turned out, I must have made the grade, for I was still there. So I said "Okay," because I had learned that was the best response to make to Johnny.

I was about to walk away when Johnny said "Call in tomorrow morning."

"You want me to stay overnight?"

"Yeah. Depending upon what you wire tonight, there may be a follow-up you can do tomorrow. If you need some cash in advance, see treasury."

I wanted to ask where the pressure for this coverage was coming from, but I changed my mind, because I'd tried that once before and got slapped down but good. That was the time the elevator fell in Eberly's department store, the largest in town, and I got it on emergency from the hospital and wrote it straight, but when it didn't appear in that afternoon's Star I asked Johnny about it, and he said: "What the hell do you think? Eberly's our biggest advertiser." It didn't take a genius to figure out that Mr. Eberly had called Mr. France, the publisher of the Star, and Mr. France had called T.D.--that's Tom Dormand, our managing editor--and that was that. The point was that Johnny made it clear that you don't ask about such pressure, because he said "Mind our own business." That had rankled for a long time, but I don't think Johnny meant it personally, because he barked it out with no more emphasis than he gave to any other order, such as: "Hey, Art, take Fred on five," when I had to put on the earphone and type Fred's dictated story from City Hall.

But this was *Opportunity* with a capital O and I wasn't so dumb that I didn't recognize it. On my own in Chesterton I could dig through the dirt until it began to pay off in terms of bylines. All I had to do was to find the angle. Johnny had indicated there was a local brawl going on, and the wheels in my head began to spin right away as words for a catchy lead formed: *Community forces here that have been united for 100 years about Chesterton's pride, the annual County Fair, are split wide open by dissent over--"* That's as far as I could get, because that was why I was being sent down there: to investigate, to probe, to dig, to ferret out, to pry, to smoke out, to use all the ingenuity of my sneaky trade to get to the bottom of the local mess and to spread in print the tale of their twisted lives, to uproot their secret prides, and to holler *Foul*, and holler it so loudly that the one hundred thousand readers of the Star would slobber over the scandal at supper, and the wire services would say: "Hey, what's going on here?" and my bylined stories would be picked up and my name, Arthur James, would be printed in a thousand newspapers across the land.

CHAPTER TWO

That was to come later. First I had to get through the morning at the courts. Fred joined me in the walk down wide Main Street, which was jammed with traffic. It was so hot that Fred was carrying his jacket. We were carefully dressed, tie and all, because proper appearance was called for by the courts. Fred was going to City Hall to pick up a story or two, which he would call into the Star later. He would also stick around for the mayor's daily statement to the press at eleven, then get back to the office and write it up. After that it would be lunch, then he would check the Star hot off the press before getting back to his beat in the afternoon to interviews concerning the sanitation story he was writing.

As for me, after trying to get to the Safety Council meeting without luck, I was off to Richland County courthouse, where I went every workday morning before going to Coroner's Court. You got only crumbs on the beat I had then, but sometimes a feature would turn up, and I hoped there would be a few one today, because then I might get a byline, and with the one I was sure to get the next day, that would make two in a row. Fred and I crossed Union Square together, where some homeless men were teasing pigeons by picking up popcorn kernels, leftovers from Sunday treats provided by kids from the nearby slums, and hurling them toward the birds as they paraded proudly on the sidewalks. Those dumb birds stumbled over one another to get at the tough kernels, nibbled at them and cast them aside, then returned to their places in front of the men, eager to be disillusioned again. Three men on a bench threw back their heads and roared each time they did it, and I suppose if it gave them some pleasant mischief in their misery it was all right, but I couldn't help feeling sorry for the pigeons.

Fred turned north to City Hall, which flanked that side of the square, and I went west to the courthouse. They were tall noble buildings, heavily pillared, monumental. Richland liked to think of this complex of civic, county and federal buildings around the square as City Center, but actually it should be called Civil Service Center, for it is the public domain of government workers of all levels. Every noon they paired up on the green, eating their sandwiches and drinking colas. I tried it once myself, pretending to a pretty young thing that I was a criminal lawyer, and she believed me. She was thrilled by my stories of the murderers I had successfully defended, but in the end her boyfriend, a City Hall clerk, came over and broke it up. I never saw her again.

A long flight of stone stairs swept from the sidewalk to the main entrance of the Court House, but no one went in that way. I went around to the right and entered by the heavy double doors there, which led directly to a ground-level corridor and to the press room. I didn't expect anyone to be there, and there wasn't. Steve Marks, who had the Star's police beat, would come over about two o'clock and we would have a game of chess before doing the rounds of the state and county attorneys offices to learn what was coming up in the various courts, but of course I wouldn't be seeing Steve that day as I was going to Chesterton in the afternoon. There were some handouts in my box, mainly copies of briefs and depositions on behalf of or against defendants, which were marked *Hold for Release* for the time they were used at trials, if there were any. Sometimes we respected the release warnings, sometimes we didn't, because we knew very well that both prosecuting and defense attorneys wanted them used by the press in order to influence juries. You will say, I suppose, that juries are not permitted to read newspapers while they are sitting, but they do, and the lawyers know they do. That's why they plant this material with us. Of course I wouldn't ever refer to a deposition as such when I wrote it up, but merely attribute the fancied facts and opinion to *an authoritative source who prefers to remain anonymous*. It has been tested in court, about a reporter's obligation to reveal his sources, but freedom of the press usually wins out, and as long as Johnny printed it, I was safe, I hoped. It was the reporter's faith that the newspaper corporation was responsible, not the individual reporter, so a great deal was possible to say in these cases without actually inviting a contempt of court citation.

After I scanned the handouts and saw that they were the usual blah of personal opinion, unsubstantiated by any sort of quotable fact, I tossed

them in the waste basket and went whistling down the corridor toward
the stairs that led to the main lobby. As usual, the lobby was crowded
with witnesses, court hangers-on and the merely curious, and it was then
I saw this character who goes by the name of Jack Bender coming toward
me. He was a handsome man, if you could call sleek handsome. His long
black hair was matted to his head and he was smooth shaven, and without
going into a long description I would say he looked something like Robert
Taylor and let it go at that.

"Hi, Art," Jack said. He waved weakly.

"Hello, Jack," I said without enthusiasm.

"What's news?" He asked with a self-conscious smirk.

"You tell me," I said as gravely as I could.

"Now, Art, you know better than that. I'm only a bystander at these
things."

"Tell it to the judge."

"I'm not kidding, Art. You know I wouldn't kid *you*."

I looked him straight in the eye. He was standing quite close to me.
"Who are you bitching for today?" I asked him.

Jack stepped back. "Now look, Art, you're a straight shooter. I know
that. I read your court stuff. Very good stuff. You always give both sides."

"Alright then. What's the pitch?"

"No pitch," he asserted, but he knew I could never believe that. "I only
want you to be squared away from something, that's all."

Now this character is as slimy as they come, and we reporters knew it.
He's connected with the rackets, floating crap games especially--at least
he was then. He got sent up recently on a contempt charge, of all things,
but it wasn't me who put him behind bars, I'm sorry to say.

"Tell me you're going legit," I said with a brief smile.

"Anyone says I am not's a liar." He usually didn't let himself get upset
like that, but I guess I was needling him too sharply.

"You're an honest crook. So what's with you?"

"They picked up Al Saturday night. He wasn't doin' nothin', see?"

"Exactly what was Al doing?"

"He was mindin' his own business, as usual."

"What business?" I asked, winking at him.

"His business. You know what Al Morton does."

"Do I?" I stepped back a few inches. "He's the biggest pimp in town, that's all." I cupped my ear, suggesting that he whisper his response.

Jack looked around furtively. He leaned toward me and spoke into my ear. "You wanna piece, Art?"

"Tell that to Johnny." Jack knew who the city editor was, because Johnny had once covered the court himself.

"Come on, Art," Jack pleaded. "What's making you so noble today?"

"I went to church yesterday," I said.

"No kiddin'? You go to church?"

"You mean *you* don't?" I asked. It was then I noticed the half-century in his hand, all balled up, but with the 50 showing through the green. His arm moved toward my left jacket pocket. I turned sort of sideways and he missed planting the bill. "Uh-uh," I said.

Jack gave me his don't-insult-me glance. "Just leave his name out of the story," he pleaded.

"Who says I'm going to write a story?"

"You mean you aint?"

"That all depends," I said as I started turning away.

Jack grabbed my arm. "I'll make it a hundred, Art."

"Now I know I'm going to write it," I said.

"You're a damn bastard, Art."

"Tah-tah!" I said, assuming Jack's own harshness. "Such language!"

I drew away from him and he made a move as if to follow, but he changed his mind and went off to a crowd of hoodlums in silk jackets. He was shaking his head sadly and I almost felt sorry for him.

As it turned out, Al got out on bail and the trial date wasn't set. Al had been in and out of court so many times it was only worth a mention in a roundup. Just the same, I used his name in my story.

I thought there still might have been some of Al's friends in the lockup, so I went across the square to City Hall, where police headquarters is located on the ground floor. The cops didn't have any of Al's pals there, but they did have a half dozen young fellows who had been picked up on the square Sunday afternoon for marching with *Get Out of Vietnam* placards.

This wasn't my territory but somehow I was intrigued, so I went to the police press room to see if Steve was around. Steve wasn't, but a Monitor reporter, Bill Williams, said Steve was interviewing the Chief about some new plan to cope with juvenile delinquents. I asked about the marchers and Bill said they were only a bunch of kooks, why bother with them? Just the same, I went out to the desk and asked the sergeant if I could visit the cells for a minute. He supposed it would be okay.

All six of the marchers were in one big cell. It didn't have any cots, because these cells were supposed to be used only as temporary lockups for prisoners awaiting arraignment. I thought the marchers must have been brought over from the jail early that morning and would be sent to court as soon as there was room on the docket. They were all of college age, so I asked the one sitting on a chair nearest the bars what had happened.

"You're our lawyer?" the boy asked. He was a good-looking chap with a sad face bristling with three-day blond whiskers. No time for a shave, I figured. "They told us they'd get us a lawyer," he said when I told him I was a reporter. "I don't know if I ought to talk to you." The other five came to the bars when they heard us talking.

"Maybe it would help you if I wrote about you in the Star," I suggested. I knew I was taking a chance because talking to prisoners before trial wasn't permitted. That's one of the things I knew about reporting: the sly confidence you insinuate when you say a thing like that. It opens mouths.

The boy told me his name was Don Archer. He was a freshman at Richland University. "Do you know when we will be called into court?" he asked me. "We've been here since yesterday afternoon."

I hardly knew what to say. Ordinarily if you've been arrested and had to be held overnight, you were lodged in the county jail, where you would eat and sleep, then taken to this police cell to await a court hearing. The students had slept on the cell floor and had not eaten for twenty-four hours. However, they were given periodic access to toilets.

They told me about marching before City Hall as a demonstration against the further testing of nuclear weapons as well as Vietnam. I had been in touch with the police all weekend. No one had told me about the arrests.

"What happened to the other students?" I asked.

"There wasn't anybody else. Just the six of us. A few guys and girls in the park marched around with us once in a while. But we were the only ones carrying signs."

He told of how the cops came out and ordered them to disperse, they were interfering with pedestrians crossing the park. The cops ordered the marchers to the station, booked them, put them in lockup and forgot about them. That was about all there was to it. I got their names and what they were studying and thanked them.

In the press room, Steve wasn't back so I decided to go up to the Chief's office to look for him. That's another thing you don't do: cross onto another reporter's beat without his permission or assignment from the city editor. I opened the door and went into the outer office where a couple of secretaries were typing. I asked one of them if Steve had been there and she said he was still inside with the Chief. I decided to wait and sat down in a chair by the outer wall. It wasn't very long before Steve came out with the Chief. Steve introduced me, although I had met the Chief before, but only when I was with a larger group at a press conference. The Chief wouldn't have remembered me. Even so, he said: "Why, of course, Art James. You write good stuff. What brings you up here, Art?" I couldn't help feeling he already knew why. He was a stout little bald man. He appeared to have a permanent suspicious grin.

"I was looking for Steve," I said. "I saw six university students in the lockup and I thought maybe Steve would be interested." I should have been alarmed by Steve's warning glance, but I wasn't.

"Oh, them," the Chief said. "You don't want to write about them."

I shouldn't have said it, but the words got out before I could think. "Why not?" I blurted. I was idealistic in those days.

"Let's go into my office," the Chief said. "You come too, Steve."

The Chief sat down in his enormous high-backed leather chair behind his desk. Steve and I sat on matching chairs in front of it. The Chief looked at us sternly. "Now, what's this all about?" he asked.

"Art's just trying to help me out, Chief," Steve said. I couldn't help notice Steve's tremulous tone. He was a stiff-lipped veteran reporter, whose stories of armed robberies, murders and other sorts of mayhem were always gems of just-the-facts reporting.

"Steve, you're still the police reporter for the Star, aren't you?"

"Of course," Steve said.

The Chief turned his attention to me. "Mr. James, have you applied for a press pass?" I shook my head. "Then, Mr. James, let Steve handle this."

I got the message. I said goodbye to Steve and fled.

I went down to the police press room and called in the story about Al Morton and a couple of other arraignments. I had just hung up when Steve came in. He seemed out of breath. He only nodded to me before sitting down before his typewriter. He was mad at me, that's for sure. He began typing and then stopped and glared at me. He removed the paper, tore it up and tossed it away.

"Art, are you nuts? What's got into you? This is my beat, not yours."

I held up a hand in protest. "I wasn't going to write anything, Steve. I wanted to tell you I couldn't play chess with you today. I have to go to Chesterton this afternoon. I talked to the students in the cell and I intended to tell you what they told me. Steve, they've been in lockup since yesterday afternoon!"

"I knew that, Art. The Chief called me last night. He told me all about the students and asked me to see him this morning."

"The Chief called *you*?"

"It's not unusual, Art."

"He asked you to report it?"

"No, Art." He looked at me as if anticipating that I would get it. "This morning he talked about the police program to put the lid on juvenile delinquency. Then he told me that would be a much better story than one about the marchers. In other words, he told me not to write anything about the students."

"He can't do that!" I exclaimed. "Suppress a story!"

"Art, you're so darn naïve! The Chief knows this would be bad publicity. He also knows he could never get a conviction, and if it got into court he couldn't stop you from writing it up, although he would try. I don't mean he would try to stop *you*, personally. Anybody. You want to know what he told me just now?"

"What?" I am sure my annoyance showed through.

"Nothing I didn't know already. He put those students in the lockup to teach them a lesson. He figures that if they get no publicity, which is what the students were after, and have to spend a rotten night without sleep, going hungry, they wouldn't try to demonstrate again."

"But the students themselves, they will tell."

"Sure, but their story won't get in the Star or the Monitor. And when they get back to the university in a paddy wagon this afternoon they will be taken directly to the dean. The Chief has already spoken to him. I bet the dean pleaded with him not to send the kids back in the wagon. But the Chief is teaching the dean a lesson. The university officials, you see, will be embarrassed by all this. The students will be further disciplined by the dean, not for marching, but for missing classes. By that time, no doubt, the university president has called our esteemed publisher, Mr. France, who is also a university governor."

"You could talk it over with Johnny," I said meekly.

"Art, it's hard for me to believe you're so ignorant. Johnny knows the score. He has his orders. Oh, knock it off, what in the world you want to get involved for?"

"It's the principle of the thing."

"Right out of the book!" Steve applauded me. "Boy, you are wet behind the ears. Still a believer in freedom of the press!"

I got mad then. I hadn't counted Steve being among the scoffers, and I know I wouldn't now, knowing him better. But I did then.

"We've still got a responsibility--" I knew I wasn't getting anywhere. Steve's fingers were flying on the keys as I left and crossed the square to the courthouse. There wasn't anything interesting going on there, such as a manslaughter case, just the routine suicide and a few accidental deaths. So I thought I had better check with the morgue, because it was getting close to deadline, and Johnny had ordered me always to call in before going back to the newsroom, just in case anything was going on and I could get over there fast. I called and there was.

Behind the courthouse was a small unmarked building with a tunnel where the morgue wagons drove through to the freezers in the back. I went in the front door. The clerk at the desk told me the wagon was going out and did I want to go along. I did, so I went through the hall and out the back door to the yard. Axel Torsing, the driver, a huge man with a gaudy tie, was climbing into the cab, so I hailed him and he motioned to me to go around the other side and get in beside him.

When we got out to Main Street he switched on the rooftop flashing red light and asked me to press the klaxon. It roared as Axel wheeled the wagon through the lunch-hour crowds, passing traffic on the left and right, with cars stopping or pulling over to the curb, and I delighted in blasting the pedestrians as we went around a corner through a red light.

It was clear sailing along the freeway, and I was so excited getting this first ride in the wagon, that I almost forgot to ask Axel where we were going. "All the way to Bixley," he said. "Got to pick up some meat on the tracks." I was still so enthralled by the adventure that my stomach didn't even give a turn, because he said it so matter-of-factly, like we were a butcher's delivery truck. I kept my hand on the horn as we screamed through Bixley. On the other side of town we turned right past the railway station and took a parallel road toward an underpass. There we stopped and got out.

A silent crowd was on the road that passed on a bridge over the tracks, and I thought I had the story right there--that whoever it was had jumped. When I saw the body I knew that's not the way it had been. My stomach turned, but I didn't throw up.

There was a cop standing near the tracks, so I kept my back turned to the rails and pulled out my notebook and pencil. I asked the cop what had happened and he told me. It received only a few lines in the Star, but the main part of the story was left out. I suppose the superintendent of the state hospital had called Max or Johnny and asked them to omit the hospital's name. So there was just the name of the man and the fact that he had been struck by a train. That's all. I suppose it didn't make any difference to the public that he had escaped his cell room and had laid down on the tracks like he was going to sleep, his head resting on one rail, his feet on the other. There he waited, not moving, I guess, until the train hit him. Well, after Axel had the body wrapped up in a rubber blanket and put it in the back of the wagon, we roared back to the morgue. I sounded the horn all the way, trying to blast the sight of the body from my brain. It didn't do any good. Only much later did I wonder what was the hurry. After all, the man was dead.

CHAPTER THREE

I picked up my car in the Star parking lot and headed down Main Street, which runs north and south through the heart of Richland. It was a 1955 Buick, in pretty good shape in spite of the years of driving for the Star. On the outskirts of the city, between the suburban towns, I was able to gain a bit of speed, and then I hit the open country and pushed the pedal until the needle showed sixty-five and held it there. On either side August fields of ripening corn and barley shone brilliantly in the sun. There was little traffic, it being Monday afternoon, and once I passed a hay wagon, wide and towering, without slowing down.

I came into Chesterton through the Plato Valley, where the town of Plato nestled among the hills, then passed through to the plain where the city of Chesterton was centered. Chesterton County was beautiful country, a high plateau, with pleasant homes stretched out along the highway, which soon became Main Street through the city. I had checked out some facts about Chesterton. The city had a population of about fifteen thousand. The Chesterton County Fair was the annual showplace for county interests, but actually it drew exhibits and participants from four surrounding counties. After one hundred years it was by far the oldest annual county fair in the state.

At the corner of Chesterton Avenue I rolled to the curb in front of the *Chesterton Times* building. It was a no-parking zone but I pulled down the right visor with *Richland Star Press* sign on it, just to dare the local gendarmes to give me a ticket. The Times was a two-story red brick building at one end of a long block of stores: Woolworth's, an adjacent shoe store, a jewelry, a men's shop, a dress shop, a drug store, the usual. I went up a flight of shabby wooden stairs to the second floor and took the first door on the left into the newsroom.

White-haired Roger Blanchard, the editor, was sitting at his desk looking over a copy of that day's Times, which had just come off the basement press. He looked up as I opened the door. "Hi! Art James of the Star, isn't it?" He had a wonderful memory.

"Yes," I said. "How are you Mr. Blanchard?"

"Fine. Just fine. What brings you to Chesterton?"

"The fair. Johnny asked me to cover it."

He laughed as he straightened up in his chair. "I didn't know our fair was *that* important."

"I know, but Johnny thought there might be a feature in it." I didn't want to tell him that I knew there was talk that this would be the last of the Chesterton County fairs. "Have you had much on it?" I asked.

"Reams," he said. He directed me to a pile of Times on a counter. There were two other men and a woman in the newsroom, but they paid no attention to me. None were typing, this being the dead period. They were all busy reading their stuff in that afternoon's paper. I wondered about that, because I did the same thing at the Star. As soon as the first edition arrived I would dash for a copy and look eagerly for my stories. Then I would read them through, groaning if they had been edited too much, but always with a knowing pride that came when I saw in print the words I had written.

For ten minutes I poured over Times back issues, scanning the contents of advance stories about the coming fair. There were items on the pavilion exhibits, the midway attractions, the groups participating in the opening parade, lists of scores of officials, and all of the same kind of stuff I had looked over that morning in the Star newsroom. There wasn't a word I could find concerning the future of the fair, not a line about the forces competing for control that Johnny had hinted at. I thanked Blanchard and said I thought I would go out to the fairgrounds, just to look around.

"Nothing's ready yet," he said. "The fair doesn't open until two o'clock tomorrow."

"I know, but I would like to see what it looks like now. There may be something interesting."

I was not disappointed. I found my way to the fairgrounds, which were only a few blocks away from the County Court House, which occupied the western side of a one-block square. The eastern side was occupied by Chesterton City Hall.

I spent an hour walking around the fairgrounds. I wrote a generous amount of notes. I took an interest in everything I saw, felt and smelled. There were scores of people everywhere, all of them busy not only outside but inside exhibition buildings. The empty areas in front of the grandstand were being worked on by a throng of cowboys and their horses. The midway was empty. I was told that everything from Indian elephants to zebras, from acrobats to midway midgets, would arrive overnight by freight train, trucks and moving vans.

I returned to the Times newsroom, borrowed a typewriter and banged out my feature story. I took it to a Western Union telegraph office across Main Street and sent it to Johnny. I thought my story might be a little off-beat, but it still wasn't what I had come to Chesterton for. After a hamburger at a nearby diner I returned to the fairgrounds. The main office was a one-story frame building just inside the fair's gated entrance, where two ticket shacks were being erected. I went up to the fair office with a wide *Information* sign on it. It was a one-story gray frame wooden structure. Two men about my age, which was twenty-five, were manning two wicket windows, answering questions being asked by a few exhibitors outside who wanted to know where to put this and where to put that. I waited patiently in line until they went away.

One of the two men was a good-looking youth, about twenty. He was a light blond with classic clean features, a smooth complexion. The other was black-haired and sun-bronzed, heavily built, with a strong jutting chin. "May I help you?" he asked. I told him who I was and that I wanted to see the fair manager.

"A reporter from Richland!" he exclaimed smugly. "You don't say?"

There was a tone of condescension in his voice that made me dislike him a little. "Come in," he said. "Door around the side."

I tried the door. It was locked. I had to wait several minutes until the older, black-haired guy let me in. He left me standing there as he returned to talk to the blond fellow. I looked around. The room was jammed with three wooden desks piled high with cardboard boxes. A fourth desk was bare except for a few notepads and pencils.

I heard my name called. The black-haired guy. "Mr. James, I'm Richard Bryson, and this is my friend, Robert Glen." I shook hands with both of them. "Mr. Stowe isn't here," Bryson said. "Is there something I can do for you?"

I took a chance. Sometimes underlings, in their innocence, will give you the lowdown on a situation. I lowered my voice as I intoned, as if delivering a secret message: "I hear there won't be a fair next year." I said, faking disinterest.

"Where did you hear that?" Bryson asked, wide-eyed. "Of course there will be a fair next year."

"That's not the way I heard it."

Robert Glen said "I suppose it's that rumor that the Grange wants to pull out of sponsorship."

That was what I wanted. Confirmation.

"That's it," I said. "The Grange folk can't get along with the Farm Service people."

"There's nothing to it," Bryson said. "There have been a few meetings, but no decision on who will sponsor the fair next year."

"Both groups sponsor it now?"

"Not exactly." Bryson leaned on the counter that ran the building's width. He kept glancing out his open window. "There's a separate corporation for the fair. It owns the fairgrounds."

"Who's on the corporation?" I asked. I removed a notepad from my jacket pocket, picked up a pencil and sat down at the unused table. I began writing.

"Some officers of the Grange, the Farm Service, the Co-op, the FGA. That's the Farm Growers Association." Bryson took a deep breath. "Also the president of Chesterton Bank, the publisher of the Times, a lawyer, an engineer, the owner of a department store, a few others. Anyway, the corporation doesn't actually run the fair. The fair has a board of directors."

"And who's on the board?"

"Same people. They are elected by the corporation."

To say I was getting confused is an understatement. "Who elects the members of the corporation?"

Young Robert Glen appeared to sympathize with my despair. "They are not elected, sir," he said. "They are appointed by various farm organizations, City Council, Chamber of Commerce, among others, I suppose."

A man and a woman were waiting outside the wicket windows. Both men turned their attention to them. When they were finished I asked them if they worked at the fair every year. "One way or another, almost all our lives," Richard said. He added that he had just graduated from Richland University, my alma mater. Robert would enter his junior year there in September. Their fathers were joint owners of a very large farm with numerous workers, including seasonal migrants. Glen's dad was head of the local Grange. Bryson's father, Sam, was head of the Farm Service. How cosy, I thought.

It was after five o'clock. I borrowed Bryson's phone and called Blanchard at the Times. He said he would wait for me. As the Buick got stuck in Main Street traffic I had an uneasy feeling that I was really onto something. Was I getting in over my head? What could be complicated about a county fair? I parked on a side street near the Times. As I was getting out of the car, I saw a colorful sticker on the car's trunk: *Have fun! Attend the Fair.* Blanchard was at his desk. I asked him if he had a list of the Fair Corporation members, and also of the Board of Directors. He introduced me to the woman reporter whom I had ignored before. "Marie, got a minute?" he asked.

Marie gave a huge sigh. "What now?" she moaned. She was a tall, skinny kid, long hair upswept, black-framed glasses. She glared at me. "What do you want?" Apparently I had interrupted a clean-up job. She continued to stack a bunch of loose papers into a neat stack. "Oh, alright." On her boss' instructions she motioned to me to follow her to a room off the hall lined with dusty wood filing cabinets. She immediately started sneezing. "I hate this place," she moaned. "Look at this dirt!" She pulled out a drawer marked "F" and dragged out a file. "County Fair, sir," she announced briskly. She placed the file on a narrow counter and switched on a hanging light. "So, you work for the Star, do you?" Almost a sneer.

I said nothing as I wrote down names of a multitude of men, all men, who played various roles associated with running the fair. Marie continued her loud assault upon my ears. "I wish I was a real reporter," she said. "I cover women's, society, cooking contests, church suppers. Trash like that. I would like to get a job in Richland. I like Richland. Nothing much happens here. My job is such a bore. I'd do anything to get a job with the Star. What do you think?" I told her the Star already had two women reporters, of a sort. She laughed scornfully as I was on my way out.

It was almost dusk by the time I returned to the fair. The sun slanted in low from the west, casting deep shadows over the fairgrounds. Suddenly street lights started going on all over. "Watch out, buddy," some male voice shouted. I stepped aside as two men hurried through the gate with a long ladder on their shoulders. I returned to the fair office. The two men were gone, replaced by a young girl who smiled at me coyly. To me she was just a kid. She said Mr. Stowe, the fair manager, would be right with me. I took out my notebook and began to read it. So far, the story added up to this: It was doubtful there would ever be another fair. The decision was up to the Board of Directors, also the Corporation members. The men involved were the same men on both groups! Dissension in one, for whatever reasons, was dissension in the other. How could I explain that to my readers? Conclusion: If the decision had not already been made, irrevocably, to close the fair, there was still hope that the fair could continue. If this was the last fair, then the permanent buildings would be torn down. Then it struck me: there were fifty or more acres here, right off Main Street, only a few blocks from downtown stores and office buildings. Chesterton had been expanding for years. The fairgrounds! Room for downtown expansion! Maybe a billion dollars worth of prime real estate! What a fool I had been not to have thought of that before.

I asked the girl, a pretty brunette who was deep in thought reading a romance novel. "Miss, is the fairgrounds part of the city?"

She smiled sweetly as she lowered the book. "I don't have the slightest idea," she said.

"Excuse me, Miss. I'm Art James, reporter, from the Star."

"I know. Ricky told me."

"Ricky?"

"Yes, Ricky Bryson."

"Of course. Nice guy."

"I'm Jenny Glen. Bob's my brother. I'm a lot older than him."

"Is that so? Well, that's interesting."

At that moment Stowe, the fair manager, appeared. He greeted me warmly. He was a good-looking man with a slick receding brow, insistently straight-limbed. He had a piercing stare, which humbled me, not in a threatening manner, but causing me to keep my distance. He gave me a cherubic smile. "I heard you had a pleasant chat with Ricky Bryson and Bob Glen. What brings you to Chesterton, Mr. James?"

I knew he already knew why, and I was annoyed by his coyness. I decided to play it cool. "You have an interesting County Fair," I said. "It's been going how long? A century?"

"Nine-nine years, to be exact," he said. He amazed me by twice holding up nine fingers. "When we open tomorrow, that will be our centennial. Why don't we go into my office?" He opened the door on the wall behind the Glen girl.

Obviously a late adjunct to the fair office, Stowe's lair was even plainer, consisting of two narrow open windows on the side walls, a six-foot dining table in the middle of the room, a few chairs and little else. We sat down at the table. Stowe picked up a pipe, loaded it with tobacco from a leather pouch and struck a match. It took him at least a minute to light the pipe. He blew a cloud of smoke into the warm evening air. Then I let him have it: "So this will be the last fair ever," I said.

Stowe stumbled to his feet and loomed over me. "It will *not* be the last!" he shouted at me. He wrung his hands. "I am the manager of this fair this year and I will still be the manager next year!"

"But I heard--?"

"I don't give a damn what you heard, Mr. James. They're all lies. Lies, I tell you, Mr. James. And you can quote me. Is that clear, Mr. James?"

"Perfectly clear, Mr. Stowe, and I will quote you, with thanks." I made sure he could see me writing that down. I determined to try another tactic. "I hear that some industries are interested in buying slices of the fairgrounds," I said.

"I don't know anything about that," he replied. "Try me again, Mr. James."

Now I was really nonplussed. Then I got it. "Could you give me the name of anyone who would be willing to give me a statement on the subject?" I asked slowly. I was silent as he looked aside. I knew he wanted to answer that particular question.

"Mr. James, I think you are a fair man, as an intelligent reporter, I mean. I appreciate your interest. You realize, of course, that my position as manager of the fair is a paid one. My duty is to assist groups and organizations who wish to sponsor events on the fairgrounds. The annual County Fair is one of those events. As an employee I am responsible to the Board of Directors. You do understand my situation, Mr. James?"

I nodded. "Of course, Mr. Stowe. "I need to know who might be willing to answer other questions that I might ask. I won't tell anyone."

"You would keep it strictly confidential?"

"Let me explain my position, Mr. Stowe. I was given this assignment to find out what's happening because the Star, the editors, think that county fairs are a wonderful institution and we would hate to see another one close down. There aren't too many left." I went out on a limb with that one. For all I know, the Star didn't give a damn about county fairs, although it sure did care about Richland industry. And about circulation, since a good hunk of the Star's readers lived in a six-county area, including Chesterton County. So I threw out the thought that the Star would be against the loss of a Richland industry to Chesterton. My remark struck a chord with Stowe. I let him have the other barrel. "Personally," I said, "I would hate to see the Chesterton County Fair cancelled. I've been delighted coming here. When I was a boy I always thought it was better than the state fair." I warmed to this lie, because I had never set foot on the Chesterton fairgrounds until that day. "There's something nostalgic about a county fair that goes to the heart."

CHAPTER FOUR

Two miles south of Chesterton the road to Castle Rock branched off the main highway. Following the directions that Ricky Bryson had given me, I came upon the farm, where its huge red barn, bathed in gold from the setting sun, edged the road. From there the rolling land swept upward to the crest of a hill, where tall elms were silhouetted against the sky. Their shadows were pencil lines on the dark meadows. Marching Indian file, a group of Guernsey dairy cattle plodded down the hill between wire fences. As I turned left into the farm, following a dirt road to the house, I noticed the name placarded on the barn: *Xenophon.* I wondered how the Greek historian figured in this. It was another indication, I surmised, of that ancient mystique of the pioneers of the new American civilization who called their villages Homer, Ithaca, Troy, Memphis, Olympia and Syracuse, and a hundred other names that spoke of conquest of the land.

At the door of the high white frame house, whose porch ran the full width along the front and around the side, I pressed the bell and waited. Samuel Bryson opened the door. I suppose I expected some bronzed leather-faced man in faded blue overalls, and I hope my dismay did not register on my face at what I did see: a six-foot handsome man with iron-gray hair, a fair, rather pale, complexion, and dressed in a dark blue business suit. I could imagine him being the town bank president but hardly a farmer. He had a high prominent nose and a broad smooth forehead, and quite piercing eyes beneath thick black brows. He seldom blinked. He ushered me into the parlor, furnished in, for me, uncomfortable Danish. I sat on the sofa and he took the low chair opposite. I found myself wondering why the chair supported so muscled a man and how he would ever raise himself from it. He sat lightly in it and I noticed his hands were not a banker's hands: they were dark and heavily veined.

"Excuse me," he said, getting spryly to his feet again, "I should have offered you a drink." I apologized when I told him I didn't drink. Perhaps he cottoned to the rumor that a lot of reporters were heavy drinkers. I don't know where that came from, because it wasn't true.

"You're the first reporter from Richland I ever met," he said. "Of course I know Walt Clark, publisher of the Times." No one in his right mind would ever think of a newspaper publisher as a journalist, but I let it pass. "I know Mr. Blanchard, the editor," I said.

He ignored that. "Walt Clark's a man you can trust," he said. "The Times gives everyone a fair shake. Yes, sir, we're mighty proud of the Times, mighty proud. Not that the Star isn't a good paper, mind you, I read it myself. But for local coverage the Times cant be beat."

"The Star admits that," I said. "Our county page tries to give the highlights. We know the Times provides the depth that Chesterton County expects." I threw in this sop to butter him up, because I really had no use for the Times, with its columns upon columns of reports on church suppers, ladies' aid meetings and Garden Club flora. Especially after today, since I discovered it was suppressing news about the fair.

"You didn't come here to talk about the Times, Mr. James," Bryson said. "And may I say it was good of you to come. I'm always glad to talk to the press." I surmised that he meant he talked to the Times publisher. He was a real pro, I thought. I had to give him credit for that. It takes one to know one.

"I learned you are head of Farm Service," I said.

"Been that for nigh on twenty years now. Great organization, really great. Does a lot for the farmers, an awful lot."

"Great!" I put my heart into that one. "I have a few questions about the fair." He nodded assent. "I heard that there won't be County Fair next year."

He didn't bat an eye. "The directors wouldn't stand for it. And if we didn't have the fairgrounds we'd find somewhere else. We always assumed there would be another fair, even during the war. The fair is a county institution. It means a lot to the people, an awful lot. Farm Service has been a sponsor of the fair for many, many years. Most farm families hereabouts are members. We always have an exhibit to show what the service does. We don't do those things ourselves, of course. More roads, research, more rural telephones and electric lines. We bring pressure to bear on the legislators, the utility companies. Where would the farmer be without price supports? Farm Service developed these. Of course we want those supports to be eliminated as fast as possible. Personally, I think farm prices should be permitted to seek their own level. Of course we have to accept government money. It's forced on us. But we're against excessive reliance upon the government. That never works. The individual must be free. Anyway, Farm Service speaks for the farmers."

He paused for a while. He could see I was taking some notes. He had gotten away from the main subject, the County Fair. I leaned forward and asked: "A hypothetical question: If the fair were to close, who would close it?"

Bryson was silent for a moment. "Certainly not the directors. The corporation would be the one to do it. As a director I have a vote that counts for several points, because I represent Farm Service. The number of points goes up or down depending upon the number of members. As a member of the corporation I have one vote. Fair management resides in the directors. The corporation doesn't own the fairgrounds. They are leased from Chesterton County. It's a sixty-nine year lease, which expires next year. However, the lease can be cancelled by mutual agreement of the corporation and county commissioners." He mustered a huge sigh of relief. He laughed. "Simple, isn't it?"

"May take a hundred years to untangle it," I said. "There's no way I need to report all the ins and outs, Mr. Bryson. To clarify, are you a county commissioner?" He nodded. It came to me in a flash. "How many county commissioners are on the fair corporation board?"

Bryson drew a deep breath. This could be as tiresome to him as to me, but I was determined to get to the gut of this web of coalitions. "There are six county commissioners," he told me. I detected his feeling of embarrassment. "They are all members of the fair corporation, which has ten members."

"The commissioners control the corporation by majority vote?" I asked. "Isn't that a problem? Isn't that unusual?"

Bryson shook his head. "Not at all," he said. "I imagine it is rather common in this state."

I found that difficult to believe, but it was true. Politics controlled the destiny of the fair. "By majority vote, then," I said, "the corporation could, conceivably, decide to break the fairgrounds lease, and the commissioners, the same men, could agree?"

"Conceivably," he said.

Bryson seemed to be sinking lower into the odd-looking chair. The sun had gone down and the room had sunk into a twilight gloom. Bryson got up, went over to the wall, and switched on an overhead light.

"This inter-locking directorate--" I began.

Bryson interrupted me. "Isn't that a loaded way of putting it?" he asked.

"The peculiar duplication of memberships might, again conceivably, act in selfish interest?"

"I don't know what you are implying by that."

"The profit motive," I said loudly.

"If you are saying that someone is trying to pull a fast deal--"

"No, I wouldn't say that," I said, looking sorry that I said it.

"If you are, I would advise you to lay off that line of questioning."

"And if I don't?" I tried to look innocent.

"It might, it just might, get you into a lot of trouble."

My back was up now. "Mr. Bryson, are you threatening me?"

"No, no, you misunderstand me, Mr. James." He gave me a palms-up signal of restraint. "I am simply saying that any story you wrote along those lines would not be provable, and would provoke a strong protest."

"Perhaps not provable, but nonetheless true?"

"Mr. James, I've been told newspapers are supposed to print only the truth, the admissible truth?"

I wasn't sure what he was getting at and I'm sure my expression proved it. "As much as possible," I said. "I like to get *all* the facts."

"Hah, hah. I don't trust the press and I never will. I've given you all the facts, Mr. James. Your interpretation may be at fault."

"We try not to editorialize."

"But the press does, by your choice of facts to print."

I could see we understood one another very well. I switched the subject. "Will the people have something to say as to whether the fair is to continue?" I asked.

"The authority rests with the directors. It is not bound to hold a fair every year. No referendum to the people would be necessary."

"In that case, Mr. Bryson, the corporation could decide not to have a fair next year?"

I could see the color rising in Bryson's face. He hesitated a moment, about to say something more, then stood up. "I'm afraid I must close this interview, Mr. James. It's getting late."

"Yes, of course, I am sorry, Mr. Bryson." He was hiding something, something really weird. I was beginning to suspect that the entire county was ruled by a clique that held the entire population in its thrall. I knew I was getting in too deep. This was my first day on this assignment. Danger signals were ringing in my head.

Even as I thanked Bryson for his time I felt that I was being manipulated by a man wiser than me, and it had nothing to do with the fact that I was in my twenties. I was encroaching on a society that had its own way of getting things done, or stalled too. I was an outsider trying to look inside a century-old way of life. I wasn't one of them. Because of that I could not possibly understand them. But that didn't mean I would give up trying.

I asked Bryson to do me a favor. He consented. He telephoned his Xenophon partner, Mr. Glen, and told him I would like to interview him, even though it was getting late. Mr. Glen agreed to see me.

On the porch I thanked Bryson and went out to my Buick. The stars were out in brilliant display. I sucked deeply on the cool night air, fragrant with meadow incense. But the stuffy atmosphere of the Bryson parlor lingered in my brain.

I pulled the emergency brake and let it go. The Buick roared to life as I turned the ignition key. The rear wheels spun furiously on the gravel. I switched on the headlights and spun around the curving road to the farm's gate, went through and turned left on the road toward Castle Rock and the Glen house. Probably it was my imagination, or I only hoped it would be, but the Glen house was smaller and brighter than Bryson's. It lay under a big clump of tall trees. There was a huge weeping willow on the corner that was sort of scary, like so many long fingers reaching for me. In the dark it was a wide shadow against the darkening sky.

Mrs. Glen, a short plump woman, answered the door. She asked me in without further ado. I followed her into the kitchen, where she directed me to take the armchair. She filled a kettle and placed it on the electric stove. The kitchen was one of those enormous white ones that had something of the atmosphere of the early farmhouse days. No doubt the Glen kitchen once had a big black wood-burning stove with a huge oven.

"My husband will be here in a minute," Mrs. Glen said as she set out cups and saucers, sugar and cream. "My son, Bob, told me you met him at the fair office."

"And Mr. Bryson's son, Richard, too," I said.

"Jennifer, that's my daughter, told me she liked you a lot, you were so handsome. And you are. Isn't she a sweet girl though?"

"Oh, I did see her there, but I didn't have any time to talk to her. I was there to interview Mr. Stowe."

"We call her Jenny for short," Mrs. Glen said with a wide smile. "She's very pretty, don't you think? She says she's going steady with Ricky Bryson, but don't you believe it. They're very good friends. After all, they grew up together here on the farm. When Ricky came home from the university in June, that was the first time I noticed." She took on a far-away look as she filled a silver teapot. She sighed deeply, a motherly sign of regret. She remained silent and busied herself with tea bags. I was beginning to think she had forgotten I was there.

"What did you notice?" I asked.

She shook her head. "Oh, yes, where was I? What did I notice? Why, that Jenny had grown up so much. She was eighteen when she went to college. Now, suddenly, she's twenty-one! Can you imagine? So fast, so fast!"

As I sipped a cup of tea, well sweetened, she said proudly "My Bob is majoring in agriculture. He wants to be a teacher." She looked at me intently. "You're not farm-bred, are you, Mr. James?" I shook my head in the negative. "I thought so. That's too bad, isn't it?" I think she felt sorry for me. I told her I studied journalism at Richland University. "Then you must have known Ricky!" she exclaimed, then nodded her head. "Silly of me. There are hundreds of students, aren't there?" I told her she was right, and that I had probably graduated before Ricky went there. "How time flies, doesn't it? Bob, has another year to go. He's a year younger than Jenny, you know."

I stood up as Mr. Glen, a five-eight figure clad in tan shirt and trousers came in. "Mr. James, I'm so glad to meet you. I love your articles in the Star!" To say I was struck dumb was an understatement. So far no one even told me they read the Star, let alone telling me they had seen my byline. I *liked* Mr. Glen. "How do you do?" he asked formally. "I can't shake hands." He showed me his upturned palms. "Got this muck in the barn. One of the cows is about to foal. I'll have to get back there soon, so let's hop to it, shall we? Shoot."

"Thank you, Mr. Glen."

"Please! Whatever you write, call me Robert, not Bob. We call our son that. He hates being called Robert Junior so much I think he wants to change his name." He hugged his wife heartily. "Don't we, sweetheart?"

"Not on your life," she said with a winning laugh. "Let's all sit down right here, shall we?" The idea of having Mrs. Glen included in the interview was a shock. But there wasn't anything I could do about it. I knew I would have to sweeten my questions so I wouldn't upset her.

"So, what brings you here, Mr. James?" Mrs. Glen asked me.

It took me a moment to set aside my planned questions. "I'm writing color stories. That's background features. I like fairs."

"Takes a lot of work," Mr. Glen said, "but it's worth it. Did you see the Grange exhibit?"

"I like the central portion," I said. "The open Bible. The stalks of wheat, the symbols of your beliefs."

"That's always at the center," he said. "Officers of the Pomona, the Grange's county unit, put up the stands. The Juvenile Grange does the rest. Did you see the Co-op display? That's a Grange organization. We package our own products, sell them directly to Co-op stores in Chesterton, Beaver, Sussex and Rutland counties."

I made a few notes. "I interviewed Mr. Bryson," I told them, "about the closing of the fair."

Mrs. Glen expressed her shock with a loud handclap. "What? That's ridiculous! The most ridiculous thing I ever heard. There's always been a fair and there always will be a fair." She folded her arms around her ample bosom. "So there!"

"Now, now, Sweetheart," Mr. Glen said. He patted her shoulder. "There's rumors about, that's all." He turned his attention to me. "Mr.

James, the Grange is a hundred percent against it. You can quote me on that. I know how Sam Bryson is leaning on this matter. We've been farming partners together all our lives. I tell you this for sure: He will move mountains, he will go through hell and high water before he would allow the fair to dissolve. He's under a lot of pressure from the business community, but that matter will be resolved. It will take time. We must be patient. The way the fair is structured is crazy. We've got to fix that, and we will. Believe me, Mr. James, we will!"

While I was furiously taking notes, Mrs. Glen said: "I know the farm people. They will never allow the fair to close. Never! The fair is our chief means of educating the public about the problems of farmers. We've got to keep some way of making contact with consumers. Urban children think corn grows in cans."

Glen told me that the Grange directors would be meeting Thursday night. "I wish I could tell you how the Grange directors will vote, but, you see, I am not free." I stood up and thanked him for the interview but he pleaded with me to stay. "Talk to Ricky, Jenny and Bob. They are the ones who would be most affected if this is to be the last county fair. They can tell you what young people think about this mess. Meanwhile, why don't you and I take a look around outside? I've got to see how that cow's doing and, well, I would like to show you why we farm folks are so stubborn about the way we see things." He laughed again. "It's what city folks might call our point of view."

CHAPTER FIVE

When Mr. Glen and I passed beyond the bar of light that flooded the porch from the open kitchen door, I was fascinated by the depth and brilliance of the star-packed sky. I lived only thirty miles away in Richland, but the night sky there was nothing like this. My boyhood sky was a scattering of only a few bright single stars here and there. There was no moon. Still, the star-clothed sky gave enough light to see, as my eyes became accustomed to it, a path leading through a meadow to a huge barn silhouetted against the brilliant canopy of the heavens. We went up a short hill toward the crest and there we turned around and leaned against a log fence. The headlights of a car ripped the darkness far away.

Under the stars the house, barn and a tall silo were dim and shadowed, but their outlines were clearly etched. Soft orange light spilled onto the grass from the kitchen windows. A single bulb blinked over the wide closed barn door. The million-voiced crickets raised a chorus in the clover, and far above a night hawk sang its long sad song. Across the valley, beyond the road, a hill swept up to the stars, where another dark house and a barn edged the ridge. When the car had passed, horn blaring at the bend, the earth stood still. Only the night creatures claimed possession of the land.

Glen swung his thick strong arm around in a semi-circle, pointing to the horizon. "The issue isn't the fair," he said. He launched into a monolog filled with musical cadences. I could not take notes in the darkness and, for that reason, I am paraphrasing what he said as best I can. I surprised myself by listening closely. I put aside my journalist's yearning to interrupt, to question, to interview, to dominate. Here is what he said:

"The issue is the land. I have tilled this soil for thirty years, as did my father before me and his father before him. My great-grandfather came over yonder hill and saw the valley, saw with practiced glance that it was good. There is a stream there, beyond the road, that flows from Chesterton to Castle Rock and farther, broadening as it goes. He hewed logs in the virgin forest and built a cabin—When the cabin was taken down the timbers were still strong and without rot. They were used to build the woodshed, which we passed coming through the yard. He was a veteran of the Civil War, fought at Gettysburg and came here, discharged, looking to the land to give him leaven and a living. He was one of many of his kind who made this valley wilderness a shelter and a home. Over there, across the river, under those trees, I helped my father bury him, and later we buried his wife by his side, a Chesterton girl who kept a diary, which I have, describing the first year of the County Fair, a one-day gathering on a farm outside the village of Chesterton that later became the present fairgrounds. That was a couple of years after the Civil War ended.

"My grandfather told me something of those early days. They were days of drudgery and monotony, without change. From one small plot the Xenophon farm expanded to six hundred acres and, with day-long labor in the sun and rain the land was cleared. When my grandfather died, he left this legacy to my father and his brothers. My father being the eldest, his brothers sold their shares to him, and they took their money and went elsewhere to buy land. All this was not done alone. There were neighbors. My great-grandfather came over the hill with a fellow soldier. They had fought together in many battles, so they say, and they settled together on the land. My great-grandfather's name was Silas Glen. His friend was Reuben Bryson. For fifty years they labored side by side, and they were closer than kin. Reuben got his six hundred acres next to ours, and when Silas died, Reuben, broken-hearted, crept across the road to the grave, crying for his loss, and died soon after. Reuben had sons too, and the eldest was Matthew, who was my father's closest friend. They carried on the farms, my grandfather, Jason, and Samuel Bryson's grandfather. Together, Matthew and Jason helped each other as their fathers had, and the farms were enlarged and prospered. Hired hands came to work in the fields, and, for the first time, migrants from the south.

"They are dead now, our grandfathers, and their sons, our fathers, and they left the farms to us, Samuel Bryson and myself. Sam and I were like our fathers, we were friends from infancy, to the land born and to the land bequeathed. When the depression came in the thirties we consolidated operations and so we were not submerged, as so many valley farms were.

After the war, with government help, we merged the farms into one, giving it the name Xenophon. The shares were divided equally among our families. I have a quarter, my wife another. The other half is owned by Sam Bryson and his wife. My half will go to my son, Bob, and Sam will do the same for his son, Ricky. So the boys will take over from their fathers, the fifth generation.

"But I have not told you of this other side of our relationship. In the last century the Grange movement started all over the country. It was established by farmers, for farmers, so they could live a richer, fuller life. We banded together in our local unit, taking the secret pledge of brotherhood, and confirming this in regular ritual. Our grandfathers were founders of the Pomona of Chesterton County. Our fathers were officers of the state Grange, and I have been a representative to the national organization. At first the Grange was used to promote the farmers' interests through cooperative effort, setting up their own dairies, wineries, warehouses, grain elevators. They campaigned against railroad and other extortion charges, but that was incidental to our cause, which was to preserve our tradition as stewards of the soil. Our fathers, we ourselves, and our sons have been raised through the Juvenile Grange, and so, you see, to us the Grange is alliance and neighbor, friend and brother.

"It was not enough. We fought for legislation, we worked with the co-operatives, but our organization was not right. We were a club, a lodge, a secret society, guarding a culture and a way of life. Economics was not central to our purpose. Some other group was needed. That was Farm Service Association. It saw the need for action in business, to the whole economic realm, in the making of laws. It became our link to government extension and experimental services, and with price support programs. Through them we have better conservation practices, rural electrification and telephones, better roads. We have backed research, both for growing, distribution and marketing of what we grow. These are the farmer's concerns, firm prices and a market. Given rain, we can grow anything in abundance. Still, we have achieved these advances at the sacrifice of others, the heaven-blessed sense of our apartness, our bond with earth and water, our oneness with the soil. In the past we contested with the earth to bring its increase, and in our victory we were triumphant over pain. Now science has conquered in our stead, and there is no joy in that, only dread that in our greed for gain we have spoiled the land and the life it yields with grain."

Glen paused and there was silence over the soil. He reached down and grasped a handful of dirt. He let it dribble through his fingers. The wind caught it and swirled it over the earth, shredded. "This is our life and our living," he said. "It is our yeast and our yearning. Dust, dear bought. Soil, sacrificed for. Earth, earned. Inheritance, cherished. Ours, alone."

We walked together down the hill, and I heard the hawk no more. The meadow lark slept, waiting for the dawn. At the house I said goodnight and went to my car. I stroked the pedal and turned onto the road. As I passed over the hill the unanswered questions hurtled through my mind. I hastened to the fairgrounds, hoping the young people would still be there.

The men were in the fair office and so was Jenny Glen. This time I really looked at her. She was incredibly lovely, a virgin brunette. She put her hand out and it was soft and warm. I held it a moment longer than I should have, and I saw her eyes were the palest blue, her features finely chiseled. Right away I determined to challenge destiny, to conquer time, to totally know her until she acknowledged that she knew me. I never believed such a thing could happen, but it did. I was smitten.

"If you have time," I said, speaking to Ricky, Bob and Jenny, "I would appreciate it if we could have a talk."

"Sure," Ricky said. "We have to put these papers away. A little work tomorrow morning and we will be ready for the parade and the two o'clock opening of the fair."

I went outside to wait for them and noted the continuous frenzied activity throughout the grounds. Lights were blazing all over. Men, women and young people were scurrying to and fro on errands. After a time the boys came out with Jenny. We went over to a tent diner with a sign over it: *Castle Rock Presbyterian Church*. A number of workmen from the sideshows were seated at small white metal tables. We went to the counter and ordered frankfurters and colas and took them to a table.

"You saw my father?" Ricky asked.

"Yes, and your father too, Bob and Jenny."

"Did you get your story?" Bob asked.

"Not everything," I said, "not yet. But I have some facts to go on. I got some things straight about the Grange, Farm Service, the fair corporation and the board of directors."

"Well, Mr. Reporter, it's rather complex, don't you think?" Ricky asked.

"Not that complicated," I said with a laugh. "It's a simple story of cooperation on the rocks."

"What's that?" Jenny's voice was firm and bright.

I was quick to ease her anxiety. "I mean it looks as if there's been a falling out among friends."

"You mean between my father and Ricky's?" Bob asked.

"Perhaps," I answered. "I got the impression your fathers are traveling on different tracks. Once they were headed in the same direction, and now one of them has changed direction."

"Which one?" Bob asked. I noted his alarm.

"I would rather not say," I said.

"A reporter's secret?" Ricky asked, somewhat sarcastically. "Read all about it tomorrow?"

"No, I wouldn't print that," I insisted. "I try not to allow my personal sympathies to interfere with my objectivity."

Ricky showed his alarm this time. "You can be objective about this?" he asked. "I thought you came here to take us apart."

"Hardly, Ricky. I don't know where you got that from, but I am more interested in the fair itself than the personalities involved." That wasn't true, of course, because I was beginning to feel that the future of the fair was very much involved with the people whose tangled lives were caught up in it. But I wanted to throw him off my trail.

"If anything happened to the fair, Jenny said. "I mean if there would never be another, I think I would just cry. I couldn't stand it."

"You like the fair, Jenny?" I asked, feigning sincerity.

"That's a weak word for it," she said. "I *love* the fair. More than that. The county wouldn't be the same without it. Ever since I can remember I've looked forward to the August fair days. You know how a child thinks about Santa Claus from Thanksgiving on. Well, worse than that. And it doesn't stop when you're grown up. It goes on all your life. My father took me to my first fair before I could talk, and there hasn't been a year that I haven't attended, not a year that I haven't been involved in some project. I remember the first time I won a ribbon, I was only five. It was for a blueberry pie. Of course Mother helped me, but I kneaded the dough myself, rolled it, spread it on the tray and trimmed the edges. I cleaned the berries and put them in the pie and laid a layer of dough on top, after I had cut a fancy design in it. Then I put it in the oven and I opened the door so many times to see how it was doing that Mother said it would never get baked. I was so proud of that ribbon. I still have it, along with others, but I am proudest of the first."

"That's the way it was with me," Bob said. "My first calf. Dad gave it to me to raise. I was there when it was born and I helped Dad. I gave that calf a name, Dandelion, because it was born in May when the dandelions were yellow in the yard. By August the calf was perfect, filled out and sturdy, with a coat that simply gleamed, I brushed it so much. Dandelion took first prize. The silver cup is in my room, surrounded by other trophies, but Dandelion is the one I cherish the most."

"The fair is more than achievement," Ricky said. "It is neighbors in competition to show their industry, their high purpose, the independence of their economy. That is what intrigues me. The girls put out their sewing, the boys their rabbits. The women enter their jellies and relish, the men their hybrid corn and wheat. In contesting for a ribbon or a trophy it is the purpose that's important, not the product. This is the American way, to vie with one another for success, to obtain reward for quality and energy, to seek recognition for daring and ambition. That's what makes the fair exciting for participants, whether they have an entry or not."

"Then all of you," I said, "would feel a loss if the fair were to be cancelled. Jenny said how she would feel. How about you, Bob?"

"I can't imagine what it would be like. Not to have the fair? And no hope for one again, ever? No, I just can't bear to think of it. Life wouldn't be the same."

"We have to realize," Ricky said, "we are entering a more sophisticated age when fairs may be passe. Not that I wouldn't be sorry to see the fair disappear. There are substitutes that are more appropriate to the space age. Last summer in Chicago I went to the International Trade Fair. That's more what I mean. Electronic gear, automatic machinery. Things that point the way to the future. Of course the County Fair has made some advances. We always have a new-car show, and some stores have appliance and furniture exhibits. But an agricultural show, pure and simple, that's somewhat anachronistic, don't you think?"

"You're asking me?" I exclaimed. Ricky looked at me disdainfully, as if I didn't know what the word meant.

"I'm asking all of you," Ricky responded.

"Wait a minute," Bob said. "I suppose when the fairs started they were places where the farmer could show off what he's grown. They were markets and as such fell into the category of advertising. When the machinery makers were invited to show their products the fair became not only advertising but also education. The machines presupposed some knowledge of the soil and climate, of seed and cultivation. They were not merely labor-saving devices. They brought in a whole new way of farming. Then, with the advent of the automobile, electric power, the telephone and rural mail delivery, the farmer was brought closer to his market, the consumer. At the same time he was driven farther away from the people he fed, for then emerged the middle man, the wholesaler, the grocer, the food broker. There was a time when everyone knew something about how the food they ate was grown. Today they seldom think about it, and if they do it turns the stomach. It's not genteel to speak of fertilizer, let alone manure, or of slaughter and quartering. No, our food comes in shining cans, all red, white and blue, or brilliant packages wrapped in plastic like candy. That there is a farmer, a tiller of the soil, behind all this is simply beyond imagining. Food, as far as the consumer is concerned, is processed, produced, or manufactured in some long low building called a plant. One would think from reading a newspaper or a magazine that it was whipped up, like a synthetic, in a laboratory."

"If the public doesn't know," Jenny said, "isn't it wrong to cut off one of the means of education we have, the fair? Farmers need friends, and at the fair we can meet them face to face."

"That's very noble," Ricky said, "but hardly realistic. Just go through the pavilion tomorrow night and count the people. It will be possible, there will be so few. Then go over to the Midway and see if you can even *estimate* the crowd. The grandstand will be full for Pete Marble, the singer, and on Wednesday afternoon there will be thousands at the stock car races, watching for some poor fellow to break his neck, being disappointed if he doesn't. They don't care anymore about agricultural exhibits. If you will pardon the expression, they are too corny."

"Then you shouldn't be disappointed if the fair disappears?" I asked.

"I really don't know," Ricky said. "I would like something better, something more modern, to take its place. Take the World's Fair in New York. That was something. I learned a lot there. It pointed the way, man in the modern world, ready to challenge the stars."

"We still need to eat!" Jenny cried out.

"Yes, we do," Ricky said. "But think of what the astronauts carry in the space capsule, food in a toothpaste tube, condensed, injected with vitamins. The farmer still thinks in terms of food as bulk, the heavier the better. But that isn't necessarily so. No, we have to develop food that has more growing power, so to speak, for children and more economic power for adults. We are weak and spoiled on pap, conscious of cholesterol and calories. Let's grow food that produces energy and still keeps the body trim. If the farmers don't capitalize on the scientific information available they will lose out to the laboratories, where dwarf grains, fruits and vegetables yield more carbohydrates and protein per ounce. And, besides, there's the increasing cost of keeping soil-grown food pure."

Bob raised a hand. "We hear a lot about the poisons in our food," he said, "but what can the farmer do? He must control the pests of nature that spoil the crop, not by destroying it, that's simple enough to cope with, but those that stunt the growth of a fruit or grain. We can grow oranges as big as grapefruit, and grapefruit as big as watermelons if we want to, and the consumer would think that was a real bargain if we could keep the price down. But the added weight would be mostly water and pulp, not good for sustenance. I've read about a plan to grind up fish that are normally cast away as the filth of the sea, but we have laws against that, because it would entail, to be economical, the use of entrails, scales, heads and all. But, properly seasoned, such dust would assure all-round nourishment."

Jenny asked: "Could I use it as flour, to make a cake?'

"Sure," Ricky said. "You could use it for anything, bread, stew, pudding. And you, my dear, with your undeniable talent, would make it taste delicious."

"You're very kind," she said with exaggerated courtesy. "But I would miss cracking the eggs and watching the wonderful yokes fall into the bowl. I would miss not having flour so white--"

"Oh, fish dust could be bleached."

"Still, it would be like oleo compared to butter. It wouldn't *feel* the same."

"That's a woman for you," Ricky said. "Sentimental. But there's no room today for sentimentality. Farming is a business and must be operated on business principles. We must know the fundamentals of our economy, the distribution and the marketing process. Those are the important things, how to make a profit out of a hundred acres, or even less. How to protect the soil from the elements, how to enrich it so that it can yield year after year without the necessity of fallow years. How to mechanize and automate beyond our wildest dreams, so that machines will not only plow and plant and reap, but also will tend and nourish as well. I speak of incubation, what we do with small spaces under glass, the so-called greenhouse. Nature by itself is a wild housekeeper. It is undisciplined, disordered, capricious. It would as soon sweep the dirt under the rug as into the dustpan. You cannot depend upon her."

Bob said: "Still, the cost--"

"Cost is relative to the need, or demand," Ricky continued. "There is the demand, all over the world. If it is true that two thirds of earth's people go to bed hungry at night, then that is a problem of distribution, of marketing, not production. Today the deserts bloom, and water can be tunneled through a mountain and over sandy plains. There is land enough to spare. No, the problem is not in the land, nor even in the lack of water. Too much water in the Yangtse creates a famine in China, too little in the Ganges causes millions to starve. Improper distribution, that's the key. Engineering is the answer."

"The cost of food is too high," Bob injected. "Oh, I know, they say the farmer does not get an even break, and that's so. A small fraction of what the consumer pays goes to the farmer. The profit is in marketing and distribution. That's why, if we share our knowledge, pool our resources, we can have our own super-stores, the co-operatives. And co-ops for distribution too, besides wholesale outlets. Through the co-ops now we buy our supplies, and the profits from our purchases are returned in shares or dividends."

"Even so," Ricky said, "the farm market is shrinking, for there are thousands fewer farmers every year. We do not buy enough, and so we cannot compete in price with the national distribution systems of the giant stores. Our warehousing is at fault."

"That is because we have relied too much on the county system," Bob said, "organizing along county lines. Transportation is the key. Shipping is the answer. If we brought together farmers from a wider area, pooled our resources, broadened our credit, we could manage trucking on our own. We could deliver food to the stores faster. I know you will ask 'What about packaging?' and I would say this too: let's do our own. If we were willing to take less profit on warehousing, that being possible with more direct routing from farm to store, then we could compete."

Jenny objected: "But people like their food prepared as much as possible in advance. Think of TV dinners."

"That's true," Bob said, "so we have to educate the consumer about the nutritional values of food, fresh food, free from contamination of some preservatives. There are health stores which, among the educated, do a fine trade. With more emphasis on body-strengthening value, and less on taste, we could do better. If I had the choice, I would be an agricultural economist and educator."

I interjected: "You prefaced your statement of ambition with the word 'if.' Do you mean you cannot become what you wish?"

"For myself," Bob said, "I see no possibility. There is the Xenophon, you see. It must be carried on."

"Must! Must!" Jenny exclaimed. "Why must it? Because our great-grandfathers, and all our great forebears did? If you want to be an economist, a teacher, then why can't you be that? To hell with the Xenophon!"

"Jenny!" her brother fairly screamed.

"Well, I don't care," she said, glancing sternly at her brother, "I know you too well, Bob. Pride in the farm and all that jazz. Well, I say let it go. If you believe so much in agricultural progress in this country, why don't you do something about it instead of just talk?"

"I have to admit," Ricky said, "Jenny's got something there. After all, anyone can run the Xenophon."

"But only the Brysons and the Glens have run it," Bob cut in. "It's been in our families for a hundred years."

"Who cares?" Ricky asked.

"May I say something?" I asked. "I have visited the Xenophon and I've interviewed your fathers. I think I care a lot now about the farm. It's a symbol--"

"Yes," Ricky said. "A symbol of sacrifice and dedication. I've been hearing that all my life, mostly from Bob's father. There's a dedicated being, like an ostrich."

Bob sprang to his feet. "Ricky, you take that back! What's so noble about Sam Bryson, I ask you." Jenny raised a restraining hand. Bob ignored it. "I'm sorry, sister dear, but Ricky started it. His father spends all his time in town, siding up to the politicians, lobbying in the courthouse. My father does all the work of looking after the farm."

"He does not!" Ricky shouted. "If it weren't for my father the Xenophon would have gone down the drain years ago. What would we do without the subsidies?"

"You mean the government bribery to keep us from doing what God gave us life to do, don't you?"

"Don't give me that Grange blah. That's nonsense, all that about God-given privileges of tilling the soil. Farming is a business, like any other business. You do it for profit, and when there is no profit, you close up shop."

Bob sat down and hung his head, as if in shame. "If you believe that, Ricky, you shouldn't be a farmer. Period."

"Don't give me that, Bob. That's why the little farmer is being squeezed out. How many acres have we got? A measly three thousand. That's a small operation. The combines, run by big corporations with headquarters in the big cities, run it the right way. They hire skilled men to run complicated machinery."

"Unskilled migrants to break their backs and lives for a pittance."

"Some day that problem will be eliminated."

"Sure," Bob said, "We will kill them all with our cruelty."

Ricky made no reply. Jenny entered the fray. "Haven't you two gone far enough?" she asked bitterly. "Please, not again, not the night before the fair. It should be a happy time."

Ricky looked abashed. "I apologize, Bob. Sometimes I get carried away. You talk so glibly about education, why don't you do it?"

"I will, but it would sound hollow without practical experience."

"How much experience do you need, Bob? You were raised on the farm. You've done all the chores. You are learning all the theories. Need you be ashamed to lecture on your beliefs because you do not have, at the moment, your hand on the plow?"

"I don't think it would be right," Bob said. "There are too many hypothetical farmers in the universities now. Take old Crombie, for instance. He's a professor at Richland, Mr. James. He's never worked on a farm in his life. But you would think he was the Grim Reaper himself the way he swings a ruler like a scythe in class. He pontificates against every known agricultural practice since the invention of the ox-cart and the grinding stone. But he forgets one thing, one very important thing, the farmer's heart. Without attachment to the soil--"

Ricky held up his hand. "I know what you are going to say, Bob. Without heart there is no hope. I will bet you think that while pitching at a dung heap."

"I could," Bob said. "There's more to farming than science knows or will admit. First, there is the farmer, then the farm."

Ricky settled back in his chair and yawned. "I know, I know. And last there is the foreclosure on the mortgage, and another abandoned farm the tourists pass by, twittering about the ghosts that haunt the crumbling farm house and barns. Farmers who believe twaddle deserve the dole."

"Any more than the teacher who loves his pupils and his classroom?" Bob asked. "Or the scientist who loves his tubes and his lab? Or the pastor who loves his people and his pulpit? Or the physician who loves his patients and his practice? Or the lawyer who loves his clients and his court?"

Jenny said: "Or the mother who loves her children and her home? Or the girl who loves her doll and her dollhouse? Or the boy who loves his dog and the doghouse? It seems to me it's all one piece. It is not something one chucks for a paycheck."

"Ah, that's it," I said. "There is profit in the land. It is the profit of the splendid spirit, the daring deed, the conscious conquest and the vital victory, the loving look. It is the tender trembling of the tree, and the terrible treasure of the task. It is the work of weakness, and the play of pleasure. It is the energy expended, and eternity experienced. Yes, it is the profit of power."

DAY BEFORE THE FAIR:

Will they ever get it ready?

But then, they always have

By Arthur James
Special to the Star

Like a city suddenly gone berserk--or an elephant trampling around in a flower garden. That's the impression you get on visiting the Chesterton County fairgrounds yesterday.

For yesterday was the day before the annual fair opens for the one hundredth time. Confusion, at least to this outsider, reigned on the fairgrounds.

All is bustle and excitement. Men and women, boys and girls, rush hither and yon carrying odd-shaped articles of every description, hurrying to set up exhibits and refreshment booths.

Down the midway, canvas lies stretched out in disarray amid a confusing welter of poles and signboards. Tractors stride recklessly down narrow lanes, pulling monster wagons. Gangs of husky men pound stakes and clamp long steel poles together.

And yet there is little actual confusion in their work. Each man and each woman seems to know what to do, knows where each pole goes and where each clamp secures a corner section. But how they will get everything ready in time for the next day's opening is a mystery. But open we know it will.

Over on the other side of the racetrack from the midway, things are a bit quieter. A horse-drawn sulky races down the track to the rhythmic beat of harnessed hoofs. A stage nears completion opposite the grandstand as men swarm over it with ropes and planks.

Over to the left a long row of silver trailers indicates the housing center of some of the traveling workmen. A few trucks are unloaded of their thousands of cases of soft drinks, as machines and hotdog grillers are installed.

Under another canopy stacks of blankets and cartons of dolls in pale blue and pink dresses are piled on the grass, prizes at a stand where players will be lined up two and three deep tonight. But yesterday a workman or two set up prefabricated shelves on which the prizes will be displayed. They string colored lights along the roof edge.

Two huge diesel generators spread their tenuous cables for scores of yards in every direction, power for the million lights that will make the fair nights bright as day.

Out of monstrous vans the multitude of pinions and rods and motors come for the merry-go-rounds. The plaster animals to seat the riders are still in the trucks.

One sideshow is ready for business. It is that of the wild midget horses. The truck has wings on it, which opens up to display enticing slogans. But where are the wild midget horses? They are in their stockades, carefully concealed from the prying eyes of non-paying guests of the day-before-the-fair.

But there are some animals on display. Here are two llamas, tied to a truck, and there are Shetland ponies which will carry the small tots around an enclosed course.

An enormous bloodhound basks contentedly in the shade, secured by a chain as a woman walks by with a pocket-size spaniel on a ridiculously long leash.

There are some shouts. "Take it easy with that pole, will you!" "Okay. A little bit higher and I've got it!" "Tighter, tighter!" And smells: rich verdant grass and clean pine-shavings, baled and ready for spreading beneath the tents, gasoline and diesel fuel, and the sweat of straining muscle.

Over there is a large faded blue tent, surmounted by a banner which says in dignified lettering: *The Eternal Miracle--What Makes Us Tick?* We are promised the show will be *As Presented at Four World Fairs*, but we will have to wait until tomorrow to witness the miracle.

In a gleaming white van, lettered in red, are Pete and Punk--the world's largest team of oxen weighing 6,300 pounds together. But not even the curious eyes of a wandering child is allowed to glimpse them.

A ticket booth proclaims Dolly Dimples, 10 cents plus two cents tax. Who is Dolly? Where is she? Maybe the fat lady? Tomorrow we shall know.

A sudden whirr-whirring from the left makes one start as two men race the motor for a skeleton of long mechanical arms which circulate dizzily up and down, up and down, in the air. To them will be attached the chairs on which fairgoers will seek roller-coaster thrills.

Back beyond the midway are more trailers and cars, in which are the performers resting up for the hectic four days ahead. There is no sight of the daring aerialists or of the dancing midgets.

Just off the midway is the cattle barn, and all the entries are in place, their owners busily placing hay and sawdust so that all will be in order by opening day. A bull of enormous heft knuckles down and glares defiantly. One approaches cautiously to inspect the chain which holds him.

A few feet away from the farm implements display, a group of youngsters hopefully raise a tent flap and, disappointed, exclaim: "There's nothing in there yet."

Shining new tractors are moved under tent coverings for the admiring tours of the county's farmers.

A long line of cars, all bearing Florida license plates, dust-covered, heavily-loaded Buicks and Chryslers, baked by the sun, speaking mutely of the long road the show people travel in their summer hike around the fair circuit.

"Something you wanted?" a raucous voice inquires, and one realizes one has really no business on the midway the day-before-the-fair.

In the education building things are a bit more familiar. School children and 4-H Club members stack up neat displays of cucumbers and radishes on inclined trays, giving an extra polish to a melon or a turnip, hoping for a prize ribbon.

Upstairs their teachers tack down colored folders inscribed neatly with schoolchild pride. Others fold aprons and jumpers on which their girls have spent many patient hours.

Dr. Joseph Patterson, county health commissioner, worries over an amplifier and speaker which fails, amid the bubble of busy voices, to register a heart-beat loud enough to be heard.

Beside him an eight-foot sheet of red cardboard, cut heart-shape, bears the admonition: "Only one to a customer! No trade-ins! No seconds!"

Girl Scout leaders flock around a couple of judges bending over camp and craft exhibits, washstands and racks.

In the main building radio engineers and announcers discuss the best place to set their microphone, and water dances over an imitation pond. Fair executives calmly nudge their way through the crowd to cajole and urge and hasten.

And outside the grounds, on Main Street, boys' bicycles crowd the sidewalk. For it's the day-before-the-fair and there is a lot to do before the crowds come--tomorrow, when it's Fair Day in Chesterton. See you there.

THE SECOND DAY

A MANTLE OF DARKNESS

CHAPTER SIX

The telephone rang. I reached out and knocked it to the floor. I fumbled for the receiver and at last brought it to my ear. "Yes?" I mumbled.

"You left a call for seven o'clock," the hotel clerk said. "It is seven o'clock."

"Thanks loads," I said. I lay there with the receiver in my hand until I heard the click. *There was something I had to do.* Somewhere I had to be, some appointment I had missed. The horrifying thought came: I had overslept and I hadn't delivered my newspapers.

This stabbed me full awake and I laughed to myself. I'd had that nightmare before. I'd wake up with the sun shining in the windows, the foggy notion sluggish in my brain, that the alarm hadn't gone off at six and that I had failed to deliver a hundred papers to my Monitor customers, something I had never failed to do for two high school years. You would think that experience would die with time, but it didn't and I still have it, often.

One thing I had missed was calling in a story to night-rewrite. It was after eleven when I left Bob, Ricky and Jenny. At the hotel I sat before my portable typewriter for a long time, trying to compose proper leads. I got as far as: *Chestertonians chuckled today at Tootsie and Toots, the fat twins, but it may be their last laugh.* I had a dozen even worse and I ripped them off the machine one by one and hurled them into the basket. I gave it up after a while, went to bed, but tossed and turned a lot as I tried to assemble some concrete facts in my bursting brain. I thought of Bryson's calculations and Glen's peculiar pride. More disturbing was the image of Jenny, not herself, but the creation of my meandering mind, a pure and innocent girl trapped in the conflict of forces beyond her knowing, of demons lurking in human hearts beyond her understanding.

I shaved and showered, dressed and took the elevator to the lobby. In the hotel dining room I sat at the counter and ordered orange juice, toast and coffee. Before the order came I went to the stand and picked up the Richland Monitor. I flipped through it looking for a story on the fair, but there was none. I really hadn't expected any, but you never know. Johnny's source might have tipped the Monitor too. Then I wondered who the source was. Had Bryson, secretly concerned, telephoned Johnny, or perhaps, more logically, Glen, seething over the land-grab by money-mad speculators? With more motive, was it Stowe, the manager, who, in a clandestine call, had sought to save his beloved fair? Or was it, with scoured conscience, Blanchard, the Times editor, ashamed and anxious for his town's integrity?

When I had finished eating I tipped the waitress a quarter, wrote my room number on the bill and went into the lobby. It was practically deserted, just one or two loungers waiting for the airport bus. I crossed the thick carpet to the phone booths and put in a call to Johnny. It was eight o'clock.

"Got your feature story," my city editor said. "Good style. Do a follow-up feature today on the opening. We could probably use one each day, which means you can stay there until Saturday."

"Give me a byline, Johnny?"

"Yes, sure. You should be able to get the Star's first edition by late afternoon. Lots of Chesterton folks read the Star. What about the fair closing?"

I told him I had done several interviews, but apparently nothing concrete had been decided. "I think a real estate deal is involved," I said, "but I can't confirm it, not yet."

"Ah, money!" Johnny said. "The profit motive. Hail to thee, free enterprise."

"You got it, Johnny. I'm going to nail some county big-wigs."

"Don't file anything until you've got it nailed down tight."

"Right. Johnny, who gave you the tip?"

"Sorry, Art. I can't tell you. Anyway, I don't think it's important."

"Maybe not, Johnny, but I think the affair is simmering now, but it could boil up into a nice fat scandal."

"Call me if you get in too deep."

Funny thing about Johnny. You could talk to him as long as you wanted on the phone, except just before deadlines, of course. But not in person. He sure was nice about it, not complaining that I didn't have a story on the fair closing yet. I wondered if his pigeon had called him again.

In my room I knocked out the big quotes that Stowe had given me, plus a few odd references to the Grange and the Farm Service as interested parties, leaving out quotation marks. That is called summarizing. However, in this present account I've used paraphrasing a lot, as you may have noticed.

I drove over to the Times office. Blanchard permitted me to search the newspaper County Fair file again. I took the file to the vacant desk of the City Hall reporter. Turning to the back of the file I found the last annual report, which listed board members and officers. Marie fetched me the Chesterton County directory, a thick black book that contained the names of county commissioners. Using my notebook, I copied the names of the six fair board members who were also county commissioners. One of them was Andrew Small, president of Chesterton National Bank. I found the bank's number in the county phone directory. I picked up the phone and asked for the president. His secretary came on the line. After considerable explanation she agreed to put Small on. There was more explaining. He agreed to see me at ten o'clock.

I turned back to the fair report and examined the financial statement. It did indeed show a profit, a small one, with a footnote that this amount was deposited to the operating expenses account. On the income side were listed admissions, exhibit space rentals, rebate from Master Shows, contributions from sponsoring organizations, and a "sundry" which was the largest amount. Under "expenditures" were: maintenance, equipment, salaries and wages, heat, light and gas, postage, publicity, sundry and insurance. The last was the largest expense category. I copied it with other accounts, without thinking about it.

That done, I reviewed the entire report, which glorified the history and tradition of the fair, paid tribute to cooperating groups, and gave biographies of Small and Bryson. I made some notes on these. As I had interviewed Bryson, I read his first, although, of course, it was on the page following that for Small. In glowing terms the sketch spoke of Bryson's outstanding contribution to agriculture, to the economic growth of the county, and to community welfare. It listed the county groups he belonged to, including Farm Service and three clubs. Oddly, it failed to mention that Bryson was also a county commissioner.

Small's biography was more interesting. It reported he was born in Chesterton. He had risen from the status of clerk at the bank, following his graduation from high school. The article apologized for the fact he had never gone to college because his father, the bank's president, needed help in running the bank. He had been a teller, a bookkeeper, a consultant on a few unnamed accounts, and had been made vice-president at the age of twenty-three. I calculated he hadn't been in any of the other jobs for longer than three months each, when he became executive vice-president. When his father, Maxwell Small, a very great man, died, he was appointed president by the bank's board of directors. That was all there was to it. No mention that he was a county commissioner either, nor of his family, if he had one. But the mention of the bank directors set me off on another tangent.

I went back to the counter and looked up the Chesterton National Bank in the county directory, and there it was, the complete list of directors. One of them was Samuel Bryson. Glen was not on the list. I recognized five other county commissioners, including Small himself, all of whom were fair directors. It was a long list, about twenty bank directors in all. I checked off the duplications on my list of fair directors. Then the thought clicked in my brain: *insurance!* I flipped to the back of the directory and looked for the listing in the index.

My head was throbbing when I found the section on insurance agencies. The list of managers was complete. There was Farm Service, an insurance organization, and under it the officers and directors. Samuel Bryson's name fairly flew off the page. And there was Small's, but the others were unfamiliar. I turned back to the index and looked up *realtors*. That was a list, and most of them seemed to be part-time agents. Under Amalgamated Properties, Inc., Bryson was listed as vice-president. Andrew Small, the bank guy, was board chairman of Chesterton Enterprises, Inc. Other names rang bells all through my head. I picked up my pencil and checked my list of county commissioners.

Besides Small and Bryson, they were Sanford Blakemore, Desmond Carter, Seymour Denis and Daniel Morris. They were all directors of the bank. They were all officers, at or near the top, of real estate agencies. The last four differed from Small and Bryson only in their apparent lack of identification with insurance.

Back at the desk I made up a list of questions for my interview with Small, thanked Blanchard, hurried down the hall and exited the Times by way of the squeaking stairway to Main Street. The shops were open. I passed by Woolworth's and the jewelry stores, not seeing any of it, the black headline with *Collusion* streaking through my mind. The pieces of the jigsaw were beginning to fit together. Rather soon, I thought, I would begin to see the picture.

The bank was at the end of the block across the street, diagonally opposite my hotel. I went through the bank's lobby to the highly polished railing at the back. A rheumy-eyed man, with the name *Vice-President* in gold lettering inscribed on a desk woodblock, looked up. I told him I had an appointment with the president. He leaped up immediately, came around the desk and opened the gate. "Come right in, sir," he said. He knocked on a paneled door and opened it cautiously. He was back in a moment to say that Small was tied up with a long-distance call but he wouldn't be long.

I suppose I sat on that chair for half an hour, switching one leg over the other, back and forth, because the chair was so high it kept catching me under the knee, making my leg go to sleep. It was after ten-thirty when the door opened and Small himself came out, apologizing profusely for keeping me waiting, but I knew damn well he did it on purpose. "That's all right," I said. "Actually I enjoyed watching the bank operations."

"Fascinating procedures," he said, ushering me to a chair. He went behind his shining desk. It appeared as big as a ping-pong table and didn't have a paper on it. The room was richly furnished with a broad sofa, upholstered in maroon leather. There was a high buffet-style cabinet at one end of the large room. I guessed it opened to a bar. On the walnut paneled walls were brilliant landscape prints, all in ornate frames with tiny lamps over them. The floor was carpeted wall-to-wall in a paler maroon.

"Banking has its own ritual," Small said. He settled back in his top-flight leather captain's chair, his hands clasped behind his narrow neck. He maintained a constant gaze at me, which startled me every time I looked up from my notepad. He was a short, spare man with graying hair, a pursed little mouth and pince-nez glasses. I guessed that he was about sixty. "There is a certain way of doing business," he continued in his lethargic way of dragging out words of more than four letters. "Yes, bank business is as formal as a Masonic initiation. Largely bank manners are unwritten, but bankers learn them from other bankers. It is passed on from father to son, and from president to vice-president. Every process has its rationale, its liturgy. That's what makes a banker so conventionally staid. It gets into their blood and effects their every waking moment. It permeates their home and social life. Correctness of manner and procedure is derigeur. It's structure, a system. It appears dependable. People expect it."

"You have been with the bank a long time," I said.

"Yes, over forty years." He told me of his boyhood in the town, how dull it was until his father took him on as a bank messenger before he had finished high school, and how he "rose through the ranks" to become president. "But that's not what you came to see me about," he said. "I'm sorry if I've rambled on too much."

"Not at all," I said. "I regard it as most interesting. In many ways the banker's life is rare and exciting, and quite essential and central to our economy. It is a service that not too many appreciate." I was really laying it on thick.

"Not many people realize that," Small said. He removed the pince-nez and laid it on the desk. Swiveling in his chair he looked out the wide window toward the intersection and the hotel. There was a distant look in his eyes. "As a reporter you know the image some still have of us bankers. They think of us as quite remote and mysterious individuals, without heart, selfish and with a lust for gold. Of course we inherit that from the past. We need a better image. Our public relations could stand improvement. Well, you have some questions?" He swiveled back toward the desk.

"You may have heard I am covering the fair for the Star."

If Bryson hadn't told him I would have eaten an edition, entire, but he said: "Oh, we do appreciate that. Publicity always helps the fair. May even bring more people down from Richland. You have a story today?"

"Yes." He was beginning to nibble, so I let him have the line and he bit, hard.

"I hope it's favorable," he said.

"Any reason why it should not?"

I perceived a reddening under his eyes on that one. "No, of course not," he said. "I'm sorry, I didn't intend to infer--"

"It's purely a color story. A feature."

"Oh, that's fine. I look forward to reading it."

"I do have a serious story in mind," I said.

"What is that?"

"About the closing of the fair." I eyed him to ascertain his reaction.

"The fair will remain open until the regular closing scheduled for Friday at midnight."

"That's not what I meant."

"What *did* you mean?" He was on to me now.

"A permanent closing. No fair next year, or any year thereafter."

"That's preposterous! Whoever told you that?"

"A usually reliable source." Of course no one had told me any such thing. It's a gimmick that often brings confirmation. But he was still cagey.

"As chairman of the fair corporation, Mr. James, I can say that the closing of the fair would be disastrous. After all, the publicity it brings the county."

"It doesn't bring you any money."

"Fairs are not supposed to make money."

"Then who pays the deficit?"

"To my knowledge the fair never had a deficit."

"Perhaps not on the financial statements, but on the books."

"Our books are audited by a most competent and trustworthy auditor. The books are open for public inspection."

"Thanks. I may take advantage of that."

"If you have any suspicion that there is graft involved, let me tell you, young man--"

"Please," I protested with a grin. "That's farthest from my thoughts. It's the intricacies of the fair control and management that intrigue me. To the innocent fairgoer it seems simple. And yet I have found it rather complicated." I tried to look innocent.

"Of course we have to apply business principles," Small said, calming down. "We have so many commercial exhibitors, so many concessions. There are over a hundred different account numbers for income alone. Nothing very large, but they add up, actually over a million dollars."

"I know. I read the financial statement for last year. Such income must mean a lot to the county."

"As I said, Mr. James, there is no profit in it. The expense more than offsets that. Actually, if it weren't for contributions--"

"You mean from patron organizations?"

"Not only those. But business, industry, commercial, and those who exhibit. They contribute money, equipment, furnishings."

"And insurance?"

"No, we have to buy that. It's a large item. Crowds can grow wild at a fair. Most of the insurance is for liability."

"Who gets the protection?"

"The corporation, if we're sued. The public is protected, if anyone gets hurt."

"Only the public?"

"Well, that includes about every person who goes through the fair gate: show people, stunt drivers, exhibitors, those who operate concessions."

"I suppose these people pay for the protection."

"No, that liability is assumed by the fair corporation."

"Do many get hurt?"

"Oh yes, we, I mean the insurance companies, have paid many claims. Mr. Stowe could tell you more about that. Liability insurance is quite expensive, especially for so short a period of time in such a crowded environment. The buildings are old, and many shelters are purely temporary. Tents and prefab structures."

"Perhaps it's getting too expensive?" I suggested.

"You mean prohibitive? Yes, it could be. The fair corporation must consider the point of no return."

"What's that?"

"When our responsibility for the safety of all those people becomes so costly that it is out of proportion to the publicity benefit."

"Is publicity the only benefit?"

"No, no. Don't misunderstand me," he said quietly. "I mean when patronage drops below a certain level. When the cost per entrant goes too far beyond the income per entrant."

"Is there a measure for that?"

"Of course it is one of those intangibles." He actually laughed, a minor giggle. "Our contributors have been most generous. I myself make a donation, and so does my bank. But there is a limit to our resources. Demands upon our philanthropic funds are growing every day. Dozens of requests a week. It is the same with every business, every store, every industry in the county. It is the same all over the country. We must ask ourselves whether we are being selfish in giving our money for publicity through the fair rather than giving it directly to education and welfare, or, perhaps with more direct benefit, business-wise, to the Chamber of Commerce."

"The fair is a business enterprise then?"

"Certainly," he said. "Oh, I know what you're thinking, Mr. James. I admit its cultural and educational origins, its entertainment value. But in each of these areas it has been superseded as a primary source by other media. I could mention newspapers for one, to say nothing of magazines, radio and television, especially television. In today's economy the fair is simply a liability, a drastic drain on the public and private treasury."

"The public treasury?"

"Certainly. Besides our private resources, we must draw upon public tax money, principally county taxes. And counties are notoriously insolvent, as you know, Mr. James."

"I don't quite understand."

"Well, take the maintenance of the fairgrounds, for example. The grounds are county property."

He noticed my gasp of surprise. "You didn't know that, did you, Mr. James? Not common knowledge, I admit, since the fairgrounds are completely surrounded by the city of Chesterton. Of course, when the fair began a hundred years ago, the grounds were outside Chesterton, which, at the time, was merely a crossroads hamlet. The fair manages the land as a public trust. For fifty-one weeks a year the grounds are largely idle. A few groups meet there, but the rental fees do not cover the cost of caretaking. There must be ground-keepers the year-round. Buildings must be repaired and painted. Roads must be patched and repaved. It doesn't make sense, economically."

"Where does Chesterton County fit in?"

"Ah, that's the point," Mr. Small said. "We must attract new industry to offset declining agricultural income. You see, there is the human factor. Fifty-two weeks of steady work for thousands, or one week of frivolity at the fair. It might come to that. We may have to make the choice."

"You are saying that the fair may have to go?" Now we were getting down to the gritty facts.

"But think of what we would gain," he said. "When you write your story, Mr. James, put in all sides. Be fair."

I laughed. "That's it then. Be fair about the fair!" I thanked Small for the interview and crossed Main Street to my hotel. Main Street's sidewalks were rapidly being occupied by people, young and old, coming downtown to view the parade. Many brought folding chairs with them, thus securing places close to the road. Others brought a variety of flags and balloons to wave. A multitude of young boys and girls chatted exuberantly.

In the hotel lobby I took a chair near a window, took out my notebook and perused my baleful English scribbles. Still no story. What could I do next? I needed to find someone who would predict either the fair's demise or its salvation. I could interview more board members, but I knew that would be fruitless, because if the two chairmen, Bryson and Small, wouldn't say anything, certainly none of the other members would. I was getting nowhere. Then the thought struck me, something Stowe had said: *Probe away, but not with me.* He had encouraged me to search, but he didn't want to be quoted. I wondered if he would give me something off the record, especially if I primed him with the implication that Bryson, Glen and Small had as much as admitted that a move was underway to sell the fairgrounds. I decided to give it a try.

As I was passing the hotel counter, the clerk called my name. "Mr. James? Letter for you." I guess he recognized me because I had chatted with him earlier when I asked if he had any phone messages for me. He handed me an envelope. I knew it was from Johnny. On a single sheet of paper he had written: *Walter Clark.* I knew what he meant. The publisher of the Chesterton Times was Johnny's pigeon. I called the Times from a phone booth, asked for Clark, but he was out to lunch. I said I would call later. It made sense: Clark was a member of the fair board and corporation, but he wasn't a county commissioner. His name had not come up on the real estate and insurance pages in the fair's directory. Perhaps he was a journalist after all. I made a mental note to ask Blanchard about him.

I picked up the Buick in the hotel's lot and drove to the fairgrounds. There was a mob in the street before the wide gateway. I continued on to the parking lot. I walked back and pushed my way through the uniformed band members, Boy Scouts, Girl Scouts and 4-H kids. At a ticket booth I flashed my press card. In the office, Bob, Ricky and Jenny were stacking red name cards. They told me they were free admission tickets for everyone who participated in the parade.

Stowe greeted me warmly and invited me to have lunch with him. "The parade is forming on the back lots," he said, "so we have enough time." We went to the place where I had eaten the day before, a diner run by Castle Rock Presbyterian Church. Over hamburgers and colas Stowe told me that the fair corporation would definitely vote Friday night on a motion to sell the fairgrounds as an industrial site.

"Tell me more about it," I said.

"Off the record?"

"Unimpeachable source."

"You may want to confirm this with Glen and Walter Clark."

"You're telling me they are in opposition?"

"They are indeed," Stowe said. "We hope your stories will stir up public opinion."

"And bring pressure on the corporation?"

"Exactly. All we need for a deadlock is to convince one county commissioner to vote no."

"Which one?"

"Sam Bryson."

"But he's in real estate and insurance, like the other county commissioners."

"You found that out?" Stowe asked. "Nice going. But Mr. Bryson's still a farmer, and almost like a brother to Mr. Glen. Family ties and all that. Their kids are doing a great job right here in the office."

"I spent an hour with them last night," I said.

"That daughter of Mr. Glen's. She's a pretty one, isn't she? Going to marry Ricky."

"I wouldn't count on it," I said.

"Well, you are observant!" Stowe lowered his voice. "Ricky's okay in most ways, but something's a little mean about him. Cold, calculating. You know what I'm saying?"

"Takes after his father, maybe?"

"In a way," Stowe said. "But I don't think that Sam Bryson is beyond redemption. No, Ricky's all for profit. His father's got it all mixed up. He's as much a farmer as Mr. Glen, but for years he's been flirting with our big business interests, got involved with Farm Service where the business forces play, then with its insurance, then real estate. Now he's more of a market manipulator than he is a farmer. Still, I think his heart is with the farm."

"And the fair?"

"Yes, I think we have a chance. If I could only reach him."

"You've known Bryson a long time?"

"For years. Once we were very close. But in recent years he's drifted away. I suppose I've argued with him too much. He's drifted from one thing to another, and now he's caught up in the web and can't get off. But just this once, perhaps, he will stand up for what he really believes."

Although we were in the shade of a canvas canopy attached to the diner's wooden frame, I began to sweat. Stowe looked like he was boiled too. His face was creased with fatigue and his eyes were shot with blood. Added to the heat there was a constant clamor all around. Last-minute tacking and stacking, wiping and polishing. Ricky's voice came over outside loudspeakers, which were set up all over the fairgrounds: "May I have your attention please! We have a small boy at the fair office. He is about three years old and he's wearing a blue shirt. Would the missing parents please come to the fair office? I repeat that: We have a boy--"

"One of the many problems of fair management," Stowe said. "Baby-sitting for little kids. Jenny often takes care of a few. She's a gem. It's not enough we have to watch out for the bawling tots of patrons, but there are the kids of the exhibitors as well. That's another fair tradition. The entire family comes to take care of a booth. A church women's group has a nursery in the agricultural building. They make a bit of money with it."

"I suppose a lot of groups take advantage of the fair to fatten their treasury," I said.

"The list runs into the hundreds, from Boy Scouts to the League of Women Voters. Apart from rentals and the cost of food or whatever, they make a straight profit, because the members pitch in to provide free labor. Many organizations would be hard hit by the closing of the fair. You might pick up some material on that, Mr. James."

"I'll go around this afternoon."

"Try some interviews with volunteers who contribute so much. Ask them hypothetical questions, for instance: What would it mean to them if there were no more fairs."

"Wonderful idea," I said. "A sort of poll."

"That's where the county commissioners make a mistake. They think they own the fair because they have custody of the grounds. You can't trample on people's rights and maintain a free society."

"I suppose," I said. "But the people have no representation in the controversy."

"They don't know about it, thanks to the Times. That's the territory of the Times publisher, Walter Clark. Ask him about it."

"I will," I said. "One point I want to clear up. About insurance. And accidents. I understand there are quite a few."

"No, surprisingly, there haven't been many accidents. We maintain a first aid station, with an ambulance and a driver on duty at all times, even after closing time, for the sake of the show people and some exhibitors who stay on the grounds overnight, the show people in their trailers, the exhibitors on cots in the animal pavilion, so they can be near their livestock, where they can guard and care for them. Also, there are the young people on the fair staff who stay in the barracks, together with their adult leaders. The Chesterton Fire Department stations a complete outfit and crew on the grounds for the entire week, and the county sheriff has a special team. Still, the insurance cost is very high. Despite precautions about accidents, fire and theft, the corporation provides coverage for every little thing. I have nightmares about what could happen."

Sweat was dripping down Stowe's face. He wiped it away with his table napkin. "Naturally we buy insurance locally," he said. "Every year the cost goes up. That means more commission, more income, for every broker. Bryson's agency gets the lion's share."

"If the fair closed he would lose all that," I said.

"Yes, and I hope he realizes it. It may make a point with him in our favor. Still, he would gain at the real estate end."

"Through Amalgamated Properties?"

"Yes," he agreed. "You have heard of Tiber Trucks?"

"Sure. It's a Richland company."

"Not well known to the public, because its trucks are used for heavy hauling, construction and the like, with the interstate highways still being extended all over the country, Tiber Trucks is expanding rapidly. They are looking for a large piece of property, close to railroad transportation. And there's the railway freight station adjacent to the fairgrounds. That's where they unload the animals with the circus show. Tiber has been looking over the fairgrounds for months. They're interested and so is the Chamber of Commerce, also the commissioners. It would mean a lot to the county to have a Tiber factory here. They need space for assembly lines, warehousing and test tracks. They are interested in the entire site. A lot of money could be made from the sale of the fairgrounds through a real estate combine. It would have to go through the agencies. Also legal fees for deed transfer and all that. I admit it's a tempting proposition. The biggest selling point would be the jobs that would be provided."

"But wouldn't Tiber Trucks bring in their own workers, those in Richland?"

"I suppose. And they would need houses. Another boon for real estate. Everyone would benefit, economically."

"Is that the only factor to be considered, Mr. Stowe?"

"No, but I'm more interested in what we would lose. It would be more than a four-day annual fair. It would be a way of life, or at least what there is left of it. Tiber Trucks would put Chesterton on the map as an industrial center. They have thousands of employees, nationwide I mean. Housing for new workers here would take up hundreds of acres of farmland. The very fact that so large a firm moved its main state plant here could be exploited so that other industries would sit up and take notice. Every industry is looking for two things today, lower labor costs and lower taxes, plus certain free community contributions. Cities are tax-shy. The cost of their services is high and still mounting. Chesterton could offer the fairgrounds free, could install utilities, free, and still make money in the long run. Communities are doing those things these days. The competition for industry is fierce. From a tax-free property the fairgrounds could be converted overnight into a site producing high tax income."

"You seem to know all the arguments for getting rid of the fairgrounds," I said.

"I've been over it many times with Mr. Bryson."

"How about Mr. Small?"

"Not him. He and I don't talk the same language. But Mr. Bryson can see my point of view. That's how I got him on the fence, at least I think I have."

"Would the people have objections to such a large industry in their midst? I mean the residents in the fairgrounds area?"

"Yes, they might object. Tiber Trucks would take any such protest into consideration. But there would be no way for such a protest to be expressed, except through petition. The Times has adopted a hands-off, ostrich attitude. The radio station is owned by the Times, so that's the same. Anyway, there would be no point to a protest. Friday night it will all be settled, one way or the other. All the preliminary studies and surveys have been done."

Beyond the gate there was the shrill cry of a whistle. "Parade's forming," Stowe said. "You going to watch?"

"I wouldn't miss it," I said.

On Main Street marching bands, resplendent in red uniforms, had lined up. There were two from high schools and between them were Boy Scout and Girl Guide units, broad strips of badges across their chests. Then came the Legionnaires, the Shriners in their fezzes, a fire truck blaring its horn, a State Guard unit, the sheriff's car, the W.C.T.U. ladies, the 4-H clubbers, the Y.M.C.A. float, with a big wooden "Y" on it, then the boys and girls of Juvenile Grange, Future Farmers, Future Homemakers, a forest ranger standing on a flat-bed truck with a statue of Smokey the Bear, Home Bureau, Farm Service with four fair queen contestants standing next to sheaves of corn. There were others far up the street, but I couldn't make out what they were.

Four motorcycles with helmeted policemen on them screamed up the street along the line of marchers and pulled into position in front of a high school band. The motorcycle policemen halted. Stowe went over to talk to a sergeant. He stepped back from the curb, took a whistle from his pocket, blew it once, a short blast. All along the line the lounging marchers straightened and shuffled into formation. Behind the band five girls in shining silver raised their batons, lifted their right legs, and, balanced there, eyes straight ahead. Stowe blew again and the bands blared *Stars and Stripes*. Flag bearers stepped in time. The police pressed their motorcycle peddles and roared ahead. The line began to move.

In a few minutes new units were coming around the corner from the fairgrounds. There was a truck with a big sign on it: *Come to the Fair! Fun for Young and Old!* Next a convertible with a banner inscribed *Mayor of Chesterton* and a beaming corpulent man in a white suit waving a straw hat. The crowd, now two and three deep on the sidewalk, cheered. Afterward, the county commissioners: Bryson and Small sitting next to one another in the back seat of a Cadillac convertible, with another four, all waving, big smiles. Then came the float of the Chamber of Commerce with a montage of photo blowups on a big board, Chesterton scenes and slogan below: *Growing Center of Industrial Enterprise.*

Afterward the Co-op, the F.O.A. with the fruit of the land piled high, then the Extension Service with a woman busily sewing a dress, and then the Board of Education with a banner *Strength Through Education*. Later, the County Council of Churches with a huge mockup stained-glass window casting colors on a cross, with a sign: *Worship Together This Week*. Then the American Legion, the V.F.W., and the Amvets in wheelchairs on a truck bed, the Parent-Teachers Association, the Junior Chamber of Commerce, the League of Women Voters with a banner urging *Register to vote*.

Another van, Navy Cadets, then the R.O.T.C., Red Cross volunteers, and a group of women dressed as nurses carrying a slogan *Stop cancer with a checkup and a check*. Blue Cross, an ambulance corps, the sight and smell of a purebred on the Guernsey Association float, a few yapping dogs on the Humane Society truck.

On and on they came, and, at last, the Bates Shows, heralded by a tumbling clown, and then the lion cage, with the shaggy animal fast asleep, and afterward the acrobats swinging on a bar, and then a truck on which dancing girls, clad in veils, were swinging to the tune of an Hawaiian band. Then the midgets and the fat lady in a convertible, two motorcyclists in black leather jackets circling madly, almost scraping fenders. Three elephants, trunk-to-tail, ears flapping, and at the end of the line the ringmaster in tuxedo, cracking a long whip and that was that, except for the children on the curb as they stepped out behind and, marching in the line, skipping, shouting, calling to their mothers: "See you later," and the mothers calling back: "Be careful. Don't get lost."

I returned to the fair office. Jenny was alone. Bob and Ricky had gone to lunch. "Did you see the parade?" she asked. She was sorting a pile of papers at her desk. I assured her I enjoyed it very much, although I had been so tired I could hardly stand. I sat heavily on a metal folding chair, which immediately collapsed. So did I, spread-eagled on the hardwood floor. I struggled to get up and failed. Then I felt Jenny hauling me upright and I'm no lightweight. Jenny was not only charming, she was strong. She laughed as I embraced her, only for support of course.

Luckily there was a heavy cot against the outside wall. "Lay down," she ordered. I did. She was blessed with a permanent smile as well as a soothing sweet voice. I obeyed. The cot was quite comfortable.

"Some evenings I get so tired I take a nap here," she said as she placed her hands under my head, held it up with one hand and slid a soft pillow under it. "Comfy?" she asked. She returned to her desk. Despite the roar of a truck engine now and then I drifted away only to be suddenly awakened as Jenny covered my forehead with a cold wet towel. "Sorry," she said. "You needed that. You were too hot." That certainly was the case.

"This place could do with some air conditioning," I muttered.

"I'm used to it," Jenny said as she spread the cooling towel over my face, wrung it out, letting the water drip to the floor, and replaced it on my forehead. I thanked her. I was still feeling shaky but I insisted on sitting up. Jenny grabbed both my hands and pulled. She only succeeded in falling on top of me, which I didn't mind at all. She couldn't stop laughing.

Later, she sat beside me on the cot. She was holding a plaque of some kind. "I thought you would like to see this," she said. "Last night you were interested in knowing why I was so keen on keeping the fair alive." She held it so that light from the window above us would fall upon it. I read aloud the words inscribed:

Exhibits are the work of our hands,
the hope of our hearts,
the aspiration of our spirit,
the symbols of our life,
the witness of our labor,
the expression of our genius.

"While I was a student at Chesterton College," she said, "I did some research on the history of community fairs. Did you know that our simple county fairs, as community events, are descended from market place festivals that go back a thousand years or more? Now you will find them or their equivalent all over the world. They are harvest celebrations, of course, but they spun off arts and crafts fairs, and every single kind of exhibit halls, museums. Long ago the fairs were parish affairs, the messe of Germany, same word as for mass. There's always been a connection between business and religion, as at Mecca and Hardwar. Think of church bazaars, the Maydays. In Scotland the fair has been called the tryst, an appointment to meet. *See you at the fair*, as we Americans like to say, means the same thing. Just think of the merchant exhibit halls at annual conventions, from electronics to automobiles to flowers. Fairs have always been celebrations, market places. Ordinary people are given the opportunity to exhibit, and that's why fairs are often called exhibitions, like the national one in Toronto, Canada. Everyone is given a chance to show off their creativity, and that's important. They exhibit for the sake of others, not themselves. Sure, they want a pat on the back once in a while. But that's still not the main reason they work so hard to display what they have created. They want to share the joy. And that is why we desperately need the fair right here in Chesterton County. People attend the fair to share their happiness with others. Sounds corny, doesn't it?"

"I had the feeling last night that Ricky wouldn't agree with you."

"You're right," she said. She looked surprised. "I guess you sensed that, didn't you, Mr. James. Good heavens! Do I have to call you mister? How old are you? Never mind. You look about my age. What's your first name?"

"Arthur. People call me Art."

"Art! Think of it. Art the artist!"

"Hah, hah. I'm just a simple newspaperman, a journalist."

Jenny looked at me closely. Her eyes widened. Surely she was putting me on. "You're first and foremost a writer, Arthur James. Shame on you. You shouldn't degrade yourself. Everyone who writes anything, literary I mean, must be an artist first, last and always. I read the papers, even the Star. I bet you're a very good writer. I have a nose for that. You're quite sensitive, aren't you? And you *like* to ask questions."

"Oh, that's my job. To interview."

"You can't kid me, Art. I've known too many of your kind. I know what you want, Arthur James."

"What?" I was really taken aback. She was different alright.

"Recognition. A byline." She looked at me without blinking.

"Jenny, you're a genius. How did you know?"

"Art, you're an open book. Psychology tells us: *By their questions ye shall know them*. There's nothing wrong with that. From infancy we're always asking why. It's human nature. And that's why the County Fair is a necessity. So there." She laughed at herself. "My goodness, I'm talking like a blooming professor! Forgive me."

"You're a born teacher, an educator, Jenny. Your mom and dad have great hopes for you. And for your brother, Bob, too. You know, you're so like your dad. I like him a lot. He knows exactly where he stands and why. And so do you, Jenny, and I appreciate it."

What I appreciated most was Jenny herself. She was the epitome of youthful understanding. She was the most up-to-date, the most modern of all those I had so far interviewed. And the wonderful thing about it was that she understood what I wanted as a journalist: the truth.

Jenny and I went out together to view the ribbon-cutting ceremony, which would open the fair officially. The sun was blinding. We put on our dark glasses. A score of county and fair leaders were gathered behind a three-inch baby-blue ribbon stretching the width of the open gateway to the fairgrounds. Traffic on Main Street was still banned. Jenny identified the mayor and Walter Clark, the Times publisher. He was a tall, heavy-set man of about sixty, with thick graying hair and a slim mustache. He was chatting animatedly with the mayor, gesturing, but in the hubbub I couldn't hear what he was saying. Jenny's father was holding gold scissors, poised above the ribbon. He handed the scissors to a man on his left. Jenny told me he was Daniel Morris, chairman of the county commissioners, who held the scissors high to prompt attention.

"It is my privilege," Morris said, his voice booming, "to declare the one-hundredth annual Chesterton County Fair--Open!" `He applied the scissors and the ribbon drifted apart. A roar went up from the crowd as they surged through the gateway.

Jenny took my hand. "Isn't this exciting?" she said.

I squeezed her hand tenderly and held on to it.

CHAPTER SEVEN

As I pressed through the crowd I said hello to Bryson, Glen and Small. I tapped Walter Clark's arm and introduced myself. "Could we go somewhere and talk?" I asked him. I waved to Jenny as she was returning to the fair office.

As Johnny's informant, the publisher of the Chesterton Times was no doubt aware that Johnny had assigned me to report on the fair dispute. The question was: Why look to the Star to investigate? Why would he allow the Star to scoop his own newspaper? He was using me for his own purpose, of course, and that was fine with me. We went to the church diner, ordered drinks, and sat down at a two-chair table. We were far enough away from other customers not to be heard.

"Mr. James, I'm glad you're here." He leaned forward. He spoke quietly. "As a member of the fair's board of directors I'm in an awkward position. I want the fair to continue forever, but, as publisher, I have my own board to contend with. That's why it would be difficult for me to take sides. So, frankly, that's why I tipped Johnny about what's going on."

I placed my notebook on the table. "I suppose a lot of people will be disappointed if the fair is discontinued," I said.

Clark brushed his mustache. He raised his dark eyebrows. "That's something we would only know in the event, wouldn't we?" he asked. "People are often apathetic about the causes that are dearest to them."

"But if it were to be proposed, and subjected to public debate, for a year?"

"Then there would be quite a debate. No doubt the Times would receive a lot of letters pro and con. But where would that lead? To a public subscription to a Save-the-Fair fund? I don't think so. The public likes popular causes, not dead horses."

"The fair isn't a popular cause?"

"What's the issue?" he asked. "It's money, isn't it? When the chips are down the public wants a payoff on an investment, something tangible: roads they can drive on, clean streets, good water, police patrols. And they want all those things and lower taxes too. But when it comes to using tax money for the fair, they couldn't see that."

I was surprised. "Tax money would be needed?"

"Of course," Clark replied. "Private contributions are for patronage."

"Still, there is citizen responsibility," I said. That was a weak remark, and I knew it.

"Oh, indeed, indeed. I suppose it is a public duty to express indignation." He paused to hear a commotion outside. A big long-haired dog was dashing through the crowd. "Where did *he* come from?" he asked. "Well, to continue. There are economic drawbacks to that idea. The Times is at the mercy of our advertisers, who could take reprisals."

"But would they? Would they dare in the face of popular demand for the fair?"

"Who could measure such a demand? Doctor Gallup? And wouldn't a poll also indicate even greater demand for more jobs, higher wages, more taxable property to make possible new schools? Oh, the list is endless. Should not, then, the county commissioners accede to the most popular demand, rather than to the lesser demand? And might not the public demand both fair and food? If it were my decision, alone, and, thank God, it's not, I would have to decide in favor of food."

I wrote that down. "Man does not live by bread alone," I suggested.

"Are you equating the fair with faith, Mr. James?"

"Something like that," I said, although I did not like being pressed to the opposite side of an argument. A reporter, by definition, is impartial, sees both sides.

"You may be right," Clark said. "But spiritual values are hard to measure, to define. As values of the fair they would be dismissed as sentimental. No, to be objective, you have to conclude that the fair would not get enough support." He paused to point out a bunch of kids waving flags and dancing along to the music of an organ grinder. He resumed looking at me seriously. "Supposing a referendum were held and the choice was between preservation of the fair or hundreds of new industrial jobs. You know how the vote would go on that. Unless protected by law, public recreational parks will be sold for profit, you can depend upon it. The conservationists, the park lovers, the recreation people, they don't carry enough weight. It has always been that way. The best sites for public pleasure are also, by position, the best sites for housing, industry, transportation, and farming. Many cities at vast expense have had to reclaim land from river, lake and marsh to find space for walks among the trees. Others, like Washington and New York, wisely set aside land for leisure. I don't condemn Chesterton for its present confusion. The choice is difficult: private profit or public good. There was a time we would have had no hesitancy in choosing. But today private profit *is* public good. Communities are *proud* of their industries, unstable as they may be. They are public assets, working for community betterment, sharing their benefits with the community, providing jobs, making possible schools, housing, sanitation, protection, all that makes life civilized."

"You mean the fair has no place in this scheme of things?" I asked.

"Did I say that? I didn't want to. I say this: Let the people have what they want. But permit them the choice. Let it be their decision. Six men, sitting in a smoke-filled room, should not have the power to decide for them."

"But they do," I protested. "Those six alone."

"They have the power," Clark said. "They were elected to it by the voters of Chesterton County. As members of the fair corporation, they say: *Speaking as a private citizen*, and not as a commissioner, as if they can divorce themselves from what they are. As much as a pastor could preach: *Speaking as a layman.* No, you see, there is this carryover of power from the private realm into the public. So the issue is clouded not only by public schizophrenia but also by the multiplicity of private roles. I sit on one board and I wear my publisher's hat. I sit on another and I wear my citizen's cap. At both I sit disguised. I am not Walter Clark, the father that my son, Timothy, knows, not the golf partner my friends are used to. I am not even the Walter Clark I think I am. I am Publisher Clark, or Citizen Clark. My mantles are dark. They cloak the truth of what I am."

"Is there no way out?" I asked.

"I would to God there was. Shall I resign my duty, my responsibility? Who can be independent? So many forces impinge upon us. But, you say, let conscience be your guide. Yes, but which conscience? As a publisher I have a duty to the public. Readers look to me to publish truth. As a fair director I also have a duty to the public. People look to me to provide for the fair's welfare. When, however, do truth and welfare coincide? In the case of the fair, who knows? One is spiritual, the other material. One is for the nourishment of the soul, the other for the body. Both must be served. Can both?"

"I think it's the duty of newspapers to publish the facts," I said. That was a cliché, but so what? That's what a lot of news writing is composed of: crisp, cute clichés. "Let readers decide for themselves."

Clark nodded. "Exactly, Mr. James." He breathed a heavy sigh, as if he had, at long last, healed the damage to a tortured spirit. "What are the facts anyway? Has a certain industry offered to buy the fairgrounds? No one will say. Has the fair corporation entertained such an offer? Not yet. Has the fair's board of directors been requested to present an opinion? No, because no one knows of any offer."

"Isn't it taken for granted that the fair directors have a responsibility to keep the fair going every year?"

"You're right, damnit! You are right! There has always been a fair. Every year for a hundred years. We don't have the *right* to end it." He paused as a tide of fairgoers noisily made their way toward the midway. He sighed again. "Darn it, it's different when you talk about the fairgrounds. They are county property. Ten men have the legal right to dispose of the grounds, with the agreement of the county commissioners. It's crazy! To think it has come to this. We should have reorganized the whole structure years ago. And I am as responsible for this mess as anyone."

"What about the fair's budget?" I asked. "I hear there will be a huge deficit this year."

Clark clapped his hands. "There's always been a deficit." he said. "The fair is run like any charity. The staff isn't paid enough and yet a few directors say they are paid too much. If we didn't have volunteers--well, you can imagine. But it's a fact there have been fewer exhibitors every year, and that's because the exhibition building has been rotting away for years. It stinks, for heaven's sake! Rich families don't even attend. And, most of all, there's been a decline in monetary support by farm organizations. I could go on."

"I get the point," I said. "Have you come to a decision, Mr. Clark?"

He shook his head. "Do you have enough to write a straight report?"

I doubted it, but I told him I would do my best. I assured him I would also write my second feature story. I thanked him for the interview and, elbowing my way through the happy fairgoers, returned to the fair office. Jenny was at her desk, counting receipts. I borrowed a typewriter and for a long time I sat before it thinking up a lead. I was aware that the Star's readers couldn't care less whether the fairgrounds were sold or not. It was possible that Johnny would simply hand the story to the State News page, where my story might be worth two or three paragraphs. My hope for a Page One byline would disappear. There was nothing I could do about it, so I started writing. It began this way:

Chesterton: The end of an era may come late Friday when the Chesterton County Fair's corporation board vote on the fate of a century-old tradition.

I finished the report in half an hour, using my notes to list the various occupations and public offices of the directors. I paragraphed the list of six county commissioners. Of course I couldn't use the name of Tiber Trucks, so I mentioned only *a large industrial company* and quoted *highly-placed sources.*

The real story was in the room with me, the split-level generation that grew up through two wars, Korea and Vietnam, whose insecure past presaged an even more insecure future, whose attachment to old values was passing with the fair, and whose conflict was not so much with the fantasy of profit as with the fairy story of success through science. Strangely, I did not feel that I was one of them, not then.

I snatched the last page from the machine, read through the copy, wrote *30* at the end and placed the three sheets in an envelope that Jenny gave me. I drove down to Western Union and my story was soon wired to the Star. If I had known then what the consequences of that story would be I don't think I would have dispatched it. But then again maybe I would, because the course of events took such a turn that there was something inevitable about it.

On the way I visited a newsstand and bought three copies of the Star. My first feature, with my wonderful by-line, was centered high on the page, not Page One, but Page 11, which was the first page of the Star's Section Two. I whistled joyfully.

CHAPTER EIGHT

For over an hour I toured the fair. Back at the office I spent a half hour writing my *First Day of the Fair* feature article. When I finished and had confined the pages to an envelope, I noticed that Jenny was looking at me closely.

"What's so curious?" I asked her.

"You," she said. "You write so fast. How do you do it?"

"Genius."

"Seriously."

"It's a trick."

"I wish I had it."

"Anybody can do it."

"I can't."

"Sure you can," I said. "All you need is a vocabulary. Write it as you think it, as you feel it."

She sat down beside me. "There are so many things I would like to write about."

"For instance?"

"Snow on the ground in winter, the way it ripples in the wind, like river waves, the whistle of wind in the maples, loosening dead leaves in autumn."

"You see, you've already written it."

"What?"

"Simply write down what you said."

"When I sit down to write the words won't come."

"You've studied creative writing, haven't you?"

Jenny laughed. "Sure, in college."

"It's a start," I said. "What would you like to write? Essays, poetry, fiction?"

"Fiction, I think. Maybe some poems."

"Then get started. Sit down and write."

"It's that easy for you, not me."

"There's no other way."

"But what shall I write about?"

"The snow, the leaves falling. Have a viewer witnessing these things."

"And tell what she's *thinking*?"

"The effect upon the viewer, yes."

"It doesn't seem like enough."

"Of course it's not enough, Jenny. But there's meaning in it that satisfies some need."

"You mean a hunger?"

"You've picked up that word?"

She blushed, unmistakably. "I suppose I did. From a course in human development. Biological needs."

"It's a good word. Yes, hunger. We are all hungry for something. All the time."

"Like hungry for fame."

That one made me laugh. "I suppose I am. And you, Jenny?"

"I can show you better than I can tell you."

"Show me?"

"Sure. Say, that's a great idea." She turned in her chair and called to Bob and Ricky, who were shuffling papers near the windows. "Bob, Ricky, could I take an hour off, please?"

We went out together. As we passed through the gate, where dozens of people were lined up to buy tickets, Jenny said: "Let's go in your car."

"Alright with me. Where are we going?"

"You will see."

From the parking lot I drove the Buick to Western Union where I hopped out to deposit my *First Day* article. On Jenny's instruction I headed south on Main Street toward Castle Rock. We were silent. On our left the sun had lowered in the western sky. We opened our windows to feel a cooling breeze. It took less than fifteen minutes to reach the road to the Xenophon, where I had interviewed both Bryson and Glen, Jenny's father, the night before. We were headed toward Bryson's house when Jenny told me to turn left onto a gravel road lined with maple trees. I slowed down as the Buick blew a cloud of dust behind us. I turned left again onto a one-lane road flanked by dense bush. "Here we are," Jenny exclaimed. It was a migrant camp.

As I pulled off the road and dipped through a shallow ditch onto a clearing I saw a long wooden building, a bunkhouse somewhat like an Army barracks. On the opposite side of the lane a number of black women and children were gathered in a barnyard.

"They're friends of mine," Jenny said. "I want you to meet them."

The children had gathered so closely around the car that we had to open the car doors carefully in order to get out. "You all get away from there," a woman called. "Come on now, git."

Jenney introduced me to Beulah as the grandmother of some of the kids. The rest of the migrants, men, women, older boys and girls were at work in the fields.

"How are you Beulah?" Jenny asked as she hugged her.

"I'm fine," the old woman said. She smiled shyly.

"You've been keeping warm enough at night, Beulah?"

"Yes, warm enough, I suppose."

"Art, come and meet a friend of mine. Beulah, this is Arthur."

"Hello, Beulah," I said. "I am happy to meet you."

Beulah put out her hand. I grasped it. I noticed that it was hard and calloused. "Pleased," she said, almost a whisper.

"May we have a look around?" Jenny asked.

"Sure 'nough. Excuse the way things are."

"Of course, I understand," Jenny said.

Girls and boys gathered in a circle around Jenny. They tugged at her skirt. Jenney withdrew a plastic bag from a pocket and handed it to Beulah. The kids surrounded her. "Later, later," Beulah said as she patted heads.

"I'm glad I remembered to bring candy," Jenny told me. "Those poor children, they have so little." She grasped my arm. "Look, Art, They're coming home."

I could hear them. A soft chorus of voices singing. It sounded like the chorus of a familiar hymn, something akin to *I'm goin' home*. From the upper reach of the bush-framed lane they came: women, men, young people, humming, chanting, then gathering together to meet us, smiling their welcome. I felt at home. They surrounded Jenny. "Hi, Miss Jenny!" She greeted most of them by their first names.

Workers walked away toward their migrant shelter. Most went out of sight to the rear of the building. Jenny whispered to me: "Latrines and wash stands back there. "Let's have a look inside the living quarters." There were two doors, one on each end of the building's windowed front. Inside were a dozen or so doors, each set in a two-storey wall running the length of the building. The wall was set back about four feet from the windowed outside wall, providing a corridor. Jenny explained that each migrant family had its own space. Other spaces were assigned either to men and boys, or women and girls, all of whom worked in the fields. Jenny opened one of the doors. On the back wall were three tiers of wooden bunks and a ladder to reach the upper two. There were a few chairs, one small table and two cabinets of drawers. "The spaces are all the same," Jenny told me. Each bunk had a thin mattress and a single pillow. The cell walls did not reach the high ceiling. "Imagine that," Jenny said. "Not much privacy, is there?"

Outside, in an area between the bunkhouse and a high red barn, one of the women was stirring something in a large black iron pot suspended over an open wood fire. The pot hung from a thick stick that looked like a pick handle. The stick was held up at both ends by forked branches. As Jenny and I passed by I noticed the pot was filled with clothing. Other clothing was strung on a wire that ran from one corner of the barn to a tree.

A rusty oil drum stood nearby. It was covered by a piece of wire mesh.

"That's the cook stove," Jenny said. "Some women have a few pots they keep in their cells. They will cook a meal for their families and others tonight. Their food is in storage in the barn. Let's have a look."

The barn was quiet and deserted, thick with the odor of dry hay. High in the loft a small barn owl floated toward its nest. "See the happy migrants in the yard," Jenny said. "See how happy they are. Strangers in a strange, alien land. Bend your back ten hours a day, eat slop, sleep on boards."

"Jenny, your father wouldn't like hearing you."

"Father! To him they aren't human. They're like the cattle, only less valuable. They are the displaced people of America, the homeless nomads in the land of the free and the home of the brave."

"Okay, Jenny, that's enough. Where do they come from?"

"Florida, South Carolina mostly. They pick oranges in Florida. They come here in July, on trucks and an old bus, a few beat-up cars. They will leave the state in September or early October. Did you know that this is only one of dozens of migrant camps in the state? This is one of the better ones. Very few of those camps have child care centers. Look at those kids there, working with their parents. They work in the fields sometimes too."

"Aren't they under age?"

"Of course they are, but the family's pay depends upon how many bushels they pick. Children are necessary, for the sake of their parents, not the farm. More hands, more pay."

"Jenny, I'm sorry. I've never been to a migrant camp before." I noted that one woman was stuffing the oil drum with newspaper and kindling. I laughed. I pointed to the oil drum. "That could be the newspaper I work for." A woman who was obviously pregnant placed a kettle above the drum's flames.

"She's due next month," Jenny said. "She will have her baby in the county hospital. A welfare nurse comes around once in a while. If the migrants leave before the baby's born she will have to stay here. The nurse says she shouldn't travel."

"When will she join her husband?"

"She's not married. Nobody may ever know what happened to her and her baby. If she has a family in Florida she's lucky. Father will give her money for a train ticket."

"They don't have much, do they?" Actually, I couldn't think of the words that could express my dismay.

"They don't have anything," Jenny said. "Nothing!"

"Surely the farm could provide better housing than this."

Jenny shook her head. "Dad says they're used to it, and they are. He says they would wreck anything better. He says it's the government's fault. Says government should pay for better housing. Besides that, he believes there is more migrant labor available than is needed. Truth is, Art, the state, with federal help, has established several model migrant camps on state property. They have doctors and nurses available, child-care centers, summer schools. There are only a few such centers in the entire state. They were supposed to be copied by factory farms and county governments. But the counties would rather have fairs." She looked keenly at me. "You're a reporter. Do something about it."

"About the migrants? Are you serious? What could I do?"

"Write about it."

"If I wrote about this camp it would hurt your father."

"Would you have to mention the Xenophon?"

"No. I could write it as from 'Somewhere in Chesterton County.'"

"Then write it."

"It would require photographs."

"Could you have a photographer come?"

"Maybe."

"It might start something."

"But my assignment is the fair."

"Who cares about the fair?" Jenny asked, looking away from me.

"I thought you did."

"I do. I really do. But I care more about, well, more about this." She waved her hand, circling the scene before us of exhausted workers lounging on a few chairs and benches set before a few picnic tables.

"Then *you* write it," I said.

"You think it would get in the paper?"

"Give it to me. I will send it in."

"Oh, would you please? I would be so grateful. I want to describe a certain night last year."

"What happened?"

"The pastor of our church, Mark Christopher, the Presbyterian, brought over a movie projector. He showed some old movies here, in the barn. Abbott and Costello, movies like that. I could write about the Sunday afternoon services that Pastor Christopher conducts."

"He comes here every Sunday?"

"Yes. He's a wonderful pastor. I wish you could meet him."

"Is that all he does?"

"Certainly not. He collects food and clothing for the migrants. He brings presents for the children. Oh, he's so good."

"How about members of the church? Do they come?"

"Only two or three, including my brother Bob."

"How do Chesterton people feel about the migrants?"

"A necessary evil. Last week I went to see the county health nurse about Lucy, that's the one who is pregnant. The visiting nurse said she had asked for financial help so that Lucy could have her baby here, but she got nowhere. So I went to town on the bus and marched right into the courthouse. That's where the county clerk's office is. And you know what he said? He said 'What are you getting so involved for, Miss Glen? They're just a bunch of niggers.' Well, I was so mad I almost hit him. I said: 'If you ever, *ever*, use that word again, I'm going to tell my father, and he will tell Mr. Bryson, and pretty soon you won't have a job.' He just laughed, and said he would see what he could do."

"Did you ask your father to do something?"

"I would have wasted my breath. Dad says the migrants come here voluntarily, they don't have to come, and we pay them decent rates, based on number of rows picked, so why don't they take care of themselves as others do. A strong, independent man, my father."

Beulah was sitting under a tree, scratching the earth off her battered shoes. The woman who had been stirring the clothing in the pot was now hanging them on the clothes line. We returned to the yard to say goodbye. Beulah looked up and smiled. "You leavin'?" she asked.

"Yes, we have to go. Got to get back to the fair."

"Movies tonight?"

"I'm afraid not, Beulah."

"But it's Tuesday, ain't it?"

"Yes it is. But Pastor Christopher has to be at the fair tonight. He's looking after his church's diner." Beulah's smile faded.

"Next Tuesday," Jenny said. "Movies for sure. And I will be here Sunday for church. Tell everyone we will come."

As I drove the Buick back to the fair I kept glancing at Jenny, who was quiet at first, a faraway look in her eyes as she sat quietly beside me. To say that I was interested in her would be putting it mildly. She intrigued me with the way she spoke to me, so confidentially, as if we had known one another for ages, confiding her feelings to me, trusting confidences. I determined to get to know her better. "Would you be very upset if they closed down the fair?" I asked her.

"I will be very upset, and worried," she told me. "But I am torn about it because it would mean more jobs and there would be more money to help tenant farmers and migrants."

"Jenny, I want to tell you something. This is only my second day here, but I'm beginning to believe that it would be a shame if this was the last fair."

"Of course," she said. "All things being equal, everyone would want the fair to live on. But all things aren't equal, are they, Mr. James?"

"To you, my name is Art. Okay? I'm concerned about your father. His name will be in tomorrow's Star. Also Mr. Bryson's. There may be, I repeat, may be, some folk who will suspect they are involved in a scheme to make money for themselves if the fair closes."

"That's absurd!"

"Some people will think *Scandal*!"

"Dad won't vote for closing."

"No, I don't believe he will."

"Then what is there to worry about?"

"If he opposes the sale he will have enemies among those who vote for it. If he votes for it, he will have enemies among those who want to keep the fair going."

"You mean that either way he will make enemies?"

"Yes, but I think he will get off better than Mr. Bryson."

I never should have engaged her this way while driving. She eyed me earnestly. "That's ridiculous!" she shouted.

"Mr. Bryson has certain business interests," I said. "The bank, real estate, insurance. He will be suspect."

"I hope you didn't put that in your story." I detected the rising tone of alarm in her voice.

"Just the facts of his connections."

"Is it your job to ruin people's lives?"

"You know how involved he is."

"Who asked you to come down here anyway, Mr. James? You've got it all figured out, haven't you? What right do you have to pry into our affairs? Let me out." She was trying to open the car door.

I had been driving slowly enough but just the same I almost missed a stop sign. I slammed on the brakes. She wasn't wearing a seatbelt. I cursed myself for that, since I was wearing mine. Jenny was thrown forward. I reached out to grab her but missed. Her forehead struck the dashboard. She jerked back and then, horrified, I saw her eyes close and her face went pale. I pulled off the pavement onto the side of the road. I turned off the engine, applied the brakes and bent over her. I pressed my fingers into her cheeks, pushing her mouth open. Panic hit me. I sounded the horn.

Perhaps I was hoping another car would stop. A car did pass by me but the driver never even looked my way. I turned back to Jenny. I pressed her mouth open again. Then, I don't know why, some reflex action learned in Boy Scouts, perhaps, I put my mouth on hers and blew heavily. My heart was racing. She exhaled. "What are you doing?" she asked, a whisper. I sped away toward Chesterton. "Where are we going?"

"Hospital," I said.

"Don't be silly. I've work to do at the fair office. Besides, I'm hungry. I will be satisfied with a hamburger."

I dropped her off as close as I could to fair's main gate. She trotted off without even a wave.

There was a parking space by a meter in front of the Times building. I slid a quarter into the slot and went up the stairs to the newsroom. At his desk, Blanchard was reading my *Day Before the Fair* article in the Star. "That's a swell story, Art," he said. "Have you seen today's Times?" He pointed to a story on Page One about fair judges and their problems this year because of the great number of *excellent* and *outstanding* entries.

Marie was busy at her desk. "Your story?" I asked her. "Very good."

"I wish I had written the feature story you did. There's never been anything like that written for the Times that I know of. There's an editorial about the fair today. I don't think it says much."

This is what the Times editorial said:

Rumor has it that the current fair will be the last in
its long and distinguished history.
If it is true--and we pray it isn't--then we hang
our editorial head in shame. Not for ourselves
(although we are guilty of editorial oversight for not
bringing this rumor to our readers' attention sooner)
but for every citizen of Chesterton County.
Is nothing sacred anymore? Must we yield to pressure
for industrial advance at the price of forfeiture of our most
precious possessions, of our most cherished traditions?
All those who love the fair, rise up! Declare yourselves
now before it is too late.

"May the Star have permission to reprint this?" I asked Blanchard.

"The Times cherishes publicity," he said.

"Don't go away," I said. "I have a few questions." I went across the street and filed the Times editorial to Johnny. I raced back again but Blanchard wasn't there. "He told me to meet him at the bar next door," Marie said.

I went out again and hit the sidewalk on the run. At the entrance to the bar I almost bowled over two old gentlemen in straw hats. I pushed by them without apology and stepped inside. It was so dark I couldn't see a thing for a minute. Then I heard Blanchard's voice: "Over here." I joined him in a side booth. "That was fast," he said. "What did you do with my editorial?" I told him. "Think Johnny will use it?"

"As a sidebar on the report I sent today," I told him, stressing that I had used the stack of names I had copied from the county directory.

"All quite factual," he said. "You may win a Pulitzer. The man who saved the fair."

"Come off it. In Richland it's not that important."

"It should be," Blanchard said. "It should be important everywhere."

"All this time you've been wanting to promote the fair, but your hands have been tied, haven't they?"

"Hardly a secret. I've spoken about it many times, at Kiwanis etcetera. They asked why the Times hasn't mentioned it."

"You couldn't tell them about Mr. Clark?"

"About the publisher's fears of a boycott? Hardly. Because half the Kiwanians would climb on the bandwagon *against* the Times. Well, I set it rolling today. Clark's probably reading it at this very moment. He won't like it, but there comes a time when an editor can take just so much. I consulted with him several times about the fair. I told him we couldn't ignore the matter forever, what with the whole county talking. It wasn't good journalism and it would sink the Times. He admitted that was true, that when readers catch you suppressing the news they are going to stop reading you. He told me we had to take the chance, because the consequences of our participating in the debate were even more horrible. Of course I can't see that at all. We have to be a newspaper first and an advertising sheet second. Besides, advertising profit is dependent upon circulation. It was as plain as daylight to me, but Mr. Clark couldn't see it, him not being an editor."

"So you dashed off that editorial just to stir things up a bit?"

Blanchard laughed pleasantly. "I didn't sleep much last night, worrying about it."

"Conscience?"

"No way." He grinned. "He could fire me for insubordination, or even breaking my contract. When you're an old man like me, that's the thing you worry about. So I keep my fingers crossed."

"I don't think you need to worry."

"Thanks for your support, Art, but you don't know Clark."

I shouldn't have told him, but we journalists had to stick together. I told him that Clark himself was the pigeon who tipped off Johnny about the scrap over the fair. "This is between us, Mr. Blanchard," I said. "Top secret," I added, laughing. "It's Clark's purpose to have the Star do what the Times can't do, that is to expose the behind-the-scenes negotiations now going on, with one side out to end the fair, and the other to protect the status quo. I just happened to be the patsy to do the job. Mr. Blanchard, I'm lucky to have the assignment. I'm becoming more and more convinced that the fair needs saving, and this is only my second day poking around here in Chesterton."

"Art, I like you." He hailed a bus boy. "Time for a beer," he said.

"Time for a meal," I said. "I'm hungry." I ordered a chicken dinner.

"I told my wife I'd be home in time for supper."

"In that case, we could continue our talk tomorrow."

"No need. I called her when you went out and told her I would be late. You know how it is, Art."

"No, I don't. I'm single."

"Never been married? That's too bad."

"Not even close."

Blanchard laughed. "You know, Marie said something today, I forget what. It was something about admiring you." He grinned. "Watch out, Art. She's a go-getter."

"I'll take my chances." The bus boy popped a couple of beers in front us. "Thanks anyway, Mr. Blanchard. I don't drink."

"I didn't order for you. They're both mine. Please call me Roger."

"Roger, when did you tell Clark that you wanted to publish an editorial about the fair?"

"A week ago."

"I thought so," I said, " because it was exactly a week ago that Johnny received a publicity package about the fair. Came in the mail. Now I know it was Clark who sent it, probably with a note from Clark appealing to Johnny to send down a reporter. I don't think he will fire you, Roger. If anyone is going to be the scapegoat it will be me."

Blanchard patted my hand. "Don't worry, Art. You're the foreign correspondent in this case. Another secret: Tiber Trucks, being a Richland company, the moguls of Richland don't want to lose it, so the company must be getting pressured to stay, being offered tax relief, as is usual. And I can't see much advantage to Tiber, but then I'm not a mogul. I don't think it's Tiber that we have to worry about. I think it's something local we don't know about or, what's worse, something we can't even imagine as a possibility."

"If you're so sure Clark will fire you, why don't you resign?"

He looked astonished. "Do you know how hold I am? I'm sixty. I know, everybody says I don't look it. I'm sixty and everything that goes with it. It's young whipper-snappers like you are getting the breaks." He breathed heavily and looked skyward. "No, I want him to fire me. I'd be proud to be fired. I can go to some newspaper that's not so spineless and I will show them my editorial and explain the situation. They will understand."

"You're sure?"

"No, I'm not sure. I'm not sure at all. In fact, I'm scared as hell." He paused a moment. "For all I know every newspaper in the country is infected with this disease, this commercialism that gets in the way of truthful reporting."

"My story will be in, I'm sure of that."

"What has the Star got to lose? It would be a different story if your county had a fair. Freedom of the press! The people's voice. Ha, ha, ha."

"The people will support you," I said. "You asked for, what was it? For all those who love the fair to rise up, to declare themselves. They will be writing tonight. Hundreds of them." That was pure hokum and Blanchard knew it. He opened his second beer. My choice was a cola.

"You must know Clark well enough," I ventured.

"Sometimes I wonder." He shook his head. "Clark covets mystery. He calls the shots on politics and who we endorse for office. Recently it's been one taboo after the other. For instance, we used to run the names of contractors who get public projects. We don't anymore. Reports on county commissioner meetings go to Clark for approval. Plenty of times he has killed our stories. He insists upon his alterations. Often we hold onto stories a day or two before he sends down his approval."

I continued writing notes. Often I had to hold up my hand to slow Blanchard down. "People around town were getting to Clark," he continued. "There was a time if anyone came into his office, demanding that we kill a story, he would throw them out. Recently there's been a regular parade of patsies gaining entry to his office, agitators I presume. They are lawyer's flunkies, bank tellers, department store clerks, court flacks. The fix is in. Plain censorship. I see it and I know it. Makes my blood run cold. Then I'm ashamed for what I have become: journalist no longer, only a printer, printing what I'm told to print."

"Still, you have the editorial page."

"Hah! Every editorial has to be approved by Clark, personally. He's the real editor. I see both sides, take none. Anything controversial, upsetting to the status quo, that's out. We view with alarm anything that upsets the equilibrium of the market. We're for the right-to-work laws, but we will defend to the death the working man's privilege of having the kind of union he wants. We're against high taxes, and for more public and private schools. We're for our precious liberties, for which our fathers died, as they say. We're against fascism, communism, even capitalism, unless it's both progressive and conservative, if it can be that at one and the same time. We're for higher tariffs and increased foreign trade, meaning you buy more from us, and not necessarily vice versa. We're for the United Nations and against foreign alliances. We're for health and liberty and happiness, and against death and high taxes. We're for an adequate national defense and against federal government interference in our local affairs. We're for mother and the home, and against juvenile delinquency and slum gangs. We're for helping the helpless and against the lazy unemployed homeless. We're against national debt and for wars against tyrants. We're for the farmer and against agricultural incompetence. We're for free enterprise and we're against unfair business competition. We're for--oh, what the hell. We're for goodness and sainthood and against crime and sin."

He took another swallow and gagged as the straight drink hit his throat. He coughed and I offered to hit him on the back, but he held up his hand in protest. He sipped the beer left in his glass and when he had recovered I said I thought he was getting tired. I felt sorry for him and I wanted to help him, but I wondered how far I should go, believing that the Times was still a competitor of the Star.

"Tell me more about Clark," I said.

Blanchard shifted uneasily. "We travel in different circles," he said. "He belongs to the upper business and social world of Chesterton, whereas I, being a citizen of the Fourth Estate, find my friends among insurance salesmen, petty storekeepers, stock brokers, cheap advertising salesmen, druggists and others engaged in pedestrian pursuits. I'm afraid I'm not one of the elite."

"Was Clark born to it?"

"Hardly. His father was a railroad switchman, his mother took in washing. Mr. Clark never went to college, didn't even finish high school. He went to work early as a messenger boy in the Times advertising department, carrying proof sheets to Main Street stores. He built up quite an acquaintance among the merchants. He was full of ideas and was given a chance to write some ads. So he progressed to become an advertising salesman. But the best thing that happened was that he married the daughter of the Times publisher, guy named Scott, who had no sons, so he groomed Clark to be his successor. When Scott died he left the Times to Clark and a few other invested properties to his daughter, Clark's wife, who divorced Clark and married Andrew Small."

"The bank president?"

"The same. Strange thing is, Clark and Small are friends, in a business and social way. Mrs. Small, being part owner of the Times, must exert some editorial influence upon Clark."

"That would account for the pressure," I said.

"What pressure?" Blanchard looked surprised.

"Pressure on you, to keep out news of a possible sale of the fairgrounds. It's Small who's putting the pressure on Clark."

"No doubt about it," Blanchard said. He was silent for a moment. He wiped sweat from his forehead. "That's it, Art. Clark wants to keep the fair but he can't publicly oppose Small, whose wife is part owner of the Times. Hah! The plot thickens!"

"And that's the reason Clark won't fire you," I said. "He's actually on your side. Maybe he's ashamed he turned the Times into such a Main Street sop."

"Perhaps a combination of both," Blanchard said. "Art, if you're right in assuming that Clark is fighting Small and the other commissioners, then there's hope. Yeah! Hope for me and hope the fair will be saved. He will have to rebuke me for running my editorial, but we will understand one another." He was quiet for moment. "Darn! I can't tell him I know he wants to save the fair."

"I have a suggestion," I said. "Tell him your conscience as a journalist got the better of you. Apologize."

"You're right, Art. And I will offer to resign dated Friday at midnight." He took note of my alarm. "Don't worry. I won't resign. Now I know that Clark truly wants to keep the fair. If he votes with the majority of the commissioners for sale of the fairgrounds, well, it will be a fait accompli, and the Times will rhapsodize about Tiber Trucks, and Clark will still be Small's weasel friend."

"And if the vote goes against the sale?"

Blanchard shrugged. "It will be only a temporary defeat for Small. He will try again next year. He will be grateful that my editorials indicate that the commissioners weren't trying to put over a strictly cover-up deal. So it all depends on Clark. When the chips are down Friday night, will he vote for or against?"

"And that will depend upon how the others vote?" I asked.

"The question is: are the commissioners united? Will it be six-to-four? Clark's vote against the fair would mean a deadlock. Four are sure to oppose: Harding of the Co-op, Keating of the FGA, Glen of the Grange, Bryson of Farm Service."

"I'm not sure about Bryson," I said.

"You mean he's on the fence too?"

"Yes, I think so. He's a director of the bank, and so may be ruled by Small. He's an officer of Farm Service Insurance, of which Small is a director. As chief insurer for the fair he has probably brokered it out among every insurance agent in town. He is also vice-president of Amalgamated

Properties, and thus has an interest in real estate, as does every other commissioner."

"The combination doesn't add up to a vote for the fair," Blanchard said.

"I wouldn't count on it."

"Clark may be our only hope."

"He may be."

"Let's get back to the Times." Blanchard smirked. "If I'm going to be fired I might as well get it over with."

CHAPTER NINE

In the Times newsroom Marie looked up as we came in. She handed a piece of paper to Blanchard.

"I know, I know," he said. "Mr. Clark called."

"I'm afraid so." she said. "He's in the fair office. Wants you to call him right away."

"Art, you know everything, probably more than I do, so get a load of this talk. You can listen on Marie's phone." He got through to Clark right away.

I listened carefully as Clark said: "Roger, I've been looking over today's Times and guess I what I saw? A little editorial."

"Are you going to nominate me for a Pulitzer?"

"You will have to do better than that, Roger."

"I suppose I won't get another chance."

"As far as the Times is concerned, not yet."

"Then I'm fired?" I could hear Blanchard breathing hard.

"Hell, no. Who said anything about that? I mean, please, no more editorials like that."

"That's all?"

"What more did you expect?"

"Everything."

"Forget it, Roger. Who knows? It may do some good. And, Roger, I'm going to have to say you were responsible for this editorial, you alone."

"I understand. Do you want a retraction?"

"No. If you get any letters, let's go over them together in the morning."

"Okay. And thanks, Mr. Clark." Blanchard and I hung up. "Art, what do you make of that?"

"I say he's on your side, Roger," I said.

"Yeah, but who's at bat?"

"Clark is. You just happened to sneak one in as a pinch-hitter. But he's the captain of your team." At Blanchard's desk I pointed to his editorial. "It's a start," I said. "I think Clark's recruited a lot of players on his team. He's got a couple of them on base. He may score a home run yet."

"I wonder what's going on in the board rooms tonight?" Blanchard said. He covered his face with his hands. "God, I'm tired. I've got to get home and get some sleep before I drop dead. Why should I care what happens to our little fair? Yes, the directors of this and the directors of that will burn the midnight oil tonight. Why else would Small be running scared? Scared enough to put the screws on Clark. When people are afraid they're going to lose, that's when they cry for suppression of the news. They do their dirty work in secret rooms, under the cover of darkness. They knife the opposition under the cloak of private business. We can't let that happen. We can't!"

"Are you going to write another editorial?" I asked.

"You heard the man. I am forbidden. We will see what tomorrow's mail brings forth."

"You don't sound too hopeful, Roger," I said with sympathy.

"I'm not. When you've been in the newspaper business as long as I have you won't rely too much upon what is popularly known as public indignation. It takes a lot to arouse that, a lot more than the issue of whether a county fair is to live or die, a lot more."

"Still, people are talking." I was trying to be encouraging.

"Yes, at this very moment, on the buses, they are opening the Times. After they glance at the Page One headlines they turn to the comics, then to sports, perhaps to the financial page. Nothing will happen. Nothing."

At last Blanchard, more exhausted than ever, left me. I presume he went home for supper and a cool shower. I had learned a lot but not nearly enough to report anything definite, so I decided to call it a day as far as interviewing was concerned. I called Jenny to hear if she was ready to accompany me on another jaunt through the fairgrounds. She was waiting for me in the fair office, so we went together from there to the midway. A crowd jostled us around a bit as we made our way down an avenue lined with freak shows and the like. I tried to hold her hand but Jenny whispered "No, someone may see us."

"Who cares?" I asked. She was so good looking, especially as the multi-color spotlights shone brightly upon her enthralling pale features. "Art, I don't care who sees us together, not really. But so many people know I'm going with Ricky. They would tell him, sure."

"You don't want him to find out, do you?" Oddly, I found that flattering.

"No, not yet. When the fair is over--"

"That's only three days away," I protested.

"It's not forever. Art."

"Do we have that long?"

"I hope so," she said. "Let's not be impatient."

I had to excuse her. She was fresh in my experience. So unabashedly fragile. Not meaning physically, not even in naivete. In sophisticated experience, perhaps. Of course, at my current age I thought of myself as being aggressively advanced. After all, Jenny was a farm girl, born and bred. And me? Well, I was city-born and bred. There had to be a big difference, right?

"Impatient about what?" I asked.

"About us, silly." She smiled and held my hand tightly. "Ricky didn't say anything. At the office, Art, didn't you notice? The way he looked so hatefully at you. He already suspects. He looked at both of us with that air of suspicion. I have to be careful when he's around. He has a hot temper, you know."

We stopped in front of the scrolled mirrors. In one we were thin and tall with very long waists. In another we were squat and short, like fat dwarfs. In the third we were neither thin nor squat, tall nor short, and it was a while before I realized that this mirror did not distort us at all. We did not laugh.

At the mirror maze I bought tickets and we walked in. Now it was alright. I held her hand. We wandered silently between the multiple mirrored walls, which multiplied our reflections to infinity. We did not get lost. In the Fun House a jet of air blew Jenny's skirt up, revealing her slim legs. I held her hand tightly. In the dark we walked a convoluting plank. She did not scream, but I did. At the top we sat together on a mat. I put my arm around her. The attendant pushed my back and we slid together down the shoot, spiraling on the turns.

I helped Jenny into a car and we were propelled into the blackness of The Pit, where, swiveled, we ducked as skeletons popped out and lights flashed. Jenny leaned her head to mine. I held her tightly and kissed her sweet warm lips until suddenly the car burst through opening doors and we blinked in the glare.

Next was the Canals of Venice with a gondola on the water. The boat rocked crazily as we clambered aboard. We drifted along dimly-lit channels where mandolins played. We clung to one another under glowing globes and lanterns. Then there was silence, and the quickened pulse, and then an end to silence and the clamor of the crowd once more.

On the merry-go-round we rose and fell in slow motion, as in dreams, intertwined, as kaleidoscopic lights swayed. To Calliope's Tales of the Vienna Woods we waltzed in time, circled the circumference of earth and around again. Along the axis of our single pole we pressed the world without. We were one, alone in the sweeping swath of light.

I bought Jenny spun sugar candy and her face was pink with it. We stopped before The Amazing Arturos and gazed, unflinching, as a turbaned man thrust blazing torches down his throat and another swallowed a sword. Beyond were three girls in veils and little else, shimmying to a Turkish melody. Jenny watched as enraptured as I. A sinuous man manipulated slimy snakes. Dolly Dimples dozed.

We emerged at last and took our time walking to the big Agricultural Pavilion. We ascended stairs to the second floor, which was almost deserted. "Doesn't seem very popular," I said.

"People see the exhibits during the day," Jenny said. "They like to see the midway at night, and the grandstand show." She guided me down a row between stands of fruits and vegetables. We stopped to observe a stack of enormous cucumbers. "Mine," Jenny said. "They should win a prize, don't you think? Largest in the fair." I agreed. "Do you know what it took to grow them so big?"

"Lots of manure?"

Jenny laughed so much I thought she would never stop. "You sure don't know much about farming, Art. It took a hundred years of soil conservation, and a hundred years of luck."

"Luck?"

"Sure. And faith. The weather had to be right for five consecutive summers. And without faith, that it might be possible, these cucumbers wouldn't be here either. We farmers have that faith, you see, unreasonable at it sounds."

"You mean it's irrational to start a project of growing the largest cucumbers in the world."

"Under natural conditions, yes."

"What about un-natural?"

"You mean, hot-house control?"

"Yes, why bother growing them outdoors."

"Ah, that's just the point. It's the glory of it."

"A morning glory," I said. "It fades with the sun."

"Not that kind. The way you feel. Like you've created something noble, like a baby. We nurture it. The life is given, a gift. We have it only for a time, and it is taken away. While we have it we must protect it, save it, pass it on."

"Like the fair?" I said.

"The fair challenges us, inspires us. Winning a ribbon is a testament to our faith. Why all that effort? Regular size cucumbers will taste as well, probably better."

"Mother earth," I said. "The womb of life. A tale as tall as time."

"I'm serious," Jenny said. "Conservation has to be practiced."

"Jenny, I'm on your side. Always have been. The world is our temporary home. To live on it we have to save it."

When we returned reluctantly to the office Ricky was there. Jenny took his place at an information window next to Stowe. Ricky invited me to have a cola with him at the usual diner. Five or six others were there. We got our drinks and settled down at a table. Ricky was not the smiling type. I knew he wasn't in a good mood, and I knew the reason was his recognition that Jenny and I had fallen for each other.

"You know I'm engaged to Jenny, don't you?" He asked, eyeing me sharply. He was a tough-looking guy, not quite as tall as me, but built like a seasoned boxer. I could never match him in a physical conflict.

"Congratulations," I said. "When's the wedding?"

He grinned. "We're not formally engaged. But we've talked about it a lot. I'm all for it. We've grown up together on the farm. But you know all that."

"Of course, I know that. Her mother told me. I like her a lot."

He grinned, a thin smirk. "And Jenny too?"

"Of course. Who wouldn't?"

"I want you to know, Mr. Reporter, that she's my girl, not yours."

I should have been cautious but I'm not the meek and mild type. "That's up to Jenny, isn't it?"

"Smart Art! You've only been here for a day. Who do you think you are? Jenny is one of us. We don't go for outsiders mucking around where they don't belong."

"And where do you think Jenny fits into your scheme of things?"

He struck the table with his fist. "Look here. Let me make myself clear. Jenny belongs on the farm. Not you or anybody else is going to take her away from the farm--or me!"

"I'm back to Richland on Saturday, Ricky. So what's all the fuss? You have nothing to worry about."

"All right then. I don't want to see you going around with her again. Understand?"

"Absolutely, Ricky. Mind if I do my job and ask you a question about farming? With you, farming is a business. Right? Do you plan to live on the farm the rest of your life, like your father and Mr. Glen?"

"Nah, that's old hat. I will hire professional manager-types to do that. It's rapidly becoming that way everywhere. Only way to make money."

"What about Bob? I hear he's keen on being a teacher, devoting his life to education."

Ricky smiled. "Temporary. He will get over it. He's got farming in his blood. Doesn't know anything else. You will see. That is, if you're around, which I doubt."

I let it go. "Is there room on the Xenophon for both of you?"

"Sure. Bob's a shrinking soul, but a good fellow in his way. I will run the place. He will fit in somewhere. I don't know quite how but we will work it out."

"And Bob's father?"

He laughed. "No problem. He will retire." I could have chastised him for that imperious remark, but I held my peace. "The Xenophon," Ricky continued, "has been in the family for a long time. It's up to me to save it."

I looked at him to see if he was serious. He was. "The farm needs saving?" I asked him.

Ricky snickered. "It's obvious. If things go on the way they're going now we will be out of business in another ten years."

"You don't think your father and Mr. Glen are doing a good job?"

"Dad's a part-time businessman. He's a farmer at heart but he doesn't have what it takes to make money at it. Neither does Bob's father. They are a dying breed."

"And, may I ask, what is your answer to this impending calamity?"

Ricky sneered. "It's obvious, isn't it? Mechanization, guaranteed markets, guaranteed prices."

"Through outlets you control, I suppose?"

"Exactly," he said firmly. "Mr. Glen owns the co-op investments. They will be Bob's. When I gain control of the Xenophon I will get control of the co-ops too."

There was no need to take notes. He had me convinced. Ricky was on the rise. It wasn't news, but it was interesting. Why was he telling me about his ambitions?

"So you gain control, Ricky. How?"

He shook his head in a manner that informed me that I was certainly too dense to know what he was talking about. "Through investment, of course," he said. "I will sell off my dad's real estate and insurance interests. He got into them as ventures to help the farmers. If I have to, I will lease the farm."

"And who will you lease it to?" I asked.

"Any good food producer. A big company that will finance improvements."

"Then you will be the manager?"

"What's the difference? I will make greater profit without the capital risk. It's the answer to our agricultural dilemma, which is production income too small compared to material assets."

"That's a pretty picture," I said, "and how does Jenny fit into your scheme of things?"

"She's a Glen," Ricky said. He had a faraway look in his eyes, as if enraptured by a welcome dream. "That name means something in Chesterton County. She will share with me in the Glen half of the farm."

"And Bob?"

"He's useless. I'll buy him off."

"Ricky, is that all?"

"No. I've known Jenny all my life. We grew up like brother and sister. The Xenophon is her home, the only home she's ever known. She will fit in, you see."

"And what makes you so confident she will marry you?" I asked tartly.

"Oh, really, Mr. Reporter. That's what our parents want. Besides, the Xenophon is in her blood. Don't you know what that name means?"

"No. Enlighten me."

"Xenophobia. The fear of strangers."

"This is the nineteen sixties, remember?" I protested. "Astronauts and Venus probes. World-wide television via Telstar. Are you sure you're one of us?"

"Oh, I am sure, Mr. Reporter. Are you?"

I left him there as he laughed and waved me farewell. I walked stiffly back to the fair office.

"Jenny," I said, "I want to sell tickets."

Jenny glanced at me and smiled. "Ricky's not coming back?"

"I don't know. Show me what to do."

"Give them a ticket for a dollar. Change is in the drawer here." She pulled out the drawer under the counter.

A man with a toothless grin came to my window. "Two please," he said. I shoved the tickets through the hole under the glass panel, then stuffed his payment into the drawer.

"What did Ricky say?" Jenny asked.

"Tell you later."

"You had a fight?"

"He's too cool for that."

"We should be able to close up soon. It's almost ten o'clock."

Just then a bus stopped outside the gate and about twenty people came up to the windows. We were busy for a while and then there was a lull. I reached over and touched Jenny's hand. She clasped mine tightly.

"How touching!" It was Ricky's voice, near the door. "Perhaps I should have knocked."

I stood close to Jenny. "He knows about us," I whispered.

"I think we can close up now," Jenny said, glancing at the big clock on the wall.

I bent my head close to the metal grill and looked out. "Doesn't seem to be anyone around," I said. Jenny pulled down her window and hung up a *Closed* sign. I did the same at my window. I stood where I was, one arm resting on the counter.

"We will have to stay here a while longer," Jenny said, "In case any exhibitors come in."

Ricky leered at us. "Perhaps you two would rather be alone," he said.

Jenny settled down in the chair behind her desk. She nervously clasped her hands. "Since you already know, Ricky, there's no reason for you to stay."

Ricky sat heavily into a chair in front of a ticket window. A shaft of light from outside illuminated his grim look of suspicion. "Now, isn't this a polite triangle?" he said. He leaned back in his chair. "Three civilized people bent on a civilized discussion."

"I'm tired, Ricky," Jenny said. "If you don't mind I would rather talk about it some other time." She bent her head into her hands as her elbows rested on her desk.

"But I do mind," he said. "I think we had better talk about it now."

"You heard what Jenny said, Ricky," I shouted at him. "Can't you see she's beat?"

"In an emotional crisis, women always feel tired," Ricky said.

"Who says I'm in an emotional crisis?" Jenny asked. "You talk as if you owned me."

"I do," Ricky said.

"Body and soul?" I asked.

"Let's not get spiritual," Ricky said. "Jenny can make up her own mind."

"Are you saying I have to make a choice between you two?" Jenny asked.

"I'm in favor of that," I said.

"Let Jenny speak for herself," Ricky retorted. "Well, Jenny?"

"I can't," she said with a sigh. "Not tonight. I'm too tired."

"Jenny!" I exclaimed. I hurried over to her. I placed a pleading hand on her shoulder. "Jenny, tell him, please tell him."

"Keep your hands off her!" Ricky barked the command.

"Leave me alone," Jenny cried. "Oh, leave me alone!" She held her hands to her head.

"Now see what you've done," I shouted at Ricky.

"Dear, dear. I made her cry."

Fists clenched, I went over to him. He was still tilted back in his chair and I thought of kicking his chair out from under him. But then he did something that was so cool, so calculated, that it stopped me cold. He reached into his shirt pocket and took out a pack of cigarettes and a lighter. He held my gaze while he was doing it, even as I felt as if my face was on fire. He pulled out a cigarette from the pack, placed it between his lips, snapped the lighter and lit the cigarette. He took a long draw, pursed his lips and blew smoke in my face.

Red with rage, I was ready to strike him--or cry. I hate to admit it, but my eyes did become wet. Perhaps it was the smoke. I heard Jenny's voice behind me, low and moaning. "Art, leave him alone."

"I only want to bust him up a bit, just a little bit," I said, letting the words escape slowly, one at a time.

"Don't touch him!" I heard her rising as Ricky blew more smoke in my face. He was impassive, except for the Madonna smile. Jenny grabbed my arm. "Sit down, Art." I staggered to my chair and sat down heavily.

"That's right, Arty boy, please be seated," Ricky said.

"So help me, Ricky, one more word--" I held up my knuckled fist.

"And you will scream, Arty?"

I started to rise again but this time Jenny had her hand on my shoulder and pushed me down. "Alright," I said. "I'll let him go. But once more--"

"I thought this was going to be a civilized talk," Ricky said.

Her voice quavering, Jenny said "Now you two stop. Cut it out. I've had enough."

"Enough of him, Jenny?" Ricky asked her. "Or will it take tomorrow before you two have had enough?"

"What's tomorrow got to do with it?" Jenny asked.

"A certain story by a certain reporter in a certain filthy newspaper that's out tomorrow."

"You've heard about that?" she asked.

"Mr. Stowe told me about it. The Star, Jenny. Your good friend here has written a story that throws mud at half the people of Chesterton County."

I laughed. "If you mean your father and the county commissioners."

"Then you admit it?" It was Ricky's turn to laugh.

"Of course I wrote it. Spend a little money, Ricky. Buy your very own copy of the Star tomorrow."

"You slimy bastard!"

"What?"

"You heard me."

"Ricky, I told you." I started toward him.

Jenny screamed "Art!"

"You expect me to take that from him?" I yelled at Jenny and I was sorry right away. Something someone once said ran through my mind: *We hurt the most those we love most.*

"No, I don't," Jenny said. She turned to Ricky. "Apologize!"

"Like hell I will. But, perhaps, if he kills the story."

Jenny said: "I can't stand this. I'm leaving." And she did. The outside door slammed.

Ricky didn't move a muscle. I wanted to follow her, but I couldn't help myself. With me it's been a rule: always attack to defend yourself. "I can't kill the story," I said. "It's out of my hands. Anyway, why should I care?"

"Because it slanders a lot of good men."

"It tells the truth about them, about their connections."

"It insinuates--"

"If it insinuates anything, that's not my fault. It's the way the cards stack up."

"Is that all it means to you, a game?"

"I was sent here to do my job," I said, "and I'm doing it. Only the guilty need be afraid."

"Are you conducting a trial? Are you judge and jury too?"

"No, but I am a witness. I report things as they are, the facts."

"Only some of the facts, Mr. Reporter. There is a lot you don't know."

"I presume that. I will find out more."

"By your half-truths you insinuated evil intention, private profit."

"You mean graft, don't you?"

"Some will make money, some will lose. My father among them."

"Your father! Don't make me laugh, Ricky. He's in it up to here." I put my hand under my chin.

Ricky looked grim. "If the fairgrounds are sold," he said, "my dad will lose a bundle."

"Can you substantiate that?"

"I know why, but it's up to him to tell you, if he wants."

"I will ask him, then"

"Of course you will," Ricky said, glowering at me. "You're great at asking questions."

"What is that supposed to mean?"

"Why don't you ask Jenny a few? Her father is in this too."

"I already have. Mr. Glen is a fair director, that's all."

"So you assume only business connections are involved."

"No, I don't. But Mr. Glen's sole interest is the Grange."

Ricky laughed. "Really? You are naïve. Perhaps that's because you're biased in favor of the fair?"

"Why should I be? The Star couldn't care less, one way or the other. But to sell the fairgrounds, secretly, without public debate, it's like stealing public property."

"You accuse my father of theft?"

"No, no. It is public corruption. I don't mean that either. Everyone is so *involved*. It's a shortcoming of society."

"Nothing personal?"

"Of course not," I said.

"I'm glad to hear that," he responded with a look of contempt. "Then your hands are clean?"

"What are you driving at?" I asked, not hiding my suspicion.

"You come down here from the big city, you poke your nose into our affairs, you try to steal my girl."

"Your girl, Ricky? That's one for the books. You couldn't care less."

"When did you arrive? Yesterday afternoon. You didn't really meet her until late last night!"

"The brevity of time has nothing to do with it."

"I can see you are a fast operator, Mr. James. Don't you know you aren't wanted here? You're a stranger here."

"Shades of serfs!" I exclaimed. "What are you? Peasants?"

"This is our country, our land. Go back where you came from. You've no business being here."

"Spoken like a medieval lord! This I should report."

There was a knock on the door. Jenny came in. "What? Are you two still at it?" She sat down heavily behind her desk. "I've been talking to Bob. He's still working at the diner. Can't we leave now? If you would both stop acting like a pair of knights on the field of contest, with the hand of the fair maiden at stake, and start acting like rational human beings."

"I'm sorry, Jenny," I said. "Of course it must be your choice."

"What are you two?' she fairly screamed. "Merchandise upon a shelf? What would you have me do? Choose by quality or price?"

"I have more than what Ricky has to offer," I said.

"That's irrelevant," she responded.

"How about character?" Ricky asked.

"You both talk like nineteenth century dime novels."

"What standards do you apply in judging, Jenny?" Ricky asked.

"Don't push me, Ricky," Jenny said. "You're no prize."

"I admit that. But I do love you."

"Is that so? Really now?"

"I've known you all my life. I ought to know."

"As Art said, time is also irrelevant."

"Is it?" Ricky asked. "Think back. The times we've had together."

"Appeal to the past, Ricky? No, I would rather make a pretense of the present, thank you."

"And a fantasy of the future? You belong on the farm."

"Who says? Just because I was born there? Am I to be chained to it for life? No thanks, Ricky."

"It's in your blood."

"Did they teach you that in university?"

"No, but it's true all the same."

"Animal psychology!" Jenny looked at me as if to ask: *Can you believe that?* "Well, I'm not an animal. I'm not one of your poor dumb brutes that know only how to give milk. Like the one you just polished for the fair. And I'm not one of your trained mares either. Don't treat me like I'm your private possession, Ricky!"

"Just the same," Ricky said. "You're mine. You always have been and you always will be."

"You've always been so darn pig-headed," Jenny scolded. "And grasping. What Ricky wants, Ricky gets. Well, I'm like that too. And you won't get me, ever!"

"We'll see about that," Ricky said. "Have your fling with your reporter friend. But you will stay with me, you will see."

"In a million years, Ricky. In a million years."

"No, on Friday night, Jenny. On Friday night you will be back."

"Why Friday night?"

"You will see, that's all."

"Now he's Mr. Mysterious," Jenny said to me, jerking her head.

"And on such a note of mystery, and threat, I think we should end this little talk," I said. "Can we close the office now?"

"We, he says," said Ricky. "Now he's one of us."

They turned off the office lights and closed the windows. Once we were outside Ricky locked the door. "That should keep the tramps out," he said. "Don't stay out too late, Jenny. We have to be in the office by nine tomorrow. That's a good girl."

We walked side by side past the Agricultural Building toward the grandstand. Because the fairgrounds were brilliantly lighted we could not see the stars nor the moon. The midway remained as noisy as it had been that afternoon. We decided to stay in the darkened shelter of the diner. My body was tired but my mind was energetically focused upon Jenny. I was puzzled, in a way, that I was so attracted to her. Perhaps it was, as I had been told, that opposites attract. I really didn't care. We were alone together and that was sufficient.

After a long silence Jenny took my hand and said: "Isn't it odd?"

"What's odd?" I asked.

"Knowing someone all your life and you discover he's a stranger. The way he behaved. Like he owns me." She gazed at me. "You're so different, Art. What time is it?" She looked at her watch, which lit up when she pressed the stem. Look at that, would you? We met for the first time twenty-five hours ago. Is it possible? No, it can't be. Art, don't you think that's strange? Being with you now, this moment, I feel I must have known you a long time. Remember the song from South Pacific? *Across a Crowded Room*. Or the other one, *It Can Happen*. Same with you, Art. I suddenly felt certain that you were the one."

"I am, Jenny," I said. But I wasn't certain. Who was I to cause a disruption in her way of life? And would I be in the wrong to take her away from Ricky, who, after all, could well be the one she loved, despite his present behavior?

"You have nothing to be sorry about, Art," said Jenny. "The best way to describe my relationship with Ricky, at least since we were in high school together, is that he assumed the function of being my caretaker. I suppose it was my fault. I've always said yes to anything Ricky wanted. And he's wanted a lot. Well, everything, really. Once when I was twelve or so I read *Wuthering Heights*. Heathcliff! And I was Cathy, his woman, but the one he could never marry. A week or so after I finished the book Ricky and I were in a field together, forking hay onto a wagon. Ricky helped me onto the wagon and we lay there together for a long time, drinking in the sun. Then he turned to me, his head on his hand. 'Jenny,' he said, 'when we grow up I'm going to build you a magnificent house. It will have tall columns and a long white porch and I will build it on the line that once divided the Bryson and Glen farms. When it is built people will see that the Xenophon as no longer two farms but one, united, merged. And you know what we will call our house? Bryson Glen. Just that. You will give tremendous parties, and everybody will come, everybody, from everywhere in the county. That was the first time he kissed me. I never denied his dream. We've talked about it over the years since. Ricky made floor plans, even where a nursery would be. Do you see what I mean? I've been a part of Ricky's entire life, and he a part of mine."

I took her hand and helped her step down from the diner. The fairgrounds was alternately bright and dark as we passed in the shadows of the great buildings and then between them where the lights blazed.

"You were children," I said. "Kids are like that."

"No, more than children," Jenny said. "We were born old, aware of each other. Totally aware of our world and our common place in it. Together we prowled the fences, looking for holes that needed repair, for toppling posts, and writing down their locations on farm diagrams. When I was fourteen we were out there once when we crossed a barbwire fence. The back of my blouse caught on a barb and Ricky said to wait, he would cut it off, and I didn't wait. I stepped forward. My blouse was pulled right off and I didn't have anything on underneath. Ricky only laughed and so did I. I tossed the torn blouse over my shoulder and we marched across the field holding hands. We were that close."

"Did you ever desert him before?" I asked.

"Like now? No. When Ricky came home from Richland in June he announced to me that it was time to get engaged. That we should be engaged a year before we were married. Our parents thought that Ricky had suddenly realized that I had grown up, but it wasn't that way at all. Ricky had thought it all through carefully, you see. He had plans for the years ahead, a timetable. The first step was to graduate from university. the second to marry me, the third to have children, so that would bind our families closer together, the first Bryson and the first Glen to marry. That would make certain that the entire Xenophon would be left to us."

"What about your brother?"

"Ricky had that figured out too. Bob wants to be a teacher. Ricky made a contract with him. Ricky will finance Bob's further education toward a doctorate degree. That will take years. Then Bob can teach for several years, and Ricky will pay him as an agricultural consultant. Oh, Ricky's going to be very generous."

"By that time," I ventured, "either Bob will have lost interest in the farm, or Ricky will have squeezed him out."

"That's probable. Ricky counts on my help to persuade Bob to go ahead with his plans to teach. Already Ricky has used all the arguments on Bob, that the Xenophon must be incorporated to make possible certain economic advances, that farming needs all the intellectual help it can get, that Bob can be the brains behind the farm, while Ricky runs it."

"And Bob's convinced?" I asked.

"He will be by springtime."

"By then?"

"If Bob is going to continue with his education," she said, "he will have to apply for deferment. Otherwise the Army will get him."

"And Bob will be off to Vietnam," I said. "How about Ricky?"

"Ricky's working on it. No doubt he will have a good argument, supported by his father's testimony, that he is needed to run the Xenophon, and so he will be deferred. Besides, we have friends in Selective Service. What about you, Art?"

"My number will come up."

"And if you're married?"

"If I have to go I will go."

"Vietnam?"

"I hope not."

We reached the soaring grandstand. At the gate Jenny showed her pass to the ticket taker and I showed my reporter's ticket. We entered though a dark tunnel and emerged next to a fence. We turned to the left to the first aisle and mounted the steps. There was a roar from the crowd. Everyone stood up, pointing. We turned around and gasped. In a net under a high wire a balding man, dressed in white trousers and a white silk blouse, was bouncing. The trapeze man's long bar lay on the ground beneath the net. Seeing that he was unhurt, the people sat down, turning to one another in breathless excitement, saying: "Did you see that? What if they didn't have a net?" I went ahead of Jenny, saying "Excuse me, excuse me," until we found enough bench room to sit down.

The high-wire man stood on the edge of the net. He dropped to the ground and retrieved the bar as the crowd cheered. He tip-toed to a rope ladder at one end of the wire and started climbing. At the top, on a little platform, a girl in glittering briefs welcomed him. The crowd rejoiced. The hero held up one hand. The crowd hushed. He grasped the middle of the bar with both hands, centered it on his midriff and shuffled it a few times to test its balance, slid one foot onto the wire and jiggled the bar. "He doesn't have to do that," Jenny whispered as she tightened her grip on my hand. The man slipped his other foot onto the wire and began to walk across the frightful abyss. Frequently he hesitated as the bar trembled and his body tipped slightly from side to side. At last, triumphant, he grasped his goal, the outstretched hand of a brilliant blond standing on the other platform. He turned around and saluted the crowd as it roared in admiration.

Over the loudspeaker the announcer's voice came: "Ladies and gentlemen, how about a big hand for the entire troupe?" White-uniformed men and women, most in tights, came onto the field in front of the grandstand and formed a line. The crowd applauded loudly, even as a vendor came up the aisle steps toward us shouting "Peanuts, popcorn, soft drinks." The troupe, skipping, left the arena. "And now, ladies and gentlemen, our National Anthem." Jenny and I stood with the others as the band in center field played. When it was finished everyone sat down.

"Is it all over?" I asked.

"Fireworks now."

Suddenly the lights, which had flooded the field as brilliantly as day, went out. The band struck up a march. In the darkness I put my arm around Jenny's shoulders. She leaned against me, her cheek on mine. There was a commotion on the track that skirted the grandstand fence, and much shouting laced with the scraping of every sort of vehicle on the dirt. Then, far to the left, a firecracker popped, and then another, then there were cannonades of exploding fireworks by the score, all at one spot. As the smoke streamed skyward there was a picture of Lincoln outlined in white, yellow and red flares. The people thundered their applause. Next came outlines of Eisenhower, then Kennedy and the last was the National Capitol with a Stars and Stripes floating over it. Even before the last portrait shed its life in glowing embers to the ground, rockets roared toward the stars, bursting in glory, their resounding clap splitting the sky.

"Oh," Jenny cried, putting her hands over her ears. "Look! Look at that!" Another rocket, higher still, climbed toward the zenith, trailing twisting smoke. Out of its gorgeous plumage other firebombs detonated with fury. The grandstand reverberated with their thunder. Then the climax as a dozen rockets soared in unison and blasted the air. I clasped Jenny to me, holding her lest the terrible tremor in my breast should break the bond between us, and I should lose her in the aphonia, the aftermath of acrid silence.

STAN MATTHEWS

CHESTERTON COUNTY FAIR OPENS

As Crowds Begin to File In

By Arthur James
Special to the Star

Well, they did it. They opened the fair today--on time.

Anyone looking around the fairgrounds 24 hours ago would have doubted that it would be possible. But, as in other years, the miracle took place and today the show is on.

And it's a big show. As they say in show business, it's bigger and better--bigger and better than ever.

For at the fair there's something for everybody. Whether you're out for interesting ideas in agriculture or hobbies, new farming and cattle-raising techniques, new sewing and cooking tips--or whether you're out for just sheer pleasure--you can't beat the fair.

It's all things rolled into one: sideshows, grandstand thrills, midway attractions, exposition and exhibits, demonstration, and, above all, entertainment. If you can stand the crowd--and for most that's just part of the excitement--you'll find something at the fair to interest you, whether you're six or sixty.

They must have worked all night to get the fair in order. A million articles had to be unloaded from vans, trucks and a train. A thousand workers had to put in place everything from frankfurters to Argentine llamas. And yet they're all there today--ready and waiting for the inspection of the curious and the thrill-seekers.

Strolling through the fairgrounds you see the transformation that has taken place in a day. There are the refreshment stands which were empty yesterday--now they fairly sizzle with inviting displays of French fries, hot dogs, mustard, relish, soft drinks, hamburgers.

And the sounds you knew would be there are there. "Come and get it! Red hot! Over here! Yes, we've got it." A dime wins a prize. Every time. "Here, mister, show the little lady how you can shoot."

And the smells--clean, fresh sawdust, spicy hot relish, sweet spun sugar candy, diesel fuel, hot blasts of air as the merry-go-round motor purrs into action.

The merry-go-round: where in the world did they ever store all those huge plaster animals that the people ride? They were nowhere to be seen yesterday.

Then the bewildering variety of fair hats--stitched with your name, for a dollar. And monkey canes, and doll canes, and all the gimcracks and knick-knacks of the midway. But where is the weight-guesser, or the fortune-teller? And--what?--no test-your-strength machine? Those we sorely miss.

Inert yesterday, the diesel motors, 15 feet tall, roar and feed the multitude of brightly colored bulbs which light the midway. Halfway down is a searchlight. Its probing beam will pierce Chesterton skies tonight.

Across the way, the Telemobile. Intricate mechanisms demonstrate the miracle of the dial telephone--soon to be all Chesterton's. A dozen kids ride the merry-go-round. Go around tonight and you will wait to get on.

Crack! Crack! The sharpshooters at the target practice booth try their skill. The clay pigeons lay down to rest. The merry-go-round is about to start. All aboard who's going aboard! Down the track races the miniature streamline train, a handful of youngsters clinging grimly to the handrails before them.

There's a motorcycle outside the Thrill Arena, but the cyclists will save their strength for the real crowds later today. Then the roar will rock the midway.

But the Tilt-a-Whirl's going, with three or four of the carriages occupied. There's a scream from a young girl as the long arms swoop down at a 45-degree angle. But she's all right. Her boyfriend holds her tighter.

Two or three boys pick up some tickets for the Fun House. They emerge giggling over being lost in the mirror maze.

The Rocket stands idle. Later it will zoom around dizzily, making its occupants cringe from centrifugal force.

Dolly Dimples is not yet in her tent. The sign was there yesterday, but today her identity is revealed. As we supposed, she is the fat lady. Her dimensions are indicated by a pair of silken unmentionables, two yards wide. "Ten Cents," says a placard pinned on them.

Past the tent where a demonstration of war tortures is supposed to be going on, the Snake Pit. But they will be open later. Then the real sideshow--Oriental Torture, King of Fire, The Great LaCordo--Sword Swallower, Leo the Lobster Boy--all the stunt men and freaks of the midway under one roof.

Tiny chairs all in a row indicate the place where the midgets will stand before the crowds and invite them in to see their show. A boy nonchalantly throws wooden rings toward a peg--but they fail to settle and he goes away disgruntled and minus a prize.

"Take a number. Any number. Eight numbers, ten cents."

The crowds follow disinterestedly past. "We will try that later maybe." And "Let's look around a bit more before we try anything."

Take your time. You can spend all day on the midway, or as long as your feet hold out. Save a little pep for the exhibits. The youngsters have all their vegetables in place now. There's not an empty rack or tray. Girl Scouts busily weave baskets. A woman runs a line down a cloth on the sewing machine.

The cattle munch contentedly on the hay. Judges meander slowly by them, their task of choosing the winners just begun.

Over on the raceway everything is quiet. Tonight it will roar to the passage of the daredevil drivers, and perhaps the scream of the less blasé spectators.

In the Midway Shows office trailer, the foremen rest from their labors of yesterday. Comparatively, it was a safe day. Only one man was injured. He lost part of a finger while unloading equipment at the railroad freight station. But he's out of Chesterton County Hospital today.

Fair officials wearily check exhibit accounts. Two office workers patiently answer the myriad questions of folk who want to know where to put this and where to put that. The ticket seller counts up 82 adult admissions in the first hour of the fair, and knowingly awaits the hours ahead when he will have no time to talk to a reporter.

Outside the fairgrounds the cars are circling to find the fairgrounds small parking lot, which is full. Tonight, for city blocks around, space for parking will be at a premium. But that's the fair on opening day--a busy hive of industry and hustling.

"Get it while it's hot! Only three days left!"

THE THIRD DAY

A TRIUMPH OF LOVE

CHAPTER TEN

The next morning I was on my way to downtown Chesterton to meet Jenny. I drove slowly through the quiet empty streets. Leaves were already turning brown and yellow and lawns were strewn with the fallen. It had been an unusually hot, dry summer. The pallid earth was crisp and scorched. The grass, once green, was stunted, broken. Dust swirled in the gutters. Cars parked at the curbs were spotted with splashed dirt. The very air itself felt parched, poisoned by August's putrefaction.

The night before, on the Castle Rock Road, under the stars, where I parked the Buick outside the Xenophon, I held Jenny close to me. While I had repeated my words of admiration, my insistence that I loved being with her, to which she had responded with confirmation that she greatly admired me, I was still bothered that her eager acceptance of my love was specifically conditioned upon the requirement that I avoid any confrontation with Ricky. She meant it all right. It wasn't an occasion to discuss it, we were so busy doing other things, but at last she asked, or rather *instructed* me, to promise that I would restrain myself, even if Ricky threatened me with physical punishment. I had my doubts but my desire for Jenny buried them. I wanted Jenny, not later. Now! If it entailed a fight with Ricky so be it.

At the Chesterton County Courthouse I pulled into the rear parking lot, got out and hurried up the high front steps where Jenny was to meet me at nine o'clock. It was a few minutes before nine. Jenny wasn't there, so I sat down on the steps to wait for her bus. A brilliant ray of sunshine lit up the round tower that capped the bright stone building. I thought how much it looked like the Richland courthouse with which I was familiar. For the first time I wondered where Jenny and I would live. I presumed we would look for an apartment. Jenny had insisted that my one-bedroom abode, which was close to Richland's downtown, wouldn't do. She was open to the suggestion that she should enroll in Richland University. I started thinking how much Ricky and I were alike. I was an only child, and so was he. We both had it all planned, he to become rich in farming and marketing, I to become a famous reporter, eventually to have a regular column of my own. Ricky planned to marry Jenny to provide the merging of their families. I would marry Jenny to live happily ever after.

A bus pulled up to the curb. I helped Jenny as she stepped gingerly onto the sidewalk. Her delightful beauty was enhanced by a pink frock that was tucked under the bodice high about her waist. "Been waiting long?" she asked.

"No, not long. It gave me time to think."

"You haven't changed your mind?" she asked with detectable alarm.

"Oh, no! Have you?"

"No, I love you, Art."

"And I love you, Jenny."

Jenny held my hand as we mounted a flight of marble stairs to the second floor, turned right down the hall. "You're sure?" Jenny asked me.

"I'm positive. Why are we here, Jenny?"

"To see Miss Herkimer. You know, the county nurse I told you about. The one who visit's the migrant camp now and then. I see her for checkups, there being a chance I catch something from the workers there. Just routine. My mother would have a fit if she knew. Our secret, Mark."

"Sure, okay."

In the County Health Department office Miss Herkimer, adorned in a white nurse's attire, rose from behind her desk. She gave Jenny a warm embrace.

Jenny introduced me. "I would like you to meet my friend, Art James. He's covering the fair for the Richland Star." She tightened her grip on my left arm and looked up at me admiringly. "He's a reporter with the Star."

"A friend of Jenny is a friend of mine," Miss Herkimer said as we shook hands. She was about forty, I guess, although her hair had a hint of gray in it. She was rather heavy, but strong-looking.

"Jenny told me about the help you have been to the migrants," I said.

"They need all the help we can give them," she said. Jenny and I sat down in small armless chairs in front of the desk. "One poor girl there is going to have a baby," the nurse said with a sigh. "She should be in the hospital now. The diet she is on! Potatoes mostly. She never sees a piece of meat. Expectant mothers should be on a diet that builds their strength."

"Will she be able to get a bed in the hospital?" I asked.

"I've reserved one for the end of September."

"That's wonderful," Jenny exclaimed. "Beulah was so disappointed we couldn't show movies last night."

"You saw her?"

"Art and I went there yesterday afternoon."

"Did they install the diesel engine yet?"

"Not yet," Jenny said.

"Why a diesel engine?" I asked.

"A generator, for electricity. It would operate heaters in the bunkhouse." She fiddled with a card on her desk. "So, Jenny, no doubt you're anxious to get that test done. Doctor Roach isn't in yet, but I can get you started, and he will finish the tests. He won't be long. Usually comes in at nine on the dot. I'll bet he's attending to our health exhibit at the fair."

Jenny went with her to a back room as I sat down on a brown leather sofa opposite the nurse's desk. It was exactly like any other doctor's waiting room, with magazines spread out neatly on a coffee table. I picked up the latest *Life* magazine with a picture of President Johnson on the cover. I thumbed through the pages, trying to focus on the photos, but they kept fading away as I saw again the look of wonder on Jenny's face the night before as we pledged ourselves to one another. It was going to be rough, especially with Jenny's parents, but a peculiar stubbornness boiled up in me. I said to myself *I don't care what they say. She's mine, all mine.* So what if I am taking her away from them? We're free to do what we please, aren't we? Ricky would have to take it and lump it.

Ten minutes later Miss Herkimer returned. She smiled at me in a curiously winsome way. She came over to the sofa and sat down beside me.

"Jenny told me you two were up quite late last night," she said. "She wants to lie down and rest until the doctor comes. Such a sweet girl. A heart as big as a mountain. You've seen what she's done for the migrants, how they love her so. All summer long she's been their best friend. As well as that, for example, she organized members of the Juvenile Grange to sing for the public patients at the county hospital. And those old folk were so grateful! It made me want to cry to see the happy look on their faces. Jenny's brother, Bob, was Santa Claus, dressed in a rented suit. They brought presents out of their own money, and they didn't miss one, not one. The boys put up a tree in the children's ward and decorated it too. Yes, Jenny is a real angel. An angel! I wouldn't want anything to happen to our Jenny."

"What could happen to her?"

"She's such a sensitive girl, so feeling about others. She wants to help everyone. I've talked to her often about becoming a nurse or a social worker, but I suppose she won't now."

"Why not?" I couldn't figure out what she was driving at and I was getting alarmed.

"She told me she loves you."

I didn't know what to say. Whatever possessed Jenny to tell her that?

"We will live in Richland and she can go to the university there."

Miss Herkimer looked at me firmly. "And if she has a child?"

"We can postpone that," I said.

"Got it all figured out, haven't you, Mr. James?" Her thin high voice had suddenly taken on a sharp tinge.

"Look, I know you don't know me," I said. "But, believe me when I tell you I love Jenny. I will take care of her."

She moved away from me and looked at me intensely. "You had better, Mr. James. Because if you don't--" She held her severe gaze. "Because if you don't, I will go up there to Richland and--"

"Please, Miss Herkimer! I love Jenny."

"You won't do anything to hurt her?"

"No, no. Why are you saying that?"

Tears brimmed her eyes. "Excuse me," she said. She tugged a tissue from a box and wiped her eyes. "Jenny means that much to you?"

"Everything. What's with you anyway?"

"Never mind, Mr. James, you will find out soon enough."

"Mystery, mystery!"

"I don't wish to alarm you, Mr. James. Jenny asked me not to tell you. But I must, I must."

"All right, so tell me, Miss Herkimer."

"You won't tell Jenny I told you? She's so young. You're older. Twenty-five. Well, you *look* mature enough."

"Please, Miss Herkimer, what is it?"

"You must remember that Ricky and Jenny--they planned to get married. At least Ricky wanted to."

"Yes, yes. I know that. I know all about it. Will you please get to the point?"

She started to cry again. "Oh, if her father and mother knew!" she wailed. "What would they say? And Ricky? He would do anything to stop you from marrying her! Or would he? Well, I don't know. He might react the opposite way, be glad to be rid of her. Oh, Mr. James, you've got to promise. Don't say I told you. Never let on."

"I promise, Miss Herkimer. Only tell me."

"Really, it's not Jenny's fault. I suppose Ricky took advantage of her and she thought she *ought* to love him—I've seen so many cases like hers. The migrant girl, for example, the one I got the hospital bed for."

Suddenly I felt my stomach heave and blood pounding my temples. There was a roar, as of the sea, in my ears as my hands began to shake. I slapped one hand on the other, gripping them tightly.

Miss Herkimer put her hands over her face. She began to sob, uncontrollably now. I grasped her shoulders and my fingers dug in. I shook her so that her head snapped back and she looked up at me with tears streaming down her cheeks.

"Tell me," I shouted. "Tell me!"

"Please! Don't shout. She will hear."

I lowered my voice, continuing to shake her shoulders. "That pregnant migrant woman! There's a connection?" The words seemed to burst from the bottom of my lungs. My mouth was going dry, and I felt my breath coming and going in deep draughts.

"Yes, yes!" She bit out the words. "That's it! That's it! Oh Jenny, poor Jenny."

"She's pregnant?" At last I got it out, and as I said it the vision of Jenny, so noble, so bright, dimmed and went out of focus, but even as the rockets blasted in my brain I saw her tilting her head to mine, and my lips seeking hers, as the grandstand thousands faded away and we were alone together, lost in love.

"Oh, yes. It's true! It's true!" Miss Herkimer's voice came from far away across a fog-bound plain. My arms rocked on her shoulders, slowly and more slowly, and I felt my knees buckling, and then I was kneeling on the floor as my head sank into her capacious lap. My hand slipped from her shoulders to her waist and I grasped her tightly as the tears came. She stroked my hair as I sobbed out my grief, but all she said was: "Poor Jenny! Oh, poor, poor Jenny."

And then it was as it had been when I came home one day from school and slammed up the stairs to my room, not bothering to close the door behind me, and I threw myself onto my bed. My mother entered quietly and came over to the bed, saying "Art, Art, oh, what is it?" And I turned to her and she clasped me to her breasts and I told her, quaking, of a girl named Lillian was moving away and I would not see her anymore, that she was taken from me, all my hope, all my dream, and my mother traced the pattern of my hair with her cool sweet fingers, and she soothed the pain away, but never the longing in my heart.

Now Miss Herkimer said: "But you must be strong, Art. You're all she has now. Don't you see? She needs you. She needs your strength. Marry her, and be a good father to her child. If you love her, you will. Does this make that much difference?"

I raised my head at last and wiped my tears with her nurse's white gown. "But it's Ricky's child, not mine!"

"It's God's child," she said.

"How can you say that? She wants to marry me because she's ashamed. And Ricky--he wouldn't do it, if he knew. And how could I be sure she loves me--now?"

"If Jenny says she loves you, she does."

"And Ricky? Can she love him too, after what he's done to her?"

"What they both did? Oh, I see, that is the problem. She's not the virgin you thought she was?"

"Please, I'm not such a prig."

"Aren't you? Didn't you fall in love with her because of what you thought she was? Once a man felt that way about me until he came to the hospital once and learned how I handled men. He couldn't stand the thought that I knew all about their bodies. How senseless! He jilted me for that."

It was true, I knew then, that the Jenny I adored was the Jenny of the movie screen, the sweet, pious, untrammeled virgin, whose first love was the last, the best. And was I to blame for that? This was the fraud, the joker, the lie to the dream foisted on the prim, the pure. I was the fool, the fooled, the naïve nexus between innocence and sophistication.

"What am I to do?" I asked Miss Herkimer, tasting the salt in my mouth.

She placed her hand under my chin and raised my head. "Marry her," she said. "Marry her while you have the chance."

"And then?" I asked weakly.

"Be her guardian, her lover, the treasure of her life. You saw how cool she was? She is wiser than you. She has accepted herself. You must do the same."

"She told you herself, didn't she?"

"Yes, she said she suspected it."

"Then she wasn't sure?"

"Yes, she was sure. She's missed two periods."

"But the doctor, he hasn't seen her yet."

"Don't think that. The doctor will be here. He will confirm it."

"We can still get married?"

"There is no law against pregnant women getting married! I suppose the law encourages it." She laughed a little, and I did too.

I stood up just in time, for there was a knock on the door. Miss Herkimer released the catch. "Good morning, Doctor," she said. She introduced me. Art is a friend of Jenny's--"

"Of course," he said. He removed his yellow straw hat and burnished his long blond hair. "Mr. James, the Star reporter. We met at the fair. Well, Jenny's friend. Isn't that a coincidence? Is Jenny waiting for me, Miss Herkimer?" He opened the door to his office. "Hello, Jenny."

CHAPTER ELEVEN

Miss Herkimer was sitting at her desk as she idled through a stack of index cards. Only the ticking of a wall clock broke the silence. Why did Jenny have to tell her? What business was it of hers? What strange pride in exhibition did she have to flaunt her condition? Perhaps it was a mean joke on me, but why? In the end, of course, there were no answers, only the questions, chasing one another endlessly, pursuing the truth.

Because there were no answers and there was nothing else to do while waiting, I asked Miss Herkimer if I could use her phone. "Got to call my boss," I said.

"In Richland? That's long distance."

"I'll leave the money."

"Well, in that case."

"Thanks," I said. I reached for the phone and dialed. It took a couple of minutes before the Star's switchboard operator put me through to Johnny. "Art, I'm going through your stuff now. Two questions: Is anybody making a move to oppose the sale of the fairgrounds, and, if so, who?"

"I haven't heard anything," I said. "What sort of move?"

"Legal."

"You mean a court injunction?"

"Seems a natural thing for someone to ask for," Johnny said.

"I'll try to find out. I'm at the courthouse now."

Johnny laughed. "Arrested, huh? Who wants to buy the fairgrounds?"

"Tiber Trucks. Maybe."

Johnny whistled. "I will ask Fred to check it out here. And, by the way, about that Times editorial. Surprising. I'm running it as a sidebar."

"Blanchard got fed up and wrote it on his own. Clark secretly approved."

"That yellow bastard," Johnny said. "Doesn't have the guts. If he wants to save the fair, why doesn't he say so?"

"Because he's a county commissioner and his former wife is married to the bank president, Small, who is a Times director. Small and his wife own a piece of the Times. Mrs. Small is the daughter of the former owner."

"Isn't that nice!" Johnny laughed. "Wouldn't that make a juicy story? What about the insurance deal? Maybe you can put it in tomorrow's story. But be careful, Art. Get it right. Say, do you need a cameraman?"

"You bet. If anything gets to court it will be wide open."

"I'll send Harry down this afternoon," Johnny said.

"Tell him to meet me at the fair office."

I felt a lot better. Funny thing, I was getting to know Johnny better on the phone than in person. Reporters get together a lot, but city editors usually don't mix with them. It preserves the boss-reporter relationship. And, of course, reporters don't chit-chat too much with editors, because they are always too busy doing their job. Of course they talk a lot among themselves. I had to admit that Johnny was getting to be a very nice guy.

Just then Jenny returned. She was wiping her eyes with her fingers. She attempted a faint smile. "Got something in my eyes," she said. Miss Herkimer handed her a tissue.

CHAPTER TWELVE

In the car, parked in the Courthouse parking lot, I asked Jenny "What did the doctor say?"

"I'm fine."

"That's all?"

"That's all."

"That's good."

I gripped the wheel tighter. Jenny was quiet. We opened the front windows. A slight fresh breeze crossed through the car. "I called my city editor," I told her as dryly as I could. I glanced at her. She was looking out the window. She breathed deeply.

"What did he say?"

"I told him that no one has filed for an injunction. That's good news. An injunction would restrain the corporation from selling the fairgrounds. It's a logical move to be taken at this time. If not by the corporation, then someone else. Your father, perhaps."

"He wouldn't go against Mr. Bryson."

"I suppose not," I agreed. I was amazed how calm Jenny was, considering what Doctor Roach must have told her. Miss Herkimer had been so certain.

"Mr. Harding is employed by my father," she said. Another complication. "You see, the Grange sponsors the Chesterton Co-operative Society, of which Mr. Harding is president. He's appointed by the Grange, of which my father is the master. As for Mr. Harding, he's a director of the society and goodness knows what else. He's a member of the Grange too. Neither Mr. Harding nor Mr. Keating could do anything without consulting my father."

"Then who does that leave? Eliminating Ricky's father. I think we can safely say that."

"I agree," Jenny said. "He wouldn't go against Mr. Small."

"That leaves only Clark, publisher of the Times. Except he's under Small's thumb too."

"What about the others?"

I started listing them. "There's Blakemore of the department store, but he's president of the Chamber of Commerce, which puts him on the side of business and the city. Carter is an industrialist and if he voted against Tiber Trucks, and Tiber got in, he would be ostracized forever. No, we can't count on Blakemore, nor Carter. Who's next? Oh, yes, Morris, a lawyer, but he's president of the City Council, so that lets him out. He wouldn't oppose progress for the city. Then there is Denis, a civil engineer. I don't know too much about him. But he's tied up with the bank and real estate, just like all the other commissioners. And that's the list. I think your father is the only hope now."

"Perhaps I should speak to him," Jenny said.

"And I could ask him, as a reporter, whether he contemplated an injunction."

Jenny frowned. "How could my father do it, unless he got Mr. Bryson on his side? If Father did it on his own, or even together with Mr. Harding and Mr. Keating, Mr. Bryson wouldn't like it, to say the least, and there would be an awful row."

"You're right, Jenny. It could split the Xenophon in two." I sighed. This was getting to be too much. "I've got to see Mr. Bryson and Mr. Small again. I hope they will see me today."

"The Grange meets tonight at the fairgrounds. Perhaps you can see Father there."

After I dropped Jenny off at the fairgrounds I turned south, picked up some gas and drove to the Times. Blanchard was there, his thick black pencil scoring copy.

"Anything?" I asked.

"Two letters," he said. "I hit it right on the nose. One letter from Small that came through Clark. Another from a little old lady. At least I think she's a little old lady. It's not signed, so we can't use it."

"You running the one from Small?"

"Since it's only one, we'll run it as a statement in a news story."

"I'm surprised," I said. "You're actually going to run a story?"

"Yeah. Got it finished, Marie?"

"In a minute, Mr. Blanchard." She was seated in front of her typewriter, pounding the keys.

"That's a double-cross," I told Blanchard loud enough that Marie could hear it. "I told you yesterday that I had a story going in today's Star. That was in confidence. I had no idea--"

"That I would have one today too? Neither did I. I'm sorry, Art, but my esteemed publisher, Mr. Clark, insisted upon it. He said we had no choice, since I had run that editorial of mine and you were coming out with the names of the people involved in running the fair. Clark said we had to counter any false impression your story might give."

"But I had the scoop on this!" I protested.

"Too bad." He laughed a little. "Never trust a newsman, especially when he's in his cups."

"You told Clark about it?"

"Sure. What did you expect?"

I could have cut my tongue out. I had thrown to the winds the caution I had shown on Monday. My hope for a scoop had been smashed. "May I see Marie's story?" I asked.

"Of course not. Read it in today's Times, Art."

"How about Mr. Small's letter?"

"Nothing doing. I can't let the Star steal our thunder in our own territory. But, here, you've been so kind, letting me know what you're up to, you can have the letter from the little old lady."

I snatched the letter from him and was about to stamp out when Marie called: "Art, a message for you."

Blanchard kept his eyes on me as I went to Marie's desk. She handed me an envelope with something written on it. She winked at me as I shoved the envelope in my pocket with the letter and stalked out.

A the corner drugstore across the street I phoned Bryson's and Mrs. Bryson told me her husband was at the Amalgamated Properties office.

"Want the phone number?" she asked.

"Let me get a piece of paper," I said. I pulled out the envelope that Marie had given me and spread it on the little counter beneath the pay phone. "Okay," I said. As I wrote down the number my eyes followed a penciled arrow stroked across the envelope and pointing to a name and address in the top left corner labeled *From*. It was a printed sticker. The name was: *Mrs. Andrew Small.*

I had to ask Mrs. Bryson to repeat the phone number, and at last I got it. I took the letter from my pocket and read it:

Dear Mr. Editor:
You asked for a protest about the closing of the fair,
which at this point looks like a forgone conclusion.
The fair is one of our most valuable assets and it
is a shame that something cannot be done to stop
the secret negotiations now going on.
I have attended the fair for so many years, and I
always enjoy the exhibits. Thank you for the editorial.
I hope you get lots of letters. A friend of the fair.

I put another dime in the slot and called the Times, asking for Marie. "I know you won't be able to say very much," I said. "The envelope you gave me. Did the letter to the editor come in that?"

"I just finished my story," she said, "and I do need a cup of coffee. Be out in a minute." She hung up.

I went out to the street and stood on the corner. She came out in a moment and I called to her. We went into the drugstore and sat at the snack counter. Except for a teenage boy sweeping the floor a distance away, we were alone. The boy rushed behind the counter and quickly served us our coffee, then disappeared behind the cash register.

"You guessed it," she said. "I couldn't talk there. Mr. Blanchard would have heard. He will fire me if he finds out."

I promised that I would never tell on her. "When did you find the envelope?"

"Every morning," Marie said, "I come in early and open Mr. Blanchard's mail. I usually throw the envelopes in my waste basket. When I heard that letter regarding the fair didn't have a name on it I searched the envelopes that I had thrown away and found this one. You can tell that the envelope matches the letter. Identical kind of paper. Often happens, people who write letters to the editor don't want their names to be used. Then, out of habit, they put their name and address on the envelope."

"What motive could Mrs. Small have?" I asked.

"She must be opposed to her husband's position. Maybe she wanted to help Mr. Clark. After all, the Times publisher is her former husband."

I laughed. "I sure would like to interview Mrs. Small," I said. "But first I have to interview Sam Bryson again." After Marie left I used the drugstore phone to call him. He told me to come right over.

I walked up Main Street to an office building a block south of the bank. I took the elevator to the fourth floor. Bryson came out of an inside office and greeted me warmly by slapping me on the back. "Thanks for coming," he said with surprising enthusiasm. His office was rather bare, furnished only with a desk, a filing cabinet, a waste basket and a pair of extra chairs where we sat down, facing one another. Bright sunlight flowed through open Venetian blinds. I took out a notebook, poised my pencil and was soon ready to start my second interview with him.

"That was a wonderful story you had in yesterday's Star, Mr. James," he said. "I mean the article about the day *before* the fair."

"There's another one today," I told him. "All about the opening day."

"Great! I'll be sure to read it as soon as I can."

I asked the question I feared to ask: "The Star is also printing another story of mine about the fair. You may not like it."

Bryson grinned and shrugged. "I look forward to seeing it anyway. I'm sure you have been factual. I have every faith in the fairness of the press."

"It's factual enough," I said. "Perhaps too factual. For instance, it lists many of your business affiliations."

I waited for the shock reaction, but his expression of indifference didn't change. "All of them?" he asked calmly. "Well, that would make quite a list. Which ones?"

"The bank, Amalgamated, Farm Service Insurance."

"Is that all? You have missed some. Why those?"

I eyed him closely. "Because I think you are in a position to be of real service to Tiber Trucks."

He didn't bat an eye. "It could be," he said. "Naturally such a large industry will need a bank, and insurance. Also, certain real estate service.

We do hope Tiber Trucks will take advantage of local business--if the vote is favorable to the sale of the fairgrounds."

"I've heard that the sale is inevitable."

"I don't know who told you that, but you have been misled. No one can guarantee a favorable vote."

"You are chairman of a fair corporation committee negotiating with Tiber Trucks?"

"I must say, Mr. James, "you have made real progress in your investigation. You are to be congratulated. Yes, you are a very enterprising young man. I suppose when you talk to so many people it doesn't take long to put all the pieces together. Still, I thought we had covered everybody in asking for silence on this matter."

I wanted to throw him off track, because I had promised the fair manager, Stowe, that I would cover for him. "The Star has checked with Tiber Trucks itself," I said.

"Well, in that case, if Tiber Trucks wants to reveal it."

"Then you confirm it?" I jumped too fast.

"No, no, I don't confirm it. I see, you don't actually have the word from Tiber Trucks yet? In that case I can't say any more about it."

"I understand," I said. "May I ask some strictly ethical questions about the insurance coverage for the fair?"

"By all means let's be ethical. Shoot."

"I notice that insurance is the largest single item in the fair's budget. Isn't that odd?"

"Not at all. The responsibility is awesome. Adequate protection comes high, but we simply must have it."

"I always thought that short-term liability was cheap."

"You only get what you pay for, Mr. James. The fair directors have taken their responsibility seriously. We could get by with less, but each year, with property deterioration, the risk increases."

"So the rates go up?"

"And the amount of coverage needed, to take care of any unforeseen eventuality."

"Farm Service insurance handles that business?"

"Yes, we are the chief broker. But the risk is spread through many companies."

"All local?"

Bryson shook his head. "No, their head offices are all within this state. They have agents in Chesterton."

"Who chooses these companies?"

"As broker, I do. It's all very much a matter of form, the practice. And it's only fair that local agents get the business."

"But the main risk is taken by Farm Service?" I insisted.

"By the company. It has headquarters in Richland. I am the county agent."

"How much insurance?" I asked.

"I don't think I should say. After all, that's done for the corporation. The books are open for inspection."

"I know. At the bank. Could I have a list of the companies that share the risk with you?"

"Really, Mr. James, no. I couldn't reveal that. It's reported to the corporation. You have the total figure. Isn't that enough?"

"Two hundred thousand dollars seems like an awful lot for insurance."

"That's for year-round coverage."

"But the main risk lasts only four days!"

"Oh, much longer than that. Intense preparations for the fair begin about a month before opening. Hundreds of people work at the fair through August. If you compare our coverage with that of other county fairs--"

"I don't think I will need to go that far, Mr. Bryson."

"I hope not. Actually, we carry a minimum amount of coverage. Just four law suits for fifty thousand dollars each would use up the premium money. Just four. In case of disaster the insurance companies could lose a great deal."

"Has there ever been such a disaster?"

"Once, in 1905. A fire burned down two exhibit buildings. Fortunately no one was injured. But someone might have been. The risk is always very much present."

I could see I was getting nowhere, so I changed the subject. "Supposing Amalgamated Properties handled the sale of the fairgrounds, that would mean quite a commission for you, wouldn't it?"

"Yes, it would. But, there again, Amalgamated wouldn't be the only firm involved."

"Who else, then?" I asked.

"Oh, practically all members of the Real Estate Board. It would involve more than the fairgrounds. There would be homes to buy for all executive levels in Tiber Trucks, and tracts of land for housing developments for the employees and their families. Also, perhaps, a downtown office building. Sellers of homes, land and buildings have agents of their own choosing."

"Still, the largest item would be for the fairgrounds itself?"

"Yes, it would."

"Have you set a price?" I asked eagerly.

"No. That's a matter for negotiation."

How much would you say an acre?"

"I really couldn't say," Bryson said. "Land hereabouts runs anywhere from two thousand to sixty-thousand dollars an acre."

"Presuming the maximum, that would be three million dollars or more."

"But you wouldn't be including the cost of the buildings and utilities already there."

Then I would have to guess much higher, Mr. Bryson. Four million?"

"That's a nice round figure."

"And Tiber Trucks would need insurance too?"

"Naturally."

"Then you, personally, would not lose by the sale of the fairgrounds?"

"You mean, on the insurance? I may lose. After all, there's no guarantee Tiber Trucks would take Farm Service insurance rather than stay with the company it already has."

"But if they take Farm Service insurance," I said, keeping up the pressure, "and Amalgamated Properties negotiated the sale of the fairgrounds, you would profit a great deal."

"You are being too specific," he said, speaking tartly for the first time. "Business is business, for profit. I don't see any sense in speculating."

"No," I said, "I think I have enough, thank you."

But Bryson hadn't had enough. "I know what you're after, Mr. James. You're looking for a deal in which I am involved. I assure you I have no commitment from the corporation or from Tiber Trucks that either Farm Service or Amalgamated will be the agents. This is a competitive field, Mr. James. Highly competitive. Why, Mr. Small himself is chairman of

Chesterton Enterprises, another real estate firm. Wouldn't it be logical that he would benefit more than me?"

"Unless there is an agreement to slice up the pie."

"Now you go too far!" Bryson cried. "The lack of public debate on this matter seems to point--"

"Please forgive me," I said.

"--to collusion, Mr. James? That's a serious accusation, very serious. I would suggest, for your own good, that you be careful on that one."

"Mr. Bryson, I'm going to level with you. Someone is opposing this undercover deal. I want to find out if it's you. But all you've told me indicates you favor the sale of the fairgrounds."

He was silent. He sighed and looked out the window. "All the facts aren't in yet, Mr. James. I want to do what is best for the county."

"But as a farmer--"

"Do I have my hand on a plow, Mr. James? You have an image of a farmer as a solitary man who runs his few acres and is independent of everyone. Well, there still is that kind in America, lots of them. But I don't consider myself one of them. I'm a businessman. The Xenophon is just one of my businesses."

"You started off as a farmer!" I exclaimed.

"That's true. And I will never give up the Xenophon until I turn over my share to Ricky, and he will be half owner with Bob Glen."

"Ricky seems to share your ideas about the farming business."

"I brought him up that way. He will do very well. He will make a lot of money."

"That's important, of course."

"Of course not. The preservation of our American way of life is important. Without individual enterprise, without the opportunity for all Americans to make something of themselves, to get a good education, we would lose our identity as a free society. That's why business has to stick together, while competing, so that our cherished rights may be preserved."

I swallowed that without taking a note. "One last question: when does your term as county commissioner expire?"

"In November."

"Will you run for re-election?"

"I'm not ready to announce that yet. Next week, perhaps."

"You mean, depending upon how the vote goes Friday night?"

"Think that if you want to. There are many factors I must consider."

I thanked him for the interview and went down to the street. It was good to feel the day's cool air in my face. It was approaching noon, so I walked quickly up Main Street to the bank and went up to the barrier inside the lobby. I told the vice-president that Mr. Small said I could look at the auditor's report on last year's fair. "Certainly, sir," he said. He opened the gate for me and I followed him to a back room where large volumes in heavy black board covers were filed on shelves. He took down one of them and carried it to the counter. "There you are, sir," he said.

It was such a massive book that I couldn't make any sense of it. "Where do I find the expenditure for insurance?" I asked.

He flipped the pages and pointed a finger toward the open page. There was a whole paragraph filled with legal-sounding language. Opposite the paragraph, in a column of figures, was: $200,000. There was no breakdown.

"Where does it say who got the money?" I asked.

"The report wouldn't say that, sir. This is only an auditing of accounts."

"Where would I find it?"

"In the fair account books, sir."

"And who has those?"

"The fair office, sir. Mr. Stowe."

I thanked him and went out. On the sidewalk it hit me: something I had seen as I turned the pages on expenditures. I raced back into the bank, told the meek vice-president I wanted to see the book again, went ahead of him into the back room and opened the book on the counter.

I turned the pages carefully. I found it. Under *Interest, amortization,* etc was a figure for interest on a mortgage paid to Chesterton Enterprises. The vice-president was behind me now. "What does that mean?" I asked him.

"Just what it says. Chesterton Enterprises holds the mortgage on the fairgrounds. I should say mortgages."

"How much?"

"I don't know, sir. Let's see. The interest last year was forty-five thousand dollars, approximately. At six and a half percent that would be something like seven hundred thousand."

I dashed out again and headed for Small's office. I knocked on the door and opened it. Two men were seated on the couch. They stood up.

"Sorry, Mr. Small," I said. "I wonder if I might see you?"

"Well, I guess we shouldn't keep the press waiting," he said. "That will be all, gentlemen." The two men, whom I took to be bank employees, pushed past me through the door.

"Yes, Mr. James," asked Small, "what can I do for you today?"

CHAPTER THIRTEEN

"Couple of questions," I said.

"Just two?" Small asked.

"Well, maybe several."

"Sit down, Mr. James. Cigar?"

"No, thank you." I sat down heavily on the plump but comfortable leather chair in front of his desk. I was so low down that, although I'm a six-footer, my eyes were on a level with Small's. He puffed contentedly on his cigar and blew the distracting smoke toward me. I choked loudly and deliberately. He apologized and turned his balding head slightly toward the huge office window to his right. It didn't help. "I had a look at the fair auditor's report," I said briskly, "as you suggested in our last interview."

"And?" He drew out the word to its ultimate length, smiling the while. "What did you find?"

"I found out that the fairgrounds is mortgaged."

"Of course," Small said. "To Chesterton Enterprises."

"And the bank is agent?"

"Correct."

"A million dollars!"

"Correct, Mr. James." He blew a dense cloud of smoke, which lingered over his desk. "I told you the fairgrounds wasn't a paying proposition," he said slowly, as if he was a coach explaining the rules of the game to a new recruit. "Yes, the fairgrounds is heavily in debt. Deficits have been made up through bank loans and negotiated through Chesterton Enterprises."

"And the bank donates over forty-five thousand dollars a year to the fairgrounds?"

"Of course not! Whatever gave you that ridiculous notion?"

"The amount of interest that the bank collects."

"That's normal interest on outstanding loans."

"It means *you* own the fairgrounds!" I said.

"Hardly," Small said calmly. "You don't think the bank put up all that money by itself, do you?"

"Then, who does own the fairgrounds?"

"Partially, Farm Services Insurance. Some Amalgamated Properties, others."

"Why don't you sell the stock?" I asked, trying to be sarcastic.

"You mean bonds, don't you? Oh, the county has plenty of bonds outstanding. The bank buys lots of those. And so do the insurance companies. What do you want me to say, Mr. James? That I own the whole county? We hold mortgages, or guarantee mortgages, on hundreds of pieces of property, mostly small tracts, some large. I can assure you that I'm not popular with a lot of farmers, even though I keep them in business."

"When Tiber Trucks buys the fairgrounds, you will receive your money back?"

"I should say not!" He rolled his eyes. "So you have heard about Tiber Trucks? It doesn't matter. You can publish it. You don't think the bank would want to lose that interest, do you?"

"But you will, through the sale, won't you?"

"I see you're no economist, Mr. James. Of course the mortgage will be refinanced. Tiber Trucks wouldn't be expected to pay cash."

"Then you will not only retain the interest, but get something more through refinancing?"

"I hope so," He replied with a satisfied grin. "I trust you are not implying there is something wrong with that."

"It looks to me as if everyone is going to get a cut."

Small puffed deeply on his cigar. "That's business," he said. "Do you think we're in business to lose money? We're in business to make money, Mr. James! Doesn't that sound ridiculous? Really, Mr. James, let's get our premises straight. The bank helps finance practically every business in town. In return, certain businessmen, whose businesses do business with us, sit on the bank's board of directors. And to help them in their business, I sit on a lot of other boards, about a dozen, I think. It's very simple. That's the way we do it in America. We share the wealth, the business brains. That's the way we get along. It's a co-operative effort."

"You also support Farm Services Insurance?"

"Mr. Bryson's agency, yes. Certainly not the state insurance company. I would be only too glad to do so, if I were asked, if we had the resources. But my bank isn't that large, Mr. James. Mr. Bryson renders a wonderful service to farm people. They get insurance at very reasonable rates, because Farm Service is sort of a co-operative itself, a mutual firm."

"But it wouldn't get along without the backing of the bank, could it?"

"I hope not," Small said glibly. "One of our best customers."

"What about Amalgamated properties?"

"Very fine firm, the best."

"It competes with Chesterton Enterprises?" I asked.

"Certainly."

"In what way?"

"Well, say you want to sell a piece of land, you can go to any real estate agent you want to. Your property can be listed with the Real Estate Board, with all the agencies, or you can have it confined to your chosen agency, whichever you wish. If you choose a board listing, the agency you choose gets the primary commission, the board a piece, and the agency that actually sells the property gets a share."

"Co-operation in that too?"

"Realtors have been doing that for a long time. It works for the benefit of both the seller and the buyer."

"What difference does it make if they are competing firms?"

"Ah, the difference is in service to the public," Small said, smiling. "You may have personal confidence in one person, not another. That person you have confidence in, the one you trust, that's the one to go to."

"Then we haven't ruled out personal friendship, or relationship, in business?" I asked. I was serious.

"Not at all," Small said with a proud smile. "That's the American way."

"Just like neighbors doing business over the back fence?"

"Exactly! You got it, Mr. James. "Rightly said! Take my word for it, Mr. James, I will take yours. In the long run, American business is founded on mutual trust and concern for one's fellow man. We take care of one another. There's more real brotherhood in business than you may imagine."

"And the fair?" I asked

"We will do what is best for the county."

"And who's to say what's best?"

Small stubbed out the cigar, for which I was grateful. He settled back in his chair and gazed out the window. I could hear the mild throb of engines and an occasional horn. "What's best? Simple answer: whatever is most profitable. Do you know what the average family income is in Chesterton County? Seventy-five hundred a year! Imagine that. How can a family live on that? We've got to raise the per capita income. People need more just to get along, to make ends meet. They've got to be able to buy better clothes and more food. And think of all those mothers working to help out their husbands. Oh, we give a lot to welfare. But when the economy's not good, it's not their fault. We've got to have a sound economy. That's basic. More jobs. It will help hundreds, thousands. Print that, Mr. James. Tell the people that we are going to have one of the strongest industrial centers in the state, right here in Chesterton County. And the best agriculture too. Chesterton County's going to be on the map. We're on the march!"

He stood up and came around to my side of his desk. He shook my hand and then grasped me by the arm. He guided me to the door. "Mr. James, you are in a wonderful profession. I wish I were a reporter myself. Tell the people the truth, son. Tell them the truth. We're going to help them. We're going to take care of them. Yes, sir!"

I think he shoved me through the door, but I can't be too sure, he did it in such a friendly way.

I hurried back to my hotel room and set my typewriter on the desk. This time my story mentioned Tiber Trucks and fairgrounds insurance policies, because that was public record. I put in various testaments to the county's ambition to grow as a haven for industry and the potential for more jobs. Overall, the story was slanted on the side that favored sale of the fairgrounds. I spotted the story's imbalance and told myself that I would fix it after I covered the Grange meeting that evening. Meanwhile, I had to discover what the Times was publishing. I certainly didn't want Blanchard to scoop me.

Back at the Times newsroom, where Marie was alone, I could feel the floor trembling as, two stories below, solidly on the basement's concrete floor, that day's Times was being printed. Marie showed me a carbon copy of her update story on the fair. It wasn't as long as I thought it would be. Most of it consisted of a brief statement by Small, in which he revealed that the agenda of Friday's fair Board of Directors meeting would deal with an offer by an unnamed industry. What the "offer" was about was not mentioned. There was no reference to a possible sale. Small's statement was a paean of praise for the long and glorious history of the fair and its important role in the life of the county. It stated that the board would welcome the attendance of the public and that any and all questions would be entertained. There was no mention of a corporation meeting.

"Nothing much in this," I commented.

"Mr. Blanchard showed it to Clark," Marie said. "Mr. Clark ordered a lot of censoring, mostly trimming background stuff, mainly facts about the directors, the way they turn themselves into a corporation, changing colors like a chameleon. Mr. Blanchard said everybody knows that, so it wasn't news. Well, I never knew that, and I don't think many other people knew it either."

I agreed with Marie about that. I told her I had phoned Mrs. Small at her home, but there was no answer. "There's a fair diner where she's a helper," Marie told me. "Maybe you could catch her there." Before going to the fair office I toured the fairgrounds again, making notes all the way. A little later, I hoped, I would have time to bang out my feature story destined for Friday's Star.

Upon entering the fair office I thought nobody was there. Unfortunately, Ricky popped up from behind a desk. "Looking for somebody?" he asked with a smirk.

"Not for you," I said.

"They're over at the Grange exhibit. Judging is going on. Today's the day Bob wins his ribbon."

"How do you know he will win?"

"Bob always wins."

"You don't sound very proud of that."

"It's boring, meaningless." Ricky turned a thumb down.

I sat down before a typewriter, an old beat-up Remington, and slid a sheet of paper into it. I was honestly surprised by his cynicism. "Ricky, I don't understand you," I said. "I assumed that the award is for the Xenophon, not only Bob personally."

"Oh, sure it is, but it doesn't improve the farm's sales." He went to a window, gazing at a long line of people at a ticket booth. "Those heavy vegetables Bob exhibits are freaks, the product of tender loving care. They are his babies. Nobody can produce vegetables that size for the market without going broke. The fertilizer cost alone is fantastic."

"Maybe by experimenting he will find a way to reduce costs," I suggested.

"Bob's wasting his time. He should concentrate on higher yield per acre, more plantings per season."

"Well, I don't know much about farming," I said, "but I will cheer him for experimenting."

"What's he trying to do? Win a ribbon, that's all. It doesn't prove anything."

"Ricky, you have a disgusting way of looking at things."

He snickered. "Oh, come now, Mr. Reporter. I thought we were friends. We have a mutual interest."

"Leave Jenny out of this!"

"How can I? She's my girl."

He was itching for a fight. I clenched my hands under the desk. Fortunately, Stowe emerged and beckoned to me to follow him into his office. We settled into chairs on opposite sides of the table. "Great feature story you had yesterday, Art," he said. "You certainly captured the thrill of the fair that a lot of folks experience."

"Thanks, I appreciate that," I said. "I had a good time myself. Seriously, Mr. Stowe, someone told you about my report that's in the Star today."

"Yes, of course," he said calmly. "You mean your first story on the suspected sale of the fairgrounds? We had a long talk yesterday, remember? It was I who told you about Tiber Trucks, off the record."

"I kept it off the record," I said. "So, who tipped you that I had written about Bryson and his business affairs?"

Stowe laughed, a trifle bitterly. "Blanchard told me," he said. "He called me while Clark was meeting with me here. Blanchard talked with Clark about Tiber Trucks for quite a while. That's when I told him about your interest in Bryson's companies. I didn't see any harm in it."

"It got right back to Bryson!" I yelled at Stowe. "When I interviewed Bryson this morning he was tighter than a clam. Ricky must have told him. You told Ricky, didn't you?"

"Yes, I think I mentioned it," Stowe said calmly. "I'm sorry, Art. I didn't realize I was saying something I shouldn't have. They will see it in the Star this afternoon anyway. What difference does it make?"

"It makes a lot of difference, Mr. Stowe. I was trying to get Mr. Bryson to confirm the deal with Tiber Trucks. But he saw through my threats. He might have given it to me off the record if he hadn't known that I had put his pedigree in today's Star. He had his back up."

Stowe looked at me bitterly. His disappointment shaded his normally pleasant appearance. It was my fault. Using the "off the record" tactic in an interview meant, to me, that I wouldn't reveal my source, and also that my source wouldn't tell anybody else that he was my source. I was simply naïve.

"So that's the way you operate, is it?" Stowe said. "Sounds like blackmail to me. Like, you tell me, or else. Did you use that trick on me, Mr. James?"

"No, I didn't," I said. "You are independent of them all."

"Am I? Supposing I told you that I am not independent?"

"But you said--" I could see it coming, but I couldn't believe it.

Stowe stared at me sternly. I know what I told you, Art. You think I never dealt with reporters before? They are always looking for scandals. Whenever anything goes wrong, guess who the press jumps on first? The fair manager! I am sorry, Art, but you had me pegged for a patsy, and I'm not going to be that for anyone, not for Bryson, not for Small, not for Clark, not even for you and the Times or the Star. I'm looking out for Number One: *me*."

"Okay, okay. I made a mistake." I took a moment to catch my breath. I boldly took out my pad and pencil. "I apologize. I assumed too much. Let me play it straight. For background, or for the record, okay?"

"Fair enough, Art. Shoot."

"So they sell the fairgrounds, put you out of a job, and you are still playing on their team?"

"I have to, Art. I will lose my job, that's inevitable. But I have to protect my career. See the difference? You play along with the powers that be. You demonstrate that your loyalty is always with the ones who pay you. The first thing an employer needs proof of is: Are you a team-player? Are you loyal? That above all. When I apply for a management job with the State Fair, and that's what I will do, I need to demonstrate those qualities.

Management skills, or whatever, are required, of course. You can see that, can't you, Art? When I apply for that State Fair job, you know who they will check with first for a reference? Bryson! If he blackballed me I wouldn't get another fair job in the country. No, I'm not going to do anything to make Bryson mad at me." He laughed. "And that's off the record, Art."

I had learned something. I had to admit to myself that I had been off center in interviewing. But I will let that pass for the time being. I needed a lead for my next report. "Thank you, Mr. Stowe," I said. I chuckled. "I know what you mean. After all, my loyalty is to the Star and the publisher who pays me. I will be more careful in the future."

"Okay, Art, what do you want to know today?"

"Why did you tell me about Tiger Trucks, even if it was off record?"

"Because Bryson told me to tell you. And Clark told me the same thing."

"Bryson!" I exclaimed. You mean he wanted publicity about that? And what has Clark got to do with it?"

"You should have figured that out by now," Mr. James. "Bryson and Clark take orders, they don't give them."

"You mean from Small?"

"You said it, Mr. James. I didn't."

All of a sudden, it added up. Small was using me and the Star to get the news out. He knew that a strictly under-the-counter deal could raise the hackles among the farm groups. But a big story wouldn't do, because Tiber Trucks had put the lid on. Only a little leak was needed. It would give Small the excuse for that editorial in the Times, and his public statement today. In this, Bryson and Clark were his toadies. Small had given them permission to tell me so much, and no more than that. That was the reason for the snow job I had been getting about supposed economic benefits to the community and all that blah. And Stowe fitted perfectly into the setup. I had to have a contact who would have a *reason* to reveal the name of Tiber Trucks and set me off on the wrong track. Stowe had a logical reason, so Stowe was chosen to detour me.

"Tomorrow the Star will reveal Tiber Trucks as the buyer," I told Stowe.

"No, it won't," Stowe said quietly. "That would require confirmation from Tiber itself. And they won't give it."

"How can you be sure?"

"How can you be sure of anything I say? Take it or leave it."

"Well, I see now that you're only a tool in Small's hands."

"I follow instructions."

"Bully for you!" I said loudly. "I hope you land a nice State Fair job. I'll go over there and roast you."

"Just try it! By the way, didn't you know that reporters need credentials issued by the fair?"

I looked at him incredulously. "Nobody gave me any."

"You didn't ask for them."

"I asked and got a press pass. What the hell are you trying to prove now?"

"Just that without proper fair credentials you cannot be allowed on the fairgrounds."

"I can buy tickets."

"I suggest you do that," he said.

"Wait until the Star hears about this!"

"Art, get wise. They already have."

"What?"

"Never mind. Write us more features, will you? They're very good."

"I've got an ace up my sleeve, Mr. Stowe."

"Aces won't help you. It's over. We got what we wanted."

"We'll see about that."

On the way out I had the urge to take a swing at Ricky, but a visitor was engaging him in an argument, so I stamped out of the office, slamming the door behind me. Going toward the Agricultural Pavilion to see Jenny I stopped at the diner where Marie had told me I might find Small's wife. I asked a plump woman behind the counter for Mrs. Small and she called to a tall woman behind the grill. She came over, her brilliant smile calming my anxiety. She was a striking beauty with long black hair. Under her white apron she wore a richly embroidered silk dress.

"I'm Art James of the Star," I said. "May I talk with you a minute?"

"I don't know as I should," she said. "You ought to talk to my husband, if it's about the fairgrounds."

"I already have. Twice."

"Oh, I didn't know." Her lashes lowered and I noticed her mascara had run a bit below her eyes.

"I have your letter to the Times," I said boldly as I studied her intently, waiting for her reaction.

"You what!" She grasped the counter tightly. "Can we go somewhere to talk, Mr. James?" She removed her apron, went over to the plump woman, whispered something to her, and lifted the hinged portion of the counter.

"I was on my way to the Agricultural Pavilion, Mrs. Small. It's cool there." She was remarkably calm crossing the space between the crowded midway and the pavilion. She commented upon the deteriorating quality of the sideshows and on the improvement of many exhibits. The coolness of the pavilion was refreshing. It took a moment for my eyes to become adjusted to the gloom. We found an empty bench in a corner between two exhibits. "Now, what's this about a letter?" she asked.

"You wrote a letter to the Times," I said.

"I thought you said you were from the Star?"

She was hedging, and I knew I ought to have done the same, but Stowe's duplicity and the entire conspiracy against me had so jolted my reason that I drew the letter from my pocket and fanned it in her face.

"This letter. See? Addressed to the Times, with your name on the envelope."

It wouldn't have surprised me if she had fainted. I doubt whether I would have stopped her from falling. For all I knew the letter was part of the plot, planted with Marie to catch me off balance, to give me a further false clue as to the nature of the frame-up.

"How did you get that?" she asked, paling. "I thought it would be printed in the Times today. Besides, it was supposed to have been anonymous. What a fool I was to put my name on the envelope!"

"Were you really surprised? How could you make a mistake like that, if you didn't want anyone to know you wrote the letter?"

"A simple mistake," she said, offering me a blank look. "I always put my address label on envelopes. It was a natural mistake. What has all this to do with the Star? Do *you* want to print the letter?"

Her features were composed, completely candid. If she was trying to pull another string to my puppet it did not show. "No, the Star isn't interested in providing a forum for discussion about the fair," I said. "I am interested in why you wrote the letter. Are you really opposed to the sale of the fairgrounds?"

"That's what my letter says, and I mean every word. Do you?"

"Mrs. Small, how I feel is irrelevant."

Several people were passing by, chatting noisily. She waited until they were gone. "I don't understand why the Times didn't print my letter." She absently shook her head.

"The Times prints only signed letters. Not anonymous ones."

"Oh, I didn't know that." She pondered that for a moment. "I don't see why they don't. Our shopping weekly prints anonymous letters all the time. Makes you wonder, doesn't it?"

"Mrs. Small, I want to get at the *why* of this story. You know, of course, that Mr. Small is laying the groundwork for the sale?"

She looked askance at me and shook her head. "I know no such thing! Really, Mr. James, closing the fair would be a great loss to the county and the state. Surely my husband must have told you that."

"Yes, he told me that when I first talked to him, Mrs. Small. He said, I believe, that it would be disastrous. But his attitude today does not seem to bear out that view. Perhaps what might have been a disaster yesterday has turned into a boon today, by what development I don't know."

"I certainly don't want to appear to oppose my husband. I do not oppose him now. But it does seem a shame that something cannot be done to save the fair. If they must sell the fairgrounds, cannot another site be found? Has an investigation been made of that possibility?"

I laughed. "Why, Mrs. Small, you would make a good reporter!"

"Well, I was married to the publisher of the Times!" She grinned. "Oh, Mr. James, can I trust you not to print that?"

"It's irrelevant," I said. Of course I knew it was quite relevant. "No, no one has told me of moving the fair to another site. And if you, Mrs. Small, haven't heard of such an event, then surely it's not been promoted."

I made a mental note to pursue the matter further. "After all," I ventured, "Mr. Small is the key man in this affair."

She looked surprised. "Why do you presume that?" she asked.

"He is chairman of the fair corporation."

"Certainly, Mr. James, but who has the most power in the county?"

"You mean Mr. Clark, because he is publisher of the Times?"

"No, although Mr. Clark does wield considerable influence over public opinion. No, I mean politically."

She was as sharp as any good reporter. I suspected she was using me for her purpose. I was pleased to oblige her. "Daniel Morris, chairman of the county commissioners?"

"Heavens, no!" she exclaimed. "Seymour Denis, the party's county chairman." She paused until the full effect of her words sunk in. "Denis is the man who gets out the votes. He controls the dominant party's local clubs. He's the man you need to talk to, Mr. James."

"Are you saying, Mrs. Small, that the county commissioners are dependent upon Denis for their positions on the county board?"

"Exactly," she said. "Why do these men have power? Because they are in banking, merchandising, insurance, real estate, agriculture, and all the rest? No, because they are commissioners. They control the patronage."

"Mrs. Small, why are you telling me this?"

"I haven't told you anything that is apparent to an intelligent observer, have I?" She smiled slyly, then gave me a knowing wink.

"No, you didn't tell me anything I should have known already. I want to thank you for pointing me in a direction I hadn't yet thought of investigating."

"You will be careful, Mr. James, won't you?"

"You can count on me," I said. "I won't tell anyone it was you."

"And the letter?"

"You can have it." I gave her the letter and envelope.

"Thank you, Mr. James. You are very kind."

"That's the nicest thing anyone has said to me. I mean of those I have interviewed."

"Was this a formal interview? It's never happened to me before. I would appreciate it if you wouldn't mention our, ah, little talk to my husband."

"Nor Mr. Clark, of course."

"Certainly. I wouldn't want him to get hurt."

"How could I hurt *him*?"

"By what you write in the Star. I mean, about my former connection with him, and my husband's association with him in business. That might be misunderstood."

"You need not worry, Mrs. Small. It's all so very personal that it would be impossible to mention it. Besides, what could it possibly have to do with the sale of the fairgrounds?"

"I would rather not say."

"Then it does have a connection?"

"I've been away from my diner too long, Mr. James. Really, I must be getting back. Perhaps we can talk again sometime."

She rose to go. I noticed as I took her proffered hand that it was shaking. She looked hesitatingly down the aisle and appeared relieved, probably because she didn't see anyone who knew her.

As I walked down the aisle and up the stairs that led to the second floor of the Agricultural Pavilion I tried to reason why Mrs. Small had told me what she did, hinting at political control of her husband and Clark. Were they also puppets manipulated by Denis? And what possible political or monetary gain was there for the civil engineer? Then something someone had told me--I recalled later that it had been Blanchard--about an interstate highway coming through the county, running to Richland, rang in my brain. Besides his interest in a real estate firm, was Denis a contractor too? And what connection did the sale of the fairgrounds have with the construction of the proposed expressway?

I reached the second floor and went over to the Juvenile Grange booth. Bob was there with Jenny, talking with a man and a woman, who walked away as I approached.

"I see you're getting some attention," I said.

"Oh, I'm so excited," Jenny said. "They were judges and they commented very favorably on Bob's vegetables, took measurements of them."

"Hope you get a ribbon, Bob," I said.

"It wouldn't be the same if I didn't win something," he replied as he placed a top-heavy turnip on the display. "This will be the last year it will happen if they close the fair."

"I still can't believe it," Jenny said, "that anyone could be so callous."

"More and more I'm convinced it's going to happen," I said. "There doesn't seem to be any way to stop it, no one who will step forth."

"Unless Father does," said Jenny.

"It does seem up to him," I said.

"What are you two talking about?" Bob asked. "How can Father stop it? He's only another member of the corporation."

"No, he's one of three," Jenny said. "Mr. Keating and Mr. Harding would go along with him."

"And Ricky's father too, I'm sure of it," Bob added.

"There's not much hope," replied Jenny. "Mr. Small has Mr. Bryson convinced. And even if Mr. Bryson did vote against the sale, one more vote would be needed to make it a tie."

Suddenly, as she said that, the thought struck me: "Does the chairman vote?" I asked. "He doesn't, does he? Unless there is a tie. And that can't happen with only nine other members of the corporation. Just supposing Clark and Bryson voted with your father and the others, that would make it five to four!"

"It doesn't seem logical," Bob said, "that Mr. Small couldn't vote."

"But it is possible," I told them. "I could ask your father about the corporation rules. And if that's the case, and something turned up that would convince Mr. Bryson and Mr. Clark that it wasn't Small who was pulling the strings, but someone higher up--"

"Higher?" Bob asked. He was eager, expectant.

"Yes, for instance the chairman of the county party organization, Seymour Denis."

Bob shook his head. "I don't follow you, Art. If anyone had the authority to command votes it would be the chairman of the commissioners, Mr. Morris."

Jenny said: "Yes, but the board elects its own chairman, doesn't it? And they elect or re-elect the chairman every three years. So the *permanent* political power is in the hands of the party chairman!"

"Jenny! You would make a terrific reporter," I said. "Of course, that's it! And, guess what? Denis is a civil engineer, right? Then wouldn't it be logical that he would have something to do with where the new interstate highway runs, whether it runs close to the fairgrounds or not? The board would look to him for guidance in making recommendations to the state highway commission. And doesn't the fairgrounds border on county property, even by a narrow road connection? That means the interstate could run right next to the fairgrounds."

"That's simple conjecture," Bob said. "Supposing Denis is involved, even on the verge of making a lot of graft, wouldn't that be hard to connect to the sale of the fairgrounds?"

"Not if Tiber has made it a condition of their purchase," I said. "The company will want some assurance from the county commissioners that they would insist on an interstate route close to the fairgrounds. In fact, there might be an extra bonus for the county if that happened. Any trucking company would want to have access to such a route for quick deliveries. And what about this: supposing Denis promised that Tiber heavy-duty trucks would be used exclusively in his share of the interstate construction. That would be a big payoff."

I knew that I was allowing the conjecturing to run away with me. I was trolling on very thin ice. Bob put his finger on the problem when he said "How can you get information on all of this? You just can't ask Denis if it's true and get an answer."

"I could arrange an interview," I said, "but that wouldn't get us anywhere. I found that out by asking a lot of such insinuating questions in the last couple of days. You're right, I've got to find it in the public records. But whose records? Where?"

"The minutes of the commissioners?" Jenny asked.

"I don't think they would be that careless," I said. "Perhaps the state roads commission, but that would take official probing, and there isn't time for that. Say, how about records of public hearings on federal highway routes? Was one held here? Well, I will have to inquire, I suppose."

"We will help you," Bob said.

Jenny said: "I know some people at the courthouse, some people who might be forbidden to talk to you, Art."

"Will you, Jenny? I'm not sure the Star would print it, but if we turned up something that was only vaguely connected to the fair it might get by."

"They will print it if you write it, won't they?"

"I wish that were true. My editor is very hard-boiled. He prints only what he thinks our readers will like, not necessarily what I like."

"That doesn't seem right," Jenny said. "You could work so hard on a story, and then not have it printed. That must be awful."

"You get used to it," I said.

"I guess there's a lot about newspapers I don't know," Jenny answered.

"Never mind. I will teach you. Are you ready for your first assignment?"

"Yes, chief," Jenny said, giving me a mock salute.

"Are you ready, Bob? I would like you to ask Denis a few questions. I will type out a few for you. No doubt he's gotten the word about me from Small. You could memorize the questions, because it wouldn't do for you to act like a reporter. You do know Mr. Denis, don't you?"

"Yes, I've met him. He's been out to the Xenophon a few times to see Mr. Bryson."

"Good. Now, Jenny, if you could scout the courthouse, find out what you can about highway hearings, anything to do with the new interstate."

"That will be fun," Jenny said. "I feel like a reporter already."

"Be careful," I said. "We don't want anyone to know you're helping the Star, do we?"

"Yes, chief," she said. "You're the editor."

"Is this the way you do it all the time?" Bob said.

"All the time," I told him. "More fun than a barrel of monkeys."

"We say rabbits around here," Jenny said. "You must see the fair's rabbits."

"I will, but right now let's get back to the office."

Only as we approached the pavilion did I remember I was barred from the fair office. "I will write out your questions here, Bob," I said. I didn't want to take time to explain. As we sat on a bench I scribbled the questions on my pad, tore out the sheets and handed them to him.

As we neared the office I saw Stowe with Harry, my cameraman. They were engaged in what looked like an argument, because Stowe was pointing toward the street and I knew he was telling Harry to get off the fairgrounds.

"Just a minute, Harry," I hollered as I waved to him. I went up to the ticket window where Ricky was selling tickets. "Two adults," I said as I passed him the money.

"As you say, sir," Ricky said. He pushed the tickets under the grill.

"Come on in, Harry," I yelled

Harry brushed past Stowe. "What the hell's with that guy?" he asked me "Said I didn't have my credentials. What kind of a hick outfit is this anyway?"

"Tell you about it later," I said. "Right now, take the bastard's picture."

Like all good press cameramen Harry already had a flash attached to his camera. He focused and pressed the button as Stowe stormed through the gate toward the street.

CHAPTER FOURTEEN

I introduced Harry to Jenny and Bob. "Photogenic," Harry said as he watched Jenny swaying her way toward the office. "Do you think she would pose for me? I mean a portrait, nothing else. She's got perfect features. Hey! She's coming back."

Jenny was brandishing a large brown envelope, which she waved in order to hold our attention. She ran swiftly up to us and handed the envelope to me. She was gasping for breath. "Art, this is an essay I wrote. Would you read it for me, please, and let me know what you think of it?" I told her I certainly would. She hastened back to the office.

I spotted Bryson on his way in. "Another of our victims," I said to Harry. We moved toward him. "Could we have a photo of you, Mr. Bryson?" I asked. We went through the gate and posed Bryson against one of the tigers. Bryson gave Harry his warmest smile. Harry promised to send him a print.

"Okay," Harry said. "Bring on the bunnies." We set off at a trot toward the Livestock pavilion. Although he was several years older than me Harry set the pace. I huffed and puffed to keep up with him. He was fairly tall and quite slim, with a dark pock-marked face. His full name was Hermanico Gardemaio.

Certainly the most popular animal exhibit was the one that celebrated the county's reputation as a Mecca for rabbit lovers. A bevy of teenage farm girls had been recruited to attend multiple pens which held, I was told, 175 rabbits, and they were reproducing rapidly. Harry followed along to grab some photos. A breeder named George Faith volunteered to be my guide. Holding a White Satin bunny, he told me: "You start off with two ordinary rabbits, then you breed several generations, achieving a variety of mutations, and pretty soon you have the same breed you started with!" Larry snapped a picture of Faith, bunny and all. I thought that Faith was quite interesting so I pulled out my pad and pencil and started taking notes.

Our guide introduced us to a two-pound Polish and an eighteen-pound Flemish giant. There were pure white New Zealands and flat-footed Alaskan, solid brown Rexes, some Black and Tan (I learned they were almost extinct in the United States until recently), some Checkered Giants.

Mr. Faith said the average life expectancy of a rabbit was only three years, although some may live to be eight or nine. Commercial rabbits have four litters a year, with anywhere from two to twenty offspring in a litter, depending on the breed. New Zealand, California, Himalaya and Giants make the best-selling eating, while the Champayne d'Argent and the short-haired Rex produce the best fur. Not all rabbits have pink eyes. Some have brown eyes and some, like the Beveran, have blue. Mr. Faith showed me an oddity: the Dutch rabbit, half black and half white, the dividing line being in the midsection. It had black ears and black around the eyes, and altogether looked rather sinister.

Harry and I had hot dogs and colas at the Presbyterian Church diner. We took our time lounging at a table while we entertained ourselves by swapping hilarious past assignments. We agreed that the bunny was the most funny.

At the Agricultural Pavilion I interviewed a woman in charge of the flower show. "I guess I walked twenty miles on these concrete floors yesterday," she said. "I was here from eight in the morning until one-thirty a.m." Yet she was back that day to arrange a new show. In the County Health Department booth Doctor Roach, clad in a surgeon's white attire, was answering questions. He smiled at me. "People are very interested in their hearts," he said, indicating a display warning against heart disease. He pointed to the Girl Scouts booth across the aisle. "That little girl, a Brownie, comes over every fifteen minutes to listen to her heart," he said.

I tried the stethoscope on myself but couldn't hear a thing. "That's me," I said. "No heart."

A rather plump woman stepped furtively on the scales. "Am I overweight?" she asked the doctor. As if to answer her questions, a sign flashed on. It warned the woman to watch her weight to save her heart. The doctor spoke a few words of comfort and admonition to her. She waddled away, sadly shaking her head.

Two Brownies were in the Girl Scouts booth. They proudly told me about their troop's handicrafts: dish mats made from rubber can rings, carefully interwoven. The Girl Scouts executive came up and I got a few words from her. Farther down the aisle was the 4-H Club agent, anxiously glancing over the fruit and vegetables on exhibit. Everything must be kept in order, he explained, even as a fairgoer pawed over the entries and a neat pile of apples came tumbling down.

So it went throughout the other buildings: teachers, Home Bureau members, Future Farmers, each giving a little color, a small quote. Harry took their pictures as we went along. As we were leaving the last building the lead for the story popped into my head: *Nice Things About a Fair Is You Meet Such Interesting People.* The story and the pictures filled an entire page in the next Sunday edition of the Star.

Back at the diner, as Harry and I sipped our colas, I took Jenny's story from my pocket. It was four pages long, typed single-spaced. I was amazed by a certain quivering, intense quality of her writing. She started the story off like a stage play, giving staging directions, setting the scene, the lighting, the sound effects, introducing the characters: thirty black migrants from Florida, men, women and children. She described a Tuesday movie night in a potato barn, with the beam of the movie projector stabbing the gloom. Then she told what living a migrant's life was like, no utilities at all, not even an inside toilet. She spoke of *the homesickness in their hearts and the loneliness that preys on their minds* and of the children's excitement over the antics of Abbott and Costello on the screen. She spoke of *the sun-baked fields and the searing noonday sun, forgotten in the hour of delight.* She described the *bleakness of the lamp-lit bunkhouse* and said the migrants were *strangers in an alien and often hostile land, the dispossessed.* She asked these questions: *And where shall they find a home? And where shall they find peace at the end of a backbreaking day? And where shall they find a friend to comfort them in their loneliness?* She spoke of their misery as *a cry going up from the land, with only a few hearing, and fewer caring.* She quoted the mother of a pregnant girl: *I depend on the Lord, for the Lord is good and surely He will see that my child is cared for.* In three sentences she summed up a Sunday service conducted by Pastor Christopher:

The dark people sing and they shout Amen and Jesus Be Praised! as the minister opens the Word of God. And as they go, refreshed and heartened, they know they will work better tomorrow, for the burden of care has been relieved, and they know they bear in common with others the task of the soil. Work is ennobled and the temple of the tender heart is enshrined.

She concluded: *The day must come when the heartache will cease and the bunkhouse give way to cottages, and the black people will come and go in nobility and dignity. Inevitably the day must come, for the hope is there, and the devotion of their white friends is there. The love is there and the love will triumph.*

With a sigh I folded the manuscript and put it back in my pocket. How could I tell Jenny that the Star could not print her essay, for the newspaper is for news and editorials and feature stories, and this was none of those? It was, rather, a petition, a statement of faith, nobly felt and feelingly written, but not the stuff with which news columns are filled.

"Cigarette?" Harry asked, pushing a pack across the little table.

"Thanks," I said. I seldom smoked and never carried cigarettes myself, but I was glad to have one then. I was glad too that Harry wasn't an obsessive talker because I wanted to think about the developments with Stowe. There were still so many missing pieces to this jigsaw puzzle. Despite my previous analysis, and despite my conjectures that led to assigning Jenny and Bob to their investigations, I still wasn't satisfied that I had found the real reasons for my sudden banishment from the fair office. It seemed beyond reason that Johnny would have had anything to do with a plot designed chiefly to make sure the fair directors would save face. The Star's interest would surely be involved, not with the future of the fair, but with the loss of a Richland industry. Still, Chesterton was within our fringe territory. Clark's link through Small with Chesterton's growing industrial economy was surely not sufficient to upset the normally balanced approach of the Star to what was, after all, an ordinary transfer of business from one county to another. Unless--and then I had it.

"Harry!" I cried out, ending his concentration on the passing parade of female beauty.

"What? what?"

"Hate to disturb your ogling, but I want to interview *you.*"

"What's on your mind?" He yawned deeply.

"Not dames," I said firmly. "Listen, you know our publisher, Ewart France?"

"Never met the guy."

"Neither have I. Do you know anything about his business connections?"

"No, only that he's a bear on the street." He meant Richland's financial district.

"Does Tiber Trucks mean anything to you in connection with Mr. France?"

"Tiber Trucks? I've been out there, some feature for financial, took some shots of a new assembly line once. You mean, has France something to do with Tiber? Sorry, I don't know. Why?"

"Tiber Trucks is considering buying the fairgrounds, that's why."

"So?"

"Don't you see? If Mr. France has an interest in Tiber Trucks, that's why I got sent down here."

"No, I don't see. If the publisher himself made this assignment, why have you been barred from the fair office? Me too?"

"The people who operate the fair," I said, "have been under orders from Tiber Trucks, I think, to keep quiet about a deal to sell the fairgrounds. But the fair people know they have an obligation to residents of the county. It's their fair, and they will be mad, to say the least, about this fair being the last one. They couldn't break Tiber's rule, but if some dumb reporter from the Star latched onto the story and got even a hint of it in the Star-- not much, just a vague insinuation--then the local paper, the Times, would have an excuse to report something, maybe only a hint, and the necessity for that would be blamed on the Star. In particular, me. That way they avoid a charge of dirty pool, excusing themselves on the basis that Tiber Trucks made no concrete proposal until the closing night of the fair. That's Friday, two days off. Well, my story is in today's Star and the Times has a story too. They both say virtually the same thing."

"What about your follow-up?" Harry asked. "Are you going to name Tiber Trucks tomorrow?"

"I put it in the story but I asked Johnny to check it out with Tiber. If Mr. France is in on this deal, then the name of Tiber Trucks will be deleted."

"I still don't see why that guy Stowe threw us out."

"You saw Bryson go in there? Stowe didn't want me to overhear anything, didn't want me to be able to barge into his office with any more questions."

"You could still do it," Harry said. "Just because he told you--"

"No, don't you see? It would mean my Star reports. Johnny knew it would be this way. It was all arranged. I can't complain, because Stowe has an excuse, the excuse that my story today was injurious to the fair."

"But it was true!" Harry said.

"He would say I broke a confidence, that he told me things off the record."

"Did he?"

"Yes, he told me about Tiber Trucks. He asked me to keep it off the record. I agreed, and I did. All the rest I got from fair reports and interviews with others. But he could say he told me all that and asked me not to print it. The bastard! He's got me cornered, and I know it."

Harry shook his head in disbelief. "Johnny wouldn't stand for that!"

"I don't blame Johnny," I said, if he was acting under orders himself, passed on through T.D. by Mr. France."

"Art, call Johnny and ask him. You've got to."

"What could Johnny say? You can't expect Johnny to admit it, over the phone."

Harry was messing around with his thatch of black hair. "I've got it!" he exclaimed. "What about France? He must be written up in something."

"Great idea, Harry. I have a friend at the Times. At least I hope she's still my friend. Let's get out of here. My hotel isn't far away."

Harry drove insanely, as always. It was the Star's company car. In my room he headed for the bathroom to shower while I got Marie on the phone. I told her I had a friend from the Star who would like to meet her. She agreed to meet us at our favorite fair diner at five o'clock.

"There's something else." I said. "Could you look up the pedigree of someone for me? Name's France. Ewart France, publisher of the Star."

"Art, are you sure?"

"What do you mean am I sure? I ought to know the name of my own publisher."

Marie laughed. "Silly! I mean, don't you think it's dangerous, messing around with the guy you work for?"

"I know what I'm doing, Marie. I only want to know if France has any connection to Tiber Trucks."

"Okay, it's your funeral." I could hear her mumbling. "Ah, hah. Directors. Yeah, he's not a director. Here it is. He's a consultant, whatever that means, to Tiber Trucks."

"It means the plot thickens. Now who's suppressing what?"

I needed time to think this through. I sat down before my typewriter, started reviewing my notes. I typed for half an hour, writing my feature article for the next day, Thursday. Sometime before I was finished Harry had completed his shower and was now dozing off on my bed. I told him that Marie was overwhelmed by the wonderful news that she was going to meet a real, live, professional news photographer.

"You're full of it, Mr. James. Knowing you, you want to pawn me off on one of those sad-sack newsroom sob sisters."

"Exactly," I said. "For now, I'm going to call Johnny."

Johnny answered promptly. "Art, I'm glad you called. I have a few questions."

I ignored that. "Johnny, what are you trying to do to me?"

"What do you mean, Art?"

"You know darn well what I mean, and I don't care if it cans me. Stowe has ordered Harry and I to stay out of the fair office, says he won't give us credentials."

"What the--who does he think he's working for? The United Nations? Who needs credentials for a county fair? He's getting kinda tony, isn't he? Tell him to go take a jump in the river. And who says you're going to get canned? You're doing a great job."

I knew I was interrupting him, but there wasn't much time. "Johnny, I'm going to level with you. This mess stinks. And I think you know about it and put me right in the middle of it. I just found out that Mr. France is a consultant to Tiber Trucks."

"Sure, I knew that," Johnny said. "What's that got to do with whatever you're talking about?"

"I told you about Tiber Trucks this morning. You could have told me then about Mr. France."

"Art, I was surrounded."

"You aren't surrounded now?"

"No, things are quiet. You think we won't print the name of Tiber Trucks?"

"That's what I think. I wrote it in my story for tomorrow, with a note suggesting you try to get Tiber to confirm it."

"Well, they wouldn't confirm it. I already had someone check. Anyway, you know there's a rule that anything that touches on Mr. France's business interests has to go to him for approval."

"Did Mr. France ask that a reporter be sent here?"

"I don't know, Art. T.D. asked me to make the assignment. He did tell me that Clark clued us on the sale of the fairgrounds."

"Are you out on a limb too?"

"I'm afraid so. Did you see today's Star yet?"

"I'm in the hotel. Should be in the lobby by now."

"Art, we've been double-crossed by Clark. Mr. France is pulling the strings. Just keep it coming, Art. Write it as you see it. I will do my best. The features are great. How about tomorrow?"

"You will have it in an hour. Early tomorrow for the report. I will probably phone it in. And, by the way, Harry took a lot of pix for a Sunday feature, roundup of fair personalities, volunteers and rabbits."

"Good. Is Harry with you? Put him on."

When Harry hung up I asked him: "What did Johnny say?"

"Told me to express my negatives and stick with you."

"Get your own room, Harry."

CHAPTER FIFTEEN

After Harry signed up for a room, we picked up a few copies of the Star in the hotel shop. Harry and I sat down on a pair of comfortable chairs. He was checking sports while I gazed, star-struck by my first Page One byline. It appeared below the headline:

Move Is Hinted to Sell

Chesterton Fairgrounds

Inside was my feature article on the fair's opening day.

The Chesterton Times carried Marie's story on the front page, spread across four columns along the bottom of the page:

Large Industry Said Bidding

To Locate in Chesterton County

There was no subhead, so I had to read the story to get the connection with the fairgrounds.

On the way to the fair I filed my feature story with Western Union and Harry expressed his negatives to Johnny. We returned to the fair diner to wait for Jenny and Bob--and Marie. Harry kept his big press camera handy. I still didn't have a lead for the next day's report. There could be something on either insurance or the interstate highway angles, and I wouldn't get anything on insurance until Johnny checked it out in Richland. Jenny might turn up something on highway hearings. However, I was really counting on the Grange meeting that night.

Harry and I were sitting together at my favorite diner table when I heard my name called. I was dozing, so at first I thought it was Harry. Then I saw the white apron of a man standing over us. "We're waiting for a couple of girls," I said before I looked up.

"You're Mr. James of the Star?" the man asked. I told him I was. He put out his hand and I stood up and carefully took it. "My name is Mark Christopher," he said. "Pastor of Castle Rock Church." He was a tall, dark-haired man of about thirty, quite slim but with strong, lean hands. I would have guessed they were the hands of a farmer rather than those of a clergyman. His eyes were a brilliant blue, deep-set beneath heavy black brows. His cheeks were somewhat sunken, his forehead broad and smooth, his chin square and determined. He was a handsome man with an intense quality about him that I wouldn't describe as exactly spiritual but as calmly introspective.

I introduced him to Harry and invited him to sit with us. He took the chair next to mine. He smiled a lot. "I wanted to meet you," he said, "because Jenny phoned me this morning and told me about you." He pointed to our copy of the Star on the table. "I haven't read it yet," he said. "Do you have another article about the fair?" I nodded. "Wonderful! Excellent writing." That was, of course, music to my ears. His voice was deep and resonant. It was one of the most commanding voices I had ever heard. "Jenny told me she gave you an essay about migrants, and I wondered if I might have a look at it."

"Certainly," I said. I fetched the article from my pocket and gave it to him. He looked it over quickly. "What do you think of it, Mr. James? I think she has the makings of an excellent writer."

"I agree with you, Pastor, but it's not the kind of article the Star would use. Not much news in it. Quite literary."

"I presumed that. We have a Presbyterian monthly magazine. I will speak to Jenny about it."

"Then why don't you take the article? I haven't told Jenny yet, but I will. She should be along soon. Her brother too."

"Two of my finest young people. When she was in high school Jenny was president of the Young People's Society. Since she's been in college, of course, that doesn't leave much time for church. Doesn't she love the fair though?"

"Too bad this may be the last fair," I ventured, just to change the subject.

"It's a shame, really. But I suppose there's nothing that ordinary folk can do about it."

"How about the clergy?"

"Do I hear a tinge of prejudice, Mr. James? We can counsel and guide, but our role is not to become involved in politics." He laughed, a touch of cynicism. "How can anyone not become involved? An impossible choice. Religion and politics have always been mixed."

"Then you view this debate as based on politics?"

"Certainly. People I know say it's economics, but I disagree. I might go so far as to say it is a religious issue."

"Religious? How so?"

"The county party in power promised to provide more jobs. It must carry out that promise before November elections, only two months from now. The fairgrounds must be sacrificed for a political promise to be kept."

"Can't the churches do anything?" I asked.

"What is a church? A religious institution to which members of other institutions belong, members of the Grange, Farm Service, Home Bureau, P.T.A. and all the rest. They don't consider the future of the fair an issue that concerns the church."

"Isn't there a religious issue involved?"

"You mean destruction of spiritual values? Certainly. The worship of materialism leads to that. The fair has been drifting in that direction for a long time. Besides the midway, what do people really want to see when they go to the fair? The new cars mostly, the latest tractors, the newest TVs. The pitchman with the cabbage shredder or the vegetable juice blender draws the most attention."

"Still, here you are," I said. "If you will pardon me for saying it, your appearance today is symbolic. Here you are in a waiter's apron helping to run a church diner for profit."

"It's true," Pastor Christopher said. "We are adding to the image of the church as another commercial organization. It's not right, but I didn't start it. My church had a concession at the fair for goodness knows how many years. It's a tradition that the pastor takes his day at the diner. So here I am, as you said, a walking symbol of all that is wrong with the church and society. If the fair goes, then at least I won't have to be a bus boy next year."

"Then you don't care what happens to the fair?"

"Not to this year's fair. I think we can live without a midway, without the stock car races, without the concessions, without the selling. I would keep the agricultural and handicraft exhibits, and the displays of various nonprofit organizations. The rest we can do without. Well, I do like the rides and rodeo."

Just then I saw Jenny, Bob, and Harry approaching. Marie led the way. She was carrying a stack of newspapers, which she dumped on the table. "We've all read them," she said.

"I see you have met my pastor," Jenny said. She introduced him to Marie and Harry.

Pastor Christopher told Jenny that I had given him her essay. "Mr. James and I don't think it will be suitable for the Star. However, I would like to send it to our Presbyterian magazine. It is a fine piece of writing. Of course I can't guarantee it will be used. I will write the editor a letter and tell him about you." He looked around the diner. "Good heavens! Look how many people are waiting to be served. I've got to get back to work. Call me when you're ready to order."

I told Marie that Harry was eagerly waiting for her to conduct him on a tour. She suggested they take in the stock car races.

"Anybody ever get killed?" Harry asked brightly as he shouldered his camera.

"What a morbid sense of humor," Marie said. "Sorry, Harry. Sometimes they only get injured. Be sure your camera is ready."

When they had gone I turned to Jenny and Bob. "What did you think of my story?" I asked.

They agreed that mine was okay, and better than Marie's in the Times. "Your story isn't what I thought it would be," Jenny said. "I am disappointed."

Bob frowned. "Listing the business connections of my father and Mr. Bryson and the others, that praises them as solid citizens, which they are."

"I certainly intended more than that," I replied.

"The story praises them as wise community leaders, worthy and important," Jenny said.

"Do you really think that's the way people will read it?"

Bob said, "I think so. I had the same impression as Jenny."

"Are you talking about the story I wrote," I asked. I picked up the Star and glanced through my Page One story. It was as I feared. My implication of collusion had been edited out. Where I had used *involved* to show the cross-loyalties of the fair board directors, the story said they had *contributed* to the business life of the county by *serving* various enterprises. The specific connections were still there, but the cutting edge of the story, its total meaning, had been blunted, my slant destroyed. It had been given this other slant by a copy editor, probably on orders from T.D., the managing editor.

"That's not quite the way I wrote it," I said. "The facts are still there, but the story praises rather than condemns."

"You intended to condemn?" Jenny said with alarm.

"No, not to condemn, only to show that these men have divided loyalties, so much so that no clear debate on the issue is possible. But the point has been clouded now."

"Maybe you can do something with what I found out," Bob said. "I went to Mr. Denis' office and we talked about the interstate. I asked him how the new highway would effect the Xenophon. He told me the route would be to the west of Chesterton, not the east, and I got out of him that it would run very close to the fairgrounds, how close I don't know."

"What about Tiber Trucks?" I asked.

"I didn't mention the name, as that might have given my game away. But I did find out that he is involved with Chesterton Construction Corporation, exactly how I don't know, and that this corporation has done some road work in the county. He talked like he knew a great deal about expressway construction, because he told me about minimum widths of media strips, about how wide the right-of-way would be, and about the procedures that would be followed to acquire land."

"Not much doubt he's got a foot in the door," Jenny said. "He testified at the public hearings on the interstate route. Mr. Morris let me see a copy of the hearing record. I used the same excuse that Bob did."

This was better than I had expected. "You said you got this from Daniel Morris, the chairman of the county commissioners, himself?"

"Himself. He was very co-operative," Jenny said. "He spoke of some legal work his firm, Morris and Sachs, was doing for Mr. Denis, in connection with the interstate. I had picked up a copy of the Times at the Courthouse newsstand, so I showed it to him and asked him about the sale of the fairgrounds. He said there was a lot of legal work to be done, but he indicated the way was clear for the corporation to make the sale, as long as the commissioners approved. He didn't say that he himself was doing the work, but he knew so much about the problems that I am sure he is involved."

"It all adds up," I said. "Denis gets a big construction contract to build the segment of the interstate through Chesterton County. Morris does the legal work not only for expropriation of the land needed for the highway, but also for the sale of the fairgrounds. Both of them will make a mint. And if Tiber Trucks is pressing for an expressway route next to the fairgrounds, then they are working together. What about the hearings, Jenny?"

"The state highway commissioners heard representatives of practically every group in the county. Some wanted the interstate on the east side of the city, some on the west. My father wanted the road between the Xenophon and the city, but Mr. Bryson wanted it to run just west of the city, near the fairgrounds. So it went."

This was getting quite interesting. "What about Small and Clark? What did you find out?"

"I didn't see their names," Jenny said. "But Mr. Blakemore represented the Chamber of Commerce, Mr. Denis the party, Mr. Carter as an interested industrialist. They all wanted a west-side route."

"Would you say," I asked, "that there were more speakers who advocated the west-side route than the east side?"

"Yes, I think so."

"Then that's it!" I said firmly. "If the state highway commission abides by the majority, the interstate will be built near the fairgrounds and Tiber Trucks will have won."

"There wasn't any mention of the fairgrounds, and none of Tiber Trucks either," Jenny said.

"I presumed that," I told her. "Any mention of either would have brought the proposed sale into the open, and the county groups didn't want that. Perhaps if your father had mentioned it, Jenny, the commission would have had some questions of its own."

Bob said: "The commission might have had some pressure from Tiber Trucks."

"That's true," I said, "especially since Tiber Trucks has the Star's backing."

"The Star!" Bob cried out. "You mean the Star is taking sides?"

I told them about Mr. France and why I had been assigned to write the story that had given the fair corporation the excuse to fly the kite statement in the Times.

"That's awful," Jenny said. "You can't trust anyone."

"Not a soul," I said, "except ourselves. We three, we are the youth of the nation. Well, you two are, being taken on a merry-go-round ride by the previous generation. They have got it rigged so we can't get off. We are riding on their backs, to their tune. If you want to get off you have to jump off, and risk being smashed. I am fed up to here."

We said goodnight to Pastor Christopher, who was behind the service counter, his hands deep in suds. Bob returned to the fair office. Jenny and I hastened through the fairgrounds to the grandstand. There weren't any ticket takers around so we were able to go beneath the stands to the fence next to the track. Some current-model cars were roaring around the curves, throwing up huge clouds of dust. A car with black numerals painted on the doors passed us. As the dust cloud settled I saw Harry on the track, approaching the middle. There he squatted, camera at the level. I presumed he snapped the shutter as a racer gunned down on him. He leaped aside just in time. The crowd roared its acclaim. He saw us as he ambled across the racetrack, swinging his camera and smiling through a cloud of exhaust fumes.

"How's that for action?" he called out. He came up to the fence and leaned on it.

"They should put you on the payroll," I said. "You're more entertaining than the drivers. Who in the world allowed you out there?"

"Nobody," Harry said. "I climbed the fence. Oh, oh, here comes trouble."

A burly man in gray-blue coveralls came up to the fence on Harry's side. "You trying to get yourself killed?" he yelled so loudly that we could hear what he said above the thunder of passing race cars.

"Risk of the profession," Harry said.

"Go on, get behind the fence," the man ordered. "I catch you on the track again I'll call the cops. You crazy newspaper guys!" He swore softly and hustled away. Jenny and I hauled Harry over the fence.

"That guy's got a nerve," Harry said. "That picture is going to make me famous."

"Who is he?" I asked.

"Run's the show. Dawson's Daredevil Drivers. He's Dawson."

I had been with Harry on too many jobs to say anything more. One time, at a fire, he climbed a telephone pole to get a better angle of a burned woman being wheeled toward an ambulance. The way he hung there by his legs, holding the camera with both hands, pointing it toward the ground, it make me feel sick. His photo made Page One and got Harry a Press Club award for the best spot news photo of the year. I've often wondered if that's why he does it, or if it was that self-destructive instinct that the psychologists talk about. As far as I was concerned, Harry was a real hero. I wouldn't have the guts to do it myself.

Marie came up behind us. "Did you see that nut?" Marie yelled above the tumult of the roaring cars. "We were sitting up there," she said, pointing to the grandstand benches. "All of a sudden Harry gets up, not saying a word, runs down the stairs, leaps the fence and crosses the track to the grassy side, with all hell tearing toward him."

"They were all going one way," Harry said.

"One way, he says," Marie bellowed. "A hundred miles an hour!"

"Nah, they don't drive that fast," Harry said.

Suddenly there was a roar from the crowd and we turned to see everyone stand up, their faces pointed toward the south end of the track. We heard the whine of metal on metal and through the rising dust made out a car caroming off the fence. It skidded across the track into the path of two approaching cars, which turned to the right to get by. The smashed car, out of control, even as we saw the front wheels turning madly, tilted slowly upward on the left-side wheels, then over, over again, and again, and finally rocked to a stop on the green, all four wheels solidly on the ground. From center field an ambulance screamed to the scene, but before it reached the spot the door of the broken car opened and the driver, all in white with a white crash helmet, stepped out. The crowd stamped and whistled as the driver unbuckled a chin strap and waved his helmet in greeting. The ambulance stopped beside him and we could see the car driver speaking to a man in the ambulance's cab. The car driver waved again to the crowd, still on its feet, got into the car, gunned the motor and speeded onto the track to resume the race.

"How about that?" Harry exclaimed. "Now there's a guy can really take it. I wouldn't change places with him for a million dollars!"

Marie and Harry took off together, hand in hand.

"Alone at last," Jenny said. "Let's get out of here. I'm getting deaf."

As we were walking toward the main gate I saw a woman who looked familiar entering the fair office. Isn't that Miss Herkimer?" I asked Jenny.

"Yes it is," she said. "I wonder what she wants."

We picked up the Buick and drove to the hotel. We were seated inside a booth in the dining room when Marie and Harry came in.

Marie was grinning at us. "How are my favorite lovebirds?" she asked." Jenny continued to examine the menu.

"Marie, please," I said. "I've only known Jenny for forty-eight hours!"

Marie covered her lips and leaned toward us. "When's the wedding?" she whispered.

I managed a choking laugh. "Marie! Marie! Stop the kidding, please."

"I know, I know, it's a secret. Okay, I won't tell anyone. Just tell me it's not so. Remember, I'm a reporter. I cover court news for the Times. I saw you two going into the courthouse."

"O my God!" Jenny cried. "I was visiting the county nurse, Miss Herkimer."

"No one else knows," Marie said, "unless you told somebody. I certainly won't. Please, Jenny, tell Art he can trust me. You know he can. Art, Marie and I have been friends for a long time. We were in the same classes at college."

"Marie," I said. "I insisted we visit Miss Herkimer to complain about the camp's sanitary condition. That's all."

Jenny was fidgeting with her table napkin. A waiter came over but we told him we weren't ready. "Marie, I pray you didn't say anything about this to Bob."

"Sorry, I did. Bob knew that Ricky was suspicious. And, of course, Bob wondered how come you two were such good pals." She laughed lightly. "Bob's a sweet boy. Whatever happens, he's on your side, Jenny."

"I must talk to Bob," Jenny said. "I don't want him to tell our parents, not even tell them I've been spending a lot of time with Art."

"That's just the point, Jenny," Marie said. "Bob is worried about what your folks will say, how they will feel. It's not that they have been mean to you or anything. They will understand that you want to escape the pressure being put upon you by Ricky. Maybe even pressure by your parents and Ricky's parents too."

"Leave my parents out of this, Marie. They will get over it."

"So you couldn't go home right now and tell them?" Marie persisted. "You don't have the courage to break it off with Ricky? How do you think your parents will feel, you telling them, Oh, by the way, I've got a new boyfriend? Your mother, especially, is very sensitive. Well, it's none of my business, of course, but I think you two are going to hurt an awful lot of people."

"I don't care!" Jenny cried. "I just don't care!"

CHAPTER SIXTEEN

Harry arrived. "I'm in," he said. "Nice hotel, nice room of my own. Come with me, Marie. These two want to be left alone." They found a table on the other side of the dining room.

"There was a stubby candle on our table. I motioned to a nearby waiter who promptly lit the candle and took our order. A warm orange glow flooded our booth. I reached across the table and took Jenny's smooth hand. "Jenny, you look beautiful."

"Thank you," she said. "You're a rather handsome fellow yourself."

"Let's celebrate," I said. "Don't tell me it's your birthday!"

"No, it's our fiftieth anniversary. We've known each other for fifty hours."

"That long? Oh my. Is that all? Only two days. So much has happened."

"Everything has happened--and nothing," I said. I couldn't stop gazing at her. Jenny was beauty incarnate. The beginning and the end. Perfection. Our days are like that, I thought. At the end of the day at work we come home and someone asks: What happened today? And we say: nothing happened, nothing at all. And yet everything has happened. We have talked to many people, influenced many lives. Our lives will never be the same again, nor will theirs. Yet we walk through life, unknowing. We see enough, but we do not care. We hear enough, but we do not understand.

"Oh, Art, it's like I've known you forever. You have been a part of my life. Once when I was very small I received a story record for Christmas. It was Sleeping Beauty. As I listened to it alone in my room, it was I who was there in eternal sleep. And it was I whom Prince Charming awoke. It was I whom he carried away on his great white charger."

"And I shall carry you off, in my great blue Buick."

"Yes, to your castle, Art. And every day, at the newspaper, you will fight valiantly against evil, conquering all with your courage and your wit."

"Jenny, I am not that courageous. Right now I am scared. I have never been in a situation like this."

It was true. I did not understand the world I lived in, with its constant threats of war. I did not understand Richland and what was the meaning of my life there as a reporter. I did not understand Chesterton and its complicated, ordered world. Where did I fit into all this? Did I fit in at all?

"It is a world we did not create," Jenny said. "We were born during one war and we were still children in another. All our lives there have been wars and rumors of wars. And what do we have to look forward to?" Two years of Army service, I thought, in a faraway place called Vietnam, and come back distraught, to pick up and reframe the pieces of my career. Would I be a reporter, an observer, all my life?

"I want to have a career of my own," Jenny said. "What can I teach? That this is the best of all possible worlds? Hardly. That world disappeared before I was born. No, I want to write, like you do, Art. I want to tell the world, so the world will know, about the cruelties we practice on one another, about the terrible poverty there is."

But this was well known. Had I not tramped the slums of Richland? Had she not seen the same in a migrant camp? Not only those, the crossroad villages where people eke out a living from an acre, the people in the hills where no one hardly ever goes.

"We can go to church at Castle Rock," Jenny said. "You don't know me until you have seen it. You don't know me until you go up a dirt road from there and see a family in a rotting shack."

I will go, and will I know you truly then? No, not even then. Years and years from now I won't know you, and you won't know me. All our lives we live within the shell of self, not wanting to be known, our thoughts our own, our tongues telling tidbits of the truth. But surely that is not enough, Jenny. I want to know you, all of you. To possess you. Be careful! Jenny is never yours to possess. She will always be Jenny Glen. Did I know myself so well? I wished I knew who I was, what I am. Once I was so sure, but not now. You see, I have been toyed with. I have been treated like a puppet, manipulated.

"Aren't we always treated so by others?" Jenny asked.

True, that is our way of life. We are under the rule, of our parents, of our teachers, of those we work for, our commanders. Ours but to obey, not to question. Why can't we question? Are they so right? Are they God? Are we tools to be treated so? No, but we are instruments of production. We are needed now, not so much for our hands or our spirits, but for our brains. We have been to the moon, and that required millions of us, working together, feeding information to computers. We are the dot, the digit in the scheme. Yes, life is a mirror maze, but we are not expected to find our own way out. Our course is planned for us. We are tested, analyzed, rated. We are scored, systematized, psychoanalyzed, counseled. Finally the experts tell us what to do, even find the job for us, the slot, where we fit in. They say we will be happiest doing that for which we are best fitted, as if we were made by hands.

"I can't stand that," Jenny said. "I won't be pushed around! No one is going to tell me what to do."

How can we avoid being pushed around if we want to get ahead? That's the way things are. The maze has been built, you see. We are fed into it. Until we reach the goal all exits are mirage. We stumble against the image of what we think we are, when we are really akin to animals in a testing labyrinth, forced to find the one way out, and then forever to race through the learned path, day by day, until the world's features blur and we go on blindly until death overtakes us.

"Well, it's not for me," Jenny said. "I will not be caught in such a game. I will make my own life. Let others serve the organizations. I will not be a cog in another's wheel."

Nor will I, although I am now. I thought I was free in journalism to be my own man, to seek my own truth, but it has come to naught. Even writing can be tailored to fit the current mode. We are not free, you see, to do what pleases us. Our protests are dismissed as adolescent, even while the world pays tribute to youth as its hope.

"What is there to hope for?" Jenny asked. "What a mess we are inheriting. An organized, structured mess."

And yet we are expected to burrow in, to correct deficiencies from the inside, for outside criticism is scorned. Insiders say: What does he know about it? He never had the problem of profit. And that is what's the matter: must everything make money? We must earn enough to live on. We must earn our daily bread. By the sweat of our brow. The laborer is worthy of his hire.

"What about the migrants?" Jenny asked. "That's exploited labor."

Isn't all involuntary labor an exploitation of the spirit? Does my pay buy me? No. I cannot be bought. I am not for sale. I loan my labor, my intelligence, and receive a living allowance in return.

"I will not be patronized," Jenny said. "The world does not owe me a living."

Really? Doesn't it? We did not make this world. Our parents, their parents, and their parents did. Having made us, requiring us to live and work in this world, let them support us.

"Our children must have our care, our home," Jenny said. She tugged my hand. "Where are you, Art? Why don't you answer me? Have you nothing to say? What's come over you?"

I jerked myself upright. "Nothing, I said. "Here comes our food."

We ate in silence for a while and once I caught Jenny looking at me furtively, a question in her eyes. I wanted her to ask me. I wanted to give her the chance to ask, to hint that I knew, but I too was afraid. If she told me, would she then be ashamed, in dread I would not marry her?

We engaged in empty anticipation of whatever action the Grange would take. Jenny laughed gaily as we joked about Harry's hair-raising adventure. We finished our food rapidly. I lingered too long. "Can we go now?" she prodded, more than once. However, as soon as we were in the Buick she cuddled close to me, but she said nothing more.

I found a parking place near the fairgrounds. Ricky was taking a turn at one of the ticket windows. Jenny said "If you say Art needs a ticket I will hate you forever. Give him a press pass." She must have cut him down with her fire, because he handed the orange card to me without comment.

"Do you think your father is here yet, Jenny?" I asked. "I would like to talk to him."

"Perhaps. There's a meeting hall at one end of the agricultural building, on the second floor. That's where the Grange will gather. Father is probably there. I must go to the office to count this afternoon's receipts. See you later."

She left me and I hustled though the crowds to the Agricultural Pavilion, mounted the stairs to the second floor. A sign was posted on the hall door: *Chesterton Pomona*. I knocked and opened the door. Jenny's father was with a small group of men standing on a podium across the rear wall. Folding chairs were set in neat rows the width of the brightly-lit room. I walked down a side aisle. Glen waved to me and descended a step to greet me.

"Good to see you again, Mr. James," he said. "And thanks for your stories in the Star. That one about opening day was terrific. Everyone I've talked to has said how much they enjoyed it." He spoke in measured lowered tones. So far, I hadn't met anyone at the fair who was more likeable than Jenny's father. "As for the Grange meeting tonight," he said. "I'm afraid we never allow reporters to attend."

"I know, you told me," I replied. "But just as an interested individual could I sit through it? I promise not to report a thing. You could tell me afterward what you want reported, and I will report that only. You and Jenny and Bob have told me so much about the Grange."

"I am sorry, Mr. James. I would be censured if I permitted it. There's nothing personal in it. The Pomona permits no one except members to attend our meetings. If I broke that rule now--"

"I understand," I said. "If you have a few minutes, could I ask you a question? I had some interesting comments today by Mr. Bryson and Mrs. Small. By the way, where did the name *Pomona* come from?"

"The ancient Roman goddess of gardens and fruit trees." We went to the back of the room and sat down on adjoining chairs. "You say you talked with Mr. Bryson and Mrs. Small?"

"The issue is the farmers against big business, isn't it?"

"Come now, Mr. James, you know better than that. I read your story in the Star today."

"Perhaps I should have said the co-operatives against big business."

"But the co-operatives *are* big business. They do lots of business every year in the United States. The difference is in ownership and profit sharing. Anyone can be an owner, and all owners share in the profits."

"A stock company is the same, isn't it?"

"Yes, but in the co-op the owners have a vote in the management. No matter whether you have one share or a hundred you have only one vote. In a stock company, the more shares you own the more votes."

"Still, the co-ops compete," I said.

"Certainly. Our main Co-op stores used to be Grange stores. We sell to anybody, of course, but only members share the profits. The more a member buys, the greater the profit. We have our co-operative associations and work with one another. That's our way of doing business."

"The more industry in the county, with more workers and more buying power, would greatly benefit the co-ops?"

"Of course. Not only that. The farmers would benefit because there would be a larger outlet for their products."

"The Xenophon would benefit?" I asked.

"You persist in asking the obvious, Mr. James. Naturally my farm would benefit. We sell a great deal to the co-ops. What's your point?" He kept looking up anxiously as more Grange leaders gathered on the podium.

I plunged on. "And you buy supplies from the wholesale co-ops?"

"Yes. But this is elementary. What are you driving at?"

"Apart from ownership and profit-sharing, there's not much difference between the co-ops and competing businesses?"

"There is a great deal of difference in philosophy. Besides, co-ops offer educational services."

"I understand that," I said. "You have co-ops for insurance, hospital care, burial, electricity, telephones, loans. What does all this mean for the fair?"

"You mean about how the farm groups vote? I may get some guidance on that tonight, from the members of the Grange, I mean. I can say this: we do not like the closing of the fair. We must think in larger terms, of the economic benefits to the community as a whole. If a compromise can be worked out, if agricultural and other exhibits could be continued--"

"A fair in miniature?" I suggested.

"--it would preserve the principal elements, the main features, of the fair, the reason for the fair's existence. Once there was no other place at which the big manufacturers of farm machinery could display their products, but now they have big stores where they are on view year-round. We have them in Chesterton County. As for livestock and food, the best place to see them would be in their natural setting, on a farm."

"Such as the Xenophon," I suggested.

"Exactly. Think of the space we have! Behind my house, where we went Monday night, there's room enough there."

"Will you make a proposal to the fair board?" I asked.

"I may, if it comes to that," he said.

"There isn't much hope for the fair, as is, then?"

"I wouldn't say that. We have two more days before the vote. I have consulted with Mr. Keating and Mr. Harding."

"And Mr. Denis?"

"Denis? What has he got to do with it?"

"The interstate," I said.

"That's a lost cause. I wanted it to go near the Xenophon."

"To bring people to your private fair?"

"Not private," he said. "It would be sponsored by the farm groups."

"Including Farm Service?"

"Probably."

As we talked the hall was filling with people. A young couple sat down beside us, depriving us of our privacy. "Time for me to get up front, Mr. James," Glen said.

Outside the hall I observed the Grange members file in. Perhaps I expected to see farmers in torn overalls, women in frumpy gowns, but they looked no different than folks attending a city parent-teachers meeting. They were young and old, and I am sure that some of the men were in businesses other than farming. Two men who looked like advertising men (gray flannel suits) stopped outside the door.

"Lorne," one of them said. "I tell you, if you say that--"

"Why shouldn't I, Len?" the other asked. "It's a free country."

Lorne and Len: Harding and Keating. I stepped toward them. "Excuse me, gentlemen," I said meekly, "My name is James, reporter for the Star. You are Mr. Harding--Mr. Keating? I am interested in knowing your views on the closing of the fair."

"Read your story today, Mr. James," Keating said. "I think I should feel slighted, Mr. Harding too."

"I didn't intend--"

"That's alright," Keating said. "We know you were concentrating your praise on the commissioners, and we appreciate that, but you made it look as if farm representatives are small potatoes compared to city big-shots."

"Except for Mr. Bryson," I ventured.

"Of course, Mr. James. You gave him a lot of space. What I mean is, you had connections listed for everyone except Mr. Harding and me."

"I would be happy to correct the error tomorrow."

"Would you?" Keating pleaded. "You might state that, besides FGA I am also associated with the Grange, that I am a state director of Farm Service, went to our state university, and also that in my spare time I run a thousand-acre farm, with the finest potatoes that are larger than those of the Xenophon. I have the finest herd of Herefords in the state. Maybe you saw my blue ribbon in the livestock pavilion?"

I had been making notes and then Harding started in: "You got me right about the Co-op. But how about my farm, and the fact that I am a thirty-second degree Mason, I used to be a county commissioner, and that I am on the board of Carter Manufacturing Company."

He rattled on but I stopped taking it all down and waited for him to finish. "Gentlemen," I said, "I think you miss the point. I did not put in the various business connections of the others to pay them a compliment."

Keating said: "It certainly showed they are important men. I'm not going to deny they have a lot more money than we have. But Mr. Glen, Mr. Harding and I also have our connections. Is it fair to give them all the publicity and leave us out?"

"I wasn't trying to give them publicity," I protested. I hope the way I spoke revealed my consternation. Did they seriously believe I was beating the drum in praise of a bunch of greedy men bent on destroying an annual event that took a hundred years to mature into a public treasure?

"If it isn't a publicity stunt," Keating said, "what do you call it? Ah, I see your game, Mr. James. You are really for the closing of the fair and you wanted to show what fine men they are, the ones who are going to wield the hatchet! Do you call that honest journalism? That's the trouble with newspapers today, they only give one side."

"I was trying to help," I said. But help who? By paying attention to the individuals involved, their backgrounds, their leadership qualifications, their achievements, was I really glorifying them, creating heroes?

"Sure, you were trying to help *them*, that was obvious."

"No, no. I am trying to help *you*!"

"Us? You mean the farm groups?" Keating asked. "Then why didn't you give us credit for being just as sharp in business as the city guys? We're not such dolts!"

They strode away from me and went into the hall. Before the door closed, I could see them shaking their proud heads in dismay. They were still chatting together as they sat down in the back row. The door closed.

I was driving back to the hotel when it struck me: the very group I attempted to please was the most displeased. It taught me a lesson that I have not forgotten: however many *newsworthy* connections a reporter has, chances are he will defend them. The more such connections, the more prominent he considers himself. I was never more mistaken in thinking that the publicity I had given the business interests of Bryson and Small and the others would discredit them. All I had succeeded in doing was to picture them as solid, responsible men. After all, they had the public's trust because of their business success.

In my room I wrote the story about the rabbits, and the other about the volunteer workers, dashed off some caption material, put them in an envelope and addressed it to Johnny. At the mailbox outside the hotel I noted that I was just in time for the final pickup of the evening. It still left me without a follow-up story on the sale issue and I began to feel a bit shaky about that, because that was what I had been sent to cover. And, now that I knew the Star's publisher, Mr. France, was on the side of Tiber Trucks, how could I write anything that would indicate that anyone had the slightest regret, the remotest sign of grief, over the passing of the fair?

It came to me, then, as I was driving through the dark streets to the fair, that I was monitoring the death of a beloved aspect of our national life. But, like mourners around a death-bed of a beloved grandmother, we were sorry to see her go, but, after all, she was old, time had passed her by, she no longer made a contribution to our progress, and it was better this way, by far, that her death not be lingering, that her suffering be brief. Our hearts would be heavy, our sense of loss sincere, but, after all, nobody expected her to live forever.

CHAPTER SEVENTEEN

Grange members were streaming from the hall when I got there. I had to wait for almost all of them to leave before I could get in. Jenny and Bob were at the front of the hall with their father. Obviously they must have arrived at the hall after I had left. They were deep in discussion, standing before a small table on which a lectern had been placed.

"What happened?" I said, asking all of them.

"Quite a discussion," Glen said. "Mr. James, you may be proud of the fact that everyone had something favorable to say about your articles in the Star."

"I hope they weren't too upset that I slighted the farm groups."

"Not that story, the other one about the fair's opening day."

"That was only a feature, a human interest story," I said.

Glen praised me by patting my shoulder. "Whatever you call them, your feature articles have created quite a stir. You should have heard the compliments!"

"That's right, Art," Jenny said. "They praised you, saying you had summed it up, why the fair had to be saved, that they wouldn't stand for the fair being scuttled."

I couldn't believe it. "You mean they *liked* my feature stories?" I said.

Bob said: "No one mentioned the Page One report, nor the one in the Times, not even yesterday's Times editorial. As far as the Grange is concerned your day-by-day stories ought to save the fair."

"That's very flattering," I said. "What did the Grange decide?"

"I got my marching orders," Glen said. "I was told to vote no to the closing of the fair."

"What about Mr. Keating and Mr. Harding?"

"They will go along with me."

"You still won't have enough votes," I said.

"Yes, we will."

I shrugged. "Who will join you? Mr. Bryson?"

"Maybe," Glen said. "If he will go along with a plan I outlined to make the fair bigger and better. But why don't we all go back to the Xenophon? I'm dead tired. I would rather be on a tractor all day than stand up two hours at one of those meetings."

Jenny went with me, Bob with his father. "What's it all mean, Jenny?" I asked as I turned the Buick onto the road to Castle Rock. I opened the front windows. We breathed gratefully as the cool evening air swept across us. Far to the east a brilliant full moon was rising.

"Everyone was talking at once," she said. "Almost all were against the closing of the fair. At one time there were five resolutions and amendments on the floor. Father had to bang the gavel almost constantly to keep order."

"They were angry then?" I asked, laughing. "Lucky that Mr. Small and Mr. Bryson weren't there."

"As a matter of fact," Jenny said, "the Pomona had nothing but praise for them and the other fair directors."

"Praise! How could they? With the directors ready to steal the fairgrounds from under their noses?"

"I said the directors, because father promised that the directors would vote to keep the fair."

"How could he promise that? He doesn't have enough votes."

"But he does. The Grange has seven votes, the FGA five, the Co-op nine, Farm Service six. Together these four have more votes than the other six directors."

"So the directors will vote to hold the fair next year? Your father suggested the Xenophon as a site. You mean--"

"Yes! Yes! That was Father's plan. But he wants to tell you about it himself. It's rather complicated, but I think he's talked it over with Mr. Bryson, and perhaps the other groups."

I turned into the driveway before the Glen house. I helped Jenny out and we stopped a moment on the porch. Jenny looked even more beautiful in the moonlight. I wasted no time in embracing her.

"No, not here," she said. "Father will be along with Bob any minute."

"How many children would you like to have, Jenny?"

"Six, I think," she answered quietly, looking shyly at me.

"Six!"

"Not enough?"

"More than enough."

"Well, how about four?"

"That seems more moderate."

"Art, I would like to have a child right away."

I was about to say I knew she was pregnant, but there wasn't enough time. But when? "That's fine with me," I said.

"Could we? Oh, that would be wonderful!"

Despite her warning I bent and kissed her. She pushed me back as the lights of Glen's car lit up the driveway. We went into the parlor to wait for them. Jenny's mother was sitting near the fireplace. She rose to greet us. "I have coffee on," she said. "I thought you would need it after the meeting." She retired to the kitchen, where she was soon joined by Jenny. Bob yawned a few times and was excused. He retired by a stairway to the second floor. Glen invited me to join him in the parlor, where he stretched out on the sofa while I settled into a matching chair opposite him. I acknowledged that it was getting late, but I needed a few more facts.

"After tonight, Art, I have a better understanding of your craft. I want you to know I admire your patience with us. Incidentally, it is because you asked me all those questions that I have been able to clarify in my own mind not only where I should stand in this conflict, and it is a conflict, but also the means by which the fair can be saved. I am grateful to you for your patience."

Jenny and her mother brought us coffee and some sweet snacks, which she placed on the coffee table between us. Jenny asked for permission to remain for my interview. Her mother reminded her husband that he had better not stay up too late. "You have a lot to do tomorrow," she said. She kissed Jenny goodnight, told me, in a motherly way, to take care of myself too, and was gone.

"Ah, it's good to relax, Art," Glen said. He removed his jacket and tie. He passed me a plate of chocolate chip cookies and a cup of coffee. "I'm ready when you are, Art."

"Jenny told me about your idea of having the fair on the Xenophon next year," I said.

"The Grange Pomona was enthusiastic about that, Art."

"Does that mean the Grange is resigned to the probability that the fairgrounds will be sold?"

"I'm afraid so. But then, you see, I told them about the annual deficits, and about how much it is costing every Grange family in terms of patronage support, so they saw very clearly that the fairgrounds was a white elephant."

"I heard that term used recently in connection with Richland's Union Station," I said. "The station is a work of art, or at least it was until the inside was plastered with neon signs and billboards."

Glen sighed. "My father told me that when he was young the fair was an orderly, quiet place where you could drift through the exhibit halls without being accosted by screaming barkers. The fairgrounds was more like a park, with trees and benches and lots of grass. It isn't like that anymore, is it? Our best picnic area was taken over by an expanded midway. However, that is one thing we could offer on the Xenophon, lots of trees and grass. Just think of it, being able to see the cattle wandering in fields instead of chained in stinking stalls, flowers growing in beautiful gardens, instead of in vases, tomatoes on vines, apples on trees, their natural setting. My plan is to offer small plots of land, where our kids, the Future Farms and Juvenile Grangers, could transplant what they have already grown on their own farms. Think of the revolution in show procedures: whole trees, whole plants, would be judged. What's the value of forced-growth tomatoes, for instance, if the process that produces them kills the plant, depletes the soil. The emphasis should be on production for the market, not on freaks."

Jenny said: "It makes sense. That's what Ricky says. I couldn't see it before, but I do now, the way you explain it, Father. Your plan has all sorts of possibilities, like demonstrations of a plow actually plowing, of a planter planting. This would be a show that would draw thousands from hundreds of miles around. And think of the commercial possibilities." I thought she was being sarcastic, but she was serious. "As it is, we have to leave hundreds of acres on the Xenophon lay idle every year because of government or market restrictions on what we can grow. Of course we have to leave some fields seasonally fallow, but we can do it. We can do it! We can hire lots more migrants to care for exhibit areas, from spring through fall. Oh, the wonderful things we can do!"

Was this the Jenny I wanted to wed? Her father had been looking at Jenny more than me. Now he focused on her completely, almost as if I wasn't there. "The Xenophon," he said, "has the support of Farm Service, the Grange, the FGA and the Co-op. Their members include almost every farmer in the county. And since these groups are the dominant sponsors of the fair they will vote for the Xenophon out of loyalty to us. Besides, the Xenophon is ideally located. It's close to Chesterton, and the interstate highway will link other counties. Think how quickly Richland people could get here!"

"Isn't it exciting?" Jenny asked as she gleefully clapped her hands. "Who needs the fairgrounds?"

"It seems I've been writing about something that nobody wants to save," I ventured reluctantly.

"But you have helped save the fair itself," Jenny said. "After all, that's what's important."

"I suppose," I said, addressing her father, "that you will be announcing your plan tomorrow?"

"Art, I will have to check it out with Mr. Bryson. This is confidential, right?" I nodded. "It may be best to hold off announcing anything until the corporation acts Friday night. We've had an ad-hoc committee working on this idea for some time, Mr. James."

"You have?" Jenny said. "I didn't know that!"

"Sorry, Jenny," her father said. "You can see why we had to keep it secret. To tell you the truth, I wasn't sure what the response of the Grange would be."

"The Grange wasn't opposed to the sale of the fairgrounds?" I asked.

"Not after I told them about the possibility of a thousand new jobs for the county, hundreds of new families to be fed. They saw that meant prosperity for Chesterton."

"So they can have both bread and circus," I said.

"What?"

"Nothing. Will there be a midway?"

Jenny said: "Oh, we've got to have a midway."

"That's something that will have to be investigated," her father said. "If it is financially possible, there's no reason why the Bates Shows couldn't set up here."

"You mean if it is profitable," I said.

"We would have to cover expenses, especially if it meant taking several fields out of production."

"What about the exhibit buildings?"

"That's where the big expense of the present fair comes in. No, I think we'd have everything out-of-doors as much as possible. A few tents, some sheltering tarpaulins, nothing permanent. But this is speculation, I'm sure the details can be ironed out. The main thing is: we have the support of the farm groups for the continuation of the fair, and that means they won't fight the sale of the fairgrounds."

"Then you weren't opposed to the sale yourself?"

"How could I have been? Mr. Bryson is my partner. We need his support for the continuation of the fair."

"Does he favor having the fair here on the Xenophon?"

"On certain conditions."

"And they are?"

"That satisfactory payments from the farm organizations can be worked out, to compensate for any loss of revenue on Xenophon land that is taken out of production. Also, the fairgrounds land here will be owned solely, and managed by, the Xenophon Corporation."

"That means the Bryson and Glen families?"

"Yes," he said. "There would be no need for a fair corporation."

"And the fair directors would vote as now. The larger the group membership, the more votes?"

"Exactly," Glen said. "That will assure the management of the fair staying in the hands of the farm groups, where it belongs."

"Still, the use of the land, what exhibits are permitted, does that power remain in the hands of the Xenophon Corporation?"

"Yes, of course." Glen smiled.

"And you will need insurance, lots and lots of insurance?"

"Mr. James," he said, "I don't get your point--"

"My point is," I said, "that the farm groups will have to pay heavily for insurance."

"Mr. Bryson is an expert on that," Glen said. "I'm sure he could give you details. Think of the possibilities! The Xenophon will be the most famous farm in four counties, maybe the entire state!"

"Ricky will like that," Jenny said.

It was time to leave. I thanked Jenny's father for the interview.

I lingered on the porch, gazing at star clusters when Jenny joined me. "We've had so little time together," I said.

Saturday will come soon enough," she said as I held her closely.

"Will it ever?" I asked. "I am beginning to doubt it. It seems so far away, so lost in time. These past two days, they seem unreal. Perhaps it's because I feel so far away from home."

"But you live alone," she said.

"I mean Richland. I miss the Star newsroom."

The past few days had dawned in dreams, merged in memory, somehow unreal.

"You lead a lonely life," Jenny said.

I had to ask her. "Jenny, will you miss the Xenophon?"

"Dreadfully."

"You think you can take it?

"I want to get away. For good, I mean. I want to get on with my life. I want to be a writer. I want to get away from Ricky. Oh, Art! I want to go to Richland University. I want to get a degree in literature. I will go to campus every day, then I will come home, cook supper, and be with you. This was meant to happen. Oh, Art, I do love you. You are so good to me!" She put her arms around my neck, held me close, and kissed me, unheeding that the parlor light exposed us--if anyone was looking. There was a murmur of voices beyond window curtains. My eyes were closed as I tried to imagine the time, only three days away, when Jenny could come with me to Richland and there we would begin a life together.

I felt a gentle tap on my shoulder. I thought it was Jenny's hand, but the tap was repeated. I lifted my head and opened my eyes, then took a step back as Ricky grasped me by the arm and pulled me from her. I raised my other arm, too late to ward off the blow. Ricky's fist must have caught me on the chin. I felt myself tumbling backward over the porch rail and falling through a bush, and then the blackness and the nothingness of sleep.

THE FOURTH DAY

A SECRET OF SHAME

No Affair Like a County Fair, You Say as You Try It Again This Year As Usual

By Arthur James
Special to the Star

There's no business like show business, they say, and there's no affair like a county fair.

Ask anybody around town at the beginning of another Wednesday workday what they see in the fair and you'll probably get a wide yawn, a vacant stare and one raised eyebrow which says more explicitly than words: "I don't ask questions. I just enjoy it."

For nobody knows why county fairs are what they are. Nobody knows how they began or why they continue the way they do. Might as well ask why we eat sitting up and not, as may be more sensible, in a reclining position like some Arabs.

It's just so, that's all. You can't fight tradition and custom. And county fairs are notorious for fostering tradition in perpetuity.

For all their flamboyancy and emphasis on the latest in thrill-providers, the county fairs are as hide-bound to tradition, as fast sticklers to custom, as unchangeable and as unchanging as the Mount Washington inclined railway.

Take Chesterton County's current fair for instance. Before we could read we were screeching under the dark canopy of the caterpillar ride. The Ferris wheel is a more standardized institution for fairs than the prize bull. The mirror-maze and the Fun House with its air jets were as familiar to grandfather in his childhood as they are to today's small fry fairgoers.

Though you've been to the fair every year since you can remember, you still look forward to it. Though you say, while nursing your corns, "Never again!" you know that next year you'll be back again pounding the midway.

And that's because you know what to expect. You want to recapture the thrill of your first fair, but you know it'll never be quite the same. So you bring the kids and, vicariously, you get the thrill as they do.

Because in America the fair is every child's privilege. It may be hard on the pocket book, but at least it's democratic. You don't have to go on those stomach-twirling machines. You don't have to meander through the dark passages of the Fun House--and think while you're doing it that you can get the same thing free anytime in your cellar.

You don't have to let the man guess your weight--and you think surely this year he'll never see those extra five pounds. You don't have to display publicly the fact that your muscles have lost something of their timbre as you pound down a mallet in an effort to ring the bell.

You don't have to do any of these things--but you do them because you've always done them. It's your annual fling, and while you say you'll not make such a fool of yourself next year, you know you'll be there. You know, while you're telling yourself there's nothing in it, that you'll get your fortune told and will try your luck at tossing rings, balls and darts.

All these things you do, not because everyone else is doing them, but because it's all part of the American way of life. No one is fooled by the ballyhoo and the extravagant claims of "It's guaranteed to make you laugh or your money back!" or "A prize every time." It's just that a little bit of tomfoolery every year never hurt anyone, and maybe the psychologists have something when they say there's a little bit of childishness in us all that needs expression.

This year you'll go home early, you say, and stagger home at 2 a.m. For the fair has a fascination that won't let you go. It's another world come to town. It's a chance to see a slice of life that's not always apparent in the workaday world. In fact, the fair is a cross-section of life itself, from people at their most freakish to people at their most daring.

Even as you watch the motorcyclists dash around their huge tub, or the daredevil drivers tilt on two wheels, you say: "That's not as dangerous as it looks." But you wouldn't try it yourself. So you imagine that's you down there on the motorcycle or that's you, topped by a helmet, in the multicolored car. And you go home feeling you've done something exciting.

You tell yourself there's nothing at the fair exhibit buildings you can't see in a department store anytime, but you don't miss a thing. You tell yourself that "the world's largest collection of wild animals under canvas" is rather moth-eaten, but still you go in and deposit, for you, a good donation on your way out.

Crowds raise your allergy hackles, and you think you'll never get in another, but once in you meet so many folks it's like old home week and a chance to be folksy and glib with remarks of derision, scorn and cynicism. But you know you aren't fooling anybody, because you're there, aren't you, and the foolish always like company.

At the fair you leave good sense behind, suspending for several hours all your faculties for reasoned action. Impulsively you say: "Let's try this ride," the while secretly hoping the last hot dog will stay down. Rashly you respond to the barker's cry that this will positively be the last show at matinee prices, the while you know he'll be saying the same thing an hour from now.

You know it's hokum, it's brash and it's cheap. But so is a large slice of life. So you get it over with and leave the pangs of remorse for tomorrow.

It's a chance to forget your phobias and your prejudices, to unload yourself of empty desires. You think you'll have a lot of fun and you do-- with reservations. For all the time you're seeking surcease from boredom, you think that just around the corner will be something that will really interest you and make you forget your tired legs and your aching head.

After it's all over, you realize that the fun has been in mingling with the crowd, in showing your will power by resisting the strident pleas of the barker, in your human disdain for it all. You realize that without a crowd a midway would be like a department store just after closing--lots of attractions but no atmosphere encouraging you to buy. It would be like a Bob Hope joke in an empty theater.

But why does the fair never change? Why always the same old chair-planes, why the same old sword-swallower, why the same old grandstand jokes? To these questions there is never any one answer--but the answer that comes when you're home from the fair, your eyes blurred with seeing and your ears deaf with hearing, when you know that there's never been and never will be anything quite like a county fair.

It may be hurly-burly and hokum, but it's also husky and wholesome.

CHAPTER EIGHTEEN

In the fiery light of dawn I opened my eyes. Overhead mad shadows scudded on the shadowed ceiling, seeking exit. There was no pattern to their shapes, no form to their slow-motioned movement. I turned my head toward the open window. A lacy curtain billowed like a sail in a balmy breeze. Suddenly I heard a door open. The curtains were sucked around the pane.

"Art! You're awake!" It was Jenny's soft voice. I turned toward the sound and for the first time realized I was not in my hotel room. "How do you feel?" Jenny asked as she swayed toward me, bright gown dancing.

"How am I supposed to feel?" I said, even as I felt a clubbing pain in my head.

"Injured," she said. "You had a bad fall."

"Is that what happened? I know Ricky hit me. Then what?"

"He ran away. I yelled for Father and he and Bob picked you up and carried you up here."

"This is Bob's room?" I asked, noting the gold and silver trophies in a bookcase.

"Bob loaned you his pajamas." I raised my arm. The pajamas were white with blue polka dots.

"Where did Bob sleep?"

"In the parlor, on the sofa. Are you hungry?"

"I don't know. I think so. I could use a cup of coffee."

"Don't go way. I will be right back."

I shifted my feet to the floor, staggered up and put on my clothes, which had been left on a chair. I opened the door and went down the hall to the bathroom, grateful that the door was open so I could tell which room it was. On the way I clung to a railing overlooking the stairwell.

Back in Bob's room I went to the window and raised the sash, breathed deeply of the pure refreshing country air, moist with the sweet odor of sunflower and Rose of Sharon. It was a perfect morning, the sun reflecting off the meadow beyond the barn, for the room was at the back of the house. I could hear birds chirping in the flaming trees behind the barn. Through the open barn doors Jenny's father appeared. I heard a screen door slam. Jenny's footsteps sounded on the stairs and I turned as she entered the room. She carried a tray with a cup of steaming coffee and a plate of toast. She set the tray on a small desk next to Bob's trophy case. I sat down on the bed. She sat down beside me.

"I'm sorry I look such a mess," I said, raising the coffee to my lips. It scalded my tongue. I felt my face. "I need a shave," I said.

"You can use Bob's," Jenny said. She went over to a walnut bureau opposite the bed and opened a drawer. "Yes, here it is." She took out an electric razor.

"Sit here, Jenny," I said, motioning to the bed. "Some things I need to know." She sat beside me and folded her hands on her lap. A bolt of sunshine suddenly lit the room, flecking her hair with gold.

"You ask so many questions!" she said nervously.

"It's my training, my profession."

"But you seldom argue."

"Also my profession. I take all answers at their face value. It's not my role to argue."

"Still, you must have opinions of your own."

"Doesn't everyone? I do my best to suppress mine."

"Why should you? Everyone has a right to their opinions."

"I'm a reporter. Since my job is to report the opinion of others, I'm not supposed to have any of my own. It's easier that way."

"Easier than what? To make up your own mind? I respect a person who knows their own opinions and sticks to them."

"Don't you respect me?" I mumbled as I bit my toast.

"Of course I do, Art. I didn't mean--"

"I know. You think a reporter is a sponge, soaking up other's knowledge. But isn't that important? Someone has to do it. I'm the means by which others communicate their ideas, their views, to the public. It's my function, an important one."

"I didn't mean to deny that," Jenny said. "But is it enough? Surely you must want to express your own thoughts."

"Oh, I do, I do. Sometimes I want to do that so much I can hardly restrain myself. Someday I will have that chance, to write for myself, I mean."

"You mean to be an independent writer?"

"I wasn't sure until now," I said. "It was last night that did it. The real meaning of what is happening in Chesterton County this week cannot be reported. The actual story that explains this shift in values is not in the bare events, it lies in history. We are observing the climax of historical events, the result of changes going on in our society that cause what is happening as inevitable."

"Including your landing in the bush?" She smiled and laughed, and I did the same, remembering. She had that way of puncturing my most profound balloons.

"Ridiculous, wasn't it? The cocksure reporter being given his just reward. Did you laugh, Jenny?"

"No, Art, I did not laugh. What a thing to say! I screamed at Ricky and rushed at him to hold him back, because he went toward the steps, intending to punish you more where you fell. I cried out for Father. Ricky took off down the driveway, down to his car. Then I went to you, and there you were, flat on your back, unconscious. You can rest here today, if you like."

"I'm fine," I said. "I have to write a report for today's Star, soon as possible."

"Stay here, Art. Rest. Let me feel your forehead."

"No, let me hold you." We laid down together.

"Only three more days, Art." For a while there was no more sun, no more birds chirping in the trees, no more pain throbbing in my head.

"Your whiskers scratch," she said at last.

"I will shave here," I said as I got up. "See you downstairs?"

"Don't be long." She went out and closed the door behind her. I plugged the razor cord into a wall outlet and looked at myself in a mirror above the bureau. My eyes were shot with red, my face haggard, my hair shaggy. Compared to Ricky's, my face was ugly. Where his was tanned and smooth, mine was scored and blotched. I leaned closer to the mirror, opened wide my red-veined eyes. "Very pretty," I said aloud. "Tough guy." Was I merely a convenient father for Jenny's child? And what of Ricky, obviously the real father? Were things so bad between Jenny and Ricky that she could not tell him? And would he not be forced to marry her, if her father knew? Would a shotgun marriage be so bad? And did Ricky already know? This last question seared the most. After all, wouldn't Ricky suspect? Had there been that one encounter only? My gentle Jenny, sullied by a childhood partner? Was it this that Ricky hinted at, that, at the last moment, knowing what I knew, I would not have her, because she bore with her always a part of him? And, hating him, could I bear it, having that part of him there between us? Was Ricky counting on this, and was that why he had struck me, not so much to punish me as to make me hate him more, and thus that part of him that Jenny had? And, hating what she carried, would I, at last, hate the carrier? She had come to me so easily. To me, no prize. Had she come as eagerly to him? Desolated by this inquisition of myself, I descended to the kitchen. I was greeted by Glen and his wife. I joined them at the table. Bob had gone to the fair and Jenny was in the barnyard talking to George, their farmhand.

"I don't know what came over Ricky to do a thing like that," Glen said.

"We had an argument at the fair," I told them. "We disagreed quite thoroughly about his ideas for the Xenophon."

"Why should you be concerned about the farm?" Glen asked.

"I meant the commercializing of farming."

"Farming is commercial."

"I agree with your point of view, that farming is a way of life. Ricky can't see that."

"It's a moot point. Still, I don't see why he should have been so angry."

"Will you be talking to Mr. Bryson soon?" I asked, getting anxious about my story.

"Going to see him now. Please accept my apology for what happened, Mr. James. I will tell Mr. Bryson about it."

"Please don't," I implored him. "Not now. Not yet."

"Yes, of course. I agree. Today is not a good day to bring that up. I'm sure that Ricky's father will take care of his son."

After Glen left I asked his wife if I could use her phone. I assured her that the call would be collect. I went to the parlor to use an extension phone.

"Art," Johnny said. "Where's your story?"

"Haven't got a lead yet. May have one soon."

"Want to give the dash matter now?"

"In a minute."

"Anything on insurance?"

I looked at my notes. "Farm Service here says that coverage of the fair was adequate," I said. "Refused to give details, says it's private business. How about the interstate?"

"No luck," Johnny said. "They aren't ready to reveal the route."

"Then I guess this lead will have to do," I said, "until I confirm it after I've talked with Bryson. Farm groups here are backing a move to hold the fair next year on a farm called Xenophon."

"The what?"

"Xenophon." I spelled it out. "It's a Greek word meaning--"

"I know what it means," Johnny growled. "Better give it to rewrite. Is that all?"

"Got my feature for today?"

"Yes, Art. Don't worry. Byline as usual. Hold for rewrite."

Frank Lawton came on the line. I heard his typewriter clacking away as I gave him the story. He could type faster than I could compose it in my head. I put in some dope on the Grange meeting, the possible effect of the hoped-for interstate route, and the fact that agreement on the Xenophon as a site for next year's fair would clear the last obstacle to the sale of the fairgrounds to a large Richland industry. I asked Frank to mark the story *Hold for confirmation.*

Jenny was in the kitchen with her mother when I returned. "I still have a few things to do around the farm," Jenny said. "Want to come along?" We went out the back door into the barnyard. We followed a worn path to the open barn doors. "Cows are in the fields," she said. "Hold your nose. I have to go in and take a look around. Oh darn, George hasn't hosed it down yet. We will go in later. You can see almost everything there is to see from here. There are forty stalls, but only thirty cows right now. Look up there. See the loft. Soon it will be filled with hay. Enough to last the winter.

Here's George now." He was wearing knee-high rubber boots. He entered from the barnyard via a smaller side entrance. He picked up the spraying end of a wide black hose and dragged it toward the deep concrete gutter that framed the rear ends of the stalls. He turned a knob and gunned a roaring stream into the gutter, blasting a river of rushing water full of cow dung all the way to the other side of the barn, where the deluge vanished into an iron pit.

"Let's go see the meadow," Jenny said. We went through a windbreak of tall poplars and turned left along the edge of the meadow, hugging a barbed-wire fence where the clover was cut low. High up an incline toward a ridge I glimpsed a receding herd of Ayreshires, their white faces pointed west.

In the slanting morning shadows of the trees we turned to one another with one intent. Jenny interlaced her fingers with mine and pressed my palm three times. "That's my secret code," she said. "It means: I--love--you." I squeezed back.

She stumbled in a gopher hole and I held her up. From the stubble, black butterflies, sun-fringed, fled our fearsome feet and grumpy grasshoppers hopped aside. We stopped at a sandy spot and, stooping, watched anxious ants scattering to store supplies in secret shelters.

Farther on we bent beneath barbed barriers and turned north toward an oak grove where already the crisp copper leaves were on the ground. On a fallen stump we sat for a moment listening to the cricket's cry. A robin warbled from on high. Before us the land lay fallow, drenched in dusty goldenrod, blond with bleached straw.

Stiff with walking, stifled by the heavy air, we crossed the hill's crest and stepped on stones across a creek. Along the banks the alder catkins shed their flowers and the willows wept above the sweeping stream. We stopped on the soggy shore and removed our shoes and stockings, then waded among water-rounded rocks.

In the cool splendor, the congenial splashing, with cajoling speech, we caressed, spawned careless plans, spun careers, star-spangled. From an alder an antlered spider sidled on a web, and across a placid pool a water bug whipped up stippling whorls as it strode.

We held hands all the way back to Jenny's house as the sky was turning deep cloudless blue.

Jenny's father invited me to sit by him on the sofa. "I think it's going to be alright," he told me. "Mr. Bryson was impressed by my plan and is willing to have it considered at tomorrow's meeting."

"Then I can announce it in today's Star?"

"Yes, as long as you say that this is only a proposal. Mr. Bryson insisted that this be said."

"Of course," I responded. "Please excuse me, I must phone my boss."

I gave the confirmation to Johnny. "Just got your features in the mail," he said. "They will carry us through Saturday. I suppose that will about wind it up."

"Just one more for Saturday," I said. "One about the fairgrounds the day-after-the-fair. Also, tomorrow's follow-up on the fairgrounds sale."

"What more is there to say?" Johnny asked.

"I've got to keep an eye on the court, and there might be some break in the Times today. Perhaps I will get something more concrete from Small and Clark. I don't know how, but I would like to look into their, ah, relationship a bit more."

I telephoned the offices of Small and Clark for appointments.

CHAPTER NINETEEN

After I dropped off Jenny at the Fair I made my way through quiet streets to the courthouse. I checked with the clerk about an injunction, but none had been sought. Returning past the health office I opened the door on the spur of the moment, thinking I would say hello to Miss Herkimer. She was seated at her desk. "Come in, Mr. James." She pointed to the chair next to her. I assumed she wanted to talk to me, so I obeyed her command and sat down.

"I'm glad you came by," she said. "I'm worried about Jenny." She looked at me curiously. "What happened to your neck?"

"A little accident. I fell off a porch into a bush."

"Don't tell me that." She came around the desk and placed her hands around my head. "Look to the left." I stiffened with pain, but I was silent. "Look to the right." This time I resisted as she forced my head slightly.

"Please, it's nothing," I said.

"Nothing my eye! That's a serious sprain. And your chin! Don't you move, hear me? How is Jenny?"

"She's fine. I just left her at the fair."

"You haven't changed your mind about her?"

"No, nothing will change my mind about that. It's all set. Saturday morning."

"You think you will both be happy, do you?"

"I love Jenny and she loves me. Isn't that enough?"

"No, it's not! Listen to me. I was in the fair office to see Mr. Stowe and I had a talk with Ricky."

"You didn't tell him?" I asked with alarm.

"When I purposely asked him how things were with Jenny, he said they were dating, that's all. Has she told you yet? No? This is serious."

"It doesn't matter," I said.

"I disagree with you. It does matter. She should tell you she's pregnant. It's not right she should run away with you and not tell you! And she doesn't know that you know. You haven't thought seriously about this, have you?"

"I have been busy."

"Busy! Good heavens, what's this world coming to? Be serious, Art, before it is too late. She will have to tell you soon, before it becomes obvious. Or else you will have to tell her you know."

"I can't do that, not yet."

"Why not? Wouldn't it make it easier for her?"

"I want *her* to tell me."

"That will make it alright, then? She can cringe and you will forgive her. And, in that act, you will prove your superiority?"

"No, not that. When she tells me I will know she doesn't love Ricky."

"And you assume that she loved him once upon a time?"

"Of course, they grew up together. I got the impression from her family and Ricky's parents that it was a done deal."

"Well, you are wrong, Art. Both of them have dated others."

"Look what he did to her!"

"If it was Ricky, they did it together. And what if it wasn't Ricky? Art, you must tell her you know. Today!"

"There will be time enough later."

"Think, Art! Think! Ricky, for whatever reasons, has ambitions. He is convinced that Jenny has a *duty* to marry him. I know that is difficult for you to understand, but you don't have the background Ricky and Jenny have. You will be breaking the rules, don't you see? Please don't be angry. It's for your own good, and Jenny's."

"I must say, I don't see why--"

"That I'm butting in like this? The reason is not what you might expect. I am afraid for you and Jenny, about what might happen."

"If you're hinting at Ricky's temper, I've had a sample of that." I rubbed my bruised chin.

"I suspected it was Ricky. He hit you, didn't he?" Now she was really alarmed.

"Last night, on the Glen's porch. It was a K.O."

"That's what I mean. What if--? But I mustn't say that, mustn't think it." She shook her head.

"That he will do it again, or something worse? Oh, my God!"

I told her I had a couple of interviews to do. I thanked her and slammed the door as I went out.

At the Times building I scampered up the stairs to the newsroom. Blanchard was at his desk but he did not look up. I continued up the stairs to the third floor seeking the publisher's office. I told a secretary my name and she went into the inner office. She returned quickly. "Mr. Clark will see you now," she said. She held the door open for me. Clark's office was paneled in dark mahogany from floor to ceiling and was dull in the light from a single window. The floor was bare wood, badly scuffed around a rather plain small desk. Once the room may have been ornately furnished to match the gleaming walls, but now it had an incongruent run-down look.

Clark stood up and came around his desk to greet me. He held out his hand. "Good to see you again, Mr. James," he said. "Your story yesterday was well done. I wish to congratulate you."

"Thank you," I said. "I hope it did what you wanted."

"The Star was not alone. The story in the Times--"

"Of course, I thought I had a scoop. But all the time you planned a story the same day mine was published, using Mr. Small's statement in response to your editorial as an excuse."

"What does it matter?" he muttered through pursed lips. "Nothing has happened. Nothing at all." He went to the window, which overlooked Main Street. "Come here, Mr. James, look down there." I crossed the room and stood by him. There were a few people rambling on the sidewalks, but no more than usual. "All those people," he said, pointing, "Don't they understand what is going on? Don't they care?"

"About the fair?" I said, looking at his stiff figure. "Why should they? We haven't given them very much to be concerned about."

"But we told them, you and I. We told them to beware, that a thief was coming to steal their heritage."

"Did we?" I asked. "Didn't we also say that a lot of noble men were going to look after their interests, to see to it that they would be taken care of?"

"Yes, we did," Clark said. "But we didn't tell them how they were going to be cared for. Here we are, above them, wondering what they really want, hoping they will want the best of life, knowing in our hearts they want profit and security."

"Must there always be that choice?" I asked.

"There was a time when I thought we could have both. Now I'm not sure. Mr. James, you are young, very young. You are one of them. Tell me, what does your generation want?"

I was silent. "Mr. Clark, I wish I knew. I wish to God I knew. I can only say what *I* want. But I'm not typical, am I, being a reporter?"

"Oh, I think you are, Mr. James. Perhaps more sensitive, more knowledgeable of your conflicting ambitions, more than most. But still, it is your generation."

"Presuming I am," I began, "then I would say this, Mr. Clark: we want what you've got. You've got a big job, probably a lot of money, a big house. You don't work too hard. You belong to a country club, play a lot of golf. You have three cars, one a big town car, the other a country roadster. You have a lot of important friends, men and women. You can travel any time you want. You have a lot of people working for you, people you can boss around. You've got a lot of connections. You've got security. In a word, Mr. Clark, you've got it made."

"That's what young people want today?" Clark asked. "Then the Lord help us. What about service to their country and the world? How about the alleviation of human suffering? How about a new idea, a new statement of truth? And what about the Russians, beating them to the moon? What about honest, efficient government, the preservation of our democracy?"

I shrugged. "People think you are taking care of that. We don't want to think about them, and certainly fear to think that you may be bungling the job. So we don't think about it very much, if at all. Anyway, it is very complex, and one thing relates to another, so we say *So what*? What's the use of it all, if the world is going to be blown up."

"Then there's not much hope?" Clark asked.

"Yes, there is," I said.. "I may be more cynical than most, but it's a pose. My generation believes in all the things that youth has always believed in. We want a better world, where everyone is given a chance. We don't blame your generation too much. After all, your millions fought and died. We were born during and just after World War Two, and we were too young to remember much about Korea. Our world is a divided one, the only one we've ever known. So we take our cue from you. You tell us we can't do business with the Russians, and that's that. But we aren't too interested in competing with them, through science, the way you want us to. We're too busy having a good time."

Clark turned wearily away from the window. He went to his desk. "I don't understand," he said. "I was born during the first world war and grew up in the twenties. That's just what we used to say about the generation of my parents. Have we made no progress at all? I thought we were making the issues rather clear."

"You are very good at stating issues," I replied, "even solutions. You propose we talk about it, that we maintain our posture of strength, warn that we will fight if necessary. And all the while its business and pleasure as usual, get it while you can, join everything in sight, and get yourself so tied up with organizations, both business and social, that you don't know who you are. Then, most laughable of all, you tell us: Set your sights high, study hard, get high grades, prepare yourself well, your country needs you, and, above all, know yourself, what your interests are, what you can do. But how can we know ourselves, when what we are is so bound up with what we do, the organization for which we work, the groups to which we belong? To say nothing about the thousands of us who get wounded or killed in Vietnam."

"In other words," Mr. James, "your generation is confused."

"No, not confused," I said. "Frustrated. Youth's ambition is to be recognized for what we are: tough individuals with minds and spirits of our own, not to be pushed around. But you treat us as if we are sub-human, idiot robots, to be fitted into your automation. You presume, you see, that this is what we want, when what we want is to be free."

"You have to assume responsibility, to take your place, Mr. James."

"Why?" I asked. "Why do we have to be responsible for the mess we didn't create? Why do we have to take our place in a niche you have cut out for us? Leave us alone, let us go our own way. We don't want your world."

"But you said young people want all the things I have!"

"We do, but we don't want to pay the price you have paid to get them."

"Hard work never hurt anyone," he said.

"We're not afraid of hard work," I countered. "That's not the price you have paid. Your generation has paid for what it has with its soul."

Clark raised his hands in protest. "Wait a minute! Now, really, Mr. James, how metaphysical can you get? My soul? I am no man's toady."

Anyway, that wasn't quite what I meant. I remained silent for a while, and as he had no more questions, I thought it time I got to work and ask him about the fair.

"You've heard about Mr. Glen's proposal that the fair be held next year on the Xenophon?" I asked.

"Mr. Small called me this morning."

"Word does get around."

"Mr. Bryson told him."

"Mr. Clark, do you think it's a good idea?"

"Mr. Small seemed to think so. As a matter of fact, he was quite enthusiastic, suggested we have an editorial about it today."

"What do *you* think?"

"I told Mr. Blanchard and he has written the editorial, of which I approved. It expresses what I think."

"You're in favor of it?"

"When you consider the value of retaining the exhibits, giving the fair a live setting, I think it's a very good idea. Also gets the fair board off the hook."

Clark gritted his teeth. "What do you mean?" I asked

"Mr. Bryson and the board can now say there will be another fair. They have looked after the people's interest. They have discharged their responsibility."

"Yes, very well put, Mr. James."

"I may quote you?"

"You may quote the Times editorial. Mr. Bryson will have a comment, I am sure, after the fair directors vote on Mr. Glen's proposal tomorrow night."

"No doubt, but I need something for tomorrow's Star."

"You will have to ask Mr. Small."

"Oh. Yes, always Mr. Small."

Clark stood up. "I think that concludes your interview, Mr. James. Good day. Thank you for your interest in the fair." He offered me his hand. His grasp was flabby. He did not smile.

I went down the stairs and entered the newsroom. "Howdy, Art," Blanchard said, looking up. "How's tricks?"

"Understand you have another touching editorial today," I said.

He didn't seem to get it. "Sure," he said. "What time is it?" He looked at his watch. "Just past noon, you can have it." He gave me a copy of the editorial:

> It has come to our attention that a proposal was
> made to the Grange Pomona last evening which
> would mean the continuation of the fair. A
> generous offer has been made by Xenophon Farm
> to provide a site for next year's fair. We heartily
> welcome this proposal as in the best interest of
> Chesterton County. It would assure non-interruption
> of a century-old tradition and the provision of a
> location for a large new industry and all its
> attendant benefits.

I stuffed the editorial in my pocket and went over to the desk next to Marie. She winked broadly. "Hi ya, lover boy," she whispered.

"Hi ya, yourself. You look sort of bleary-eyed."

"That Harry. Did we have a time!"

"I'll bet." She looked at me quizzically. "Who are you afraid of, Art? Ricky? I was in the fair office this morning. Jenny told me about it."

"About last night? Of course I'm afraid."

Marie laughed. "Maybe you need a bodyguard."

CHAPTER TWENTY

Within fifteen minutes I was in the bank. Small was still out to lunch so I waited in a soft red leather chair outside his office. Fifteen minutes later he hailed me with an enthusiastic "Hello, Mr. James!" The bank president apologized profusely.

In his office he invited me to join him on a remarkably comfortable leather lounge beneath an extensive row of framed color photographs, each of which showed him in a different pose playing golf. I showed him my copy of the Times editorial. "Any comment?" I asked.

"For publication?"

"Yes, I need a lead for a story tomorrow," I said.

He shifted his svelte body a few times, seeking a satisfactory position. I laid my notepad on one knee and poised my pencil.

"You may report that I am very pleased with this development. For some time I have been seeking a way to guarantee that the fair will be held for years to come. I suggested to Mr. Bryson, in his position as chairman of the fair's board of directors, that he seek another site for the fair. I told him that my bank would consider financing the acquisition of a property as long as it was reasonably priced. Mr. Bryson and other county realtors surveyed the entire county. After considerable legal research, it was determined that the Xenophon was ideally located for the purpose. Mr. Bryson appointed a special board committee to investigate the possibility of leasing the required acreage from the Xenophon, for one year only, on a trial basis, with the option of continuing the lease for another five years. The board of directors has made this proposal known to the fair's patron organizations. The fair board will vote upon the committee's proposal tomorrow night. That's it, Mr. James. Any questions?"

That was like asking a man dying of thirst if he wanted a drink. "This proposal was not Mr. Glen's personal proposition?"

"As a co-owner of the Xenophon, he, like Mr. Bryson, was not a member of the committee that studied the matter. That committee was chaired by Mr. Blakemore and included Mr. Carter and Mr. Morris, in consultation with Mr. Keating and Mr. Harding."

"This study must have taken considerable time."

"It was started last June. You see, we have given the matter considerable attention."

"Of course. But isn't it strange that the Xenophon was chosen?"

"You mean because of Mr. Bryson and Mr. Glen being members of the fair board? That point was thoroughly discussed. We were aware, of course, that there were some who might contend that we were giving the lease to the Xenophon on the basis of favoritism. However, when all the facts are known--for instance, the substantial subsidy required of the Xenophon because the rental will not cover the cost of preparation of the grounds--it will be seen that Mr. Bryson and Mr. Glen have been most generous. You may say the county owes them a vote of thanks." Small looked nervously at his watch.

"What's new on Tiber Trucks?"

"A representative of the firm will be present at tomorrow night's meeting."

"And he is?"

"I am not at liberty to say."

"He will address the corporation?"

"Yes. That will succeed the meeting of the fair directors."

"Oh, I thought that would be held first."

"The directors will meet first, then adjourn to meet as the fair corporation. Then, most likely, will meet again as directors. Naturally the directors cannot act on this proposal regarding the Xenophon until the corporation has made a decision on disposal of the fairgrounds."

"The directors will be made aware of the Xenophon proposal first?"

"They are aware of it," Small said. "A report preceding the meeting of the corporation would be a formality."

"Is that in order, I mean for this informal conference technique to practically guarantee acceptance of the fairgrounds sale?"

"It wouldn't be right for the members to come to the meeting ignorant of what is to be proposed. Each member has a responsibility to argue for or against the proposal. As chairman I have the responsibility to give each member ample opportunity to examine the proposal and to prepare their opinions."

"Each member has received information on the proposal?"

"You mean regarding Tiber Trucks? No, Mr. James, please do not misunderstand me. This has been done by word of mouth. We have received no proposal from Tiber Trucks. The proposal we expect, although here again we have no assurance, will be made by a Tiber representative. All we have is a request from Tiber Trucks to make a presentation."

"Surely you are aware, Mr. Small, of what the presentation implies?"

"We have had overtures from Tiber Trucks. We have indicated our readiness to listen. There have been meetings between the parties concerned. There has been correspondence."

"Then the groundwork has been well laid for the sale?"

There was little doubt that I was getting on Small's nerves. "This is a complicated affair, Mr. James. All the fair corporation can do will be to hear the proposal and then vote on whether to explore the proposal further. It cannot, will not, vote then and there to sell the fairgrounds. That sort of transaction takes time."

"Still, presuming an affirmative vote," I said, "the basic decision having been made, the sale would go through."

"Considerable work would have to be done. Tiber Trucks will want to study our counter-proposal. The negotiations could take weeks."

"But," I persisted, "presuming all goes well, and you come to terms, the fairgrounds could be turned over to Tiber Trucks this fall?"

"Under the best of circumstances, yes. Please remember the matter of additional studies that would have to go into housing, utilities and all the rest."

"I would have thought the county and the city had that in hand."

"Of course. We would not be so inefficient. Mr. Morris and his firm have written a voluminous report."

"Would you say that Mr. Morris, being chairman of the county commissioners, has an inside track on the *way* in which they will vote on the sale?"

"Naturally, Mr. James," Small said with a sigh. "After all, it is county property. But Mr. Morris has found nothing that stands in the way of the corporation's legal right to turn control of the fairgrounds back to the county, which can then dispose of it in the manner specified by the corporation."

"Then the corporation," I persisted, "says to the commissioners: Sell it to Tiber Trucks, and that's the way it will be?"

"Hardly, Mr. James. The commissioners can approve or disapprove, as they see fit. After all, they are an autonomous body, not to be dictated to by anyone."

"Of course," I said. "They are absolutely independent."

CHAPTER TWENTY-ONE

"Hello, slugger," I said to Ricky through the bars of the ticket window. I showed him my press pass. He smiled, a twisted smirk. I went around to the side door, opened it, and saw Jenny at the desk. She was counting dollar bills. She looked up, smiled, and kept counting, moving her lips with each bill. When she had finished she wrote down a figure on a yellow ledger. Ricky, standing at the wicket, his back to me, was busy passing out tickets.

"How are you, sweetheart?" I called to Jenny, loud enough that Ricky heard me.

"I'm fine, darling," she said with a warm smile. "May we go to Castle Rock now?"

"Alright, but first I want to talk to Bob."

"He's at the Exhibition Pavilion," she said.

"I won't be long," I said. "How's my esteemed friend, Mr. Stowe?"

"He's been around but he had to go out for a while. You want to see him too?"

Ricky turned around. "You're off your beat, aren't you, Mr. Reporter?"

"Want to throw me out?"

"I don't handle trash," he said. I stepped toward him, but Jenny intervened. "Please, Art. I had it out with him this morning. He promised not to do anything like that again."

Ricky came toward me, fist held tightly upright, leaving a customer on the other side of the barred window. "Something happen to your chin, Mr. Reporter?"

I wanted to grab him by his tie and twist it around his neck, but Jenny was standing between us. Just thinking about it, my stomach did a flip-flop. "You must have been drunk," I said flatly.

His head jerked back. "I don't drink," he said. "I've never been drunk."

"Ricky, you're so drunk you smell!" I cried out.

He tried to push Jenny aside. I was ready for him. "Stop it! Stop it!" Jenny screamed. "You had better go, Art."

"I will be back," I said defiantly. I backed toward the door, glaring at Ricky as steadily as I could all the way. I banged into the door, turned, opened it, and went out. My face was burning all the way to the Agricultural Pavilion.

Bob was talking with a couple of teenagers, a boy and girl. They were admiring a huge cabbage. "You can grow one even larger," Bob was saying. "Keep a warming light on them for six hours after sunset. That's why they grow so big in Alaska. Around Fairbanks. Sun doesn't go down until almost midnight." Bob spotted me as the pair left. "Hello, Mr. James, see my cabbage." He held it up. It was wider than his shoulders.

"Bob, last night, I didn't get a chance to ask you a couple of questions."

"What about?"

"The fair, of course. I know what your father thinks, Jenny too. How about you?"

"I don't like what's happening," he said. "Not a bit. A farm should be a farm, not a place for entertainment. If Father and Mr. Bryson have their way, leasing a lot of acres for the fairgrounds, and the fair gets bigger and bigger every year, as it has for the last hundred years, it wouldn't be long before we would lose the entire Xenophon. I hate to disagree with Father. He says the Xenophon itself would be on exhibit. Everything we grow would be on display."

"What's wrong with that, Bob? Your dad says that the Xenophon would be famous."

"And ruined," Bob said. "The Xenophon has been setting the pace in Chesterton County for a hundred years. We should be helping others to come up to our standards. We should share, freely, what we know."

"That's exactly your dad's idea, isn't it?"

"At a dollar a head? They would have to charge more than that, a lot more. Placing the fair on the Xenophon is a terrible idea, and I don't want anything to do with it. It's Father who would like me to quit university now, when I have only two more years to go, so that I can help prepare the Xenophon for next year's fair. Only thing I want is for the Xenophon to be a model farm, not a super farm. I want a farm that demonstrates how modern agricultural techniques, good conservation, can make the land pay handsome dividends, provide a way of life. All that would be impossible if our efforts were directed to making it a showpiece."

"Your father says the profits of the fair could be plowed back into research."

"Spoken like a true businessman!" Bob shook his head. "Research for what? On how to run a farm and have more leisure time? How to preserve moral values and courage, despite the rotting of these qualities everywhere in the world? How to find a way to send our surpluses to the hungry in other lands without injury to our economy? How to increase generosity and decrease selfishness? That's what is important. My father's plan would enslave a farmer to his so-called leaders. He thinks that what is good enough for the Xenophon should be good enough for any farm. Turning the Xenophon into a fairgrounds would destroy the farm. The farmer toils to produce food, of course, but he also must be a steward of the soil. In the end, the soil is all we've got."

I thanked Bob for the interview, knowing it was only good enough for background, but at least it was reassuring me that my generation was not so blindfolded by the profit motive that it had forgotten its indebtedness to Mother Nature. I meandered around the pavilions to pick up more stuff for the next feature story. I stopped at the Castle Rock diner for a snack. It was after two-thirty before I returned to the fair office.

Approaching the office I saw Stowe coming out and he saw me. He stood there waiting for me. It was too late to turn away. "How are you, Art?" he asked cheerfully, as if yesterday's tirade had never happened. He gave me a cheerful grin.

"I'm fine," I said. I did not smile.

"I thought you might be in to see me today."

"Look, yesterday you practically threw me out of the office. Now what gives?"

"Your story in today's Star."

"You mean I have succeeded in making you happy?"

"Very. The story on the meaning of the fair sounds exactly like me." He said it with a twinkle in his eye.

Jenny had the Star on her desk, opened to Page One. There was a two-column headline above my byline:

New Site Proposed
For Chesterton Fair

She flipped the page and there was my other story, the big quote from Stowe, with Harry's photo of him storming through the fair gateway and looking quite business-like. My feature story appeared on Page One, Section Two.

"I think we're in," Stowe said. "We will have another fair next year. Art, these stories you've been writing are terrific!" He patted my shoulder. "Let's forget what happened yesterday, shall we? After all, you did threaten to roast me, as I recall, and I was under considerable pressure. I apologize for the way I behaved. I think we understand one another better now, presuming you know all that's been going on."

"I have a good idea," I said. "You were caught in the middle, same as me. I shouldn't have tried the same tactics on you that I did on Bryson and the others. You're too smart for me."

Stowe offered his hand and I shook on it. "Actually," he said, "as it turned out, your story yesterday was quite accurate." He sucked deeply on his pipe and blew the smoke away from himself. "I assumed your reporting was going to roast everybody connected with the fair. Despite Mr. Clark's precautionary statements, your reports were accurate, for which I am grateful. I was given the job of steering you toward the Tiber Trucks story, which I did, after I first gave you some feature stuff on the fair itself. What I hadn't counted on was your probing into the lives of every last one of the fair directors. I was called onto the carpet for that, because they thought I had led you into it. They couldn't believe you would go so far on your own. They feared the worst, but a few editorial touches on your story was turned into a bonanza of publicity for the county. Now it's even better, because your story today shows Richland that we intend to keep our fair, to preserve our countryside atmosphere."

"Is that important to Tiber Trucks?" I asked.

"Indeed. Must keep the workers happy. Promise them a home in the country. That's what everyone wants. They will be crazy about moving to the fresh air of Chesterton County, to escape Richland's smog."

"Richland doesn't have any smog," I said.

"Well, whatever it has that Chesterton doesn't. Lots of space, trees, hills, fishing. And a real, live, honest-to-goodness county fair. What more could anyone ask? This way the company will have the unions on its side."

"How come you know so much about Tiber Trucks?"

"Why didn't you ask me that before?" Stowe said. "Even on Monday you could have asked it and I would have told you. Men from Tiber have been swarming all over the fairgrounds since June. There's a couple of them here today."

"There are!" Down the drain went an image of myself as the hottest reporter in four counties.

"Didn't I tell you?" Stowe asked. "I used to be a reporter myself. Worked on a small daily in Indiana for five years. That's how I got connected with fairs. They had one there, and I did what Marie does, turned out the publicity. I fell in love with fairs and I haven't fallen out of love since. The fair is family to me. Almost literally, since I don't have a family. Being single, I can work these ungodly hours. Come back tomorrow, Art. I think we can promise some good background for tomorrow night's meeting."

Somewhat dazed, I went out with Jenny, and it was only outside that I realized Ricky hadn't been in the office that afternoon. I asked Jenny about that.

"He was in Mr. Stowe's office," she said. "I saw you coming from the Agricultural Pavilion, so I asked Mr. Stowe to stall you at the door for a minute while I practically shoved Ricky in there." She laughed. "I told him I would beat him up if he didn't."

"I will never understand you Chesterton people, never. You certainly do stick together, don't you?"

"For love," Jenny said, "we will do anything."

In the Buick, on our way to Castle Rock, I filed my feature story at Western Union, then drove past the Xenophon. Jenny was silent as she gazed at sunny fields, which rose sharply from both sides of the highway. Here and there a white farm house gleamed, side by side with high red barns and towering blue silos. A slight breeze was blowing over the hills as clouds gathered in great wide puffs. Still the sky was blue and bright, the air warm and scented by the odor of dry maple leaves.

We rode through vast acres of waving green corn and bright stands of sunflowers.

"Isn't this gorgeous country, Art?" Jenny asked.

The changing brilliance of hardwood trees, bright with yellowing red leaves, the harbinger of harvest and eventual snow, now flashed by. We rose to higher ground with steep hillsides darkening the road ahead.

"I was wondering if Ricky is jealous about you, Jenny," I said.

Surely, not jealous of Jenny. She inspires everyone. She is the fairest of the county, a precious treasure, the gift of earth. One might as well be jealous of a summer flower. It is admired, glanced at, mantled, its presence enjoyed. It is photographed, painted. But we are not jealous of its beauty, we do not covet its comeliness.

"Flowers are fading," Jenny said.

Yes, they wither on the vine, their beauty is no more. Perhaps that is why, if what she said is true, then I am perishable, fragile too.

"Strange, isn't it? Jenny said. "Seasons change, flowers perish."

I want you to stay with me forever, Jenny. Do not change with the season. O Lord, every generation should enjoy you. Your beauty is for all to see, transparent. All see you, but do not know your meaning, how deep is our desire that you should not change.

"I suppose all beauty has its season," she said.

Remove beauty from its natural setting and it is quickly spoiled, like the rose petal, pinched. I do not like cut flowers, they die in a day, two days, a week. In the garden they may be seen in season. Smashed, stricken, crushed. A flower that bloomed, saw the sun, and, in darkness, was cut. Was the beauty banished by our living lust, our driving duty, our haunting hunger? Was Jenny doomed to fall, thus, with the leaves of autumn, to pale with winter?

"You know, it is my brother Bob who loves me most," Jenny said.

But that was family, fraternal love. Raised as brother and sister, a command to love. But why? Her heart, unhurt, yet sheds tears, though her tissue's torn. We mourn the passing of her beauty, needlessly, for she breathes life, invites pity, broods on her brother. He speaks little to Ricky. He is empty, a shell.

Suddenly the spell was spoiled. A dog ran at the car's wheels along the side of the road. I swerved as he snapped at a front tire, too late. I heard him squeal, slammed the brakes. We got out down the road, turned back, stooped over the quivering animal in the grass, as a boy, about seven, with tossing hair, raced from a farm. He knelt in the grass, cradled the dog's head in his lap, as the brave heart gave out and his friend was still.

"You killed him! You killed him!" the boy screamed, even as his tears flowed.

"Oh, I'm sorry," I cried. "I didn't mean to. He came out of the grass and ran barking at the wheels. I tried to avoid him, but I couldn't. I'm sorry."

Jenny bent to him and caught the boy's head to her bosom, and there they sat for a moment, swaying with the wind, the dog with the boy, the boy with the girl, and I cried a bit inside, thinking that the boy's head now rested on another life, just begun, and that if he knew he would not be sad.

CHAPTER TWENTY-TWO

Through a narrow defile the highway led directly to the heart of Castle Rock Valley. From one side of the highway the hills climbed high toward the upland farms. The land on the other side dipped slightly, then was flat for half a mile before rising again to the higher hills to the south, where the clouds had bunched in dark formations. Between the hills the village of Castle Rock spread out on half a dozen streets, all of which could be seen along the road that was known, of course, as Main Street.

"There it is," Jenny said. I parked the Buick by the curb opposite the tall brick church across the road. A square tower surmounted the porch and to the left was the peaked roof of the sanctuary. Three stained glass windows, each tall and narrow and topped by a gothic arch, ran almost the full height of the church's front wall. On the lawn, next to an enormous oak, a black-framed sign on stilts announced the subject of Sunday's sermon: "The Web of Life." Above the title was the pastor's name: *Mark Christopher.*

"That's the manse," Jenny said, pointing toward a white bungalow before which I had parked. We got out and crossed the street to the church. On the porch I turned and looked down the road. On either side, toward the east, there was a single block of stores. I made out two groceries, a hardware, a gas station, a tavern, a furniture store, and a variety shop.

I opened the heavy wood church door and let Jenny pass in first. The hall was dark and cool and smelled of newly-laid wax. We went down the hall toward two swinging doors at the end, pushed through them and entered the sanctuary. From the rear the floor sloped toward the raised chancel. On the left was the pulpit, on the right the lectern. Between was a Communion table clothed in green. A brass cross and two brass candle holders decorated the cloth. Behind was a dark brown drape, about two feet high, hung on a brass rail, partially concealing the choir stall and a small organ.

Jenny took my hand as we padded down the center aisle and sat in one of the cushioned pews. Jenny bowed her head in prayer. From the side windows, whose panes were tinted mauve and orange, a warm glow of sunlight spread over the curving pews. I looked up at the high vaulted ceiling, painted turquoise, and then the deep and easy silence of the sanctuary closed in upon me, and in the hush I whispered: "It's beautiful."

"I love this church," Jenny said. "Right down there, you see the baptismal font, that's where I was baptized as an infant. And in front of the Communion table I knelt to be confirmed. I was thirteen. This is our family pew. We call it ours because we always came early with Father and Mother to claim it. All my life, except for the years when I was very little and was taken to the nursery, I sat here in this pew with my family every Sunday. It became part of me."

We got up and went into the hall at the front of the church and entered a door on the right. It was a large hall, carpeted in linoleum, and was bright with colored light from the stained glass windows that I had seen from the street. At the bottom of each window was a panel inscribed with the names of persons whom the windows memorialized. Three saints were portrayed in the leaded panes above: Andrew on the left, Paul in the center, and Peter on the right.

"This is where I go to Sunday school," Jenny said. "It is held before the service." She pointed to several wooden panels mounted on wheels. "Those dividers are set between the classes. Over there is the kitchen." We crossed the room and opened a door and peered into a smaller room lined with a gas cooking stove, a refrigerator and an enormous sink. "The women cook the church suppers here," she said.

We went to the hall again, crossed it and opened a door under the stairway that led to a floor below the hall. In the basement was a room fully as large as the Sunday school above. "This is the young people's room," Jenny said. "We meet every Friday night, except in the summers. I was president of the society during my last year in high school."

From the upper hall we went up the stairs. At the top a glass panel was set into the right of the landing, and the words *Pastor's Study* were painted on it. I had no sooner stepped onto the landing than the door opened and

Pastor Christopher said: "I heard you coming. How are you, Mr. James? I'm glad to see you again." He hugged Jenny lightly. "You look tired," he said to her. "I hope you aren't working too long at the fair."

"I am beginning to feel the strain," Jenny said.

His study was a long room with a view of the old oak. "I would like to talk with you both and then one at a time," he said, "so come in and make yourselves comfortable."

I saw right away that we were in for a formal counseling session. However, he didn't use the usual commanding method of sitting behind his desk. Instead, we sat uncomfortably in a circle of hard metal folding chairs. "Art, Jenny told me you plan to take her away to Richland."

"Jenny!" I cried out.

"I had to, Art," she said. "It didn't seem right without telling Pastor Christopher."

"We have to consider her parents, Art," he said. "Of course all this is confidential with me, you are assured of that. Still, there may be some things you would both like to talk over with me before--well, before taking such a serious step. I wouldn't put any roadblock in your way, Art. You are perfectly free to do what you wish. My concern is for your happiness, that you are both sure you are doing the right thing."

Jenny said, looking at me, her eyes pleading: "I think it's best, don't you, Art? There are some things I want Pastor Christopher to know."

"I suppose it's okay," I said reluctantly. "I didn't know we were coming here for that."

"I wanted you to know what this church means to me."

"I don't see anything wrong about it," I protested. "We need time together, pastor, to get to know one another. Jenny wants to attend Richland University, that's all."

"Please understand," the minister said, "I've known the Glen and Bryson families a long time. I am therefore concerned about what happens, that you have a successful marriage, if that is your intent. I am stating my reason badly. Perhaps you will understand, Art, when we talk alone."

"All right, let's get to it," I said.

"I would like to speak with Jenny first."

"How long will you be?"

"Give us an hour. There's a small library in the hall."

I looked grimly at Jenny. "It's all right, Art," she said. "You will see."

I left them and went out to the street. The clouds that had mounted high above the southern hills had shifted to the west and, even as I watched, the sun drifted behind a cloud and the sky darkened. I walked along a sidewalk toward the library, crossing an intersecting street called Mountain Drive. I noted from a signpost that I was now on East Main Street. Looking back I noted I had left West Main Street. How odd! This was the Four Corners. Here was the crossroads of Castle Rock. The very heart of an ancient village. The Presbyterian Church occupied one crossroads corner, an Episcopal Church the other diagonally opposite. Right in front of me was a two-story building ringed by long porches. A large white sign on the grass told me the building housed a library. Clearly the library had once been the typical crossroads hotel, where Wells Fargo stagecoaches may well have tarried overnight. The library grounds were surrounded by high iron palings, split in the middle by a gap where a gate had once hung. I went up the brick path and mounted the verandah steps, crossed and entered the building. From the hall an open door on the left led to a large room, probably at one time a tavern, where a gray-haired woman was sorting cards on a counter.

"May I help you, sir?" she asked with an intriguing smile.

"Do you have something on the history of Chesterton County?"

"Yes, indeed." She came from behind the counter and went over to a shelf of books by a window. She reached up and took down a slim volume. "This is my best," she said, "A history published in connection with the county's centennial several years ago."

I took it from her and went over to a table covered with current issues of popular magazines. I began to flip the pages of the book, starting from the back. In the middle I found the masthead: the *Historical Souvenir,* published in 1900.

Following many pages of brown prints of Chesterton County's roads, industrial establishments and stores, I came to a long paragraph on early settlers. It told of Silas Johnson, who built a sawmill on Chester River, and who was later appointed surrogate and county clerk; of the first blacksmith, Jacob Hubbard; the first jewelers and silversmiths; the first harness and saddle maker; the first newspaper publisher; the first tanner.

An interesting paragraph caught my eye. I took out my notebook and copied it: *Every town's growth increases the value of property, widens the range of trade and raises rents. It makes for increased attendance at church and school. It means more mouths to feed, more bodies to be clothed, more people to be amused. Communities compete today in growth as much as tradesmen."*

There was an ancient history story about the competition of four villages: Chesterton, on the Chester River, Castle Rock, Port Attica and Plato, for selection as the county seat. Chesterton won when Jonathan Small donated the site for the courthouse. There was a brief item on the *Chesterton County Agricultural Society Fair.* Actually, I discovered the society held fairs as far back as the eighteen forties, the first being held in the Owl Tavern and later on the courthouse grounds. The present site was secured in 1892. The paragraph continued: *Enclosed grounds cover many acres. Buildings are erected in a modern and substantial manner. A graded half-mile track is the scene of many interesting trials of speed. The grand stand was erected at a cost of 5,200 dollars. There are commodious buildings for display of exhibits and good stabling facilities. Twenty thousand admission tickets are said to have been purchased in 1899.* That meant *daily* tickets.

Apart from a paragraph each on the Farmers' Club and the Grange there was no mention of agriculture as a county industry. Most of the book was devoted to descriptions of the City of Chesterton's industries, merchants, churches and their wide variety of organizations, the Normal School, clergymen, banks, barbers, physicians, public officials, fire companies, sheriffs and their deputies, and two undertakers, both of whom also operated furniture stores, which made not only furniture but also wood burial caskets.

In the introduction there was this declamation: *Chesterton is a city of business and its growth has been the work of creative business enterprises. However, never in its history has a crude mercenary spirit possessed it. Its humanitarian impulses have never been blighted by the wealth of self-seeking men who aim to rule or ruin. As an industrial center, Chesterton provides unique advantages. It has many inducements, not the least of which is the large available manufacturing space still available. Chesterton aims to be a flourishing center of great manufacturing and a splendid mart of trade.*

I returned the book to the shelf, thanked the librarian, who nodded, and went out. Now the sky was overcast, a drab gray from horizon to horizon. I was laughing to myself as I mounted the church steps. The Smalls, the Blakemores, the Brysons, the Clarks of the nineteen-sixties were no different from the men of the same names I had encountered in the book. But what good had the appeal for industry done them? In 1900 the population of the county was 29,000. More than sixty years later it was 65,000. Taking into account the natural increase, the population had merely marked time.

As I ascended the stairs to the pastor's study, I heard Jenny's covered sobs. I looked through the glass and saw her bending into her cupped hands, her shoulders heaving. I knocked, then turned away. Pastor Christopher came to the door, opened it a crack. "Come back in a few minutes, Art," he whispered. I crept down the stairs, holding tightly to the banister, to the Sunday School hall. Bright with colored light before, it was almost dark now, the gloom relieved only far up near a high ceiling where the lone lamp on the minister's desk shone through a window. Shadows of two chain-hung globes penciled the wall above the kitchen door.

There was an ancient player piano to the left of the door from the hall. I sat down on a wobbly stool, lifted the cover from the piano keys and tried to pick out chopsticks, the only piece I had ever learned to play, but my fingers couldn't find the keys. I pressed the pedals below the console and there was a wheezing gasp of air behind the lower panel, and that was all. I pushed open the panels and saw there was no paper roll. About as useless as a clock that doesn't tell the time. I closed the doors and the keys' cover and tried whirling myself around on the stool, as I used to do at home when I was a kid. I went round a couple of times, my heels digging into the floor. The stool's worm gear jammed and I almost fell off.

Has he told Jenny she can't marry me? I thought. *Did she tell him she was going to have a baby? Why was she crying? Did he threaten to tell her parents, after all? Well, he can talk all he wants. Nobody is going to take her away from me. Nobody.*

I heard her footsteps on the stairs, approaching so slowly that I knew she must be halting on each step. She was leaning against the wall, her right hand gripping the banister, her left holding a tissue to her eyes. It was so dark on the stairs that I could hardly see her face. "Jenny! Jenny! What is it? What did he say?"

"Pastor Christopher will see you now." I put my arm around her waist and she leaned heavily against me. I clasped her to me. "I'm sorry," she said. "I don't mean to be such a crybaby. But I'm so happy!"

"Happy?"

"Yes. Pastor Christopher will explain it to you. Oh, Art, I should have told you. Pastor Christopher is right. So right!"

"Told me? Told me what?" But I knew what.

"I will let you know later," Jenny said. "Pastor Christopher said it was best for me to tell you after he speaks to you."

Her sobs became less frequent and then stopped. "You all right now?" I asked. Strangely, my voice quavered and I suddenly felt shaky.

"Yes, don't worry. I'm okay. I will wait for you. Only, don't be long."

"I won't," I said, although I knew that how long it would take wasn't up to me.

I left her sitting on a chair in the enfolding darkness. Going up the stairs, I tripped on the landing. The minister came to the door. "I had no idea it was getting so dark," he said. He flicked a switch next to the door. A bulb flooded the stairway with light.

"I think we're going to have a storm," I said.

He resumed his chair in the study and I took one opposite him. He gazed quietly at me for a moment, his eyes dim pools in the shadowy room. His glance, beneath thick dark brows, was barbed. I dropped my gaze.

"Don't be upset about Jenny's crying," he said at last, his voice low and sonorous. I half expected that ministerial tone I was used to hearing at church funerals. But his voice was far from funereal. Rather than that it had a rich musical quality, like a cadence of the sea. "Jenny had something surprising to tell me," he said. "She asked me to prepare you for it. She wants to tell you herself." I knew she was pregnant. It had to be: she wanted to call the whole thing off. "This will be difficult for you to take. I told her this would not make a difference. She agreed about that. She also said she loves you very much. You are very fortunate, Art. Jenny is a very fine girl."

I let him go on like that, just to learn what he had to say. I interrupted him: "Pastor Christopher, I already know," I said as steadily as I could manage. "After Jenny had her physical, the nurse told me."

He looked steadily at me, curiously instead of surprised. "How do you feel about it?" he asked.

"Feel! At first I couldn't stand it. I felt sorry for Jenny, mad as--hated Ricky Bryson."

"And sorry for yourself?"

"Then it was Ricky?"

"You aren't sure, are you?"

"It doesn't make any difference," I said..

"You want to marry her just the same and be a good father to her child?"

"Absolutely."

"What about Ricky? How do you feel about him?"

"I'm indifferent to Ricky. What's happened has happened. It can't be undone."

"Abortion?" he asked.

"I don't know. I hate to think about it, and I haven't thought about it. What can I say?" I could feel the heat rising to my face. "Isn't that up to Jenny?" I hesitated. "No, that wouldn't do. If her life was in danger--"

"Complicated, isn't it, Art? You see, you haven't had time to think it through. That's dangerous, Art. Human nature is a strange thing. We think that love will conquer all. Well, it can't. It takes a lot of mature, mutual understanding. I know that sounds mundane, and it is."

Yes, we would be bonded by love, stronger than the pull of earth, brighter than the glance of sun, more lasting than the rock of time.

"Think about this, Art. The shadow of the father of Jenny's child will effect your love for one another, a deep dark everlasting shadow. I'm not saying that the shadow won't fade away. It will, given time. A lot of time. This need not be an impediment to your marriage. Lots of young couples learn to accept it, raising a child fathered or conceived by a third person still alive. The rest is up to both of you. Come to see me anytime, Art--"

But I had enough. I left him and went down the stairs to the hall, pushed open the door to the Sunday School room. It was very dark. "Jenny," I called. There was no answer. I went outside and saw that the clouds had blackened. The air was very still. Jenny was nowhere in sight. In a panic, I returned to the church hall, bounded up the stairs and thrust open the study's door. "Jenny," I exclaimed. "I can't find her."

"Didn't she tell you?" the pastor asked. "I suggested she wait for you in the manse."

"Thanks a lot," I said. I turned to close the door. Pastor Christopher was reading an open Bible. "You should know," I said. "It's going to rain. A storm, I think."

"In that case I better leave myself." He turned off the lamp on his desk and we went down the stairs together. As we crossed the street I felt a splash of rain. He unlocked the manse door. I went in ahead of him. The door led directly into the parlor. Jenny rose from the sofa.

"That didn't take too long," she said calmly. We thanked Pastor Christopher, who loaned us an umbrella.

"Good luck," was all he said.

We dashed for the car as thunder rolled in from the west. Rain descended heavily. I opened the Buick's front door, helped Jenny in, then raced around to the other side. Behind the wheel, I turned the key. The engine roared. I switched on the headlights and wipers, put the car in drive and made a u-turn. "Darn rain," Jenny said. "I wanted to show you more of the countryside. Think what it's like at the fair!"

We were silent again. The rain pounded the roof and splashed off the windshield. Lightning split the leaden sky. We passed the spot where I had killed the dog. Jenny looked past me, peering toward the grassy area on the other side of the road. "It was a fine dog," I said.

"I used to have a dog of my own once," Jenny said. "She was a little thing. I loved her more than my favorite doll."

"What happened to her?"

She died, of old age."

"You never got another?"

"No. I didn't want another. It couldn't take Patsy's place."

"That's what you called her? Strange name for a dog. There's a special meaning for that name."

"Her real name was Patricia, I called her Patsy for short. What does Patsy mean?"

"A dupe. A victim of deception."

CHAPTER TWENTY-THREE

The dirt road to the Glen house was flooded. I slowed down as much as possible, splashing water all the way. Fortunately the rain had turned into a dense drizzle. I parked the Buick within a few feet of the house. We scrambled up the steps to the porch. The house was dark. Jenny tried the door, then knocked.

"Oh my gosh," she said. "I forgot. This is Mother's day to go to the fair. There's nobody home, and I don't have a key."

"What will we do?" I asked.

"What I've always done when I've been locked out. We go to the barn and wait." The rain let up and the sky brightened.

We sloshed our way from the house across the muddy driveway, finding our way easily to the barn. We were a few yards away when a light over the barn door went on. "Automatic," Jenny said. She pushed the latch and the door swung open.

I could hear the cows munching quietly in their stalls. Jenny held my hand, leading me. "This way," she said. "Up here." She guided my hands toward a wooden ladder with rails built against a wood partition. As my eyes got used to the gloom, there was just enough light to see dimly. "I will go up first," Jenny said. "Follow me, but be careful. The steps are slick."

I gained the first two steps and halted. "Where are you?" I called.

"What are you whispering for? There's no one here but us mice." Her voice came from far above me. "All right, I'm up. Now, you come."

I reached high and grasped a rail and kicked for the bottom step, found it, mounted, and started climbing. I must have taken a dozen steps when I felt Jenny's hand on my head. I gave my hand to hers and she helped me up and above the last step. I fell into a soft pile of hay.

We climbed a few feet higher into the hay and lay down side by side. I gasped for breath. "That wasn't difficult now, was it?" she said. In the still blackness, looking toward a window under the eves, I felt the quietude like a warm embrace that was more than physical.

"Isn't this great?" Jenny said. "Feel it? I call it home in the hay."

I laughed. "It is sort of comforting, isn't it?"

The shuffling of cattle hooves, the damply warm, soothing, sweet smell of hay: I was a stranger to it, but it was home to Jenny.

"You've been up here often, I suppose," I said.

Jenny cuddled to my side. "Oh, yes, since I was a little girl. Father used to scold me for climbing the ladder. He was afraid I would fall, but I never did. I come up here whenever I want to be alone, which is often. I come here to think, to get away from the constant busyness in the house. I used to think that I was hiding from them, but they always knew where to look, and Father would come in and call up: 'Alright, alright, Miss Muffet, come down. I know you're there.' And always I wondered how he knew, at least until I got bigger. It's still my favorite place. It's always too dark up here to read, even when the barn doors are open. Once late on a summer afternoon I fell asleep, and I didn't hear Father call, and he came up and shook me. At first I didn't realize where I was. I had been dreaming I was Snow White and when I opened my eyes I thought sure it was Prince Charming come to carry me off."

"Next time it was Sleeping Beauty, I suppose."

"Same thing, isn't it? Anyway, that's the way it was. Since then, when I come here, I always think of that time. It was so pleasant and peaceful, as if the whole world was shut out, as if I was a different person."

"It doesn't happen any more?"

"Not any more. Not since last June. That's what I want to tell you."

"How it happened?"

"Yes, and where. It happened here."

I felt my stomach quake again. "Right here?" I am sure she caught the tremor in my voice.

"Never mind," Jenny said. "I'm not superstitious about it. Why don't you lay back? I will feel more comfortable if you do. I can talk easier then." I nestled into the hay by her side. "Take my hand," she said. We waved our hands in the air, trying to find one another and at last our arms met and I grasped her hand. "Please don't say anything until I'm finished. Promise?"

"I promise."

"It was right after Ricky was graduated from university, only a few days. I saw him the first day he came home, because he came over to see Bob. I don't know what came over him, because I'm a year younger than him, but he took one look at me--we were in the yard--and it was like a line in the movies: 'Is his Jenny?' he said. 'Is this the little girl I've known?' He picked me up, like he used to when I was small, like he hadn't seen me for years, as if we had never been together before. He swung me around like Father used to. I yelled to him to put me down, he was making me dizzy, but he kept swinging me around, and my legs went out from under me and my dress came up and I'm sure my panties were showing. It was like in the circus. He was really fierce about it. I had my arms around his neck, and I was scared he'd drop me. While he was swinging me, crazy like that, and my head was starting to swim and I thought I was going to be sick, I closed my eyes, and then the first thing I knew he was kissing me, right there in front of Bob, and we were still going around like that. He kissed me real hard, too, and wouldn't let up until I heard Bob calling 'Okay, that's enough,' and finally he circled more slowly and dropped me to my feet, but he had to hold me up or I would have fallen right down on the ground."

She paused a moment and the only sound in the barn, other than the labored breathing of the cattle, was the drip-drip of water on the tin roof, I suppose from branches of the overhanging poplars to the north.

"That very night," Jenny went on, "he took me out on our first real date. In other years we had been out together, but always with our neighborhood or church gang. But growing up, before high school and university, Ricky was like a god to me. I even had a photo of him on the wall of my room. You know how young girls worship movie stars or popular singers, well, that was the way I felt about Ricky, It was something my girlfriends in senior year at high school kidded me about, that I was something special because I had a romantic attachment to a university man. I used to talk a lot to them about Ricky, boasting I suppose, trying to make out I was a cut or two above them. This got around among the high school boys and I never had a steady date after that. They thought I was spoken for, when I really wasn't. I wouldn't have made it to the graduation prom if it hadn't been for one of my girlfriends. I told her--she was real popular with the boys--that I didn't have a date, when it came two days before the dance.

225

I was desperate by then, so she found out who didn't have a date among the boys and I got the rush from the ugliest ones around. I accepted one of them and was taken to the prom in this broken-down car of his. But it was better than not being able to go at all. My friends were surprised that I'd go with that guy--he's from one of the farms in the hills south of Castle Rock, but he's in the Army now. He tried to date me again after that, but Bob wouldn't let me go with him. So you see, if it hadn't been for Ricky, in a way, I would have had more dates and perhaps a steady all through my last two years of high school, like my girlfriends had. I covered up my lack of dates by saying Ricky wouldn't like it, so one thing led to another."

She rubbed my hand with her palm. "Your hand's so warm," she said. "It is warm up here, isn't it? You could sleep here and not need a blanket. Well, to get back to the day Ricky came home, we went out to this ritzy place in Chesterton; it's over a block from Main Street and costs a fortune just to get into the place. They have a sort of floor show, just a sexy girl singer and a three-piece band. Ricky ordered the most expensive dinner on the menu, without asking me what I wanted, but I couldn't eat a thing, because I was so excited just being there with him, and being treated so well and everything. I had on a party dress Mother had bought me for the prom, and he had on his best suit. It was really my first big date, although Ricky kept saying I must be used to that sort of thing, and he really couldn't believe it when I told him I'd never been in that place before. After dinner we danced through almost every dance and he whirled me around the floor, he's such a marvelous dancer, and I wondered whether there wasn't anything he couldn't do really well, I mean superbly. One of my girlfriends was there for a while with her boyfriend and we went to the ladies room, to powder our noses, as they say, and she said she never really believed that Ricky was my boyfriend until then, and I was very pleased about that, and I told Ricky. He said sure I was his girl, that I'd always been, and I believed it because I wanted to believe it, because then all those years wouldn't have been wasted. He had come home and swept me off my feet, and even then I had this notion that maybe it would happen, that he'd marry me, although I didn't hardly dare hope he would. I thought he was so far above me, and that having been away from home for so long he must have been going with all sorts of girls, which he had, and why should he pay any attention to me, because I hadn't finished college and I was just a kid in his eyes. While we were dancing he kept exclaiming how beautiful I was, and, oh, it was such a line as you never heard, that I was quite gone on him by the end of the evening, if I hadn't been before. And he said he couldn't believe how I had changed, that when he'd gone away the summer before I wasn't grown up at all, and now I was, except, of course, he'd seen me last at Easter. I was getting giddy with the dancing and I didn't think about it. He had bought me this corsage, really beautiful, and he said the flowers were ugly compared to me. He never said he'd fallen in love with me or anything like that, although he got it out of me that I thought he was the most, and that just to be there with him was like an answer to my dream. I don't know why I said that, except that he kept questioning me about how I felt about him. I suppose Bob had passed on to him all these things I've been telling you, and he wanted me to confirm them, like 'Did you miss me while I was away?' And 'What were you thinking about me?' Questions like that.

"When I woke up the next morning I felt as if I had dreamed it all, that it hadn't really happened, and then I heard the phone ringing, and Mother calling up the stairs that it was Ricky. I grabbed my dressing gown and dashed down the stairs and I was so excited and out of breath that I could hardly talk. Ricky asked me if I wanted to go for a ride in his car, and of course I said yes, so I hurried with the things I had to do for Mother, and packed a lunch before Ricky came at noon. We drove out past Castle Rock and went up into the hills--that's where I'd like to go tomorrow with you, Art--and we picnicked on the very top where we could see the entire valley spread out before us. It was glorious in the sun and I was delirious being with Ricky while we talked about his ideas for the Xenophon, or at least he talked and I agreed with him that it was wonderful what he wanted to do. I didn't see, then, that I was part of his plan, that he had it all thought out, how I would fit in. It was then that he first told me of his idea for Bob, that Bob could continue with his studies and, after teaching for a time, come back and be manager of the Xenophon. It was only later that he told me of my part in his plan, that I was to be a very important part of it. That happened in the evening, while we were eating at his place. I had been to the Bryson's often for supper or Sunday dinner, but always it had been with Mother and Father. But now I felt as if I were on display, that Ricky had insisted that I be there so that his parents would be prepared for the day when they would be called upon to pass judgment on me, the day he told them that he wanted to marry me. It was only then that I began to understand what he really intended, that he was preparing me, too, without ever having asked my feelings in the matter, as if he assumed that I would say yes to whatever he had in mind. And that wasn't only to marry him, but to become a sort of partner, to be the one who would bring our two families, the Brysons and the Glens, together, I mean through inheritance, that once we were married that, naturally, he would be named to get his father's share of the farm, and I would get half of my father's share, with Bob getting the other half. Not that anything like that has been decided by my father, as far as I know, but Ricky said as much, speaking of my part of the share as if I already owned it, and how when we were merged into a single corporation that there would be better opportunity for efficient management. I didn't guess, even then, that he wanted to squeeze Bob out, I was so full of thinking of what he was, and trying to figure out what he really meant to me, whether this was only an infatuation or whether I really loved him.

"Afterward we sat out on the Bryson porch for a while and then went for a walk among the trees up there, a lovely grove of oaks, and in the moonlight he told me more about his ambitions, how he really wanted to do something for the farm people of America. No, more than that, for everyone in the whole country, and even the world. He wasn't at all like the Ricky I had known, or thought I had known, for of course he'd never talked to me like that before, and I had been preparing such plans of my own, having just gotten out of community college, that I was breathless listening to him. You know how smoothly he talks, so sure of himself, so certain that everything he said was definitely going to happen, like there was no doubt of that at all. He talked as if, as if all this had been revealed to him in some way, you know what I mean? He didn't say God had a plan for his life, but he gave me the impression that all this was foreordained, that there wasn't anything that could stop it from happening. Of course we are both Presbyterians as it used to be preached, but that might be the closest I can come in describing his attitude, that he was predestined to be what he was going to be, and his pleasure was all in waking to each new day to witness what part of the plan was to be fulfilled. That is why he is so sure you and I, Art, won't be married, you see, because it was not intended that I should marry you, only him. It gives him patience, not the kind that bears burdens without complaint, for, as you learned, he can lash out in anger like the rest of us, but the kind that waits for things to happen when they're due to happen and does not expect them to happen before their time.

"Some of this he said and some of it he implied. Perhaps it is mixed now with my own feelings about him, and my own love for the Xenophon, for he was talking about home, and I want the Xenophon to be finer and grander than it has ever been, for that responsibility is upon me too as much as upon him. Since the days of my great-grandfather, our great-grandfathers, the Xenophon has been constantly enlarged and improved. Our fathers taught us since we were very small that they looked to us, including me, to carry it on and see to it that the farm progressed, because unless we progressed we would go backward. There could be no standing still. So always there was talk around the meal table at both our homes of what new crops would be experimented with next year. Always it was next year, this year was not enough. In another year there would be a larger yield per acre, in another year there would be greater milk production per cow, in another year a building or two would be remodeled. Always something to do, always some improvement to be made. Our progress in school was closely monitored, and even as closely were we expected to report on our contributions to the Juvenile Grange, the Future Farmers, the Homemakers, and always we were reminded that the world belonged to us, because we had been born to a great heritage, a responsibility and a duty greater than our parents have, because we would inherit more than they had.

"The next day Ricky called for me again and we went over the whole farm together as we used to do summers when we were younger, patrolling the fences, looking for breaks or rotting posts just above the ground, and taking notes as we went so the farm hands could be sent out to make repairs. I made the notes as Ricky called out the spots where attention was required, and we were partners again just like it once was. It was while we were walking together that he spoke of what *we* would do together to make the Xenophon better, and he mentioned the mansion we would build together, and asked me if I didn't think the parlor should be named the Great Hall and should be two storeys tall, because there we would hold the October ball and invite the neighbors from miles around. You would have thought that he was master of a great plantation, the way he talked, and I did not deny that I would relish such a role as mistress of a mansion. He even got me imagining myself in an immense hooped dress standing on the porch, with bright lanterns hung all round, welcoming the guests as they drove up the circled drive in their Cadillacs, and the men bowing and kissing my hand, paying their respects to the greatest lady of the county, and paying compliments to the squire for his immense good fortune in having me for his wife.

"If this was Ricky's dream, then it became mine too, and as we stood on the ridge before the stream and his pointing finger traced the horizon, he said all this would be ours one day, and he put his arm around my waist and I leaned against him there on the hill, and we swayed together a little in the breeze, drinking in the sight, not as it was, but as it would be, with the best of everything planted as far as the eye could see, and imigrants bent to their work in the long rows, and there was pride in me as I looked at him, as if for the first time, as the handsome hero come to share this grand life with me, to give me the gift not only of himself but also of his definite dream. I swear that if this was not love, then I will never know what love is, and yet it was not the love I have for you. There must be more than one kind of love, for I have felt both deeply, and I still must for Ricky, although I know now it is not for me, because I am not what he thought I was, not the queen to his king., the princess to his prince, but still only the little girl he once knew, grown, not changed. So, on the way back from the hill to my house, and although I had lived there all my life, and must have known how ill-favored it was compared to the Bryson's, still I had never thought of it as slightly tarnished, ill-kept. But then I was aware how common it looked compared to the finer Bryson house, and I wondered why it was so, Father being equal partner in the Xenophon, but I did not raise the question and haven't ever, for that's the kind of secret you keep to yourself, knowing that it's so, not daring to probe the reasons why. But it made a difference with me, because I felt, in a way, that I was Ricky's inferior, not as clever, and perhaps he was some sort of god sent to earth to deliver me from what was, after all, a rather shabby home, and that he should think me worthy of sharing his dream! The glory of it shone upon me, and if I was radiant with it, as he told me I was, then it was because I stood in his shadow. And that is strange, because I felt I should not touch him, but only gave him my hand when he offered his, only put my arm around him when he first put his arm around me. And when, in the evening, we came here to the loft to talk and it had grown dark, and he had reached for me and took me without request, it was as if it was his natural right, that this was predestined too, and no invitation was needed on my part, none expected, that it was the inevitable climax of those three days, it fitted in."

She was silent. Her breath came heavily on the damp air and it had been so long listening to her that I felt transported from the loft to some downy cloud, where we rested while the earth floated past, far distant, as unreal as the unknown sea.

"And now?" I asked at last.

"And now you know, will you forgive me?"

"I forgive you."

"And love me?"

"I will love you forever."

"Then hold me." She turned to me and clasped me fully. From the eaves the last rain fell, seeping to the rich fertile earth. Through the webbed windows of the loft, by the stalls the moonlight shone, and the wind moved smoothly on the black hills. In a far corner the cattle moaned, a sigh, and the silent night was slowed, the heaving rhythm of its motion paced by our song of love.

I think we were both dreaming when the whine of a car's engine notified us that the Glens had returned from the fair.

THE FIFTH DAY

A WAY OF KNOWING

Many Interesting People Do
Lots of Work to Make Fair
A Success, Reporter Finds

By Arthur James
Special to the Star

Nice thing about a fair is that you meet such interesting people

And we don't mean the *Lobster Boy--Alive!* either.

We mean the local folk who put in the 16-hour days all this week to keep the fair wheels turning. While thousands mill around in the aisles, these people stay behind the scenes.

Without them there wouldn't be a fair. Those thousands of exhibit items don't just happen. Somebody has to arrange them. And the somebodys turn out to be hundreds of men and women and young people deeply interested in the progress and prosperity of Chesterton County.

They don't get anything for their effort, except maybe a headache and sore feet. But they're the most energetic, patient, alert representatives of the county's citizens.

There are the folk of Castle Rock Presbyterian Church who are pitching in to keep their canvas-covered diner open 24 hours a day.

"Pretty soon everyone in the congregation will have a turn serving," says Pastor Mark Christopher with a flashing smile. He reveals that he was there until 2 a.m. opening day, serving the last of the day's visitors and fair workers.

"You know, you may think some of these carnival workers are pretty callous," he says, "but we got talking with one of them last night and our talk lasted an hour and a half. They get pretty lonely sometimes. It's a tough life traveling around all the time as they do."

Two men stay at the church's diner all night, catching what sleep they can while they're there. Proceeds go to the church.

Just inside the Agricultural Pavilion, Mrs. Seymour Denis supervises the flower show.

"I guess I walked 20 miles on these cement floors yesterday," she says. "I was here from 8 a.m. to 1:30 a.m." Yet she was back again today, opening a new showing.

In the education building, Carl Richards, a health instructor at Chesterton Community College, awaits visitors at the County Health department's stall. He alternates throughout the day with Dr. Roach, county health officer, in answering the public's questions.

"People are quite interested in their hearts," he says, indicating the display which warns folks to take care of their blood pumps. "Little girl, a Brownie, over there in the Girl Scouts booth, comes over every 15 minutes, and wants me to listen to her heart," he says.

We try the stethoscope ourselves, but can't hear a thing. "That's us," I say. "No heart."

A rather plump woman comes up. She weighs herself furtively on the scales. "Am I overweight?" she asks, somewhat fearfully glancing at a flashing sign which warns that folk should watch their weight if they want a good heart.

After a few words of comfort and admonition from Mr. Richards, she waddles off.

Two Brownies are in the Girl Scouts booth. Both eight, they shyly display the handicraft of their troop--dish mats made of rubber can rings, carefully interwoven.

They plague their leader, Mrs. Peggy Weaver, to tell everyone who made the mats, but Mrs. Weaver isn't telling because the mats are troop entries and to the troop, not the individual, goes the credit.

The girls are delighted to be "on duty," taking their turn among dozens of others at the booth. In their Brownie jumpers, they're really "official."

With them a great deal of the time is Miss Elizabeth Warner, Girl Scout executive, who has spent uncounted hours in preparation for the exhibit. She's proud of the handiwork of her girls.

Down the aisle, Carl Bratton, 4-H Club agent, anxiously glances over the fruit and vegetable exhibits. Everything must be kept in order. Nothing must spoil the patient hours of effort which went into making this 4-H exhibit the best ever.

So it goes all up and down the aisles of the exhibit buildings--manufacturers, teachers, Home Bureau, Farm Bureau, Future Farmers, shopkeepers--they're all here.

Yes, the most interesting thing about a fair is the interesting folk you meet. Last Day, folks. Let's go to the Fair!

CHAPTER TWENTY-FOUR

It was after ten when I awoke in my hotel room. I bolted up, looked at my watch and leaped from the bed. I went over to my closet to retrieve a paper that Jenny's father had given me the night before. I picked up my phone and asked the operator to get me the Star.

I fidgeted with the telephone's wire. "Johhny? I'm sorry I didn't get a chance to write up the story for today. I'm ready now to give it to rewrite." He told me to hold the line and get back to him when I had finished.

"Okay, Frank here." I heard him fiddling with his earphones. "Shoot," he said. I dictated the story on reactions to the proposal to use the Xenophon as a site for the fair, giving him quotes from my interviews with Small and Clark. Then I dictated Bryson's entire statement.

Frank switched me back to the city desk. "Got your story," Johnny said. "Looks okay. Also using your fourth-day feature, *Interesting People*. Good headline. Anything from the courts?"

"I will check," I said, "but it looks as if the whole thing is sewed up. Turns out everybody's been working on the scheme for months. Cut and dried now."

"Stay awake, Art. Surprises do happen when there's a feud going on."

As I was driving slowly toward the fairgrounds I tried to make some sense out of the tangled net that enmeshed so many of the people I had met, including the score I had interviewed. But a *feud*? Wasn't this the nineteen-sixties? I knew that Small's wife was silently opposed to her husband's designs, to which the fair would fall victim. Were Small and Bryson feuding? If so, Ricky's role in the feud was to neutralize any possible injury that Small could cause to his father's supple ambition to be the founding father as Chesterton County transitioned from rural eminence to urban, industrialized majesty. And it was Ricky's role to be the ordained crown prince.

At the fair office I stood by the counter while Jenny, at her desk, finished tallying a long column of figures. She smiled up at me. "I'll be with you in a minute," she said. Now I knew her I wondered why she was stranger still. When I first saw her there on Monday afternoon (so long ago, five days!) she was just another girl, a clerk, courteously showing me into Stowe's office. I wondered why I had not paid more attention to her. If, last Monday morning, I had seen Jenny at a desk in Richland, perhaps in a courthouse office, would I have looked at her so little? Were there other Jennys in Richland whom I had passed by, unseeing, because they were so familiar, so close, so available? Then why had this happened?

Bob was counting change at one window and Ricky was at the other, selling tickets. Stowe came through his open office door. "Art," he called. "I have something for you." I caught Ricky's eye as he turned to observe me. His stare was defiant, hard and cold. In his office, Stowe handed me a stapled sheaf of mimeographed paper. "My report for tonight's meeting," he said. "I thought you would like to have some time to digest it."

He sat down on his chair and motioned me to the one beside the table. I started glancing through the report while Stowe picked up his pipe, filled it with tobacco and tamped it down tightly. He struck a match and blew great puffs of smoke into the air. "Let me show you something," he said. He reached toward me to get the report and as he did his arm hit the pipe, knocked ashes over the papers on his desk. "Darn, I'm always doing that," he said. He picked up a paper weight and stamped out the glowing embers. I gave him the report. He flipped through the pages. "Here," he said, "Page nine." He held up the page so I could see the figures. "These are estimates of attendance, based on the first three days. Of course we won't know until late tonight what the totals will be. Notice that they are broken down between adult tickets and children's tickets. Our definition of a child is anyone twelve years old and under."

"All right," I said. "I'll be careful to report the figures. Perhaps I can pick up the final tally in the morning. And how about comparison with other years?"

"You will find it there. My estimate is we have set a ten-year record. Of course it's far below the pre-war years, before World War Two, I mean. Will you see me after tonight's meeting? I will have a statement for you."

"What about?"

"I might as well tell you now. If it goes as I think it will go, it will be a statement giving the reasons for my resignation."

"You're going to quit? Couldn't you move over to the Xenophon?"

"Haven't you heard? Ricky's going to be the fair manager."

"How can he?"

"Oh, his father and Mr. Glen will carry on for him, doing the preliminary work that will start right away. But Ricky will take over fulltime as soon as the legal work is done, papers signed, etcetera. I say full-time, but of course that's a relative term. If Ricky follows in his father's footsteps, as we know he will, he will get two assistants to take care of the details. Another thing. Ricky's against using volunteers in the fair office. Say's they are too amateurish."

"Excluding himself."

"Well, he's realistic about it. You can't command volunteers to be here all the time you need them. Take Jenny, for instance, she's given almost all her time for weeks, but she was gone all afternoon yesterday afternoon and evening."

"I'm to blame for that."

"It's all right. She's young. You can't expect a girl to stick to it sixteen hours a day, standing much of the time, the way Ricky and Bob can. Jenny's a wonderful worker. I just state it as a problem we have to contend with in using volunteers. I've never had enough budget for a full-time staff. Even when the fair's not on I only have a part-time secretary. Well, all that will be so much water under the bridge for me. I'm going to apply to the State Fair for a job. Get references from Mr. Small and Mr. Bryson."

"They know about it, then?"

"We had our final conference this morning. They wanted me to stay on through the winter, but I pointed out that if I was going to move, now was the time, that it would be too late next spring to start looking for a job. They understood and said they would recommend the acceptance of my resignation tonight. That's a formality. They couldn't keep me here. What I need is the board's recommendation. That's the way it goes. Chesterton, farewell!" He looked past me to the door. "Yes, Jenny?"

She winked at me. "I've finished accounting this morning's receipts, Mr. Stowe. I will finish this afternoon's later, I promise."

"That's fine Jenny. You want to leave now?"

"If I may."

"Certainly. See you tonight."

I stood up to go with her. "See you after the meeting tonight, Mr. James." Stowe said.

"I will be there."

I was about to leave the building when I heard Ricky call out. "Just a minute, Mr. Reporter." I turned as he came slowly toward me. "A word with you, if you please. Shall we go outside?"

To Jenny I said: "I'll be right back."

Ricky followed me out. We stood face to face under the hot sun.

"Well?" I asked.

"You're taking Jenny with you?" He placed his hands on his hips.

"Yes."

"Don't. I'm warning you." His voice was steel-edged.

"Ricky, don't threaten me. But it you want to have it out right here, I'm ready." I tightened my hands into fists.

"Don't be ridiculous. I will flatten you in a second. I told you, Mr. reporter, Jenny is my girl. She will never leave me."

"Jenny has made her choice, Ricky. Go find yourself another girl."

Suddenly I was falling. It was only on the hard earth that I felt the pain rising along the nape of my neck. It had been fast, faster than the time before. I felt myself struggling up in a sort of fog and then going down again as his second blow caught me on the chin. Then Jenny was bending over me. "Lie still," she commanded. I was conscious of several people standing around us. With Jenny's help, I made it to my feet. I looked around. Ricky was not there.

"Let's get out of here," I mumbled. I staggered through the fair's main gate to the street and along the sidewalk, holding to the fence with one hand while Jenny grasped the other, until we reached the Buick.

"I will drive," she said. I fumbled in my pocket for the keys and handed them to her. She opened the right door for me. I clambered in and sat down heavily. Jenny went around to the other side, unlocked the door and sat behind the wheel. I tried to open the window, but a pain in my elbow that I couldn't explain caused me to cry out. "It's stuck," I said. Jenny reached over me and turned the handle. A welcome cool breeze swept over me.

We were silent as we passed slowly through quiet streets and entered the Castle Rock road. "Wow," I said at last. "What happened?"

"You know very well what happened! I warned you not to get into a fight with Ricky"

"You call that a fight? It was a massacre." I attempted a smile, but gave it up as the contraction of my jaw muscles sent a bolt of pain through my head. We reached the Xenophon and passed over the hill toward the Glen house. Jenny turned the car into the driveway. Why are we stopping?"

"First aid, silly."

I waited in the car while Jenny went inside the house. She returned ten minutes later. She doctored my bloodied chin with stinging red drops from a tiny bottle, then applied a sticky bandage. "Stay put," she said and returned to the house. Five minutes later she came back carrying two heavy suitcases, placed them on the ground, reached inside for the car's keys, opened the trunk and heaved her luggage inside.

"Let' go, Art. Abscond with the runaway bride."

CHAPTER TWENTY-FIVE

Jenny piloted the Buick slowly along Main Street East in Castle Rock, braked and pulled over to the curb. "Over there!" she cried. "Beside the church."

The majestic oak, which had towered higher than the church spire, no doubt a century-old landmark, the pride of Castle Rock, lay flattened on the church's lawn. It rested on its virulent side, top branches pointing north, broken, smashed, irretrievably dead. What was left of its magnificent strong trunk was broken, splintered, gashed open by a lightning strike, unknown, unheard by Jenny and I while we nestled in the safe embrace of a Xenophon loft.

Jenny pushed the gas pedal and we idled slowly through the quiet town, through the business block, past the library, past the gleaming white Methodist and Baptist churches and the Catholic chapel, past the cemetery, until, the town behind us, we entered farm country, where vast fields of corn stretched for miles, their greenery reaching free and high.

Jenny was sobbing. "I will miss that oak," she said. "All my life, it's been there. Now it's gone. Why now? Oh, Art, I am afraid."

"Never mind, we came out here to enjoy the scenery," I said. Jenny turned the Buick onto the side of the road, braked and cut the engine. "Look, look over there, Jenny, that cattle herd under the tree. Tell me, why are they all looking in the same direction?"

"Oh, who cares?" She dried her eyes with a tissue. "Follow-the-leader, I suppose. That's just the way cows are."

"People too," I said.

Jenny was looking at me curiously. "Your chin's bleeding," she said. She handed me a clean tissue. I dabbed my wound. "It's okay," I said. "That Ricky! He needs help."

Despite everything, Jenny laughed. She couldn't stop laughing.

"He's weird," I said.

"Maybe so, but he's no different than a lot of people I know. I don't have to tell you to stay away from Ricky tonight, do I?"

"You too, Jenny."

"Bob will take me home."

"Good."

"Here's the road," Jenny said.

I turned into a dirt road on the right. Jenny threw the stick into low as we went up the hill, following the twists and turns carefully. We were silent all the way, and at last we reached the crest and stopped on a grassy spot off the road. We got out, crossed the road into a field. The wind blew swiftly on the hill, tossing our hair. A score of yards across the field we sat on a rough log in the shade of a pine tree. Below us the vast panorama of the Castle Rock Valley was spread out in all its green glory. Far away on the left was the village itself, a white blotch, with the tower of the Presbyterian Church rising over the fallen oak.

"It's beautiful up here," Jenny said. "Doesn't it feel far away from everything?"

"Not far enough," I said.

"I wonder when we will be able to return?"

"When your mother and father accept us."

"That's the hard part, doing this without them knowing."

"You can explain it to them. I'm sure they will understand."

"Will they? Will they think you are the father of my child?"

"That is what we will tell them," I said. "In fact, they will presume that, won't they?"

"I hope so." She laughed a little. "Quick action, they will say!" She turned toward me and I cradled her in my arms. "Oh, Art, you're so good to me."

"I'm not taking you away from here to be good to you."

"I know you will be good to me."

"I will. I will marry you because I love you."

"Do you? Do you really?"

"Yes, yes. No need to question me, Jenny. I mean it. I love you."

"I love you too, Art. We will be happy together, won't we?"

"As happy as two people can be."

"You don't sound very convincing."

"Jenny, do we have to question everything? We have each other. We are leaving here together. Let's accept it."

"I still can't believe it's happening. It's been so fast, so sudden."

"We had no choice," I said uneasily.

"No, we didn't, did we? Then it's not our fault?"

"Fault? Why should we be at fault? You've got to get over feeling that way. It's peaceful here. Let us be at peace too."

I reached for her hand, raised it slowly and kissed it. He slim fingers trembled in my grasp and so did mine. Despite her spoken assurance that she was *just fine* I felt a slight shimmer as we held one another tightly. She exclaimed, with a shy laugh, "What are you trying to do, Art? Smother me?"

What was I trying to do? Escape, perhaps? Take Jenny with me on the morrow under the circumstances? What circumstances? She was shivering slightly within the orbit of my embrace. The sun slid under a long dark cloud, casting a shadow upon us.

"Let's talk about something else," Jenny said. "What shall we talk about?"

"About you, Jenny, I said. "I want you to go to Richland University as soon as you can, okay?"

"Okay," she said cheerfully. "What about the baby?"

"My mother will look after him--or her."

"She must be very nice."

"She is. She's crazy about kids. I'm an only child. She made no secret of it that she had wanted a girl. Mom and Dad tried, but they had no luck."

"I want to have lots and lots of them," Jenny said.

"Four, remember?"

"You won't spank the children, will you?"

I wasn't ready for that one. "No spanking. We will spoil them."

"I was only spanked once, when Mother caught me doing a naughty thing."

"Naughty, huh? And what was that?"

"Never you mind." She shifted easily in my arms and turned her face to me. I kissed her lightly on the cheek. "Anyway, she spanked me, but that was the only time."

"You were too good."

"No, I wasn't. I was always mean to my brother. I used to tell Mother that Bob was bad. For instance, when I got out of bed at night to go to the bathroom, and I saw a light shining under Bob's door, I would tell Mother that Bob was reading when he should have been asleep. Bob would get scolded, and afterward Bob would do something mean to me, like hiding my hairbrush."

She went on, telling me other stories of her childhood, and sometimes I was listening and sometimes I wasn't, because I was brooding whether Jenny's fears were well founded, and wondering how I could protect her through the long night ahead. She paused in her recital.

"Let's talk about tomorrow," I said. "Where shall we meet?"

"At your hotel, I suppose."

"You will take the bus to town?"

"Sure. It goes down Main Street, stops at the hotel."

"Then I will meet you in the lobby." I paused. "Oh. I almost forgot. I have to go to the fairgrounds tomorrow morning."

"Whatever for? The fair will be over."

"I have to do a windup feature about the day *after* the fair. Well, I can get there early, the earlier the better. My story will have more color."

"You're going to pick me up at ten o'clock, and you want to work before then?"

"It's my job."

She closed her eyes. I held her close. In the trees the birds sang fitfully, calling to their mates. Around the edges of the field the crickets chorused. High up, a swallow soared, and far down the valley a car horn sounded, subdued. But that was far away.

CHAPTER TWENTY-SIX

As soon as I entered the hotel lobby I saw Bryson and Glen. I hurried after them. Why don't you come with us, Mr. James?" said Bryson. We mounted the stairway to the second floor. "Want to meet the representative of Tiber Trucks?" he asked. "He should be here by now. I invited him to sit through the meeting. You received Mr. Stowe's report?" I nodded. "Here we are." He opened the door to Parlor C and we went inside. There were already a half dozen men there, including Stowe, Small and Clark. I went around the big rectangular table and shook their hands.

"Good to see you, Mr. James," Small said. He introduced me to Carter and Blakemore, a tall guy with balding black hair, slicked back, and wide black-rimmed glasses. Carter was a short man with steel-gray hair, crew-cut. Then it was MacDonald, the Tiber Trucks rep, who, surprisingly, was only about thirty. He had a bland, open countenance and a wide smile. He was snappily dressed in a gray smoothly-pressed suit.

"May I see you for a moment, Mr. James," MacDonald said. We went off to a corner. "I have been instructed to give you a statement following the meeting of the corporation," he said. "Meanwhile, if there is anything you would like to know."

"Perhaps some facts about Tiber Trucks," I said. "Of course the Star already has a lot of material on your firm, so there won't be any trouble filling in the background."

"Of course. I do have a little folder here that contains the basic facts about the company, its officers, when the company was founded, production, that sort of thing." He opened his attache case and gave me the pamphlet. I glanced through it.

"Just what I need," I said.

"Only if the corporation votes favorably."

"Naturally."

"We wouldn't want any unfavorable publicity if the vote is negative."

"I'm sure the Star will treat you kindly," I said with a smile. "As a matter of fact, I imagine that Richland would rather have Tiber Trucks stay in Richland."

"I appreciate your understanding, Mr. James. There are so many public relations problems connected with the transfer of a plant from one community to another. One thing I might reveal in confidence is that you will find in the statement a plan for maintaining production on a decelerating basis while operations are built up here. That is, there will be a gradual transfer to Chesterton, rather than an abrupt move. We will give very generous severance payments to any worker who desires to remain in Richland rather than move to Chesterton County. Of course we will pay moving expenses."

"You expect to take care of all your employees?"

"We will help those who need assistance in acquiring comparable employment, yes."

"I mean you will employ as many people in Chesterton as you now employ in Richland?"

"Oh, no, Mr. James. That's why we are moving. The possibility of modernizing our Richland plant was carefully explored, very carefully. It was not economically possible. It proved more economical to build new facilities at another location. The Chesterton plant will be as automated as we can make it. This will mean an increase, a vast increase, in production per worker, but with a sharply reduced staff. It will place Barclay in a favorable competitive position with Michigan, very favorable."

"How many employees will you be transferring to Chesterton?"

"That is difficult to say. We have already commenced a retraining program, using automated equipment of the type that will be established here. The better-trained workers are, of course, more adaptable to re-training. Others, unfortunately, are not so adaptable."

"And these will be let go?"

"As I said, we will make every effort--"

"I know, to get them jobs. What about the employment of Chesterton people?"

"We plan to establish an employment office here at the earliest possible date. Applications will be received from all who wish to apply. These will be screened and those who are found adaptable to the new type of equipment will be hired first, before others from elsewhere."

"You mean you will have to hire workers from other parts of the country?"

"Of course. This has been assiduously explored. We will need a large number of graduate engineers. Already we have been in touch with the great technological institutions. The engineering staff will be greatly augmented here, more engineers per worker than in Richland, many more."

"Then how many jobs for Chesterton people will your plant make available?"

"That would be difficult to ascertain, most difficult. It all depends upon how many of our present staff are available, how many are willing to move. But I want to assure you that Tiber Trucks will be a good citizen of Chesterton, very good. As our statement will indicate, we think Barclay trucks will be a boon to Chesterton's declining economy, a big boon."

"Declining?"

"Oh, yes. We have studied that thoroughly, quite thoroughly. That is one of the attractions. Taxes are low, quite low. Yes, Chesterton will be an ideal location for Tiber Trucks, most ideal."

A gavel banged behind us. Bryson raised the gavel again. "Shall we come to order, gentlemen? Mr. James, you may sit with us, if you wish. I believe there are plenty of chairs at the table. I looked around as the men began shuffling into their chairs. Keating and Harding sat side-by-side with Jenny's father and Stowe. There were two other men I hadn't met. I presumed they were Seymour Denis, the engineer, and Daniel Morris, the lawyer, chairman of the county commissioners. I walked around the table and sat down in a chair near the door. Just as I did, the door opened and Marie came in. She sat down quickly in the chair next to mine.

"We welcome Marie, representative of the Chesterton Times," Bryson said.

"Well, hello," I whispered to Marie as I leaned toward her.

"Greetings," she replied cheerfully.

Bryson was standing in the middle of the long side of the table, opposite me. "Gentlemen, and lady, if you are ready." He banged the gavel on a wooden knocker. "I declare the one hundredth annual meeting of the board of directors of the Chesterton County Fair--open!" There was a scattering of applause. He banged the gavel again and sat down. "I believe you have received the minutes of the last meeting? Do I hear a motion that they be approved?"

"I so move," Blakemore snapped.

"Second," said Carter.

"All in favor of receiving the minutes as printed and distributed?"

"Aye, aye, aye," rang around the table.

"Hearing no nays, the motion is approved. Mr. Secretary." Bryson looked toward Glen.

"I'm taking notes, Sam," said Glen laconically without looking up. He had a small sheet of paper before him and was writing on it.

"Then I believe we may distribute the agenda." He picked up a sheaf of papers before him, split the pack and handed half to Small on his right and half to Denis on his left. Each director took a sheet and passed the remainder down the line.

"My apologies, gentlemen," Bryson said. "I believe I forgot the first item. Shall we stand?"

I stood up and pulled out Marie's chair for her. "Let us pray," Bryson said. All heads bowed. I noticed that almost all the men clasped their hands before them. All eyes were closed. "Our Father," Bryson began, "we pray Thy blessing on this one hundredth annual meeting of the board of directors of the Chesterton County Fair. Amen."

There was a clearing of throats all around as we resumed our seats. "Now, let's see," Bryson began. "The report of our manager. Mr. Stowe?"

Stowe stood up. From two stacks he picked up one of his reports in each hand and dealt them out like playing cards. The reports were passed out from one to another until everyone had a copy, including Marie and I. "I need not bore you, gentlemen, by reading the report," Stowe said, glancing around with a smile. The directors did not smile back. "However, I would like to touch upon a few highlights. If you please turn to the summary on Page Three." He waited until all had found the page. "You will note that estimated fair attendance this year has set a ten-year record, the highest since I have been in your employ. Likewise, the figures for total number of exhibits, both commercial and voluntary, have set a record. Receipts, although not final, are expected to exceed those of last year. Any questions?" He sat down.

Carter said: "I notice you said receipts exceeded last year's. How about other years?"

"Our peak was reached five years ago," Stowe said. "Since then, except for this year, there has been a decline."

Bryson said: "Any other comments, gentlemen? Yes, Mr. Morris."

The man beside Carter said "There is no deficit, then?"

"That all depends how you look at it," Stowe replied. "We expect to break even. Contributions are up, as are concession fees. Minus the contributions, of course, we are in the hole."

Bryson said: "I think you may use more technical language, Mr. Stowe."

"Sorry, I mean there is a deficit, yes, if we set aside contribution income."

Morris said: "Then I wish to submit, Mr. Chairman, that the fair is riding on very thin ice, responsibility-wise. Should a rise in contribution income fail to materialize in another year, we'll be sunk!"

"A good comment, very good," Bryson said. "Do I hear any other comments? No? If not, do I hear a motion to receive the report with thanks?"

"I so move," Keating said.

"Second," said Harding.

"Aye, aye."

"And may I take this opportunity to commend Mr. Stowe on his usual excellent presentation? I am sure we will all study this report most thoroughly, and inwardly digest, as the saying goes. Now--"

"Mr. Chairman!"

"Yes, Mr. Stowe?"

"I have something else to say."

"Let's put it under other business?"

"Alright," Stowe said.

"Now, the reports of the patron organizations. Mr. Glen."

Glen stood up and divided a shallow stack of papers before him. He passed them around, starting with Keating on his left and Harding on his right. "The report of the Pomona is before you, gentlemen. Shall I read it, Mr. Chairman?"

"I think we can dispense with that, if that is agreeable to you, gentlemen?" There was a nodding of heads all around. "Do you wish to say something Mr. Glen?"

"Only that the Grange is honored and proud to be a patron of so worthy an organization as the Chesterton County Fair. Our report indicates the interest of the Grange, the Juvenile Grange and our members in the continuation of the fair, and the preservation of a glorious tradition."

A few hear-hears rang out around the table. "Thank you, Mr. Glen. Do I hear a motion to receive?"

"I move it," said Keating.

"Second," said Harding.

"It is received," said Bryson. "Any other organizations wish to report? Mr. Keating."

"If the board will agree, the FGA report will be mailed to the directors," said Keating.

"And the Co-op, Mr. Harding?'

"Likewise."

"Agreed?"

"Aye, aye."

"Before going on to other business, a most important item tonight, I venture to propose that this board go on record with a vote of thanks to the Times for the excellent publicity on the fair. Do I hear a motion?"

"I so move," said Small.

"Second," said Blakemore.

"Agreed?"

"Aye-aye."

"Yes, Mr. Clark?"

"I wish to thank the Board for its expression of praise. And may I assure the Board that the Times will always stand ready to support a worthy community enterprise."

"Thank you, Mr. Clark. Now, other business. Mr. Denis?"

"A motion of appreciation to the patron organizations is in order?"

"I move it," said Carter.

"Second," said Denis.

"Aye, aye."

"How about the business exhibitors?" asked Carter.

Bryson said "Gentlemen, we can be here all night passing resolutions of appreciation, and we all know we have a more important, that is more pressing, business to take care of. Can't we wrap it up in one motion, Mr. Glen?"

"I will be glad to frame, it, Sam."

"All in favor?'

"Aye-aye."

"Is that all? Then we can adjourn."

Stowe said: "Uh, Mr. Chairman."

"I was about to say, Mr. Stowe, that we can adjourn this meeting of the directors, go into corporation, then reconvene as directors. Do I hear a motion?"

"I move it," said Small.

"Second," said Blakemore.

"Aye, aye."

"Thank you for being present, lady and gentleman of the press," said Bryson. "We will call you when reconvening."

Marie and I stood up to leave and so did Stowe. As I held the door open for Marie I noticed that Small took Bryson's place.

In the hall, Stowe said: "I wanted to get my resignation out of the way so I could get back to the fair. It's the biggest night and the kids will need me. But I suppose the corporation meeting won't take long. We should be able to get a cup of coffee. How about it?"

We went down the stairs to the lobby and crossed into the coffee shop. We sat down in a booth, Marie beside me. "So, Mr. Stowe, you're going to quit?" she said.

"Told Art about it this afternoon," Stowe said. "I don't understand why Mr. Bryson put it off like that."

"Looks like they're putting off all the goodies until the second round," I said. "The first round was pretty cut and dried."

"It's always like that," Stowe said. "By the way, Art, good stories again today."

"Thanks," I said. "That reminds me. I haven't seen the Star or the Times yet."

"Terrific story in the Times," Stowe said. His sarcasm was clear. I bought both papers at the lobby shop. I flipped open the Times first, to be polite. "Bottom of Page Three," Marie said. There it was, a one-column box, two inches deep, only a notice that the fair board was to meet. "That's all?" I asked.

"That's all," she said. "Of course there will be a story on the action tomorrow. I will be writing that. I'm so embarrassed. That stupid board resolution, thanking the Times. They didn't mention the Star and you have given the best coverage, Art. The Times has done so little, I mean real news."

I opened the Star. My report had been relegated to Page Three. Beside it was my feature article about the fair's volunteers.

"What happened to your chin?" Marie asked me.

I felt the bandage. I had forgotten it was still there. I pulled the edges and ripped it off, stinging my skin. "Oh, nasty," Marie said.

"Art ran into a door at the fair," Stowe said.

"Thank you, Mr. Stowe," I said laughing. I turned to Marie. "It was Ricky."

"Not again!" Marie exclaimed.

"I saw you on the ground," Stowe said. "I wasn't that concerned. I thought it was a little argument you were having with Ricky because you had a couple of dates with Jenny. I'm sorry, Art. I apologize. I knew Ricky has a wild temper. I should have done something."

"Forget it, Mr. Stowe."

In the hall outside Parlor C we stood waiting for a while. Marie pulled me to one side. "Please don't start anything with Ricky tonight, Art. Promise."

"Sure, Marie, I promise," I said. The last thing I wanted was another encounter with the future manager of the fair.

The door opened. Bryson told the three of us to take our seats at the table. Bryson went to the presiding position. "For the benefit of the press, let's proceed to a report from the corporation. Mr. Small?"

Small stood up and thanked Bryson. "I will skip the details," Small began. "Present corporation officers were re-elected. A proposal from Tiber Trucks was presented and considered. A motion was made and unanimously adopted. Mr. Chairman, Mr. MacDonald has a statement for us and the press, and I have one myself on behalf of the corporation."

MacDonald reached into his case and took out bundled sheets of paper. They were passed around the table. Small's statement followed.

I glanced quickly at MacDonald's statement. It stated the gratification of Tiber Trucks for the opportunity to build a plant on the fairgrounds. Small's statement welcomed the firm to the county and expressed the conviction that Chestertonians could be proud of their industry.

Small called for the board's attention. "Perhaps I should read the resolution, for confirmation, before releasing it to the press?"

Bryson told him to go ahead. Here it is:

The Chesterton County Fair, Incorporated, petitions approval of the Board of Commissioners of Chesterton County to enter into negotiation with Tiber Trucks Corporation of Richland with regard to the sale of the property known as the Fairgrounds, situate entire within the said County of Chesterton.

Bryson said: "You have heard the report of the corporation."

Morris said: "I move it be received with thanks."

"Second," said Denis.

"Aye, aye."

"We are still under other business," Bryson said. "Does anyone have a report they would like to give at this time?"

Stowe said: "Mr. Chairman."

"In a moment, Mr. Stowe. Mr. Glen?"

Glen said: "As chairman of a committee appointed by Mr. Bryson, I have a report to present." He picked up another pack of white paper and had it passed around. I looked at my copy. It was headed: *Site of Chesterton County Fair.*

"Do you wish to read it, Mr. Glen?" Bryson asked.

"I don't think that will be necessary, Sam. Briefly, the committee finds and recommends that the fair be held next year on the Xenophon."

Bryson said: "Take your time, gentlemen. Read the report carefully. Meanwhile, perhaps we may have a motion?"

Keating said: "I move we accept the committee's recommendation."

"Second," said Harding.

Bryson said: "Any discussion? Ah, you have the floor, Mr. Small."

Small said: "For the record, I consider this to be one of the finest and most generous gestures for the benefit of the county that has ever been made by our illustrious agricultural organizations. I'm in favor of the motion."

"Question!" called Morris.

"The question has been called for," Bryson said. "Are any opposed? No? I think this calls for a show of hands. I will put the question: All in favor of acceptance of this recommendation by the committee signify by raising the right hand. I shall abstain, due to conflict of interest."

Glen said: "I abstain. Same reason."

Seven directors raised their right hands.

"The motion is passed," Bryson said. "I see it as unanimous, barring abstentions. Mark that down, Mr. Secretary." He turned to address MacDonald. "The representative of Tiber Trucks has requested an opportunity to address the board. Motion, please."

"I move it," said Glen.

"Second," said Small.

"All in favor?"

"Aye, aye."

"All opposed?"

Silence.

"The motion is carried. Mr. Macdonald, thank you."

MacDonald stood and bowed. "Gentlemen, I have been authorized to announce, in the light of your favorable vote on the new site for the fair, that Tiber Trucks desires to share in the expense associated with the movement of certain fair equipment, including furnishings and other goods, to the new site, and I wish to present to you, sir, our check as the first installment on our fair contribution." He took an envelope from his pocket and handed it to Bryson.

"Shall I open it now?" Bryson asked.

"By all means," MacDonald said.

Bryson opened the envelope, took out the check and held it high. "Gentlemen," he said boldly. "The contribution is in the amount of fifty thousand dollars."

There were glances and nods among the directors and a whistle or two. Glen beamed. "This is certainly a pleasant surprise, Mr. MacDonald," Bryson said. "I am sure the board will wish to express its appreciation in the most audible manner." The directors clapped enthusiastically and then thumped the table. MacDonald remained standing and bowed graciously, humbly.

"I have a request to make of the board," MacDonald said. "Is this in order, Mr. Chairman?"

"I will ask the board," Bryson replied. "Gentlemen?"

"I move approval of the request to be heard," said Keating.

"Aye, aye," they shouted.

MacDonald cleared his throat and smiled agreeably. "The request concerns the necessity that the fairgrounds be kept in safe operating condition until such time as the property may be sold to Tiber Trucks, assuming that the esteemed county Board of Commissioners deems it wise to concur in your recommendation, of course. We wish to employ a person who is completely familiar not only with the good citizens of Chesterton County, and with the fairgrounds, but also has your complete confidence and support. I need not emphasize before you how important it is that an orderly and expeditious transfer of the fairgrounds equipment from the property will be helpful to Tiber trucks. Therefore, I am authorized to suggest--suggest, I stress--that we may be permitted to borrow your efficient and respected manager, Mr. Stowe, for the term of one year, to act as our Chesterton properties manager at the annual salary of thirty-five thousand dollars."

I looked at Stowe. He appeared to be in a state of shock.

"At the same time," MacDonald continued, "we realize that this board will desire to continue his employment in order that the business of the fair, while in transition, may be completed. Therefore, Barclay trucks would be prepared to enter into negotiations regarding his time schedule so that a mutually satisfactory arrangement may be arrived at. Thank you."

Bryson said: "I see Mr. Stowe squirming a bit, and I don't blame you, Vic. This is a high honor indeed. I want to assure Mr. MacDonald that we will be very happy to talk with your people concerning Mr. Stowe's continued service with us. Meanwhile, there is the question of a one-year contract."

"I'm sorry, I should have made that clear," MacDonald said. "The contract would be for one year, but it would be renegotiable for a three-year term through mutual agreement. Also, the title of the position would be vice-president in charge of plant relations."

Bryson said: "Mr. Stowe--Vic--you wanted to make a statement. Would you like to make one now?" The directors turned their attention to Stowe. They smiled a lot.

Stowe stood up. His face was solemn, flushed. It was hard to tell whether he was going to laugh or cry. At last he spoke: "I, I don't know what to say. I need time to think it over."

"Of course," Bryson said. "This is between you and Tiber trucks, Vic. As far as the board is concerned, we are perfectly agreeable to whatever time schedule you can work out. Gentlemen?"

"Aye, aye."

"You see? Give your answer to Tiber Trucks, not to the board."

"Thank you," Stowe mumbled. "Thank you all, very much." He sat down heavily and gazed at his clasped hands.

"This is a heartfelt note upon which to conclude this meeting, gentlemen," Bryson said. "But I would not want us to do so until we express our appreciation in a formal way for all that Vic Stowe has done for the fair and Chesterton County through the years. Do I hear a motion?"

"I move it," said Small.

"Second," said Morris.

"Aye, aye."

The directors pounded the table until Bryson gaveled for order. "There being no further business, I declare the meeting adjourned," Bryson said. "Thank you, gentlemen."

The directors stood up, then milled around Stowe. They shook his hand. They patted him on the back. They offered their congratulations. Stowe blurted out his thanks.

When all had left the room except Bryson, Glen and Small, who were conferring with one another, I went around the end of the table. Stowe stood up. I held out my hand. "You have my blessing," I said.

"Et tu Brute," he said.

"Don't bite the hand that feeds you," I said. "You've been bought."

"Don't I know it! Thirty-five thousand! That's more than twice as much as I get with the fair. I would never make that much, even with the State Fair, if I lived to be a hundred."

Marie came over. "Congratulations, Mr. Stowe. It couldn't happen to a nicer guy."

"Thanks, Marie. Say, how would you like a job with Tiber Trucks? I will need a smart assistant."

"Just let me know the salary," said Marie.

"How about fifteen thousand as a starter?"

"You're kidding!"

"No, I'm not kidding. They're sure to let me choose my own staff."

"When do I start?"

"Soon as I sign with Tiber Trucks."

"Yikes!" Marie exclaimed. "What do you say about that, Art?"

"It was nice knowing you, Marie," I said.

Stowe said "Come with me to the fair, Marie. We don't want to miss the fireworks. First, I have to pay my respects." He went over to Small and shook his hand, then Bryson's, then Glen's. They said a few words together. Stowe returned, jauntily took Marie's arm and went away.

"Oh, Mr. James," Small called out. "Do you have a moment?" He came over to me and shook my hand. "You have my statement, and Mr. Bryson's? Any questions?"

"Can't think of any."

"Good. I look forward to seeing your report in the Star tomorrow. And thanks again for your help."

"Don't mention it."

I went into the hall and took the elevator to my room. I phoned the Star and asked for the newsroom's emergency desk. Frank was on duty. "How's it going?" he asked.

"The autopsy's over," I said. "The corpse has been nicely sliced. Who you got can take the story?"

"Fred Sussex. Just a minute."

He transferred me to Fred. I dictated the story, using the decision about the sale of the fairgrounds as the lead. I followed it up with reactions about the Xenophon deal. I was finished in twenty minutes.

Suddenly I heard a blasting noise from the fairgrounds. The fireworks had started. I glanced at my watch. It was almost eleven. Jenny would be waiting for me. I dashed from the room, hurried out of the hotel, found the Buick in the parking lot and drove away toward the fairgrounds. As I approached the gate I saw a red light in the sky, so I pressed the pedal down and went over the speed limit.

I was vaguely aware of a crowd in the car-lined street. I presumed they were there to watch the fireworks. Then I saw the flashing red beacon of a police car. A traffic cop demanded that I turn right into a cross-street. I drove quite a distance before finding a parking spot. I walked back to Main Street and on toward the fair, which was jammed with a crowd fleeing the fair. Beyond the gate a fire truck's horn blasted a fearsome warning. I started to run. I pushed my way through the outgoing mob. I was stopped by the crush. "What is it?" I asked a woman holding a huge doll. She shook her head as she squeezed by. I rammed the mob again and started shouting "I'm a reporter!" They let me pass. I ran along the side of the fair's high wooden fence until I stumbled over a knotted fire hose. Then I saw it: the fair office, flames shooting from the roof even as firemen sprayed it with thick jets of water. An ambulance was parked next to the church diner. I ignored the shouted warnings of firemen as I hurdled more hoses. I made out Stowe's spare frame standing near a police car.

"Jenny!" I screamed at him, even though I was too far away and there was too much noise for him to hear me. I closed the distance between us and grabbed his arm. He was gazing, as if hypnotized, at the flames shooting from the windows of the fair office.

"Jenny!" I cried again.

Stowe stared at me with dazed eyes. Reflected flame reddened his dumb look of astonishment. He began to moan. "It happened so fast--"

"Was Jenny hurt?" I yelled into his ear.

"Burned. I didn't see her. I was coming back from over there." He pointed toward the Agricultural Building. "I saw the fire. Someone had hit the fire alarm. Maybe Ricky. Oh, all my work!"

At that moment, far away above the grandstand, a burst of sparkling fireworks zoomed into the dark sky, booming and crackling.

"Where did they take her?" I shouted.

"Hospital," Stowe said, almost a whisper. "County Hospital. Ricky and Bob went with her."

CHAPTER TWENTY-SEVEN

When I reached Main Street I kept to the center of the road, walking as fast as I could, cursing my luck that I had to park the Buick so far away. I bucked my way through the gawking crowd, who, eyes raised, screamed with unabashed glee as rocket after rocket blasted the sky. No one knew about the fire. No one cared. I kept going, jamming my elbows rudely into men, women, boys and girls, unaware they were blocking the way of a madman intent on rescuing his sainted, beloved, heroine. I struck out wildly, arms akimbo, elbows braced for attack, until I reached the street where my faithful Buick waited obediently for its master and a ride of destiny.

My hit-and-run elbows ached. I fumbled for my keys, cursed the darkness, finally found the tiny aperture into which I thrust the proper key. Seated at last, I turned it and, joyfully, the Buick started: backward. I had smacked the bumper of the car behind. I didn't care. Now I had enough room to maneuver the Buick down the street. I managed to get back to Main Street and turn toward the hotel. Suddenly I realized I hadn't the foggiest idea where the hospital was.

I stopped at a gas station and raged as an attendant ignored my honking. He came over at last and I yelled for the location of the hospital. He gave me vague directions and I headed off the way he had pointed. I passed the courthouse, which he had given me as a landmark, then went south on the street behind it. A light at the Castle Rock Road loomed red but I went right through it, not even looking to see if anything was coming, and two blocks further on pulled up in front of a high red brick building. I really didn't know whether it was the hospital or not, but I lurched out of the car and ran up the walk and bounded the steps three at a time. At the top I snatched open the door and made a nurse wait while I went through.

The faint antiseptic odor hit me all at once and my head began to swim and I felt the hot flush on my face. There was an information counter halfway down the hall. I pounded on the counter and screamed: "Jenny! Where is she?"

A gray-haired woman in a stiff white uniform rose from behind the counter. "Jenny who?" she asked owlishly.

I was really wild by then, because all I could say was: "Jenny! Jenny, stupid!" I couldn't think of Jenny's last name. It was like sitting through a long movie in which the hero and the heroine call each other by their first names all the time, and then you come out and you try to tell someone about it, and all you can say is: "Rock said this, or Elizabeth said that," and you can't remember the names of the characters those actors played.

Eventually, of course, the nurse at the desk understood that I meant the girl who had been burned. I don't remember what I said, but it must have been something about the fire, because she told me that she had heard from Emergency that an ambulance had arrived from the fairgrounds. She directed me to the stairs and I remember only seeing the red light blazing *Exit*, and then I knew I was going down again, but this time I held onto the banister. The stairway had a nasty turn in it and I smashed headlong into a wall, ignored it, and leaped down the final flight.

Across the corridor opposite the stairway was a glass-paneled door with the word *Outpatient* on it, and I wondered why those departments were marked *Out* when they handled only patients coming *in*. I snatched the door open and went inside.

To my left along the wall there was a long bench and seated on it was a boy of about sixteen holding a pad of rolled bandages on his forehead. The bandages did not wholly cover a blotch of dried blood. A disheveled woman of about fifty leaned against the back of the bench, her eyes closed, snoring heavily. On the right was a long counter and behind that a desk with a bright lamp on it. There was no one at the desk. I sat down on a nearby bench more out of habit than because I wanted to. I had been in many outpatient departments before and I was used to seeing horrors, like the time the Old Folks' Home in Richland burned one winter, and I was covering hospitals for the Star. I never saw the fire, although I visited the ice-coated ruins the next day and saw where the roof had fallen through the third floor, where most of the deaths occurred. The ambulances shuttled back and forth from the fire for two hours; the worst cases were those who were not only burned but also frostbitten. There wasn't room for them all in the outpatient clinic of Civic Hospital, so a public ward was cleared and the injured were put in there, being taken up on stretchers in the elevator that exited to the outpatient waiting room. So, if an ambulance had come up the driveway, outside the room I was sitting in, and they had started bringing in more victims of the fairgrounds fire, I wouldn't have batted an eye.

A door from another room behind the counter opened and a nurse came out. I leaped from the bench.

"Jenny! Jenny Glen!" I shouted at her. She ignored me and sat down at her desk.

"You don't have to shout," she said, not looking up. She was about twenty-five or so, with a round, smooth face. "Miss Glen will be alright. Superficial burns, that's all."

"I would like to see her," I shouted. "Now!"

"Certainly not! She is being taken to a room. Her parents are with her, also her brother. You're a friend, are you?"

"Yes."

"Name, please."

"Look, I just want to see her! Tell me her room number."

She got up and came over to the counter. "You obviously haven't been in this hospital very much, otherwise you would know our procedures. Visiting hours are tomorrow afternoon from two to four, with doctor's permission."

"Are you crazy?" I shouted.

"What? What did you say?"

"I said you're crazy." I left her with her mouth open and dashed toward the stairway.

In the main foyer I asked the woman at the desk for Jenny's room number. She didn't look up at me as I rested my arms on the high counter. She continued to concentrate upon her task of writing notes on a bunch of patient forms.

"Miss Glen has been taken to a room," she said. She still didn't look up at me. "No visitors are permitted at this time."

"I'm her brother," I said.

"Oh, in that case, let me call the duty nurse on her floor." She dialed the phone and I heard her say: "Yes--yes--I see--thank you."

"Well?"

Finally the woman looked up at me. She eyed me suspiciously. She was an older woman with a quaintly firm smile. "The nurse will go to Miss Glen's room to request permission for you to visit. She will call back. Please have a chair."

"I don't want to sit down!" I fairly screamed. "I've been waiting five minutes already."

"If you are concerned about your sister's condition, sir, I can assure you that she is not seriously injured."

"How do you know?"

"I have the report of the outpatient department."

"Let me see it."

"It was verbal. And even if I did have a written report I could not let you see it. That is against the rules."

"The hell with your rules!"

"What?"

"You don't hear very well, do you, mam? Want me to repeat it?"

"You needn't bother. Really, Mr. Glen, you have my sympathy, but there is no need for you to--"

Her telephone rang. She turned away and picked up the receiver. "Yes--thank you, Mildred."

"You said you were Miss Glen's brother?"

"That's right."

"The truth, please."

"Alright, I'm not her brother. I'm a very close friend."

"If you had said that in the first place you might have been permitted to see Miss Glen."

"You mean, I can't?"

"Her family requested that no other visitors be permitted tonight, and her physician, Doctor Roach, concurs."

"Who else is with her?"

"Her brother, her real brother, and another man, I didn't catch his name. Richard somebody or other."

"Bryson?"

"That's it."

"But Jenny will want to see *me*!"

"Really! The duty nurse identified Mr. Bryson as Miss Glen's fiance."

"I'm going up."

"I will call the guard, right now, sir!"

I knew I was beaten. I heaved a deep breath and lunged in again. "Night nurses have a hard job, don't they?" I said soothingly.

"It's no picnic."

"I know a nurse who works very hard. Hardly ever has a day off. Perhaps you know her. Miss Herkimer?"

"The county health nurse? Of course. She used to work here."

"You say Doctor Roach is attending Miss Glen?"

"Yes."

"Then perhaps Miss Herkimer is with him. If so, she should be coming down soon, I would like to see her."

"Well, that's better. I see you are calming down a bit. Believe me, Mister--"

"James. Arthur James."

"--Mr. James, we have no wish to be harsh with friends of our patients, but our first concern must be their welfare."

"Oh, I agree. How could you treat accident cases if everyone who knows the victim barged in at once?"

"Exactly. She needs quiet and calm, and rest. It's as important as the treatment, a part of it."

"About Miss Herkimer," I said.

"Oh, yes. Let me call the floor again." She dialed the number and talked for a moment. She turned to me: "Miss Herkimer will be told you are here and wish to see her. Now, Mr. James, will you please be seated? It will help you to think more calmly, to compose yourself."

"Thanks," I said. A few yards down the corridor there was a small alcove with a bay window. A horseshoe-shaped plastic-covered couch enclosed the waiting area. I entered it and sat down. I picked up a magazine from a table in the alcove's coffee table, tried looking at the pictures in the dim light, but gave up. I thought of all the people I knew who probably had been at the fair at the time of the fire, and of how I was busy on a phone while Jenny was trapped by the flames. Where had the others been while Jenny was in the office? Probably the Glens and Brysons were in the grandstand waiting for the fireworks display, the grandest of the week because this was the closing night. And where had Stowe and Marie been? Had Stowe been squiring her around the fairgrounds? And what about Bob and Ricky? Were they with Jenny too? And if they had been, how was it that they had escaped being burned, as I presumed they had?

For the first time it occurred to me that unless Jenny was well by morning and was released from the hospital we could not escape together. If her burns were minor, and I had no reason to suspect they were not, then she could leave with me. I began to plot how I could come to her hospital room in the morning and take her away with me. I thought of calling the fairgrounds, seeking Stowe, but then, of course, the telephone would be out of order. Marie! I stood up and was halfway down the corridor before I remembered that I did not have her telephone number, if she had one, and that she probably was still at the fairgrounds reporting on the fire. I returned to the couch and picked up another magazine.

I heard approaching. steps. "Hello, Art," Miss Herkimer said. "Have you been waiting long?"

"I don't know," I looked at my watch. It was one o'clock. "About half an hour," I said.

"Doctor Roach just finished," she said, her voice warm, tender.

"Is she badly burned?"

She sat down beside me. "No, not badly."

"She can leave today, this morning?"

"No, Art. She must be here for a few days."

Suddenly there was no thought in my head at all, only a widening void.

"I know what this means to you, Art."

I looked at her blankly. She looked so different. She was wearing a dark patterned dress. I thought how shadowed she looked without her white uniform. She touched my hand. "You mustn't worry, Art. You may be able to visit her tomorrow afternoon."

"I'm expected back at the Star."

"She will be home in a few days. You can come back."

"Can I?"

"Why not? She will be well. After all, you two have only known one another for a few days. Two or three weeks won't make that much difference."

"Weeks!"

"It will take that long,"

"But Ricky!"

"What about him?"

"He said something would happen."

"No one could have predicted this, Art."

"Ricky did. He set the fire!"

"No!" she declared. "You can't say that."

"He did. I know it!"

"Listen to me, Art. I was with Jenny in the ambulance. She told me what she knew. Mr. Stowe and Marie arrived at the fair office after ten o'clock. Both Ricky and Bob were manning the office information windows. Jenny was working in Stowe's office almost the entire evening. Why? Simply because it was quiet. Mr. Stowe worked with her for fifteen minutes or so, while Marie waited for him. Mr. Stowe had asked her to go with him to the grandstand. They didn't want to miss the fireworks. Neither did Ricky and Bob, so they went outside to watch, but stayed close by. Jenny locked herself in Stowe's office, to be safe while she finished her work. Only twenty minutes later Ricky saw smoke coming out the window of Stowe's office. The window had been left open, just a few inches. Ricky and Bob didn't know Jenny had locked the door. They tried to get in that way. They ran around to the window, braving the smoke. They were able to open the window. They climbed through it and found Jenny on the floor. They opened the door from the inside and carried her outside the building. They set off the fire alarm and the fair firemen came quickly. Meanwhile, I was summoned to the scene. In the ambulance I gave her first aid."

"Was Jenny badly burned? Nurse here told me that it wasn't too bad. Where was she burned?"

"Art, I'm sorry you had to ask. It was her face, her cheeks, her forehead. She will need skin transplants. Oh, Art, I'm so sorry!"

I attempted to hold back my tears. I clung to her.

"Did Jenny tell you how the fire started?"

"It was Mr. Stowe. No sooner did he sit down in his office, to review Jenny's work, than he lit his pipe. Apparently he was smoking until Marie pestered him by saying she didn't want to miss the fireworks, that was why she was waiting. Jenny said Stowe knocked ashes from his pipe into the big ash tray he always kept on his desk. Some of the ash must have landed on the papers she was working on. Mr. Stowe left the building, leaving Jenny to lock the door behind him. A couple of papers on the desk burst into flames. The fire spread so rapidly that she was soon inhaling dense smoke. She tried the single window. She was unable to raise it high enough. She pounded on the door to arouse Ricky and Bob. She didn't know they had gone outdoors. She stayed close to the floor, as she had been taught to do in case of fire."

Where had I been? What had I been doing? In my hotel room, dictating to Fred for 20 minutes my final story about the last county fair! If only I had returned promptly to the fairgrounds! Jenny had been waiting for me! I would have saved her!

"Firemen were still pouring water on the fair office when I arrived," I told Miss Herkimer. "I spoke to Stowe. He was in a sorry state. My God, I wonder if he suspected that he had caused the fire?"

Miss Herkimer handed me a tissue. I wiped my tearing eyes. "What are you going to do now, Art?" she asked.

I shook my throbbing head. "I don't know. I've got to see Jenny, the sooner the better. They won't let me see her now."

"Ricky still be with her?"

"So I was told."

"Beware of Ricky," Miss Herkimer said. "He hit you again today, didn't he?" She looked at me carefully, as if waiting for my reaction.

"I will be careful." I laughed bitterly. "I don't want to get beaten up again."

"Art," she said quietly. "Ricky knows."

I was startled and I showed it. "Knows what? Oh my God, not that! Not that Jenny was pregnant! You told him?"

"Yes, for his sake. And yours. I thought he had a right to know, being the father."

I stared at her, unbelieving. I laughed again, a titter. "Isn't that hilarious, Miss Herkimer? First, Jenny knew, then you knew, then Doctor Roach knows, then I knew, now Ricky knows. Only later does Jenny know that I had known. Then our question was: Did Ricky know? If he didn't, then what reason did he have to be sure I wouldn't take her from him? He counted on that, that I would find out, somehow, and then I wouldn't want her. Don't you see?"

CHAPTER TWENTY-EIGHT

Avoiding the main entrance, I crept close to the wall, where the darkness hid me, turned the corner into the driveway and slowly stepped forward until I could see through the glass doors into the hospital's outpatient department. The waiting room was empty and there was no one at the desk, so I pushed on the door and it opened without a sound. I slipped through and tip-toed slowly across the room. A quick glance told me a nurse was at the desk behind the counter, her head bent to her work. Two more steps and I would have been through the other door to the hall, but she must have looked up then, hearing me.

"Where are you going?" I heard her say.

I did not stop to answer. I thrust my shoulder against the door, ran low across the hall and loped up the stairs, rounding the turn without accident, then cautiously up the last flight until I could see the information counter in the main floor corridor.

I peeked both ways, crouched and sprang around the banister and leaped the steps to the second floor. There I paused, drew myself erect, crossed the hall, acting as if I were the inspector-general himself. I demanded of the wan nurse at the little desk there: "Miss Glen's room, please." She stood up, startled: "Not this floor, sir, must be on the third." I thanked her with a slight bow and almost clicked my heels. Walking as if I couldn't care less, I mounted the stairs to the third floor where a girl who might have been the twin of the other was guarding the corridor. There was a paperback on the desk and her head was poised over it. I saw the smoke even before I saw the cigarette. She raised it from behind the desk, put it to her lips as if she was kissing fire, snatched a puff and lowered the cigarette again below the desk. She blew the smoke out in one exhalation and it hung there in a blue cloud, quite visible in the circle of light girdling the lamp on her desk. Seeing the smoke hover there, she swished her left hand through it, back and forth, but she might as well have tried dispersing a morning mist. It was then she saw me, taking the few steps needed to reach the desk. I saw the cigarette drop to the floor and then the soft pat of her foot as she tamped it out. "Yes, sir?" she said, her eyes wide.

"Miss Glen's room, please." I spaced the words with authority.

"Three thirteen," she said. She pointed the way. As I stepped aside I turned my head and saw her bending to the floor to pick up the butt.

At the door to Jenny's room I put my ear to the panel and listened. There was only silence, so I turned the knob, not knocking, and slowly opened the door wide enough to back through. I closed the door quietly, facing it, then turned. A few feet away from me was a high white curtain suspended on a bar, which, in turn, was held by two upright poles supported by bases with three prongs on swivel wheels. A dim light glowed from behind the screen. There was no sound in the room, except for human breathing, including that of my own laboring lungs. Thinking Jenny must be sleeping, I tip-toed on the polished floor, leaned slightly, and looked around the curtain.

"What the hell!" I said, stepping out. Jenny released her grasp and Ricky raised his head from her breasts.

He had been sitting on a chair next to the bed, and, leaning over, had been clasping her shoulders.

Jenny looked wide-eyed at me.

White bandages hid her face from her forehead to her neck. Only her eyes and nose were uncovered.

"Art!" she gasped.

Ricky stood up and stepped toward me. I fully expected a swing from his upraised fist. I backed away.

"Don't be afraid, Mr. Reporter," he said quietly. "Do you want to see her? I will wait downstairs." He turned toward Jenny. "I will be back," he told her. Jenny blinked.

He left the room quietly as I stood there, transfixed, the palms of my hands flat against the curtain behind me.

Her quaking voice came from deep in her throat. "Art, it was good of you to come," she said with shocking formality. "Please sit down."

Her eyes were full upon me, and if it had not been for them I would not have known it was her. I slowly moved away from the curtain, reached out, grasped the back of the chair, leaned heavily and sat down uneasily.

She looked at me, not pleading, rather with interest, as if I were the injured of whom to be afraid, waiting for the reaction to sympathy expressed, not knowing whether it would be rejected or received. We looked at each other for a long time. How long? I do not know. Time flowed. Time passed me by. Memory played its tricks. We exchanged words, insufficiently expressing feelings that cannot be expressed fully and completely in words. Perhaps many words such as these:

"You *are* hurt," she said at last.

"Would you expect me not to be?"

"Ricky was so sorry. He needed comforting."

"That's what you were doing?"

"No, he pledged his love anew."

"I understood he had never pledged it."

"Did I tell you that, Art? Not so. He gave me love."

"Then abandoned you?"

"I do not know. How can I decide? A woman's heart is not a violin, to be plucked at will. It responds to love."

"Then, with us, it is finished?"

"No, Art, it never will be. You will go home and forget me."

"Never!"

"There is a way of knowing, for a woman."

"And a man, too, I think."

"Then you know why I cannot marry you?"

"Because of what happened?"

"Yes, though not the burning. Ricky cares for me, he really does."

"More than I?"

"Yes, more deeply."

"But our love was broad. On the hill, it filled the valley. In the loft, it voided the gulf. By the stream, it broke the web."

"It had no roots, Art. Therefore, it was not strong. Against the thief, the storm, the fire, it could not stand. Yes, it was love. It is. I love you, Art, now."

"Jenny!" I took her hand. "I cannot give you up. I won't!"

"I was never yours to surrender. Don't you see? You came a stranger to these parts, were given the hospitality of these high hills. You were guest and I the host. You invaded privacy, though I welcomed you in. Still, though loved, you were a visiting stranger."

"And Ricky is your family, he is your home?"

"Yes. Now the long wait begins. The damage has been done, something lost, something gained. New life awaits. It will not be as it was before. What we took for granted was a value, now lost. Only the ghost remains."

"I grieve for that. And for you, Jenny."

"Do not be sad, Art. We have had four days. We will never be the same again."

"You are so wise, Jenny. You have a deeper knowledge than I have."

"It comes from being what I am." She closed her eyes.

"Does the light bother you?" I reached to pull the chain on the lamp above the bed.

"No, I've been in darkness long enough. I am content, except for this." She touched the bandages on her face.

"Does it hurt?" I took her hand.

"No. It is numb now."

"How horrible!" I cried.

"You should not think that. Shall I tell you how it happened?"

"No. I heard. You were alone, a prisoner there."

"I could not find the key. And then, falling, it was relief and no more pain."

"Ricky and your brother saved you."

"Yes. They were very brave. Did I never tell you? It happened once before. Do you remember the well behind our house? When I was ten, the well was uncovered to be cleaned. I was told not to play nearby. But I was curious and I lay flat to look. The water had been removed, and so the well echoed to my call. I imagined it was another girl, destined to live out her life there until the wicked enchantment was broken. I reached far over to grasp the dangling rope, thinking I would pull her up. I toppled and but for my grasp upon the rope I would have fallen in. So I swayed there, the dark pit below, my legs on the edge, screaming, and the well's voice mocked me. Then I felt my ankles clasped and I was pulled back. Ricky and Bob, together, held me."

She was silent, her eyes still closed. I touched her smooth hand.

"Your hand is cold," she said.

"Your hand is warm."

"They say I have a fever."

"Then you must rest."

She opened her eyes. "No, don't go."

"Ricky's waiting."

"I may not see you again."

"I will come again tomorrow."

"No, do not come. Leave me now with the dream we had."

"The dream has died?"

"Don't they all? With the light, they pass away."

"And if we had left together tomorrow--today?"

"Has the new day come? The fair is over, isn't it?"

"Yes, it is finished. It is after one o'clock."

"So long until dawn! It was a dream, Art. Not meant to be. Ricky was right."

"Only because he knew you were pregnant!"

"How so?"

I could not tell her; there was that between us, let it go.

"I love you, Jenny, love you more."

"Then let us part this way, loving one another. You have your duty, I mine."

"You will marry Ricky?"

"In due time."

"And your child?"

"He claims it as his own."

"Then I think you will be married soon."

"Perhaps. He has not asked me."

"He never will, not with words. But he will marry you. He has the right."

"Then you do see, Art?"

"Yes. I am an intruder here. Beloved, wanted perhaps, but not needed. In your own time, Jenny, in your own way, you will work it out, you two."

"You will come to the wedding?"

"No, I am too weak for that."

"Then kiss me goodbye."

I stood and bent over her, pressed my cold lips to hers. She did not put her arms around me.

"Goodbye, Jenny," I whispered.

"Goodbye, my darling."

From behind the mask I thought I heard the sound of tears, but her eyes were dry. The tears were mine.

"I will always remember you, Art," she said.

I turned to go, but she caught my hand. I felt the squeeze, three times.

THE SIXTH DAY

A CLOUD OF SMOKE

CHAPTER TWENTY-NINE

For an hour, that Saturday morning, I toured the fairgrounds. The fair itself had disappeared. A thin cloud of smoke rose from the fair office toward the overcast gray sky. Stowe and I sat together at a damp table, one of the few items left at the church diner.

"Will you fix it?" I asked as we surveyed the ruined building.

"No, it would have to be torn down anyway. I will put a desk in a corner of the Exhibit Pavilion, the only one that will have some heat. Come winter, we'll need it. He took his pipe from his jacket pocket, removed a pouch from another, pulled the zipper and began filling the bowl.

"Then you've decided to take the job with Tiber Trucks?" I said.

"How could I turn it down? It will be the most money I've ever earned in my life. This way I will be able to set quite a bit aside and retire in a few years."

"You will hardly be of retirement age."

He struck a match on the side of a small box, but the wind blew it out. "I've always wanted to retire early," he said. "I would like to move to Florida, maybe California. Just relax, fish, hunt. Here I've never had much time. Oh, I've had the odd trip in the fall to the Adirondacks with some Chesterton friends, but only weekends. No, I would like to take things easy for a lot of years, while I've still got my health. Being with Tiber Trucks, I will be able to do it." He struck another match, cupped his hands and got his pipe going. He blew smoke into the air. It hung there a moment, motionless, then the breeze caught it and swept it over the ground.

"Won't you miss being manager of the fair?" I asked.

"Yes, I will, but it did get to be routine. With Tiber Trucks I will have the opportunity to do something new, something different. It's a real challenge. But I will keep my hand in. Ricky will need a little help. He will need me around to sort of guide him."

"He looked across the cleared space toward the Agricultural Pavilion and the empty midway. "You don't learn how to run all this in the summer," he said. His arm went out to gesture, struck his pipe and hot bits of tobacco scattered on the metal table.

"Did you do that last night?" I asked.

"Do what?"

"Dump burning ashes on your desk, while Jenny was with you?"

"I'm always doing that. Careless, I know. Last night? I don't know."

"Think: In your office--"

"Why, yes, come to think of it, I did. But I don't see--"

"The fire started in your office. Think!"

Stowe blew another puff of smoke. "O my God!" He laid down his pipe on the table. He covered his face with his hands. He was silent for a long time.

"It must have been me," he muttered. "The police asked me. I told them I couldn't imagine how the fire started. They asked about the electric wiring, and I said it hadn't been too good, that I had noticed a spark once or twice when I plugged in a cord. Art, must you report what I did?"

"Certainly not," I said. "That's up to the authorities. Right now, as far as I'm concerned, and Jenny too, it was an accident. Careless, perhaps, but an accident."

"If they bring charges-if Jenny tells them--my new job!"

I looked at him coldly. Cruelly, perhaps. He raised his head from his hands, but avoided my eyes. He looked at his watch. "It's noon," he said. "I have to make sure the farmers get all the cattle out by two o'clock. If there's nothing more, Art?"

I stood up. "No," I said. "There's nothing more."

"Then I will say goodbye. And, thanks, for everything. Let's keep in touch."

"Sure thing," I said. The wind had gone down. He lit his pipe. He went off, trailing smoke.

I went over to the phone booth. I dropped a dime into the slot, dialed long distance, gave the operator the number for the Star's newsroom.

"Hold everything," I told Johnny. "I'm coming home."

I drove to the Times and gave Jenny's two suitcases to Marie. She promised to return them to her.

A couple of hours later I was at my desk, banging away the final feature story on Chesterton's last county fair. Here it is:

THE DAY AFTER THE FAIR IS A SAD DAY

One as Reporter Goes Over the Grounds for the Last Time

By Arthur James
Special to the Star

It's a sad day, the day after the fair.

You wander around the empty fairgrounds and the wind whips bits of paper trash around your legs, and the sounds of the fair that were there yesterday echo in your ears.

Gone--yet not quite all gone--are the vestiges of the fair and all its trappings. Gone are the thousand men and women who performed the stupendous job of taking down the fair.

But the signs of their coming and going are here. Across the quiet acres (you wonder how they got everything in that small space) is an unbroken expanse of litter: paper, glass, and plastic.

Over there a few workers methodically sweep the grass and place the debris in cartons. A little further a group of boys kick casually through the shreds of paper, looking for souvenirs.

Gone are the three thousand folk who came to Chesterton to stage the county's one hundredth fair. But they did not leave without mementoes of their passage.

No tents, no rides, no bright lights, no savory sweetness of spitting frankfurters now--but one vast landscape of rubbish. Empty booths proclaim the departure of 350 concessionaires and 850 show workers. Crickets have repossessed the land.

All that is left behind to remind you of the bustling, hustling four days of the fair are a few smashed auto bodies on the race track, a battered sign here and there, two hens forgotten in the henhouse, some cows in the cattle barn. And the lonely wind whistling through the trees, bringing back memories of the hurdy-gurdy's dancing melodies and the barker's raucous cry.

Where the merry-go-round circled to the delighted cries of her up-and-down riders, now only a circle of ticket stubs, cast off by the collector as he weaved among the bobbing animals, taking the tickets, tearing them and throwing half of each to the ground.

A mass of broken balloons marks the place where hundreds of fairgoers tested their skill at dart-throwing. By the number of punctured balloons you know many won trinket prizes.

On the dangerous eastern turn of the track a yawning gap in the fence where a stock car went through--and over there unpainted planks hastily nailed on the posts where a midget-race driver was pinned in a flaming pyre.

And everywhere broken light bulbs--yellow and blue and red--the glow of the fair that lit Chesterton skies until after midnight every night. Shiny new coat hangers bunched carelessly on the grass where the dancing midgets had their tent. And here a pair of shoes--and way over there another pair, and another and another.

Everywhere, the grass, once green, is darkened by pools of oil, where dozens of big trucks stood, and the fifty trailers and cars of the fair folk. The grass is creased yellow where the miles of electric cable lay.

An empty paper bag spirals over the ground--soon even these remnants of Chesterton's fair will be no more. At night the fairgrounds will be black and lonely. It will be as if the fair had never been.

THE END

Printed in the United States
By Bookmasters